"After working here, and then at the diner, you get to do homework duty at night?" Matt asked.

Callie glanced up and nodded, as if perplexed. "Of course."

He'd have given anything to have had a mother like that, a mother who was invested in her kid. He'd tackled his difficulties in school on his own and failed miserably. "That's amazing, Callie."

She glanced up. Their gazes met.

She went still, her eyes on his.

And she read his gaze, his thoughts. It was there in her slight intake of breath, the way she blinked, the quick flex of fingers as if realization just struck.

"I've got to reload the nail guns," she said, breaking the connection. But that was good, right? Neither one of them had the time or energy to put into whatever was flaring between them, so it was best to ignore it.

But there was no way in this world he'd be able to ignore Callie for the coming weeks, and a big part of him didn't want to try.

And that spelled trouble for both of them.

Multipublished bestselling author **Ruth Logan Herne** loves God, her country, her family, dogs, chocolate and coffee! Married to a very patient man, she lives in an old farmhouse in Upstate New York and thinks possums should leave the cat food alone and snakes should always live outside. There are no exceptions to either rule! Visit Ruth at ruthloganherne.com.

Belle Calhoune grew up in a small town in Massachusetts. Married to her college sweetheart, she is raising two lovely daughters in Connecticut. A dog lover, she has one minipoodle and a chocolate Lab. Writing for the Love Inspired line is a dream come true. Working at home in her pajamas is one of the best perks of the job. Belle enjoys summers in Cape Cod, traveling and reading.

Yuletide Hearts

USA TODAY Bestselling Author

Ruth Logan Herne

&

Reunited
at Christmas

Belle Calhoune

LOVE INSPIRED
INSPIRATIONAL ROMANCE

LOVE INSPIRED®

INSPIRATIONAL ROMANCE

ISBN-13: 978-1-335-42500-3

Yuletide Hearts and Reunited at Christmas

Copyright © 2021 by Harlequin Books S.A.

Yuletide Hearts
First published in 2011. This edition published in 2021.
Copyright © 2011 by Ruth M. Blodgett

Reunited at Christmas
First published in 2016. This edition published in 2021.
Copyright © 2016 by Sandra Calhoune

This edition published by arrangement with Harlequin Books S.A.

For questions and comments about the quality of this book, please contact us at CustomerService@Harlequin.com.

Love Inspired
22 Adelaide St. West, 40th Floor
Toronto, Ontario M5H 4E3, Canada
www.Harlequin.com

Printed in U.S.A.

CONTENTS

YULETIDE HEARTS

Ruth Logan Herne

This book is dedicated to my mother-in-law, Theresa Elizabeth Blodgett, a woman who has never been afraid to put her hand to any task, large or small. Her strength and devotion are a constant inspiration to me. She's one of those gals who could have settled the West single-handedly and would have coffee waiting for the crew at day's end. Merry Christmas, Mom!

Acknowledgments

Big thanks to Bob Dean of Dean Remodeling in Hilton, New York, known affectionately as "Bob the Builder." Bob's advice on construction and his dedication to a job well done helped lay the foundation for Cobbled Creek. Huge thanks to Karen and Don Ash of the Angelica Sweet Shop and The Black-Eyed Susan Café in Angelica, New York, for getting behind this project. You guys are truly amazing! Hugs and gratitude to Major Tony Giusti and his lovely wife, Debby (my Seekerville sister), for their sage advice on military basics. I'm spoiled to call so many experts friends.

To Beth for finding silly mistakes… And there were several! To Mandy for being my right-hand gal on road trips and for giving me a namesake. I love both! To Jon, who has taken on stove and refrigerator duty. You rock! To Stacey and Lisa for the spontaneous gifts of coffee: you have no idea how that spurs me to work into the night. Thank you! Hugs and thanks to Kyle and Casey Kenyon. I don't know what I'd do without you guys. And always to Dave, whose work ethic inspires my own: thanks for the sandwiches. And the coffee, dude. And for being there, night and day.

My son, if your heart is wise, then my heart will be glad indeed; my inmost being will rejoice when your lips speak what is right.
—*Proverbs* 23:15–16

Chapter One

Complete and utter desolation.

Peering through a driving November downpour caused by remnants of Hurricane Karl, Matt Cavanaugh surveyed what might be the biggest mistake he ever made as sheeting water sluiced from unprotected roofs. Wind-driven storm rains pummeled gaping window openings. Expensive, irreplaceable topsoil washed down unprotected berms, each muddy water trail sweeping centuries of rich, organic soil into the watershed.

Basically he was watching a large share of his life savings wash away. What had he been thinking?

"I see merit here, son."

The memory of his grandfather's reassuring voice eased the tension snaking Matt's back, crowding his neck. Simple words from a gentle man, an industrious construction worker unafraid to lift a hand to any task, great or small, including the gift of unconditional love to his bad-boy grandson.

Matt clenched his jaw, then realized that would only fuel headache potential. Surveying the muddy mess he'd just purchased with significant help from the bank, he fought the urge to run hard, fast and long when a banging screen door drew his attention to the left.

A boy raced out of the faded farmhouse facing the neglected subdivision. A dog chased after him, a black-and-white spitfire, his non-pedigreed look perfect for the place and the boy, a pair of mutts enjoying the tempest.

Within seconds they were soaked, the rain blurring their features, but the combined excitement apparent even from this distance.

The boy aimed for the uncompleted subdivision, the dog racing alongside. Too late, Matt realized their intent.

The kid dived through a window opening.

The dog followed.

The kid emerged from a door opening.

So did the mutt.

Then back in another window, a little higher this time, the crazy game of follow the leader probably not the smartest of ideas for a kid and a dog around a construction site. Matt left his truck at the now-unnecessary roadblock and raced downhill. "Hey! Hey, you! Kid. Stop."

Visions of leftover two-by-fours, nails, screws and abandoned tools raced through his head, the innocence of youth unfettered by the hazards of life. As the new owner, Matt didn't have the luxury of relaxation. Construction insurance rates skyrocketed with a claim, and the kid and the dog were a hospital visit waiting to happen. "Kid. Stop! Now!"

The driving rain swallowed his voice and the thickening mud did a similar number on his feet. The dress shoes he put on for the bank closing weren't meant for tromping around construction sites.

He lost visual of the quick-paced pair as he neared the skeletal houses, his descent and the rising rooflines blocking his line of sight. He wasn't sure if the storm made it impossible to hear the kid and the dog or if they were just unusually quiet. Since unusually quiet might mean unconscious, Matt increased his pace. "Kid! You hear me? Come out of there!"

No answer.

Matt continued along the road, mud-slicked shoes slowing his progress. The graveled areas would have been inconsequential in his boots. In worn dress shoes, the rough curves and sharp points of stone reminded him that if new shoes hadn't been on the list before, they'd gain a spot now, and all because some fool didn't have sense enough to keep their kid out of harm's way.

Kind of like his mother.

He refused to flinch at the memory. His mother was no June Cleaver, but he hadn't been a choirboy, either. He had the juvie record to prove his stupidity before Grandpa Gus realigned him with old-fashioned hard work, faith and fishing.

A movement drew his attention left. He darted between two incomplete houses, saw the kid about a house-and-a-half away, yelled again and took off in pursuit. The boy appeared fairly savvy about dodging among the half-built homes, so Matt ducked through a window and raced across the subflooring to the front door of the house, burst through and collared the kid just as he angled toward the house Matt had cut through.

"Hey! Hey! Let go! Let me go!"

"Not until we've had a few words, kid."

"Let me go! Let me go!"

Matt held tight.

The dog raced into the fray, tail wagging, obviously unconcerned about his young owner's welfare.

"Jake? Jake? Where are you?"

The dog's tail flagged faster. He dashed to the front door of the house, barked a welcome, then raced back, his gaze expectant, his angled doggie look wondering what was going on.

Which reflected Matt's feelings to a tee.

A disheveled woman strode through the nonexistent front door, her hair a mess, her shoes not quite as bad as Matt's, her jeans rain-spattered, her fleece pullover soaked.

"In here, Mom! Someone's got me!"

"Someone's got you all right." Matt sent the kid a look meant to quell and refused to relinquish his grasp, despite the fire-breathing mother striding his way. Her purposeful gait seemed militaristic even though she wore somewhat impressive heeled boots, which meant she'd most likely served at some point in time. If that assumption proved true, she should know enough to keep her kid where he belonged. He raised his chin, noted she almost matched him in height with the shoes on, met her glare and stood his ground, refusing to scowl, letting his stance make his point. "This your kid?"

"Let him go."

Matt ignored the command. "Do you have any idea how dangerous it is to have a kid running around a construction site? The things that could happen to him?"

The woman's gaze returned his look, one on one. "I'm well aware, thank you very much, although Jake knows his way around construction sites. Usually." She leveled a tough, knowing look to the kid, shoulders back, feet braced, her posture adding evidence to Matt's guess that she'd been in the military at one time. "Were you supposed to leave the house?"

"N-no."

"And what if something happened to The General?"

The General? Matt frowned, followed her glance to the dog and realized it must be the dog's name.

The boy snorted, a pretty gutsy act for a kid being collared by an absolute stranger while his mother reamed him out from a few feet away. "The General knows all the enemy hideouts. He's trained to sniff out snipers and UXBs."

"UXBs?"

The woman kept her gaze on the boy, her profile taut, worry lines marring a perfect forehead over sea-green eyes. Light brown hair fell to her shoulders, a side clip meant to keep the bulk of it out of her face, but the storm had outmaneuvered the clip's potential. She shoved the errant hair back, obviously irked. "Unexploded bombs. London. The Luftwaffe."

"I get the war reference." Matt switched his gaze from her to the kid as he released the boy's collar. "What I don't get is how *he* gets it. You're what? Seven? Eight?"

"Almost nine."

"Which means eight."

The kid's glare matched his mother's, obviously a genetic trait. "You can't play around these houses. It's off-limits," Matt told him, his voice stern. He turned his attention to the woman, realizing she was probably chilled through, the November day wretchedly wet and cool. "You'll keep him out of here?"

"Yes." Something in her look told Matt she didn't say things lightly. That quality reassured him. She turned and hooked her thumb toward the door. "Jake, let's go. The banker's got better things to do than chase you around where you don't belong."

Her words registered as she neared the door, the kid following, head down, chin thrust out, forehead furrowed. "I'm not a banker." Matt strode forward and yanked down a bill of foreclosure notice attached to the front window. "I'm the new owner."

Her head jerked up. She stared at him, then the house, then him again, utter disappointment painting her features. Wet, bedraggled, rumpled, cold and wickedly disappointed.

Her look grabbed a piece of him, the air of disillusionment needing comfort and joy, but at the moment, confronted with the enormity of what he'd undertaken less than two hours ago, Matt's personal comfort level had nose-dived into incredulity.

"Seek and ye shall find. Knock, and the door will be opened, son."

Gus's wisdom reminded Matt that he wasn't in this alone, that despite Gus's death while Matt served in the desert sands of Iraq, he'd never be alone again, not in spirit anyway.

"You bought this house?"

The reality of the recent transaction tightened his neck, his look. "I bought the subdivision."

"All of it?" The kid's air reflected his mother's again, a shadowed starkness making Matt feel like a crusty headmaster, cold, cruel and crotchety.

The cold part was accurate, his wet clothes and the

brisk wind a chilling reminder of what was to come. He met the kid's eyes and nodded. "All of it. Yes."

"But, Mom—"

"Stop, Jake. It's all right."

"But—"

"I said stop."

The kid's baffled look made Matt feel like scum, but why? Why should it matter if…

"You bought Cobbled Creek?"

A new voice entered the fray.

Matt swung around.

Three older men stood at the back door opening, backs straight, heads up, their posture definitely not at ease.

Military men, despite the paunch of one and the silver hair of another.

The man in the middle stepped forward, drew a breath and extended a hand. "I'm Hank Marek."

The name sent a warning bell of empathy. Hank Marek of Marek Home Builders, the now-defunct contractor that started this project over two years ago.

Matt wasn't a sympathetic person by nature. He'd hard-scrabbled his way up the ladder of success despite illegitimate beginnings followed by a fairly miserable upbringing, but coming face to face with the man who lost his dream so that Matt could have his, well…

He hauled in a breath and accepted Hank's hand. "Matt Cavanaugh of Cavanaugh Construction."

The older man's face revealed nothing of what he must be feeling inside, the loss of his work, his livelihood, his well-designed subdivision the victim of over-extended loans and the burst of the housing bubble.

The other men stepped forward, concerned.

Hank moved back, nodded and directed a look beyond Matt to the woman and boy. "There's stew just about ready and the temperature's supposed to dip lower tonight before coming back up tomorrow. Jake, can you help me fire up the wood stove?"

The boy scowled Matt's way, scuffed a toe, huffed a sigh, then trudged past Matt, the dog trailing behind, their mutual postures voicing silent displeasure.

"Callie? I'll see you at home?"

"I'm on my way, Dad." She pivoted, her mud-slicked heel tipping the move.

Matt started to lean forward to stop her fall, but she managed to right herself despite the wet floor and the mud. High, flat, wedged heels marked her departure with a tap, tap, tap as she hung a right turn at the door. She strode up the drive to her car, the soaking rain deepening the pathos of an already melodramatic situation.

Matt watched her go, then headed to the back door opening. The older men and the boy trudged in measured steps across the banked field, faded flag stakes symbolizing the wear and tear of waiting through too many seasons of sun, wind, snow and rain.

Matt watched their progress, his brain working overtime, the reality hitting him.

Hank Marek lived alongside the subdivision he had tried to create in the beautiful hillside setting, the curving road nestling the homes in the ascending crook of the Allegheny foothills.

It was that eye for setting that drew Matt to the initial showing, then the ensuing auction, his appreciation for the timeless, reasonably priced and aesthetically pleasing housing, a plan that not only fit the terrain but added to it, a rarity.

But he had no idea Hank lived in the quaint, small farmhouse on the main road, just steps away from the sign labeling Cobbled Creek a community of fine, affordable homes.

He pinched the bridge of his nose, muttered a prayer that combined a plea for understanding and a silent lament that he might be following the foolish imprint of the older man's footsteps, and headed to his truck, the cold, soaking rain a reminder that winter loomed, and he had an amazing amount of work to do in a very limited time frame.

Which was probably something he should have thought a little more about before papers were signed and money exchanged, but the delayed closing was the bank's fault, not his. Matt understood the time constraints he faced, but God had guided him this far. Someway, somehow, they'd get these sweet homes battened down for the winter.

As he crested the rise to his truck, the woman's car backed toward the roadway, a wise decision on her part. Mud-slicked shoulders weren't to be trusted in these conditions, and when she curved the car expertly onto the road, then proceeded to the farmhouse beyond, he recognized the meaning behind Hank Marek's words.

The woman and the kid probably hated him for who he was and what he'd done. On top of that, they appeared to live across the street from where he would take over Hank's dream because he was lucky enough to be in the right place at the right time.

The hinted headache surged into full-blown reality, a niggling condition spawned from a really nasty concussion while fighting in Iraq, a grenade explosion too close for comfort. But if occasional bad headaches were his worst complaint after a double tour in the desert, he really had no complaints at all.

Dad's dream is gone.

Callie steered the car into the drive, angled it between the catalpa tree and Tom Baldwin's classic Chevy, then headed inside, determined to put on a happy face despite what just happened. The smell of Dad's stew reminded her of how often her father had been there for her, supportive, honest, caring and nonjudgmental.

Returning that respect was imperative now.

The men trouped in, their footsteps heavy on the back porch. Callie pulled out a loaf of fresh-baked Vienna bread crusted with sesame seeds, placed it on the table and settled a plate of soft butter next to the bread, her mama's custom because cold butter seemed downright unfriendly.

Right now a part of Callie felt unfriendly, but not to Dad and the guys. Or Jake, her beautiful son, her one gift from a sorry attempt at marriage to a fellow soldier.

Hank dropped a hand to her shoulder. She looked up, sheepish, knowing he'd see through her thin attempt at normalcy. "It's okay, Cal. He's young. Looks competent. And he must have the numbers behind him because the bank signed off. Those homes need someone now, not next spring when things might look better for us."

He was right, she knew that; she'd been handling his books for three years, and truth be told she did as well with a nail gun as she had with an M-16 and a computer spreadsheet, but—

"The important thing now is to save the houses. I'm hoping Matt Cavanaugh and his crew can do that."

She nodded, not trusting herself to speak.

Hank had personally planned that subdivision to honor her mother, the name reminiscent of her mother's childhood home along the shores of Lake Ontario, the quaint family cobblestone a salute to artisans of old. Hank had been determined to carry that classic neighborhood warmth throughout Cobbled Creek, his plans lying open on a slant board he'd erected at the back of the family room. He didn't glance their way now, and neither did she, the thoughts of all that time, effort and money gone in the blink of an eye, a slash of a pen.

Hank lifted the stew pot onto the center of the table. Tom and Buck grabbed bowls, napkins and utensils, the old-timers a steady presence at the Marek homestead. Jake put The General on the back porch and shut the door. He ignored the dog's imploring whine and triple tail thump, a sure sign The General would rather be curled up on the braid rug alongside the coming fire, but the smell of wet dog didn't rank high on Callie's list.

An engine noise drew her attention to the north-facing kitchen window.

Matt Cavanaugh's black truck sat poised at the end of Cobbled Creek Lane. Sheeting rain obscured her vision, but something about the truck's stance, strong yet careful, imposing yet restrained, reminded her of the man within, his shoulders-back, jaw-tight stance just rugged enough to say he got things done. His dark brown eyes beneath short, black hair hinted Asian or Latino, maybe both, his look a mix that defied the Celtic last name. She'd faced him almost eye-to-eye in three-inch heels which put him around five-eleven, not crazy tall, but with shoulders broad enough to handle whatever came his way.

She refused to cry, despite the disappointment welling inside. Stoic to the end, she'd been practicing that routine for years now.

Too long, actually, don't you think?

Callie pushed the internal caution aside. Survivors survived because they manned up, took the shot and stood their ground. Four years in the military taught her how to draw down the mask, put on the face, pretend disinterest as needed.

"Great bread, honey. Thanks for picking it up."

Callie turned, flashed the men a smile, laid a gentle hand on Jake's shoulder and nodded. "You know I'll do anything to keep you boys happy. Any word on when this storm's going to let up?"

Jake took her lead, such a good boy, so much like his grandpa. "Supposed to be nice tomorrow, Mom."

"Perfect." She smiled, ruffled his hair and sank into a seat alongside him. "We've got to finish the front of the house while we can, get it cleaned up so we can decorate for Christmas. We'll save cleaning the gutters—"

"Again?"

Callie sent Jake a "get serious" look and nodded. "Yes, again, they're filled with leaves and maple spinners. You know we can't leave them like that for winter."

"We don't want ice damming that porch roof again," interjected Hank.

Tom took up the thread, his face saying he'd play along, pretend everything was all right. "I remember Callie up on that roof last winter, luggin' that smaller chain saw, cutting through the ice."

"Bad combination of events, all around," agreed Buck. "To get that much snow, then warm up just enough to get a quarter inch of ice. Rough circumstances."

"But nothing we couldn't handle," Callie reminded

them all. She'd used the short chain saw to hack through the pileup, pretending she didn't recognize the risk of being on a roof bearing thousands of pounds of unwanted ice, chain saw in hand. The roof's shallow slope helped steady her, but that flattened slope caused the initial problem, the lack of height allowing snow to gather and drift beneath the second-story windows.

"Exactly why we used steeper roof pitches on the subdivision," Hank reminded them. His expression said he was determined to face this new development like he handled life, head-on. "Quick water shed is crucial in a climate like ours."

"It is, Dad."

"Right, Grandpa."

Mouths full, Buck and Tom nodded agreement, pretending all was well, but Hank's old buddies were no fools. Faced with the new realization that Hank's dream was in someone else's hands just beyond the big front window, Callie was pretty sure that nothing would ever be all right again.

Chapter Two

"What do you mean you've got no crew?" Matt asked his roofing subcontractor the next morning. "I can't do a thing until we get these places under cover with good roofs. We've got water-damaged plywood to replace, it's November and I need the crew you promised today. Not next April."

Jim Slaughter, the owner/manager of Slaughter Roofing and Siding sighed. "I'm tapped out, Matt. Fewer housing starts and reroofs. I'm filing for bankruptcy restructuring and hoping I can keep my house so we're not tossed out on the street. I had to let the guys go."

Matt's marine training didn't allow temper tantrums or bad vibes, even though he was tempted. "Who else might be available?"

Jim went silent, then offered, "You've got the Marek family right there, and Hank is friends with Buck Peters. They've all done roofing."

Ask the guy whose dream got yanked out from under him to finish that dream for someone else? Matt didn't have the callousness to do that.

Did he?

Matt eyed the farmhouse across the way. A ladder leaned up against the front. While he watched, the woman came out of the house with a bucket. She climbed the ladder, the unwieldy bucket listing her to the right until she settled it on the ladder hook. She pulled out a large green scrubbie and began washing the faded paint systematically, until she'd extended as far as she could, then she climbed down, shifted the bucket and the ladder and repeated the process despite the cold day.

A scaffolding would be so much easier. A power washer? Better yet.

He clenched his jaw and shook his head internally. "Another option. Please."

"I've got nothing. Literally. There aren't a lot of roofing contractors close by and making time for your job would be hard with a clear schedule. For anyone with jobs lined up, getting yours in would be next to impossible and a lot of people let their crews go from November to March because of the holidays and the weather. I was hoping to hold out, but the closing took too long."

It had, through no fault of Matt's. Bankers didn't comprehend weather-related restrictions and rushed work meant shoddy work.

Matt didn't do shoddy. Ever. He inhaled, eyed the house across the street and released the breath slowly. "If I get help, can you crew with them?"

"If it means fighting my way out of this financial mess, I'll work night and day," Jim promised.

"Can we use your equipment?"

"Absolutely."

Matt made several futile phone calls, carefully avoiding people who wouldn't give him the time of day for

good, if old, reasons. And while plenty of construction
workers were laid off, most had left the area, unable to
survive on nonexistent funds. Half the remaining sub-
contractors were the type Matt wouldn't trust with his
hammer, much less his livelihood, and the others were
too busy to take on a huge project like Cobbled Creek.

Matt eyed the Marek place again and squared his
shoulders, determined to find another way. He took
two steps toward his truck, then gave himself a mental
slap upside the head.

Jim made two very important points earlier. Was
Matt willing to risk his investment on the possibility
of bad workmanship?

No. His intent was to implement the appealing design plan that drew him initially. Of course it was less
than beautiful now, and that had steered other devel-
opers clear. But Matt saw the potential and was determined to watch this pretty neighborhood spring to life
under his guidance.

But rot problems would continue if the homes sat
unroofed for another winter, and in the Allegheny foothills, rough weather came with a vengeance. He could
complete inside work between now and spring, but outside endeavors were dictated by conditions. Lost time
meant lost money, an unaffordable scenario to a guy
who'd just invested a boatload of his and Grandpa's
money into this venture.

He pivoted, then headed across the front field, his
gaze trained on the house facing him, uncertainty and
determination warring within.

Callie strode into the house after her lunchtime waitressing stint and came to an abrupt halt when she saw

Matt Cavanaugh seated at their kitchen table, sipping coffee like he was an old friend. A heart-stopping, good-looking old friend.

Except he wasn't.

"Callie, Matt needs some help."

Callie bit back a retort, trying to separate the tough-as-nails guy before her from the situation that wrested her father's dream out of his hands.

Nope. Couldn't do it.

She moved past the table, set a couple of plastic grocery bags on the counter and headed for the stairs. "I'll leave you men to your discussion."

"It's a family decision, Cal."

Callie swallowed a sigh, one hand on the baluster, her feet paused, mid-step, then she shielded her emotions and faced them, albeit slowly. "About?"

"I need a work crew for roofing," Matt explained. His deep voice kept the matter straightforward and almost a hint detached, as if this wasn't about as insulting as life could get because he was talking about roofing *their* homes, *their* dreams, *their* project. "Jim Slaughter's run into bad times, he had to let his crew go and you guys know how crucial it is to get these houses roofed."

Hank nodded. "It broke my heart to see them sitting unprotected. Uncovered."

Callie knew that truth firsthand; she'd lived, breathed and witnessed her father's depression. His Crohn's disease had contributed to the ruination of what could have been a beautiful dream, a feather in his cap. She'd prayed, promised, cajoled and bullied God and this…

She swallowed a sigh, eyeing Matt, trying to look beyond the tough-guy good looks, the steel gaze, the take-charge attitude so necessary in a good contractor.

But right now this man represented their failure through no fault of his own other than being fiscally sound at the right time. While she couldn't hate him for that, a part of her resented his success in light of her father's failure.

A pessimist sees the difficulty in every opportunity; an optimist sees the opportunity in every difficulty.

Churchill's quote stuck in her craw. She crossed the room, poured a cup of coffee, moved back to the table, sat and eyed the two men. "I'm listening."

"Matt's offered some good money if we can crew alongside Jim Slaughter while his business is restructured."

So Jim's company had succumbed as well, and he had a nice, hardworking wife and two kids. Callie choked down a sigh. "Good money as in?" She turned Matt's way, keeping her affect flat, her gaze calm. Extra money was worth getting excited about for a combination of reasons, but taking it from the victor who now owned the spoils?

That cut. Nevertheless, her twenty-five hours of waitressing offered small monetary respite, not nearly enough to get by on, and she'd crewed for her father and his construction friends for years after leaving the military.

Matt's calm expression went straight to surprise. "You crew?"

And there it was, old feelings rubbed raw, his look reminding her of her ex-husband's disdain, how Dustin found her unfeminine and unappealing. She met his gaze straight on. "Yes."

The bare-bulb wattage of his grin should have come with a warning label. Sparks of awareness flickered beneath her heart, but she'd served in the military for four years and good-looking smiles had been a dime a dozen. But something about his...

"Well, that's an unexpected bonus."

When she frowned, he explained, "Numbers-wise. I knew your father was experienced, and his friend Buck, but to have a third person." He raised his shoulders in a half shrug. "That's clutch in roofing. And Jim Slaughter will help, too, so that makes five of us."

"Six, actually."

Matt turned back toward Hank.

"Tom Baldwin might be on in years, but he's a solid roofer. I know that firsthand."

"Excellent." Matt swept Callie another quick smile, just quick enough to make her want to shift forward.

Therefore she pulled back. "Except I haven't said yes."

"That's true." Matt stood, his shoulders filling the tan T-shirt beneath a frayed brown-plaid hooded flannel, the plain clothes adding to his hard-edged charm. "Here's my number." He handed her a business card, reached across and shook her father's hand, his frank gaze understanding. "Can you let me know by tonight?"

"Of course." Hank stood and walked Matt outside. "Let me talk to Buck and see if he's available. Tom, too."

"And, sir..." Matt hesitated, then turned, his eyes sweeping Hank, then the subdivision across the road. "I know this is difficult," he began.

Hank cut him off. "Things happen for a reason, son. Always did, always will. I can't pretend I wasn't disappointed by my run of bad luck, especially because it affected more than me."

Callie knew he'd shifted his gaze her way, but she kept her eyes down, not ready to rush this decision, although seeing Matt's grin on a regular basis wouldn't be a hardship. No, she'd definitely go to delightful. Maybe even delicious. But seriously off-limits.

Like you're all that much to look at in hoodies and jeans with a tool belt strapped around your waist? Step back into reality, honey. Been there, done that. Bad ending all around.

"But I've wound 'round God's paths all my life," Hank went on, "the ups and downs, the back-and-forths, and we've always come out okay in the end."

"Good philosophy," Matt noted. He moved across the side porch, then down the steps. "I'll look forward to hearing from you."

"I'll call," Hank promised.

Callie stared at her coffee, not wanting it, not wanting to be broke, not wanting to work for the attractive guy across the street who seemed bent on getting them involved in his success while facing their loss.

"It's a good opportunity, Cal." Hank laid a hand on her shoulder, his gentle grip understanding.

"The location's convenient."

"Yes."

She sighed and stared out the window, seeing nothing. "And the money's good."

"And welcome."

"I'll say." She paused, drummed her fingers along the table top, then slanted her eyes to his. "I know we have to say yes, Dad."

He winced, then shrugged, understanding her mixed feelings.

"But I have to recount the reasons why before I do it."

"Like bills to pay?"

"For one." She nodded toward the school bus lumbering down the road. "I spent my Christmas budget on school clothes and supplies for Jake. He grew so much this summer that nothing fit, so I had to totally re-outfit him."

"And my little stash went toward truck engine repairs."

Two relatively minor things had dissolved their meager savings. Callie hated that, but then gave herself an internal smack upside the head.

Jake was strong, healthy and athletic, a good boy who loved traipsing off to a fishing hole, who behaved himself in school and accepted the necessary extra tutoring with little argument. He knew his way around a hammer and saw, a Marek trait tried and true, and wasn't afraid to don a hard hat and be a crew gopher.

Her father's health had returned with his colostomy, and if he continued to do well, they'd be able to reverse the procedure mid-winter. And while his appetite waned occasionally, she couldn't deny that good old-fashioned hard work was the best appetite builder known to man, and that getting back to work was in her father's long-term best interest.

The General dashed off the porch to greet Jake, his fur blending to grays in pursuit, the flash of white tail fringe the kind of welcome any boy would love.

"But the needy will not always be forgotten, nor the hope of the afflicted ever perish."

The words of the ninth Psalm flooded her, their comfort magnified in simplicity.

Callie liked things simple. She loved the feel of crewing on a house, walking scaffolding, climbing lad-

ders, working a rooftop. Her father had affectionately
called her his "right-hand man" from the time she was
big enough to eye a square alongside him, and they'd
laughed at the expression.

*But you stopped laughing when Dustin walked out,
citing your lack of femininity as a total turnoff.*

Jake's dad had tossed her over for the former Liv-
ingston County Miss New York entrant, a petite gal
who'd promptly given him two daughters in their sub-
urban home in Rhode Island, neither of whom Jake had
ever met. Dustin made it abundantly clear that his first
family was an anomaly in an otherwise perfect life,
therefore best forgotten.

Jake's entrance stopped her maudlin musings. She
stood, smiled, grabbed him in a quick hug, then examined the papers he waved her way. "Another hundred
on your math test?"

His grin said more than words ever could.

"And a plus on your homework sheets." She ruffled
his hair, nodded toward a plate of cookies and the refrigerator. "Grab a snack, there are fresh apples in the
crisper. I'm heading out front to get more of that mold
washed off."

"Can we work on my science project tonight?"

"Absolutely." Halting her work on their home's west-
ern exposure for dinner, dark and homework left her
little time to make progress, but Jake's enthusiasm over
schoolwork outranked everything. His excitement came
after years of grueling practice, nights when he hated
her, mornings spent crying, not wanting to get on the
bus because school proved too difficult.

"Success is not final, failure is not fatal: It is the
courage to continue that counts."

Churchill's words uplifted her, World War II a favorite study topic for Jake, and having served in Iraq, Callie understood war rigors firsthand. While hyped battles might gain more press, small battles, fought daily, wore down the enemy, except when the enemy came from within.

She pushed that thought aside, refusing to revisit old feelings that should have abated long past. Sure, she'd been dumped. Callie was adult enough to handle that. But Dustin dumped Jake, too, and despite prayer and her best efforts, what did she long to do?

Give her ex the quick kick he deserved for abandoning a God-given miracle. The first gift of Christmas. A child.

But Callie refused to dwell on Dustin Burdick's shortcomings, although that proved harder at holiday time. She was home, safe and sound, with a beautiful son, a warm house and good friends. What more could she need?

The sound of a generator drew her gaze across the street. A light winked on in the model home, the only home near completion, and she caught sight of Matt Cavanaugh trekking back and forth from his truck to the pretty Cape Cod house, lugging things inside.

She pulled her attention back to the task at hand and climbed the ladder with her bucket and thick, green scrubbie, determined to get as much done as she could despite the chill, waning light.

Determination. Valor. Perseverance. She had the heart of a lioness and the grit of a soldier, two things vital to soothe the scarred soul of the woman within.

Chapter Three

Matt recognized Hank Marek's name and answered his phone quickly, praying for a "yes."

"We're in, Matt."

Thank you. Matt breathed the thought heavenward, knowing what even a day's delay could mean this time of year. They'd already been hammered by squalls packing hail, wind and rain. Time was of the essence.

"Everything's being delivered tomorrow morning," Matt told him. "I started roof examination today, but my day got chopped by having to order supplies."

"We'll be there at eight," Hank promised. "Callie works the lunch shift in town, but she's got Wednesdays off, so we'll have her all day tomorrow."

"What about Thursday?" Matt asked, assuring himself it was strictly a job-related inquiry.

Yeah, right.

"She'll split things up. She'll crew with us, then the diner, then back here."

Matt knew how abbreviated days curtailed time frames, but did his frustration stem from Callie's prior commitment or...

No.

He refused to go there. Callie would be working for him. Matt didn't mix business with pleasure, no matter how intrigued he was by soft brown hair and gold-green eyes.

"That's her job," Hank continued.

It didn't take good math skills to realize roofing paid more, but Matt liked people that honored their commitments. His mother forgot she had a child when the world discovered he was Neal Brennan's illegitimate son. He was eight years old when life capsized. His mother sought solace in a string of random men, while his stepfather found comfort in a bottle. That left no one around to raise an eight-year-old kid with learning problems. Jake's age, he realized.

"But Buck and Tommy are available whenever. With respect to Tom's age I wouldn't put him on the tallest roofs, but he's sure-handed and has a good eye. And quick."

"He's welcome, then. Anyone else you can think of, Hank?"

A moment's hesitation followed, then Hank offered, "Your um—" indecision lingered in the older man's voice, his tone "—father's in town."

"Stepfather, you mean."

"I guess."

Matt didn't blame Hank for sidestepping the issue. When your biological father turns out to be the wealthy but drug-using, gambling vice-president of a local big business, Walker Electronics, the poor guy who'd been publicly emasculated took a hard hit. Don Cavanaugh became the classic definition of deadbeat dad, but because he *wasn't* Matt's dad, Matt guessed the expression didn't apply.

But it hit hard when the guy you called dad for eight

years walked away and never looked back because of biology. That hurt, big time.

"He crewed with me a few times when I really needed help," Hank explained further.

"Then you know he's fairly unreliable on a day-to-day basis."

"When he's drinking, you're right. He's sober right now."

Sobriety was temporary in Don Cavanaugh's life, a hit-and-miss condition Matt would rather miss. "I can't trust him."

"Then I won't mention this when he's around. He'll notice when you change the sign, though."

"How?" Matt's father had no reason to be this far out of town and he hated the cold and snow. He'd race to Florida once the weather turned just like he had years ago, leaving Matt with his drama-queen mother.

Face front, eyes forward. No flashbacks, got it?

"Don comes by for coffee and soup with the other boys from time to time."

Which meant he'd see them working on Matt's new project, and the inevitable face-to-face meeting. "I can't have him over here, especially right now. I've got to get my bearings for this job. Find my comfort zone."

"I understand."

"Thank you, Hank."

"See you in the morning."

Matt disconnected the call and walked outside the house, eyeing the gloaming shadows beneath a waning gibbous moon.

A noise drew his attention to the Marek place. In the almost dark he saw Callie's silhouette, captured by the porch light. She clambered down the ladder, a bucket in hand, its weight making the descent awkward. At the bottom she splashed water onto the street, then headed for the side porch, humming.

Pride and strength embraced her maverick beauty. The idea of working for him obviously bothered her, but if she was as experienced as Hank made out, he was glad for the help.

Lights blinked on in the front of their house and he caught a glimpse of Callie and the boy, heads bent, eyeing something, a family moment that resurrected all he'd missed as a child. A father's love. A mother's touch.

He headed into the nearly complete model home, studied the mattress and box spring on the floor, the small generator outside giving him power for minimal light and heat. He'd surrendered his apartment in Nunda because the commute would eat up too much time. And saving nearly seven hundred dollars a month was nothing to take lightly. Wear and tear on the truck, his equipment? That took their toll over time.

No, better to headquarter himself here, on the job site, guarding his investment.

The house wasn't certified for dwelling, so Matt would have to sequester his sleeping arrangements when the inspector came by, at least until he could get a certificate of occupancy on the model. He'd complete that once the roofs were in place on the other houses, his first-things-first mentality key to this situation. Then he'd set up properly upstairs, but for the moment, this would do. He set his alarm clock early to take a shot at bookkeeping, not one of his strongholds, and burrowed under the covers, burying dreams of heat. And a woman with gold-green eyes.

* * *

"He's staying over there." Callie jerked her head west, her hands plunged into soapy dishwater the next morning.

"Makes sense," Hank replied as he gathered their tool belts and supplies. "Why pay rent when you've got a nearly finished house?"

"Because Finch McGee will be all over that if he finds out," Callie replied. She wiped her hands, waved goodbye to Jake as the bus approached, then headed to the table.

"Finch is a little power-hungry," Hank admitted.

"A little?"

Hank shrugged. "He's got a job to do, Cal. You know that. He just does it with more zeal than most."

"Maybe Matt will be lucky and Colby will be his inspector." Colby Dennis had taken the job as Finch's assistant two years before, and he was a decent guy on all levels. Finch?

Callie'd been privy to more than one run-in with the divorced building inspector, and she knew a jerk when she saw one. She'd kept him at arm's length, but he'd taken to coming into the diner at lunchtime lately, when he'd always eaten at the Texas Hot before. And it wasn't a fluke that put him in her section, day after day, any more than it was coincidence that she traded tables with the other servers, keeping him at bay.

"Finch won't let the new kid on the block oversee this." Hank shifted his gaze to Cobbled Creek as they headed down the stone drive. "And while his inspections are all right, he doesn't have a lick of common sense when it comes to balancing economics."

"Ready, guys?" Buck grinned at them, crumpled his coffee cup and set it inside his truck cab.

"I am," declared Tommy, a knit hat drawn over his bald head, a thick flannel layered over a turtleneck.

"You expectin' a blizzard, Tom?" Hank teased.

"I'm expecting it's cold now and warmin' up later," shot back the older man, "and I've crewed with you often enough to know that cold and number of hours don't mean all that much."

"I knew I liked you." Matt smiled as he approached the group. "Supplies are due to arrive in three hours and Jim Slaughter should be here anytime with his equipment. Hank, can you get these guys together on inspecting the roofs, marking any part that needs to be redone while I finish a few phone calls?"

"I'm on it."

They spent the first hour setting up ladders and scaffolding, then split into two groups, checking for damage.

"We've got a problem here," Callie called out midmorning as Matt passed by below. He clambered up the ladder, saw what she'd uncovered, and grimaced. "We'll have to take this section back down to the rafters."

"I'm on it."

She'd been amazing and quick, working hard and long beside the men without a break, and in her hooded sweatshirt and loose-fit blue jeans, no one would even know she was a girl.

So why couldn't Matt get it off his mind? *Focus, dude.* "You really have to go to the restaurant tomorrow? No chance of getting someone to cover you?"

Callie looked up. Had he tempted her? Heaven knows he tried. She shook her head. "Sorry, can't be helped. But I'll see if one of the girls wants to pick up my shifts

next week because working here pays better than waiting on the lunch crowd at the Olympus."

"If you can do that, lunch is on me every day next week."

"For all of us or just the pretty girl?" Tommy wondered out loud.

"Everyone." Matt shot Tommy a quick grin of appreciation as he jerked a thumb in Callie's direction.
"Although she's easier on the eyes than the rest of you
lugs." He headed back toward the ladder, the crew's
work ethic easing his concerns. "I've got a friend who
works at the Tops deli in Wellsville. She can hook us
up with some pretty good eats."

Tommy exchanged a grin with Buck. "I had a few
of those friends back in the day."

Matt laughed and discovered it felt good to laugh
with a crew like this, as unlikely as they appeared. A
gray truck turned into Cobbled Creek Lane, the town
emblem emblazoned on the cab doors. Matt swung onto
the ladder, his features relaxed.

Callie stepped toward the roof's edge, then squatted alongside him as though checking something. "It's
Finch, the building inspector."

Matt paused his descent and nodded, wondering how
the scent of fresh-sawn wood could smell so agreeably
new and different to a longtime contractor like himself.
Or was it her strawberry-scented shampoo?

"You're not from around here, but he's a little high
on himself."

Relief tweaked Matt. She obviously didn't know he'd
grown up here a long time ago. He chalked it up to their
four or five year age difference. The old Matt Cavanaugh
was best left forgotten, although that wouldn't be completely possible. He'd messed up big time back then. Now?

Now it was his turn to make things right. Make Grandpa proud. His newfound peace with his half brother and half sister, Jeff and Meredith Brennan, was a good start. Glancing down, he swept the gray truck a quick look. "Overzealous?"

"Bingo. And you can't let him see you have stuff in the model, that you're staying here."

"How did you…? Never mind," Matt continued.

Of course she'd notice, she lived across the street. His truck had been there all night and his lights were on before 5:00 a.m. "I'll steer him clear."

"Five-hundred-dollar fine," she muttered under her breath. "No contractor wants to waste a cool five hundred."

She was right. He'd traded off the apartment to save money, not throw it away. He climbed down the ladder, nodded his approval at the scaffolding Matt rigged in front of house number seventeen and stuck out a hand to the inspector. "Matt Cavanaugh. Nice to meet you."

"Finch McGee." The guy looked around amiably enough, but Matt hadn't tap-danced his way through the marines. Friendly snakes were still snakes, and Hank's daughter had this one nailed. That only made him wonder why, but he'd ferret that out later.

"I examined the initial plan when it came before the zoning commission." Finch surveyed the half-done houses with a thin-eyed gaze, then rocked back on his heels. "I wanted to give myself an up-to-date visual. You've got the copy of town code my assistant gave you?"

The demeaning way he said "assistant" tightened Matt's skin, but he tamped that down and sent McGee a comfortable look of assent. "Yes. How much leeway do I need with your office to set up inspections?"

"Forty-eight hours should do it. We're not slammed right now."

Not slammed? Talk about an understatement. The town had been literally asleep for the past eighteen months. But Matt heeded Callie's warning and gave in easily. "Forty-eight hours it is."

"You've got Hank Marek helping you?" Finch turned Matt's way. His approving expression insinuated that having Hank working on this project was some kind of power-hungry badge of glory. "Gutsy."

"Necessary." Matt clipped the word, needing to get back to work. "Hank knows this project inside and out. Who better to have on board?"

Finch shrugged. "Just seems funny, but no worse than hanging out in that farmhouse watching this place get ruined."

"Well, it's in good hands now," Matt told him, ready to cut this conversation short. "Mine and Hank's." He wasn't sure why he included the older man in the statement, but realized its truth right off. Despite hard times, Hank Marek was unafraid to put his hand to the task, a guy like Grandpa, tried and true. That kind of integrity meant a great deal to Matt.

"Nice outfit, Callie."

Matt turned in time to see the wince she hid from McGee as Callie came down the ladder.

McGee's words pained her, but why would a pretty girl like Callie Marek be hurt by a little teasing? Two thoughts came to mind. Either Callie'd been hurt before or McGee's words came with a personal tang.

"She's working for you?"

Matt turned, not liking the heightened interest in McGee's tone but not willing to make an enemy out of the building inspector who would be signing his certificate of occupancy documents. "Yes, they're a talented family."

McGee acknowledged that with a nod as he headed out. "They are. I'll stop around now and again, see how things are coming along."

Translation: I'll stop around now and again to see Callie and maybe find you cutting code.

The latter insinuation didn't bother Matt. He refused to shirk and never used slip-shod methods in building. That had kept his reputation and business growing heartily in the northern part of the county. Now back home in the southern edge of Allegany County, where teenage bad choices dogged him, he'd be choirboy good to erase those dark stains on his character.

But realizing McGee would be stopping by to check Callie out?

That scorched.

And while Matt knew Callie was off-limits, the way his neck hairs rose in protest when Finch McGee eyed her said his heart was playing games with his head. The way she'd faced the decision of crewing with him, upfront and honest, the way her hair touched her cheek, the brown waves having just the right sheen, like newly applied satin-finish paint...

Words weren't his forte, but feelings...those he got, and since he was fresh out of a relationship with a woman who'd wanted to change every single thing about him, he wasn't ready to charge head-first into another one, especially in a place where everyone knew his name and all the baggage that went along with it. With an employee. Nope. Wasn't going to happen for a host of good reasons.

"If you can trust yourself when all men doubt you, but make allowance for their doubting, too..."

Kipling's famous poem soothed the angst McGee stirred up, the poem a gift from Grandpa back in the day. Matt had to trust himself. He couldn't afford mistakes or missteps. He'd already made his share.

"Matt, you wanna cut those sections we removed or have me do it?"

Matt turned, grateful for Buck's interruption. "Have at it, Buck."

Buck nodded and swung down the ladder. "Be right back."

Matt climbed back up, inspecting each seam before they added the underlayment and the shingles. A mistake now would cost time and money later, every builder's nightmare.

Do it once, do it right.

By the time Matt glanced at his watch again, it was nearly one o'clock. "Hey, guys, lunch."

Hank waved a sandwich from the roof across the street. "Got mine right here, boss."

Tom did the same thing.

Buck straightened and rolled his shoulders to ease muscle strain. "I'll bring mine up so we can keep going here. You want something, Matt?"

Their dedication touched Matt's heart. He'd worked with a lot of crews over the years, good and bad, and from both ends of the spectrum as low man on the totem pole and supervisor, but this...

He cleared his throat and nodded to Buck. "I've got a sandwich inside the truck. And some of those snowball cupcakes."

"I love them," Buck declared.

"Bring the box, we'll share. And see if the other guys want some."

"Hank won't. Coconut bothers him since he got the Crohn's, but Tom will dig in. So will Callie. She loves chocolate. Thanks, Matt."

"You're welcome."

Callie headed across the roof just then, a soldier's satisfaction marking her gaze, her walk.

A really good-looking soldier.

With great hair and pearl-soft skin.

Stop. Now.

He couldn't afford to mess up this job. He'd seen the careful way Hank handled his daughter, although this woman didn't seem to need protecting.

The image of her quick wince revisited him, the way she'd cringed at McGee's teasing, and that brought back another Grandpa Gus-ism. "If you respect women, you'll respect life."

Maybe Callie Marek *did* need protecting and was good at hiding it, but either way, she was off-limits. Her warm voice reenforced that notion a short while later. "Jake's home."

A yellow bus rolled toward them, lights flashing. Jake climbed down the steps, let the dog off the porch, then hurried their way with The General racing alongside. "You guys got a lot done today!"

Matt grinned as the pair drew closer, their enthusiasm contagious. "We did, but it's easy with a great crew."

"I can help." The boy's excitement made it tough for Matt to say no, but—

"We'd love your help," Callie told him, staving Matt's refusal with a sidelong glance. "First, get changed. Put on proper gear including your boots and hard hat, then head over here. There won't be much time, but you can work on cleanup."

"Okay."

The kid dashed across the open lot at a run, the dog streaming alongside, his pace pretty solid for an eight-year-old. Matt turned Callie's way, disapproving. "I—"

She held up a hand to thwart his argument. "I know what you're going to say, but trust me on this. Jake understands construction sites. He's been working side-by-side with us for years with no harm, no foul. He's great on cleanup duty and this is a much better choice than television or computer games, right?"

"Yes, but..." Matt met her gaze, decided that was dangerous because her eyes made him remember how lovely she was, even in roofing gear, and he didn't want to go there. No woman in her right mind would find his teenage police record a good thing to have around an impressionable kid like Jake. A *good* kid, Matt reminded himself. "Doesn't he have homework?"

"Yes." Callie nodded, chin down, focusing on her work, talking easily. "But he's got some processing problems so school doesn't come easily. We'll do it together, step by step, after supper."

That's what they'd been doing last night, Matt realized. "After working here all day, you'll do homework duty at night?"

She gave a brisk nod. "Of course."

He'd have given anything to have a mother like that. He'd tackled educational difficulties on his own and failed miserably. "That's amazing, Callie."

She turned, surprised. Their eyes met.

She went still, her eyes on his, her mouth slightly open, the parted lips looking very approachable.

And she read his gaze, his thoughts. It was there in her slight intake of breath, the way she blinked, the quick flex of fingers as realization struck.

Amanda Slaughter created a welcome diversion by pulling into the tract with promised coffee.

Matt was pretty sure he didn't want to be diverted.

Callie turned toward the ladder, breaking the connection. That was good, right? Neither of them had the time or energy to put into that quick flash of recognition. Obviously they'd be smart to ignore it.

But he caught her shifting a surreptitious glance his way moments later, and that confirmed what he'd been struggling with all day.

Working side by side with Callie Marek meant he couldn't ignore her. And the over-the-shoulder look said she wasn't oblivious to the spark of attraction.

But a kid like Jake deserved to be surrounded by the best examples possible. Matt had been anything *but* a good example for a long time. Sooner or later Callie would discover his past. No self-respecting woman wanted a guy with a record setting an example for her kid, and Matt understood that. Respected it, even. He needed to remember he was in the southern sector of the county for two things only: to make amends to those he'd hurt and help Cobbled Creek become what Hank Marek meant it to be.

And although he was thrilled by the skill level and dedication shown by Hank and his crew, no way, no how was he looking for anything else. Especially where Callie Marek was concerned.

Chapter Four

MᴄGee's truck reappeared while the crew grabbed coffee from Jim's wife. He braked quick, scattering stone, then climbed out, strode their way and met Matt's gaze head-on, his expression taut. "You living here, Cavanaugh?"

Matt's face showed surprise, not a good thing, but Hank's quick reaction spared a clash. "Of course he is, Finch. Wouldn't make sense to travel back and forth to Nunda while daylight hours are scarce, winter's closing in and every penny he's got is invested in Cobbled Creek."

"You don't have a C of O," Finch barked, his typical attitude more evident this afternoon. "There's reasons we've got regulations, Cavanaugh, although you were never real good at following rules, were you?"

Matt's flinch surprised Callie, but then Hank sighed and frowned as if wondering what the clamor was about. "Finch, I don't know any rule that says Matt can't live with us while he gets the model done and inspected. It makes good sense, all in all." Hank kept his voice easy and his surprise genuine, as if taken aback by Finch's intrusion.

Callie swallowed a lump in her throat the size of a small two-by-four. Live with them? Was her father kidding?

"He's staying at your place?" Finch swept Callie a look, then drew his gaze back to the two men.

Hank shrugged, sidestepping the truth. "We have extra room. Matt needs to be on site. It works out for everyone."

Everyone but me, Callie wanted to shout. She was having a hard enough time keeping her distance from Matt in the short time they'd been working together, but to have him staying at their place?

"A perfect solution," Matt added, as if everything was suddenly hunky-dory. "And just so you know, I'm ordering us a fresh turkey for Thanksgiving."

Finch scowled.

Hank grinned.

Tom covered a laugh with a cough.

Callie decided more coffee would only tax her already-twining gut and headed back to the roof, trying to untwist the coiled emotions inside.

Yes, she was attracted.

No, she shouldn't be.

And having him under their roof, sharing their home, their food?

Way too much proximity and she had too much to lose, but Hank had extended the invitation and Hank Marek carved his word in stone. He kept a General Patton quote framed on his dresser: "No good decision was ever made from a swivel chair."

Great. Just great.

Finch would be annoyed, which meant he'd annoy others. She'd have Matt underfoot which would entail having her guard up 24/7. And the guys were clearly delighted with the prospect of having Matt around, his friendly grin and storytelling a welcome addition to their circle, a perfect match.

But she'd found out the hard way there were no perfect matches. Not for women who strike a different path, a career that includes tool belts weighted with claw hammers and tape measures. Nails and utility knives. Unfeminine suspenders to distribute the tool weight appropriately.

Some lessons a girl never forgot.

Matt's footsteps followed her. He crouched by her side, pretending to work, his gaze down. "Hey, if it bothers you that much, I'll just get a place in town. Or stay at my brother's house in Wellsville. That way I'm not breaking the rules and McGee won't have anything to complain about."

Finch would dog Matt's steps, Callie knew. He wasn't above pestering contractors he didn't like, and he'd had his eye on Callie for the last several months. She'd kept it cool and friendly at the diner, but Finch added another component in an already-complex puzzle. She didn't want Matt targeted by the zealous building inspector, but she didn't want him living with them either.

Nevertheless, the invitation had been extended, and Hank wasn't a man to go back on his word, a quality she shared.

She bit her lip and swallowed a sigh. "It's fine. It just came as a surprise."

"I'll do my own laundry."

His earnest words almost made her smile. "You bet you will."

"And I can cook."

"Excellent."

"How big a turkey shall I get?"

"You weren't kidding about that?" She turned to face him and felt the draw of those deep, brown eyes, tiny hints of gold sparking warmth and laughter. "I got a couple of frozen turkeys at Tops while they were on sale. That's a lot of good eating at a bargain price. Fresh birds are expensive."

"Have you ever tasted one?"

She brushed that off and turned back to the task at hand. "Turkey's turkey."

He grinned and moved a step away. "It's not, but I'll let you discover that next week. And now—" he shifted his attention back to the nail gun "—we need to get back to work. Can you help your dad and Buck get started on number twenty-three?"

Across the street and two houses up. Just enough distance to calm things down. Smooth them over.

"Sure."

"And Callie?"

She turned at the ladder and arched a brow, waiting for him to say more.

He eyed her a moment and shifted his jaw. "You do good work."

His awkwardness told her he meant to add something else but thought better of it. Just as well. Too much fun and teasing could be misconstrued. She headed down to ground level, crossed the street, moved up the block and joined her father on the elongated roof covering the well-designed ranch house. Hank noted her presence with a welcome smile and nod.

"Ready?"

Ready for roofing?

Yes.

For having Matt's teasing smile, his easy manner, his firm jaw around every day?

No way.

But Callie had withstood basic training and a deployment in Iraq. She could handle this.

She adopted a noncommittal look and started handing her father shingles, pushing thoughts of Matt aside, but with the steady pop of his nail gun keeping time with his whistling, she was mostly unsuccessful. Luckily no one knew that but her.

He'd be moving in tomorrow.

Ignoring Matt's light proved impossible as Callie helped Jake recognize consonant–vowel patterns for his language arts class. Her chair faced the front window, overlooking Cobbled Creek and the unshaded reminder of Matt's existence.

Change chairs, her conscience scolded.

She could, she supposed, warm yellow light pouring from the uncurtained windows of the model home. But...

"Mom, can I help Matt this weekend?" Jake asked, pulling her attention away from cute guys and broken dreams, definitely in everyone's best interest.

"We'll all be working this weekend, as long as the weather holds," Hank told him. "Your mom has a couple of shifts at the diner—"

"I switched them up with Gina," Callie cut in.

Hank eyed her, speculative.

"I make more crewing and we have no guarantee on the weather this late in the game," she explained to Hank, then turned her attention back to Jake's word list. "Yup, short *I* words here, long *I* there. Perfect."

Jake beamed. "Mrs. Carmichael told me to picture them like puzzle pieces, looking for clues."

God bless Mrs. Carmichael, Callie breathed silently. Between Hannah Moore's tutoring and Jake's teachers, he'd come a long way academically, and since his ADD prognosis, his continued progress thrilled Callie. She knew strong middle school academics required a solid foundation now, and she'd worked extra hours to pay for his tutoring, his book club, his interactive educational games, anything it took to surround him with learning opportunities.

So far, so good.

She smiled, ruffled his hair, tried not to glance out the window and failed, then said, "Yes, you can help, but The General can't be over there all the time, okay? We can't have someone's attention diverted when they're on a rooftop."

"Okay."

"And I want to get those Christmas lights strung this weekend. Thanksgiving's next week and I'd rather do it before we get big snows than after."

"That's a good idea," Hank agreed. "If we use both ladders we can do it together and get it done in half the time."

"True." The ladders were about the only thing not seized when Hank's business bellied up. The bank had considered them household use instead of business inventory. "I want to finish scrubbing that side, too. Get rid of the mold."

"Not much sense if we don't have time or the right temperature to paint," Hank told her.

"It looks better when it's clean." Callie didn't elaborate, but something about coming home to that worn facade weighed on her. Painting could wait until spring, but decorating for the holidays with the front of the house looking tired and worn...

That didn't sit right.

"When can we get our Christmas tree?" Jake's eagerness refused to be contained.

Callie laughed and stood. She stretched and fought a yawn. "Let's tackle Thanksgiving first, okay? And decorating the front of the house."

"Can we put up Shadow Jesus?"

Hank exchanged a grin with Callie. He'd created a plywood Holy Family years ago, the images of Jesus, Mary and Joseph done in silhouette, then painted black. Two spotlights tucked into the grass bathed the cutouts in light at night, making their shadowed presence appear on the white house. The simple, stark visual was an eye-catcher for sure.

Jake had referred to the infant in the manger as "Shadow Jesus" from the time he could talk, a sweet memory and a good focus on the true meaning of the upcoming holy season. "Next weekend," Hank promised. "It doesn't take long, but let's get the outside lights up first."

Jake nodded, satisfied. "Okay. Good night, Grandpa."

"'Night, Jake."

He was such a good boy, Callie thought as Jake headed upstairs to bed. She would never understand

Dustin's cool disregard for his beautiful son, but then she hadn't understood Dustin for a very long time.

Maybe ever.

"He's doing fine, Callie." Hank drew her attention with a nod toward the stairs. "Don't borrow trouble."

"I know. It's just rough at holiday time, when most kids get presents from their dads. Visits. Cards."

"He's happy enough."

"But he wonders, Dad." When Hank went to speak, she held up a hand to pause him. "I know he's content, but it weighs on his mind from time to time. His birthday. Christmas. When they do father-son events at school and church. And those are the times when I could wring Dustin's neck for brushing him off."

"And brushing you off."

She shrugged. "Not so much. We married young, we were both in the service, we thought we could conquer the world and when that didn't work, we grew apart."

Hank's snort said more than words ever could. "In my day skirt-chasing was called just that, and it didn't involve growing apart. It involved breaking vows, going back on your word. A good soldier never goes back on his or her word."

His righteous indignation struck a chord with Callie. "You're right, Dad, but it's in the past and I've moved on. We all have."

"And the future is ripe with possibilities," Hank reminded her. "Seek and ye shall find. Knock and the door will be opened unto you."

Callie leaned forward and planted a kiss on Hank's bushy cheek. "Are you letting your beard grow to keep your face warm on those rooftops?"

"Yes I am." Hank scrubbed a hand across the three-day stubble and grinned again. "One of the advantages of age and gender. I can grow my own ski mask."

Callie shook her head, laughing. "And I'm just as thankful I can't." She headed for the stairs. "I'm turning in early so I can work on the front of the house before first light. I'll turn on the small spotlights to help me see. Another few hours of washing should do it."

"If we had a power washer…"

Hank's quiet aside made her shrug. "We don't want to disturb the paint too much anyway. It's pretty loose in spots and a power washer might peel it off. Hand washing is fine for this year."

Hank hugged her shoulders and planted a kiss on her cheek. "You make me proud. You know that, don't you?"

She did. And she appreciated Hank's commonsense take on Dustin's behavior, but the image in the mirror once she climbed the stairs showed a strong, rugged woman, a laborer. And while her father's approval was a lovely thing, and Callie took pride in her work, her dexterity, her intrinsic knowledge of building, some days it would be nice to look in the mirror and have downright beautiful looking back at her, the gracious swan that evolved from the misunderstood fictional duckling.

But that wasn't about to happen.

Startled awake, Callie stared at the clock, rubbed her eyes and peered again.

She'd overslept the alarm. Not only would she not be scrubbing clapboard that morning, but she'd be lucky if she got lunches made before the bus pulled up for Jake. And what on earth was that noise?

Her father sent her an amused smirk as she ran down the stairs in her robe. "Tired?"

Grr.

Hank held up Jake's lunch bag. "We're good to go."

"Thank you." She gave him a half hug as she kissed his cheek on her way to the coffeepot. "I have no memory of turning the radio off or hitting the snooze bar. I must have zonked. And what is going on out there?" She jerked a thumb toward the subdivision.

Hank shook his head. "Not there." He pointed toward the street side of the house. "Here."

Here?

Callie followed the direction of his finger, pulled back the curtain and stared.

Matt Cavanaugh had brought over a small power washer. Using care, he splayed the jet of water against the siding in a slow and steady back-and-forth sweep, his attention locked on the task at hand.

"Pretty nice of him." Hank's words drew her gaze around.

"Very."

"Must have seen you working out there."

Callie was pretty sure the flush started somewhere around her toes and worked its way up. "Probably just wants to make sure we can use daylight hours on the subdivision."

"Most likely."

"Dad, I—"

She stopped as Jake clamored down the stairs, his expression a mix of surprise and delight. "Matt's washing the front of the house!"

"He is, yes."

"Then we can put up the Christmas lights this weekend!" He raced for the door and barreled across the porch, then down the steps and around the front. Callie watched from inside, pretty sure Matt couldn't hear a word Jake was saying.

It didn't matter. Matt's grin said he understood a little boy's excitement. He nodded and sent Jake a quick thumbs-up as he guided the spray around the windows. He spotted Callie watching and for a quick beat he forgot to move the water wand.

Oops. His look of chagrin said he'd peeled a bit of paint.

He swept her one more quick look, barely noticeable except for the wink. And the smile, just crooked enough to be endearing.

Callie rolled her eyes, shook a finger at him and tried not to smile. She couldn't feed this flirtation and she had plenty on her plate dealing with Jake and Dad, but...

She let the curtain fall into place as Jake raced back in to grab a bagel and his lunch. "It looks great out there, Mom." He switched his look to Hank and raised both brows. "So we can decorate this weekend? Right?"

"When we're not working," Hank promised.

"Perfect." Jake gave Callie a quick hug and pointed toward the clock. "Matt says you've got fifteen minutes before you have to be at work and that you might want to get your coffee to go."

"Oh, he did, did he?"

Jake grinned and headed outside. "He's funny."

Funny. Right. She shooed Jake on. "Have a good day."

"I will." She heard him hail Matt as he headed for the road, The General at his heels, his voice upbeat. "See you later, Matt!"

She refused to check out Matt's reply, to see if he heard the boy's call.

She never overslept. Ever.

Her father poured a fresh cup of coffee into a thermal cup and swept her and the clock a look. "Twelve minutes and counting."

Laughter bubbled up from somewhere far away, a different kind of laughter. Sweet. Girlish. Kind of silly, actually.

But nice.

She hustled up the stairs, donned her layers and refused to think about the nice thing Matt was doing, saving her work, saving her time, precious commodities these days. And the joy in Jake's step…

That thought nipped the gladness. She didn't want Jake hurt. He'd taken a shine to Matt, but Matt was only temporary. If Jake grew too close…

Are you worried about Jake or you?

Both. Callie tugged her hoodie into place, grabbed a pair of fingerless gloves and headed back downstairs.

Matt's grin was the first thing she saw as she rounded the bottom step, his shirt cuffs damp from the sprayer, his hands wound tight around a mug of coffee. He flicked a gaze toward the clock, then back to her. "Right on time."

She faced him, tongue-tied. Despite her efforts, she couldn't get beyond that smile to create a quick comeback. And he saw that. Recognized the reaction. Probably because girls fell at his feet on a regular basis. His grin widened, lighting his eyes.

Not me, not now.

Callie grabbed her insulated coffee mug, not ready to play this game. Maybe she'd never be ready, and that might be okay. She headed out the door with Matt following, but as she passed the front corner of the house, she couldn't ignore what he'd done. She turned back and caught him studying her, his gaze curious. Maybe a little concerned. "Thank you." She waved toward the front and a hint of his smile returned.

"You're welcome."

"It looks much better."

He nodded, quiet, still watching her, one eye narrowed as if wondering something.

She pointed over his shoulder and slightly left. "Except where you peeled the paint above the window."

His smile deepened. Softened. He shrugged. "Distracted."

Talk about smooth.

Again the flush rose from somewhere deep and low, the pleasure of having a man flirt with her awakening sweet memories.

Memories that crashed and burned, honey. This guy's way cute, but he's here today, gone tomorrow. Let's not forget that.

She headed across the road, chin down, knowing he followed a pace behind, not hurrying to catch up. Was he waiting for her to come back? Match her pace to his?

Or just enjoying a walk with his coffee?

"House looks good, Matt." Buck smiled and nodded appreciation toward the Marek place as they drew alongside. "And that means we can rig up Shadow Jesus soon, I expect."

"And the lights," Hank added. "Jake sure is excited."

"I got that." Matt grinned, took a sip of coffee and settled an easy look Callie's way. "He's a good kid."

"Thanks. Same assignments as yesterday, boss?"

A muscle clench in his chin said he recognized the marker drawn. "Sure." He headed right while she moved to join her father and Buck on the roof they'd begun the previous day, but his light whistle followed her, the tune young. Bright. Carefree. It called to her, but she'd put carefree aside a lot of years ago and it would take more than clean clapboards and perfect teeth to bring it back. Most days she was pretty sure it was gone for good.

So much for maintaining a distance, Matt thought as Callie headed across his roof on steady feet a few hours later. "Tom said you needed a hand over here."

Matt nodded, brisk, pretending immunity. "I do, thanks. The pharmacy called to say his wife's prescription was ready."

"And he didn't want her waiting." Callie adjusted her gloves, flexed her fingers and squatted beside him, close enough to notice how her lashes curled up on their own with no help from mascara. "That's Tom, all right. And since Dad and Buck are capping twenty-three, I was the logical choice. Looks good, Jim," she noted, raising her voice so Jim could hear. "And it's almost straight."

Jim made a face at her. "Ha, ha. Do I have to remind you that I've put on more roofs than anyone else in Allegheny County?"

Callie laughed. "Since there's no one here to argue the point, I'll let you stake your claim. In the meantime," she turned her gaze toward Matt.

"Do you want to feed or nail?" he asked.

"I'll nail. Then we can switch so neither one of us ends up with a backache later."

"And you didn't leave for the diner today. How about tomorrow?"

Callie shook her head, eyes down, working the nail gun as they edged right. "Nope."

Matt fought off the quick glimmer of appreciation her answer inspired. *Focus on your work. Remember that you're on a rooftop and concentration might be in everyone's best interest.* But he'd be lying to say that Callie wasn't a pretty nice distraction, totally against the norm of women he'd known.

"I switched with Gina," she continued, working as she talked. "She's a single mom, too, and she can use the extra shifts. She'll do doubles, which will help her out at this time of year."

"Christmas."

"Christmas and winter clothes," she told him as she shifted her angle to give him more room. "With kids you go right from back-to-school clothes to winter clothes and then Christmas. There's no such thing as saving a dime in the fall. Not with children."

Tom's truck pulled back in a few minutes later. He climbed out, surveyed their progress and whistled, appreciative. "Nice work."

Matt grinned, showed a thumbs-up and jerked his head toward Hank and Buck. "Can you finish up with Hank and Buck?"

"And let you have the pretty girl all to yourself?" Tom drawled. He tipped his wool hat toward Callie, ever the gentleman. "Good thing I'm a happily married man. I might be giving you a run for your money."

Matt shook his head, pretending indifference, but when he glanced Callie's way, twin spots of color brightened her cheeks.

The wind, he decided.

"Ready here."

He started feeding her shingles again, her speed and concentration commendable when it was all he could do not to notice how she moved, the way she handled the nail gun as though born to it, her manner decisive, her gaze intent, her lower lip drawn between her teeth as she squared up each section.

She didn't talk, she worked, and Matt appreciated that. Talking slowed things down, and they were already racing the clock. Callie understood the time line and stayed focused on the job at hand while Matt had a hard time focusing on anything but her.

A car pulled up. Amanda climbed out, toting a drink tray of fresh coffees from the convenience store at the crossroads.

"She's a lifesaver," Callie muttered from behind Matt.

Matt met her gaze and smiled. "I'll say. Now if she only thought to bring doughnuts…"

Amanda set the tray of large coffees down on the saw table tucked inside the garage of number seventeen, then headed back to the car and pulled out a big box of doughnuts.

"No wonder he loves her."

Callie laughed out loud, Matt's easy humor a comfortable draw. "And times aren't easy for them."

"Exactly." Matt nodded her way, before tilting his gaze toward Amanda. "But they go the distance. That's why I contracted Jim initially, but the closing took weeks longer than expected and he was already treading water."

"Tough business climate for builders," Callie noted as she climbed down the ladder ahead of him, pretending not to notice how nice he looked from behind in his jeans, his movements sure and steady. A guy who looked that good in denim ought to be doing TV commercials.

This is a work relationship, it's money in the bank, Callie. It's a chance to get through this winter in the black, instead of the red. You can't afford to let anything mess this up.

She knew that, but couldn't deny the pull. She'd been a soldier for years. A good soldier learned to assess and acclimate, then decide.

She'd assessed Matt, all right, and she was tempted to get a little more acclimated, but when it came to the decision-making part of things, she had one job first and foremost: to take care of Jake and her father.

She couldn't afford to tip this job into negative territory, and romance gone bad could do just that.

Nope, she'd be friendly, work hard and hope Matt kept them on as he proceeded to finish the homes her father had started.

Matt turned and handed her a coffee. Their eyes met. He stood, holding the coffee, her hand skimming his, their gazes locked, electrifying the moment.

"Cream?" He half choked the word, then rolled his eyes, smiled and leaned forward, his voice soft. "I don't think my voice has broken like that in nearly twenty years, and I was talking to a pretty girl that time, too."

Callie accepted the coffee, slanted him a wry glance and reached for two little creamers. "Twenty years between girls? That's so not normal. You get that, right?"

He grinned and added sugar to his coffee before sidling her a look. "Maybe it depends on the girl."

"Makes men choke." Callie nodded, stirred her coffee, put the lid back on to help ward off the cold and

turned his way. "I'll put that on my list of attributes if I decide to go on one of those internet dating sites."

"Or you could spare yourself the trouble and just go out with me." The look he sent her said he was only half-teasing.

An offer she'd love under different circumstances. She'd figured that out when she'd found him sitting at their kitchen table, firm but at ease, decisive, but kind when pushed to ask for their help. Matt's warmth and self-confidence spelled "good guy" in bold letters, but this good guy was also her boss.

"I never date the boss," she told him, keeping her tone easy but her answer firm. "If things go bad it makes for a rough work environment."

His look said he agreed but wished he didn't. He handed her the open box of doughnuts and indicated them with a glance down. "May I offer you first choice in doughnuts at least?"

She grinned, wishing she could have said yes to going out, but glad he recognized the dangers, too. "That's quite chivalrous of you."

"The least I can do, ma'am." He tugged his wool hat slightly, the maneuver endearing, but Callie couldn't risk endearment.

Could she?

Not when he controlled the paycheck.

Chapter Five

Callie walked into the familiar setting of the Jamison Farmers' Free Library for the weekly fundraising meeting that evening. In partnership with Walker Electronics, the towns were raising funds to upgrade and expand the tiny library tucked in the vintage village. Callie loved being on hand to help raise money for the good cause because Hannah Moore, the former librarian, had tutored Jake the last two years, inspiring him, laughing with him.

And now Hannah was engaged to Matt Cavanaugh's brother, Jeff Brennan, her cochair on the library committee. Which meant Callie couldn't stop thinking of Matt while seeing Jeff and Hannah.

But she was having a hard time not thinking of Matt without Jeff and Hannah around, so tonight wasn't much different than every other night this past week.

"Callie." Hannah sent her a quick grin of acknowledgment and handed off meeting minutes from the previous week. "Do you mind setting these around for me?"

"Glad to." Callie laid a copy on each chair while Hannah finished measuring coffee.

"Done."

"Me, too." Hannah crossed the room and grasped her hands. "Hey, I wanted to say I'm sorry about your father's subdivision. It's got to be hard, watching it being developed right across the street from you."

"Actually…"

"We all know how hard you worked on it…"

Callie grasped her friend's hand to shush her. "Hannah. Pause. Breathe. Dad and I are still working on it."

Hannah frowned. "Huh?"

"Matt hired us to crew with him."

Hannah's frown turned into surprise. "Gutsy move. Not like that should surprise me." She sent a wizened look toward the door as Jeff walked in, looking confident and happy to see his future bride. "They are brothers." She refocused her attention on Callie as Jeff paused to talk to Melissa, the young woman taking over Hannah's job at the library. "Are you okay with all this?"

Callie's hesitation outed her.

"Oh, honey." Hannah made a face of concern. "You don't have to work for him, you know. Not if it's that hard."

Hannah had clearly misunderstood her pause in conversation. As Jeff moved into their area, Callie hedged. "It's fine, really. Matt's amazing and we're already making great progress on the houses. And that's good for Dad, mentally and physically."

"Glad to hear it." Jeff slipped an arm around Hannah, planted a soft kiss to her hair, but kept his attention on Callie. "And I told Matt he could stay with me, but he said he was going to finagle a spot onsite because he can't afford to lose time with the short days now."

"And that's a fact." Callie didn't mention that Matt

had moved into their extra room, and that his burly presence added a whole new dimension to their home. That his laugh shook the rafters and his smile…

Oh, that smile…

Luckily other committee members began trouping in, saving her from making a complete fool of herself. Jeff moved off to greet people, but Hannah stayed put. She swept Callie an up-and-down look before nodding. "Hmm."

Callie frowned. "Hmm?"

"Hmm."

Hannah tossed Callie a knowing look over her shoulder as she set pens around the table. Callie shook her head, firm. Resolute. "No hmms. Strictly business."

"I know exactly what you mean." Hannah jerked a thumb toward Jeff in the crowd of new arrivals. "A few months ago I was fighting tooth and nail to get off this committee. Now I'm marrying my cochair. Oh, I get it, Cal."

"I barely know the guy," Callie protested.

Hannah leaned closer, grinning. "I think that must be one of their special gifts, honey. And I can't say I'm a bit sorry. But because they are aggravating, industrious, somewhat know-it-all men…"

"With a great sense of humor."

Hannah acknowledged that with a brisk nod. "Call me if you need me. Or if you just want girlfriend time."

"Aren't you busy planning a wedding?"

Hannah laughed and lowered her voice as others approached. "Dana took over."

Callie grinned. Jeff's mother was well-known throughout town, a pillar of the community, a stalwart, God-loving woman unafraid to get dirty or put her hand to any task.

"Leaving me free to teach science." Hannah tipped another smile Callie's way. "And see my fiancé."

"Perfect."

"It is." Hannah gave Callie's hand a light squeeze. "And Matt, well..." Her smile deepened. "Dana raves about him, and I'd trust her opinion on anything. I'm just getting to know him myself, but he seems like one special guy."

Callie didn't need that reminder. Still, it was nice to see the approval and appreciation in Hannah's eyes because Matt was sharing their home, their food, their table. She faltered, then dropped her gaze to Hannah's hands, Hannah's soft skin tweaking her. "Do manicures help?"

"Help?"

Heat rumbled up from somewhere deep inside Callie. Not that she cared about what her hands looked like, but soft skin, pretty nails...

"My hands take a beating," she confessed. As committee members started to settle into seats, she held up her hands. "Construction work is tough and this cold, dry weather isn't exactly friendly to the skin."

Hannah tilted her head, smiled and winked. "You need a little Meredith time."

Callie frowned. "Jeff's sister?"

"Jeff's sister ran a posh spa in Maryland until a month or two ago. Let me set up an appointment for you."

Callie shook her head. No way could she justify spending money on a frivolity like that when cash was so tight.

"And don't worry about the money," Hannah added as if reading her mind. "Meredith's a sweetheart and she'll do it just to help her brother's friend. We can do it at Dana's place. Or mine."

"Um…"

Hannah's laugh said she realized she'd railroaded Callie and didn't care. Callie had never met Meredith Brennan, but she knew Hannah. Trusted her. She had a hard time imagining people spending hard-earned money on fancy nails, a true skeptic when it came to anything construed as froufrou.

Except a great pair of heels. Those she understood.

The press of committee members pushed her back into meeting mode, a good thing when talking about Matt just made it easier to think about Matt. Better for both of them to keep him out of sight, out of mind.

And definitely better from a paycheck perspective.

"I think the rain will shut down roofing tomorrow," Matt announced the next evening. He set two bags of groceries on the counter and laughed when Jake zeroed in on the Christmas tree snack cakes.

"I love these!" Jake exclaimed, eyes wide. "Mom, can I—"

"First, no, it's too close to supper. And second, they're Matt's, not ours."

"Rule number one," Matt said. "Any food I buy is up for grabs."

"Sweet." Jake mimicked Matt's grin and Matt high-fived him like they'd put one over on her.

"Still, not before dinner. Either of you."

Matt sent her a look across the room, a look that said more than words. He gripped Jake's shoulder and nodded toward the homework table. "If you've got home-work, I'd be glad to help."

"Sure."

"He's been here two days and already he's replac-ing me?" Callie asked Jake, a hand to her heart, feign-ing hurt.

"That way you can have some downtime after sup-per," Matt advised. "Maybe we can play Yahtzee. Or UNO." He scanned the game shelf. "But watch out if you take me on in war." He pumped up his chest and drew his shoulders back. "Me being a soldier and all."

"Mom was a soldier, too," Jake chattered as he pulled his agenda and binder out of his book bag and laid them on the window table. "So was my dad."

Callie kept her wince hidden, but something about Matt's analytical gaze said he saw too much. He carried the discerning air of a marine, and while that should be a comfort, Callie didn't need anyone discerning too much. Not now, not ever.

She lifted the soup pot lid and breathed deep before spearing a carrot. "Almost done, so you guys have about fifteen minutes. Because I've been replaced, that is."

"Only temporarily." Matt flashed her a teasing grin, but his words reminded her this was a short-lived setup, not a permanent convenience.

She'd tried ignoring him for the first twenty-four hours he lived there.

Fat chance.

Then she tried treating him like a brother.

That didn't even come close to working.

Friends, she decided that morning. Good friends.

They'd worked side-by-side all day and now had only

two houses left to roof. With Thanksgiving approaching, the guys would need time to be with their families.

The weather forecast didn't look great, and each day meant the odds against them were growing. They needed two solid days, maybe three of decent weather.

God, please, asking you to govern the weather seems a little bossy with all you've got going, but please... Help us get these last two homes covered.

"If it's raining we can install windows."

Matt nodded, pointed out a problem to Jake and turned her way. "Exactly what I was thinking. That way we don't lose time and prevent further damage. And the Tyvek wrap will help keep external walls from getting damaged over the winter if we can't side them right away."

Not getting them sided would disappoint him. He'd laid out his plans the first night in their house, showing the time line to Hank and Callie after Jake had gone to bed.

Hank had eyed the plans and made a skeptical face. "It works if everything goes perfectly."

"Exactly."

"So if it doesn't," Hank continued, turning a frank look Matt's way, "We prioritize. Roofing. Tyvek. Windows. Get them sealed as best we can. Then interior work over the winter won't suffer damage."

"And with a four-month window to get the Tyvek covered," Matt observed, "we can apply siding when the weather starts to ease."

"Yes." Matt's respect for the manufacturer's guidelines earned him Hank's approval. "Warranties remain in effect and the town doesn't cite us for not following code." Hank's expression changed as he realized what he'd said. "You, I mean. Not us."

Matt had offered him a straight look. "I wouldn't be here if it wasn't for you, Hank. Your vision. Your plans. Your project. Having you on board makes my life a whole lot easier right now. I'd be foolish not to realize that, and I finished being foolish a long time ago."

Matt's words eased her father's strained expression, and Callie blessed him for guarding the older man's ego. Hank's self-esteem had taken a beating these last two years, first from a debilitating and somewhat embarrassing illness that left him wearing a colostomy pouch, followed by losing the business he'd spent thirty years building. And because Callie had worked for Hank's company, the double loss of income spelled near disaster.

Matt's investment in Cobbled Creek changed all that.

His presence in their home was changing more than her business perspective, but she'd made a firm decision to keep her distance. Her father and son had been through enough, and adding romantic drama to an already-tense life would be foolhardy. Hadn't Matt just mentioned how he'd stopped doing foolish long ago?

Well, so had she, about the time Dustin walked out leaving her with an eight-month-old baby and little money.

Matt's engaging laugh drew her attention to the man and boy profiled in the window, heads bent as Jake worked out a word problem. Matt fist-pumped when Jake got the answer right, and Jake's answering grin reaffirmed what Callie had shared with her father the week before. Jake didn't know his dad enough to miss him, but he missed *having* a dad. That was evident in the shine he took to Matt, the way he tried to emulate Matt's moves on a house. If she wasn't careful, Jake would fall in love with the square-shouldered, sturdy builder and have his heart broken once Cobbled Creek was complete.

She couldn't let that happen, but she couldn't deny Jake the chance to hang with Matt, talk with him. Chat with him. Matt's positive influence was good for Jake. She recognized that. And while life handed out good and bad, some rough turns could be character-building. A boy didn't grow to be a man without scraping a few knees, and Jake was no exception.

"Done." Matt grinned at the boy, satisfaction lighting his face.

"Done." Jake echoed, exuberant. He glanced at the clock. "And we did it quicker than Mom does. She talks a lot."

"I do not."

Matt held his hands up in surrender, his eyes bright with humor. "I didn't say it." He jerked a thumb Jake's way. "He did."

"'Cause it's true," Jake added as he put his notebook away.

"She's mighty quiet on those rooftops," Matt noted as he withdrew plates and bowls for the table. "Hard to imagine her a chatterbox here."

Callie sent him a faux-withering look. "I talk as needed."

"And then some," offered the boy.

"Jake."

He laughed and dashed off to the living room to call Hank and Buck.

Callie eyed their study table and shifted her gaze to

Matt as she piled biscuits into a napkin-lined basket. "He might be right. I tend to go overboard, always explaining. Showing him the whys and wherefores."

"That's not a bad thing." Matt took the basket from her, lifted it to his nose and breathed deep, appreciation brightening his dark eyes. "These smell wonderful."

She grinned. "Good change of subject."

"I do what I can, ma'am."

Callie paused, one hand reaching for the soup kettle, Matt's words and tone sparking a memory of life in the service. Soldierly reparté.

"You okay?" Matt gazed at her, puzzled, a brow thrust up.

"Fine." Callie shrugged, grabbed the soup with both hands and shook her head. "Just a déjà vu moment."

Matt set out spoons and butter knives like he'd been setting tables all his life, but the look he sent her was only half-teasing and not at all unappreciated. "Cal, trust me on this. If we'd met before, I'd have remembered."

She felt the blush rise from her chest, staining her face and neck, and despite her best military ways, she couldn't tamp it down. "Artful flattery, marine."

"Yes, ma'am." He smiled across the table as the older men lumbered through from the living room. "Two tours in Iraq taught me to plan for the future but live in the moment."

"Good advice, son." Hank nodded approval as he sank into the chair, breathing deep. "Cal, this smells wonderful."

"It does," Buck chimed in. "And I grabbed some ice cream this morning. It's in the freezer on the porch. I thought someone might like a sundae tonight." He targeted Jake with a grin of appreciation. "There's fudge sauce in the cupboard 'longside the sink. And whipped cream in the fridge."

Jake beamed. "Thanks, Buck. I thought you forgot."

"No, sir, I did not." Buck ladled his bowl of soup, set it down and passed the ladle on to Hank. "When this old soldier makes a promise, he keeps it and you worked hard to make that honor roll."

"He sure did." Hank smiled approval at the boy. "Hard work pays off. Got your homework done already?"

Jake waved toward Matt. "Matt helped me while Mom finished supper."

"Ah."

Her father's partial word said a lot, maybe too much, but Matt took it in stride. "The smell of this soup prevailed on me, sir. A good marine does what he must to facilitate great food."

"Amen to that," added Buck. "And speakin' of amens, if you'd bless this food, Hank, we could commence to eatin' and I for one am mighty hungry after workin' rooftops all day."

Hank offered his typical short, clipped blessing and Callie sent him an "Are you kidding me?" look.

He grinned and dipped his spoon into his soup. "No need to look at me like that, daughter, I spent my day praying on that rooftop. God understands short and sweet as well as he does long and drawn out."

"Can't have the biscuits cooling off," Matt chimed in reasonably.

"Would be a cryin' shame," added Buck as he slathered butter across his. "Though Callie's biscuits are fine hot or cold."

"A good selling point," Matt noted, grinning.

"Yet totally unnecessary when nothing's on the market." Callie kept her tone light but directed a pointed gaze at Matt.

"Duly noted."

"Good."

"Did they come and switch up those shingles for number thirty-one?" Hank asked Matt, shifting the subject to Cobbled Creek, a change Callie welcomed.

"First thing in the morning. I'm glad you caught the mistake, Hank." Matt shook his head. "I can't believe I almost missed it."

"The three and the eight in the code looked mighty similar, but gray shingles in the midst of all these other homes?" Hank made a face. "That would have been bad. This way they're here in time and we don't waste a day. If the rain holds off."

"And I can be here only Monday and Tuesday next week," Buck explained, his tone reluctant. "We're headin' down to the daughter's place for Thanksgiving and won't be back until Saturday. Mother's got to have her shopping day with Jeannine while Bob and I hang out with the kids on Friday."

"Family time's important." Callie smiled at Buck, then shoulder nudged him lightly. "And you know you love wrestling with those boys."

"Though they're too big for that now," Buck admitted. "Tim's in sixth grade, and Tyler's a freshman in high school this year. Seems funny to have them that grown."

"Family is meant to be enjoyed," Hank assured him as he went back to the soup pot for seconds. "The good Lord wouldn't have it any other way."

* * *

Hank's choice of expression struck Matt.

Nothing in his family had been enjoyable. Hank's words shone a new perspective on his parents' choices. Neither one held any belief system holy or sacred, neither one invested time in anything but themselves. Matt hadn't known the warmth of a candlelit church service until Gus took charge of him, and it took the rough stint in juvie to put him back on track.

But he'd done it. Finally. With help from his beloved grandfather.

He felt Hank's gaze on him, measuring. Assessing. That single look said Hank knew his past and understood his present, and Hank wouldn't have invited him to live under their roof if he didn't trust him, right?

But Hank knew Matt's stepfather, which meant he knew the clutch of drama surrounding Matt's parents. The two fathers left a legacy of drinking, gambling and womanizing. It wouldn't be a big leap to wonder if Matt carried either man's hard-hitting characteristics. Half the town knew Matt had been headed full-bore in that direction as a young man.

He'd stopped that train of self-destruction, but folks had long memories. His past would intrude on the present, which meant he had to make the here and now as pristine as possible, no hassles, no hurries, no mistakes.

And sitting at the Marek table, Matt never wanted anything more.

"Uh-oh."

Callie peered at Hank as she shimmed a window from the inside while Hank and Buck adjusted the outside the following afternoon. "What?"

Hank jutted his chin toward their house, visible through the back opening. "Don's here."

Callie followed his gaze. "And that's bad because?"

Her father made a face, then pushed out a breath that sounded long overdue. "He's Matt's father."

"He's…" Callie paused, squinted toward the window, then faced Hank. "He's what?"

"Matt's father. Stepfather, actually. In a convoluted weird kind of way."

"You either are or you aren't," Callie corrected him. "It's a legal term. So, is he or isn't he?"

"Is he or isn't he what?"

Perfect. Just perfect.

Callie turned toward Matt's voice, mad at herself for talking about him when he wasn't there. Except he *was* there.

"Don's at the house." Hank pointed toward the road. "I was just explaining to Callie…"

"No sense explaining what can't be understood." Matt rubbed his hands against his jeans, two wet stripes darkening the denim. "I lived it and I still don't get it."

"I'll go talk to him," Hank said. He made a move toward the door and Matt caught his arm.

"I'll do it."

"But you said—"

"I know." Matt studied the view beyond the window, the older man climbing out of his truck, heading toward the house. "But there's no time like the present to have this said."

"You sure?"

Matt shook his head and made a face. "Not by half, but I'll do it anyway."

He strode out the door, climbed into his truck and

drove the quarter mile, wind-whipped rain beating on his truck, the wipers slapping up and down in furious fashion. Callie turned toward her father. "I don't get it."

"Neither do I," Hank admitted. He turned his attention back to work. "But it's Matt's story to tell. I just happened to know some of it."

She sent her father an incredulous look. "You're not going to explain this?"

"Nope. Sorry. Gotta ask him."

That wasn't about to happen. She'd managed to keep personal conversations to a minimum so far and...

So far? You're on day five. Not exactly world record pace.

Oh, she got that. But it *was* significant because she'd fought off the inclination to share sweet banter with Matt, knowing he could get under her skin.

Worse, he recognized the ploy. She saw it in his gaze. The set of his chin. The tilt of his head, the tiny muscle that twanged now and again in his jaw.

Knowing his marine background and his patient demeanor, she'd sidestepped anything that might be of import conversationally.

But now, seeing him climb out of his truck and mount their side steps, she kind of wished she knew what was going on.

"I've got the rest of the windows unpackaged." Buck's voice interrupted her wandering thoughts. "Callie, you need help?"

"I'm good, thanks."

Buck stared out the window and then met Hank's gaze. "Uh-oh."

"I said the same."

Callie swept the pair a look of disbelief. "You both know what's going on?"

"Before your time, I expect." Buck helped Hank balance the living room picture window as they lifted it into place from outside. "Cal, can you give us a hand here?"

Callie helped leverage the lower edge of the window into the expertly cut opening. "Nice job, Dad."

"Thank you. And I'm still not telling you. A man's got a right to privacy."

"She could ask him herself," Buck supposed.

Like Callie needed to hear *that* again. "Or not."

"Suit yourself." Buck nodded approval of the window fit as Callie leveled it from inside. "Kind of nice to have an uncurious woman around. Refreshing, you might say."

Uncurious?

No way.

But she refused to feed the gossip mills at anyone's expense. The thought that Don and Matt were related shouldn't be a surprise with the same last name, but lots of Irish had settled into the lower counties of New York State. Cavanaugh wasn't exactly rare.

But she'd noticed the pained look that crossed Matt's face before he hardened his jaw. That flash of emotion said the past colored the present, and Callie understood that reality tenfold.

Chapter Six

"**M**att." The older man's face paled when Matt strode into the Marek kitchen, giving Don an unhealthy hue. Not that Matt cared.

"Don." Matt kept his voice calm, his effect flat, and refused to use the term *Dad*. That title had been forever tainted in his mind by both men, but he was beyond letting their callousness affect the boy who lingered within. Most days. "No one's here right now."

"What are you doing here?"

"Working." Matt jerked a thumb west. "I bought Cobbled Creek from the bank. Hank and his buddies are helping me get things winterized."

Don lifted his chin, surprised. "You own Cobbled Creek?"

"Yes."

Don passed an aging hand across the nape of his neck. It didn't tremble. A good sign, Matt supposed. "Hank was hoping to buy it back himself."

Matt stayed quiet, his silence punctuating the obvious.

"You need help over there?"

A part of Matt's gut seized. Another part froze. Did the guy who walked out on an eight-year-old boy who'd known him as dad just ask for a job?

Matt conquered his instincts and shook his head, wondering if he could locate a punching bag nearby. "Got it covered, thanks. Hank's invited me to stay here." He waved a hand, indicating the house. "Until I get the model certified."

Don's expression hinted at the sorrowed man within. But Matt had endured more sorrow than a kid should ever have to, so Don could just take his angst and—

"...forgive us our trespasses as we forgive those who trespass against us...."

The sweet words of The Lord's Prayer proved wickedly hard to follow right now. Matt would discuss that with God later, but for the moment... "I've got to get back to work."

"Oh. Sure." Don hauled his wet hat back onto his balding head with two hands. "I'll get on, then."

He'd put on weight. And lost hair. And his teeth could use work. Matt saw all that and tried to equate it with the guy who played catch with him in the backyard. Who took him to Little League games to cheer on the home team. Who promised him the world until the day he realized he had no legal responsibility for Matt and walked out the door, never to be seen again.

Old anger resurged, too sharp to be considered controlled.

But Matt managed it. As he led the way out, he waved toward the subdivision again. "I expect this will take a while."

"I see."

Don's expression said he understood what Matt

didn't say. *Keep your distance until I'm out of here.*
He nodded. "Good luck on your project."

Matt refused to acknowledge that. He didn't need
luck; he had faith. He didn't need handouts; he needed
workers. And God himself knew that Matt didn't need
a pretend father hovering on the outskirts of his life,
one who should have been holed up in Florida collect-
ing unemployment checks until spring.

If I was a father...

Whoa. Matt put the brakes on that train of thought
in whipcord fashion. He carried enough bad genes to
ruin a dining room table full of kids, so the idea of
procreating?

Wasn't gonna happen.

Nope, he'd stop the craziness of passing on Neal's
and his mother's self-absorbed genes right here. He had
his work. His company. His service buddies. And a host
of construction people in the northern section of Allegheny County admired him for his pledge of excel-
lence and work ethic.

His brother, Jeff, and his new fiancée, Hannah, could
produce the next generation of Brennan blood.

Guilt speared him as he approached 17 Cobbled
Creek Lane. His grandfather had loved his Latino heritage. And he'd married an Asian woman who taught at
a local preschool until her untimely death from ovarian
cancer. Matt only knew her in pictures, but Grandpa's
praise painted a rosy picture.

And his mother had been beautiful. But looks only
go so deep, and if he had to hunt two generations back
to find goodness in his family tree, that was too far.
Being upfront about that saved a whole lot of wasted
time and emotion.

He parked the truck, climbed out and ducked inside the house, damp chilled air surrounding him.

Comfort later. Work now.

That's how he got through the Corps. And through the early days of forging his own company. And through the lean times of project start-ups. He should be used to it by now.

"Need help over here?"

A new warmth stole over Matt. He turned.

Callie stood inside the door. She indicated the house across the street with a nod. "Dad and Buck have that one just about done and I figure we've got a couple of good hours of daylight left, even with the rain."

"Did you have lunch?" Matt didn't remember seeing her leave or eat, so...

"Work first," she told him, moving inside. "Plenty of time to eat once it gets dark and you stay warmer if you keep moving."

A part of Matt respected her stance. Another part wanted to bundle her in a blanket by a cozy fire and make sure she was warm. Fed. Comfortable.

Red alert. You've entered a "no cozy fire" zone. Proceed at your own risk.

"You're right." He headed outside as she moved into the great room area. "Let's see if we can get this done before Jake gets home."

Callie laughed. "He's spending the night at Cole's house, so I'd hope so. I figured that worked out well because we can't put the Christmas lights up in this rain. But maybe tomorrow."

Matt wanted to help with that. He wanted to see Christmas through Jake's eyes, the eyes of a beloved child.

"We'll make sure they go up tomorrow, one way or another," he promised. "I'm not afraid to get wet. As we're about to witness."

"Thanks, Matt." She smiled his way and the warmth that flickered when she walked in the door intensified. "I can manage the lights, but it's easier with two people."

"Yup. Hank and me. You can make supper, or something."

She sent him a "get serious" look as she unpackaged a window. "Keep the little woman in the house? Are you kidding me?" She flashed a glance around them. "You get what I do, right? Climbing a ladder to hang Christmas lights is no biggie."

"Even so." Matt double checked the window dimensions, snapped his tape shut and raised one shoulder. "It wouldn't hurt for you to be warm one day out of seven."

A spark of pleasure brightened her eyes, but she quenched it pretty quick. Not quick enough, though, and Matt wondered how long it had been since anyone had taken care of Callie. Treated her like a woman. Treasured her.

Seeing Don must have lit some emotional fire within him, a flicker of flame that better get squelched quick. He needed the Mareks to make his dream happen. They needed him and his paychecks to survive their current situation. No one on either side could afford to muck this up. So he wouldn't, plain and simple.

Although catching her gaze through the rough-cut window opening made him want to rethink his position.

Time to change the subject. "I figured church first thing. Then a few hours over here. Then Christmas lights and football."

Callie laughed out loud. "After the week you've put in, I'd call football well-deserved entertainment."

He winked in agreement. "Monday's weather looks clear. We can resume roofing then. And if we get this house enclosed by tomorrow night, we're better than halfway done."

"And making sweet time."

"Which brings me back to tomorrow's schedule."

Callie helped stabilize the window as he lifted it into position from outside. "Yes?"

"You in an apron."

She blushed, shook her head and slid thin wooden shims beneath the frame, eyeing her carpenter's level.

"With some kind of great Sunday afternoon meal going," he continued, raising his voice to be heard through the window and over the rain.

"An apron?"

He widened his grin and flicked her outfit a glance. "Saves wear and tear on your flannel shirts."

She didn't answer right away, and when he balanced the window and glanced down, she wasn't smiling.

"Hey, I was kidding. You can get your flannel shirts dirty if you want to. They're washable."

Something flashed in her face, the pain he thought he'd seen the week before, as if...

He had no idea, but he felt bad. And stupid. "Hey, Cal, you don't have to cook." Was her lower lip trembling?

No. She wouldn't do that, would she? Get girly on him?

"Actually, I'll cook," he added hurriedly, anything to put off the possibility of a woman's tears. Nothing in the corps taught him how to deal with those, and that seemed downright wrong and maybe dangerous because he didn't know a male soldier that muscled up to a crying woman. "And put up the Christmas lights. And finish the windows. Just don't cry, okay?"

She scowled, blinked and shrugged, eyes down. "I don't cry."

Right. Matt refused to argue the whole shaking-lip thing. He knew what he saw, but God had also given him a working brain and arguing with an emotional woman? Not smart. "Well, good. So I'll cook…"

"I'll be glad to cook." She finished the shims, assessed the level, then whacked the excess shim board away with more energy than required. Like double that. "I like cooking. Occasionally."

Something wasn't adding up. "Then why the long face?"

"No long face." She straightened and sent him a reassuring look. "See?"

Oh, he saw all right. He saw a soldier that knew how to draw down the shield, a gallant woman who'd learned to quell emotion. And normally he'd praise that talent, a skill not easily attained, but here? Now?

He wanted to help. He longed to ease the flash of hurt and insecurity. Inspire her laughter. But seeing Don face to face left him fresh out of funny things to say.

Cut him some slack, Callie's inner voice advised. *That meeting with Don couldn't have been the easiest thing in the world.* And something she'd like to know more about at some point in time. But not now, when she'd already gone girly and emotional over an innocent comment about her work clothes that should have been funny.

But it wasn't.

Callie moved to the next window, then drew up short. "Oh, I forgot."

Matt checked the frame size before he looked up. "Forgot what?"

"You got a call on the house phone."

"Oh. From?"

"Reenie."

He sent her a puzzled look, one that almost looked sincere, and it wasn't as if Callie cared who called him. Or what they looked like. How they dressed. Really.

"What did she want?"

"Does secretarial pay come with the job?"

He grinned, which meant she let too much emotion creep into her voice, a trend that occurred regularly around Matt Cavanaugh. "Under 'hazard pay' in the fine print. Better read your contract more carefully next time." He held the window in place while Callie leveled it. "So?"

Silent, she winged a brow through the glass.

Matt heaved an overdone sigh, playing along. "Did Reenie leave a message?"

Callie was tempted to pretend she hadn't, except because she had no vested interest in Matt Cavanaugh, why would she even consider such a thing? "That she's fine with next week and your cell phone was out of service."

He pulled out the phone, scanned his bars and made a face. "Signals get choppy down here."

"Sometimes. That's why we kept the landline. Something to think about when you get your C of O on the model." She bent low, then made a quick sure cut, her home-building confidence intrinsic.

Her self-confidence?

Whole other kettle of fish, but she wasn't going to get into that with Matt. Hopefully he'd chalk it up to bad timing or whatever. And she could care less who Reenie was.

Liar, liar, pants on fire...

She stood back as he positioned the next window, shushed the inner voice, then nodded approval. "I've always loved these house plans. Each one distinct despite the neighborhood similarities."

"That's what drew me to Cobbled Creek." Matt sent her a frank glance of approval. "Your dad has a great eye for manipulating design just enough to maintain a neighborhood feel but leave each house unique. And the hillside setting, leaving established trees in place." Matt's appreciation for the aesthetics raised Callie's confidence a notch. "A perfect draw."

Callie slanted up a knowing smile. "He had help."

Matt read her inference and grinned. "You?"

She nodded. "I love that kind of thing. Setting. Blending. Coordinating."

"Interior stuff, too?"

She shook her head. "Decorating's not my forte. But home design. Placement. Light filtration. And kitchen setup. That stuff I get."

"That's a gift, Callie."

"I know." She moved to remove the casing from the dining bay windows. "And Dad was never afraid to let me use it. I love that about him."

"So you do that with Jake."

"Is it obvious?"

He nodded. "Definitely. You draw the best out of

him, but don't smother him. You let him find his way. That takes guts."

She shrugged, not wanting to explain too much, but grateful for Matt's compliment. "I want him to feel independent. It's hard for kids who need extra help in school. It gets embarrassing."

"It sure does."

His wry note drew her closer. "Don't tell me you struggled in school, marine."

"Ha." He moved to the east side of the house and measured, then remeasured before grunting satisfaction. "School came hard. That's why I think it's cool how you help Jake. Teach him. Coach him."

Callie heard what he didn't say, that no one had bothered to do that with him. Her heart pinched at the thought of his little boy struggles, how challenging it must have been. And yet he'd conquered those dragons. He must have, or he wouldn't be standing here today. "Somewhere along the way you caught up."

He winced. "Took too long. Wouldn't wish that on anyone, so you just keep doing what you're doing. Jake's a great kid."

The unspoken part of that comment said he hadn't been a great kid, and that quiet admission nicked Callie's work-hardened reserve a little more. "Thanks, Matt."

He didn't reply, just angled a look toward the far side of the window. "Can you catch this when I slide it into place?"

"Sure."

They inset and leveled the five tall, slim windows framing the dining space. When he finished setting nails in the last one, he grunted approval. "It looks good and it's getting dark. Done."

"I love the look."

She gathered tools and left the mound of wrapping. "We'll stow it all once we're finished with windows." They headed down the walk, then the stone drive. As they hit the road, Callie turned. "It's starting to look like something, Matt."

"It is." Matt's approving tone made her feel good, which was silly, really, and yet…

"Which one is your favorite?"

She didn't need to consider the question as they moved into the street. "The model, of course. That's why it's the model, it's the one I pictured living in. Hearth and home, classic Cape styling, paned windows, stone front." She turned and waved a hand to the rest of the street. "These are all good designs, but when I tweaked the model I tried to incorporate everything I'd love in a home, starting with the feel. The emotional response it creates in people."

"Women, mostly."

She laughed and bumped shoulders with him. "Probably, yes. But is that bad? What man doesn't want his wife to be happy? Or what woman wants to scrimp on the home she's worked for years to get?"

"But you kept it affordable." Matt paused and turned her way as they reached the Marek driveway. "That's a rare talent, Callie."

She started to shake her head, but he paused the action with a hand to her shoulder. "Don't shake me off. It's true. Especially now, with mortgage lending tight and housing needs tanking. You managed to make these homes something that invites investment, promotes families and is affordable. That took knowledge and a keen eye for placement. Thank you for that."

His words rang sweet because she'd adjusted the original plans for all his listed reasons, but gazing up into his eyes, those deep, dark pools of chocolate, his grateful expression put a hold on her heart. And her tongue. For the life of her, she couldn't wrap her brain around anything to say, not when he held her gaze and her shoulder, the strength of his grip something to lean into. Rely on.

"Callie…" His attention slipped from her eyes to her mouth, his expression wondering. Maybe hoping.

Callie took a firm step back, unwilling to wonder, not daring to hope, refusing to play in waters that nearly drowned her before.

Matt stood strong and silent, watching. Waiting. Giving her a chance to move toward him or step away, and despite how badly she'd like to take that first step in his direction, she moved back and quieted a sigh. "We had an agreement, remember?"

"I was hoping you'd forgotten."

"No, you weren't." Callie pulled her flannel closer and swept the subdivision a look. "We both need this done. You need to guard your investment, I need a paycheck. Dad, too. And muddying the waters would be ill-advised. Besides, the guys all kind of look out for me."

"Because your husband left you alone to raise Jake while he traipsed around with another woman?"

She smacked his upper arm and refused to feel bad when he cringed in pretend pain. "Leave it alone. Please. And have you noticed that while I've guarded your privacy like an M.P. at the gate, you've managed to dig up half my life history? Level the playing field or change the subject."

"First, that's some left jab you've got there." He sent a look of overdone admiration to her left arm as they climbed the stairs to the side porch and rubbed his arm, pretending she'd really hurt him. As if. His corded upper arms were steel bands and looked mighty good in a T-shirt. Not that she noticed.

"And second," Matt continued, "I think it was the guys' way of issuing warnings. Letting me know they stand to protect you from other stupid men who don't appreciate how wonderful you are."

"I don't need protection." She made that pronouncement as they approached the door. Matt paused her with a hand to her arm again.

"What *do* you need, Callie?"

Need? Want? The list was too long to articulate, but she'd trained herself to keep things to a minimum. She leaned forward, just enough to let him think she was reconsidering the glance he'd sent to her mouth, then tapped him on the nose when he drew close. "A paycheck. And peace on Earth would be nice, too."

She stepped back, gave his knit cap a gentle tug and headed inside, leaving him to follow.

As she shed her outer layer of work clothes, the memory of that near kiss played with her heart. Her head. But she knew better than most what fickle things men were, so she'd keep herself focused on the task at hand. Home-building. Roofing. And while a little flirting might not be a bad thing, she couldn't risk upsetting this apple cart of opportunity.

"I'll start a load of heavy stuff."

She turned straight into one of those dull brown T-shirts he favored, muscled marine chest and shoulders straining the worn seams, the soft cotton fabric needing a good washing at the end of the day.

And he was still appealing.

She didn't need an air raid siren or blackout curtains to remind her she was in grave danger, but she couldn't quite remember the last time danger felt this refreshingly good.

Obviously she was food-deprived.

Hank saved the day by walking in with an extra-large pizza. Callie headed for the kitchen while Matt started the washer, the mingled scents of pepperoni, sausage and cheese replacing cotton knit.

But even after skipping lunch, there was no way Callie could fool herself into thinking the pizza smelled better than the well-worn shirt, and that spelled trouble.

Chapter Seven

~~

Matt studied the five church choices facing the park green, a sweet template despite the bone-chilling rain. And from the steady stream of cars rounding the circle and pulling into backyard parking lots, Jamison folk weren't about to be deterred by the seasonal drizzle.

What's your goal?

To pray.

Soldiers didn't need a church for prayer, but Matt wouldn't confuse Jake by staying home on a Sunday morning. He also wasn't about to go to Good Shepherd with the Mareks, not when so many people from his past were members.

He wasn't after confrontation, just peace and quiet. Solace.

He slid the truck into a parking space along Main Street, climbed out and approached the White Church at the Bend, second-guessing himself.

Maybe he should have headed north. Route 19 went straight to Houghton, a sweet college town with several churches, but that extra twenty minutes meant productive time wasted.

It also ensured privacy. Matt was less likely to meet his past on the streets of Houghton. Jamison and Wellsville?

The past met the present at every corner.

Man up, marine.

Matt entered the small church, found an innocuous seat on the far left and sat, eyes forward, determined to pay attention to nothing but the service.

The sound of dripping water thwarted his vow. A spreading damp spot encroached the plastered ceiling over the altar. The budding smell of mildew shouted wet basement.

And was that a taped-up electrical connection on the left?

The old place had seen better days. Flaking paint above the congregation meant damp wood. The floor was older than dirt and looked it.

The little church needed help, and a construction guy like Matt knew how quickly things went from bad to worse if left too long.

"Gettin' worn around the edges, ain't it?"

Matt turned toward the outside aisle. A small woman with a cane stood alongside his pew. Matt moved in to make room, and when she had trouble wrestling her cane into submission, he helped hook it on the pew's back.

She breathed a sigh of gratitude as she sank into the seat. "Thank you."

"You're welcome."

She nodded forward, then leaned back against the cream-colored pew. "You're in for a treat this mornin'."

"Am I?" Matt settled back and smiled. "Good."

"Katie's playin' for us."

"Ah." He nodded politely, ever the gentleman.

"Her father don't like that she comes here, but Katie ain't never been one to listen to his harping on this, that or the other thing."

Matt twitched inside. He'd come to pray, not catch up on local news, and he was just about to sidle right when a young woman entered the sanctuary area from the left.

Katie Bascomb.

Guilt power-washed his heart.

A C-clamp seized his lungs, the turning screw tightening with each breath.

His fingers went numb, the adrenaline rush pouring pins-and-needles energy into his extremities.

She looked lovely, and that beat the way she'd looked the last time he saw her. Broken. Bloodied. Bruised.

Memories blindsided him, images streaming like a bad video feed, showcasing what he'd done.

But mostly what he'd failed to do.

He started to leave, feeling certain he had no right to be here, invading Katie's life. Her time. Her peace.

The old lady leaned closer. "Do you mind helpin' me out when service is over?" She skimmed the cane and the rain a cryptic look. "I'm not as steady as I used to be. I live a few doors down Main Street. If it's not too much trouble," she added, as if asking for help pained her.

He wanted out, big time.

But he couldn't deny this grandmother's petition. "I'd be glad to, ma'am."

Her smile soothed a little. Or maybe it was God. Or memories of Grandpa Gus hugging his shoulder and saying, "We all make mistakes. Then we learn from them and go on. Or not." He'd nod and grip Matt just a little tighter. "The choice is ours."

Katie positioned herself in front of a stool. Two clips held her long, blond hair back from her face, a face that seemed too serene for what she'd suffered because of him.

A long, flowing skirt rippled its way to the floor in some crinkled material, a blend of bright fall colors vying for attention. An earthy necklace hung against a pale sweater, its chunky beads accenting the colors below.

She looked beautiful. And mature. And peaceful, a violin grasped in one hand, a bow in her other. She quickly glanced at the small but growing congregation as if teasing them, as if guarding some fun-loving secret from her vantage point at the altar.

Shame wrenched his gut because he knew that under the placid beauty lay a broken woman.

His fault. All his fault.

He had to leave.

A young couple with two small children edged into his pew from the right.

Blocked.

Unless he *wanted* to be noticed and he could guarantee that was the last thing on his to-do list that morning. Why hadn't Katie stayed at Good Shepherd where her parents had gone forever?

Sweet notes sang from the front, single haunting notes inviting prayer.

Right until they jumped into quick succession, the small congregation grinning as if in on the secret. Katie's hands flashed the bow across the instrument. As one, the congregation stood, keeping time, heads bobbing, wide smiles matching hers. Clapping.

Obviously Matt had landed in a place that *looked* like

Jamison but became some sort of "sixties"-style Celtic fair once you walked through the double oak doors of the White Church at the Bend.

The old woman jutted his arm. "Ain't she somethin'? And our new pastor, well, he's got people comin' in to do all kinds of things now. Nothin' slow or easy 'bout his way of doin' things and I say good for him!" She punctuated her approval with a firm nod that looked almost grim. "'Bout time we had someone rile up this old church. Best we've been doin' lately is diggin' holes, settin' one after another to rest. Now we've got young families comin' in. Bringin' their babies." She grinned across him to where two preschoolers eagerly awaited whatever was going to happen next. "New life."

And that's what he wanted, wasn't it? Why he'd come back to Jamison? To atone for the old and make way for the new.

A young man wearing a black-and-gold football jersey and wide grin strolled onto the small altar as Katie picked out a foot-tapping arrangement of "When the Saints Go Marching In."

The small crowd erupted, singing and clapping, welcoming the man despite his presence in the heart of Buffalo football fans. Matt grinned in spite of himself.

It took a gutsy guy to claim his team in enemy territory, but the young pastor's face said he'd handle whatever came his way. Matt liked him immediately, an uncommon occurrence for a marine.

By the time the atypical service concluded, Matt was sure of two things.

Katie was doing okay.

And Jamison had changed.

"Loretta, you've found yourself a new beau," the

young pastor exclaimed as Matt assisted the aged woman out the back door once the life-affirming service had concluded. "And you're new here." The pastor clasped Matt's hand, grinning an amused welcome.

Matt swept the town a glance. "I grew up here."

"You did?" The old lady shot him a look of shrewd interest.

"Then you know how wonderful it is firsthand." The pastor pumped Matt's hand with an easy vigor. "A great place to settle down. Raise a family. Or come home to. Right, Loretta?"

"Yessir."

Because Matt wasn't inclined to do any of the above, he hedged. "Nice to have you here, Reverend."

"Si," the other man corrected. "Simon MacDaniel, but everyone calls me Si."

"But you *are* a reverend, right?"

Si grinned. "Got me a nice diploma from one of those mail-order places to prove it."

"Oh, you!" Loretta's grin lit up her face, easing the chronic line of worry.

Matt grinned despite himself. "Then I should expect reggae next week?"

"I'll get Katie right on it," the pastor affirmed as he turned to greet the next person. Matt hoped Si turned quick enough to miss his reaction. As he headed down the front walk, commotion across the leaf-strewn park said his timing had gone awry.

The doors of Good Shepherd swung open opposite them. Either Reverend Hannity cut his sermon short or Si had waxed on. Matt glanced at his watch and made a face.

Si's fault, which made him a good preacher in Matt's

book, but that proved small comfort as streams of people headed toward vehicles parked creatively here, there and the other place. While the five churches created a postcard-like ambiance to onlookers, the Sunday morning reality became a logistical nightmare, guided by a sheriff's deputy in rain gear, allowing traffic into and out of the circle.

Only in Jamison, Matt thought, but as confusing as the moment appeared, he found himself longing to belong. A huge part of his life had been lived in this town, like those unfinished houses he now tended.

He'd been rough-cut. Unpolished. Not plumbed to fit anywhere, so he'd made up his own rules and crashed and burned, taking Katie and two of his buddies with him.

The guys had walked away with barely a scratch.

Katie hadn't walked away at all. Not for a long time, and then it took a prosthetic and loads of therapy. She'd been doing physical therapy while he did time, but in the end, he gained his release and walked free.

Katie was still missing a leg.

He longed to move quickly, berating himself mentally for not going to Houghton, but the aged woman's pace urged caution.

Jake ran their way, oblivious to the rain, a wide grin lighting his face. "Matt! Did you see this?" Waving Matt forward, Jake stopped in front of a large sign. "They're doing Christmas lights in the park! And sleigh rides! In the dark!"

Jake's voice spiked the exclamation points to new highs, his enthusiasm contagious.

"Looks fun, bud."

"A little pricey," Loretta noted.

Matt eyed the ticket cost and saw Jake's expression dim, but the boy didn't wallow or pout. He manned up with a stout smile and said, "It is kinda pricey and who wants to go see old lights anyway?" He turned a bright gaze up toward Matt, his earnest expression pulling Matt in. Brave. Stoic. Sturdy. What a kid. "And we're putting our lights up today, right, Matt?"

"Right. But let me get this nice lady out of the rain, Jake, and I'll see you at home."

He raised his gaze and saw Callie watching from the edge of the park green. A hint of winsome softened her smile, as if wishing… wondering…

Hoping?

Back off, dude. Would that pretty lady be looking at you that way if she realized what you had done? Who you were?

No way.

You there, God? I thought this was a good idea. I thought I'd come down here, make amends, fix things and move on. But maybe I'm being selfish. Maybe my presence will hurt more than it heals.

Matt passed a hand across Jake's head, escorted the old woman to her door, then headed back to his truck, eyes down, pretending oblivion.

"Cavanaugh."

Most civilians didn't realize how dangerous it could be to sneak up on a marine. Matt stopped himself from putting a hold on the middle-aged man, but just barely. "Mr. Bascomb."

"What are you doing here?"

Since Katie's father served on the town council, he knew why Matt was in town. Howard Bascomb had tried to nix Matt's zoning approvals for Cobbled Creek but couldn't, and that bit deep with the older man. Because Matt was responsible for what happened to Katie two decades back, he couldn't say he blamed him. Still… "Going to church."

"Katie's church."

Matt raised two hands, palms out, in surrender. "I didn't know that until she stepped onto the altar."

"Stay away from her." Howard took a step forward, his gaze menacing, but Maude McGinnity must have sensed something was up. She bustled through the door of the Quiltin' Bee, her sewing and quilt shop that pulled in tourists from all over. "Howard, good morning. And Matt." Maude reached out and gave him a hug, an obvious move meant to quell Howard's angst. "So good to see you. I hear you're doing some fine work up there on Dunnymeade Hill. We'll all be happy to see Cobbled Creek finished, Hank Marek most of all."

"Yes, ma'am."

She grinned and tugged him inside, leaving Howard in the rain. "May I show you something?"

"Yes." Matt elongated the word, reading her ploy. "And thank you," he added as Howard trudged in the opposite direction.

"You're welcome." She kept drawing him forward and Matt paused, puzzled.

"You really have something to show me?"

She frowned. "Yes."

"That wasn't just a maneuver to break up the drama on your front step?"

Her knowing smile confirmed his guess. "That, too." She led him into a room where racks of hand-sewn quilts were displayed away from the south-facing windows.

"Wow." Matt eyed the walled display, then the racks.

He arched a brow and angled Maude a look of admiration. "Amazing work."

"My Amish women." She nodded, brisk, and moved several poled quilts aside. "But this is the one I wanted you to see."

He stepped forward as she singled out a beautiful coverlet arrayed in a mix of quilted and embroidered flowers. "Mama's Flower Garden," she told him, a fond smile crinkling her face.

The blanket was a virtual backyard of color, tone and warmth, the three-dimensional feel of some of the blossoms a salute to warm, sunny days. The vibrant mix of hues heralded spring, and in the dank, gray days of November, spring seemed a long time off.

"It's lovely." He fingered the quilt again, then turned, puzzled. "But why are you showing me?"

"Hank Marek commissioned this for Callie before everything tanked. It was a Christmas present for her, but then he couldn't afford it, so I put it out here."

Matt flipped over the price tag and winced. "The most expensive one of the bunch, of course."

"Let's call it creative financing." Maude grinned at his hiked brow. "I didn't want anyone else to buy it, so I discouraged the purchase. Think half what you see and it's yours."

"Mine?"

"If you're interested, that is." Her facial expression read "all business," but the gleam in her eye said "yenta."

Matt took a broad step back. "Hank might want to get it himself."

"Possibly." Maude's look said she wouldn't push, but

it also said she didn't think it likely that Hank could put together over five hundred dollars for a blanket.

Matt started to turn away, but reached out for one more touch. "He really commissioned this for her?"

Maude regarded the quilt, then Matt. "He said when Callie came back from Iraq, she was different. More subdued."

Matt could understand that. War could change people, but because women weren't allowed in combat, he didn't think the effect held true for them. Maybe he'd been a little simplistic in his assumptions.

"And that she missed color most of all."

That statement hit a note as well. The flat, dull tones of desert duty held none of the warmth and drama of Allegheny County, its beauty ever-changing in the dance of seasons: "That's true."

"Callie's mother loved to garden. She had a knack, that's for sure. That's why Hank picked this design." Maude flicked the quilt a quick, dismissive touch. "Well, you know it's here. That's really all I meant to do."

"And break up the confrontation with Howard."

She mulled that as she walked him out front. "Howard's not a bad person, but he's unforgiving. And Katie had a rebel streak in her that he tried to squelch six ways to Sunday."

"But—"

"No buts." Maude turned a firm gaze his way. "I've known that girl since she was in the cradle. And Howard's as responsible as any for her wild years. He knows that, which is why he needs to blame you. Howard Bascomb isn't about to shoulder that responsibility himself."

"I was sixteen, driving the car and drunk." Matt laid out the facts with no defensive strategy. "I'm going with my fault."

"Huh." She sighed and looked aggrieved. "You're such a leatherneck."

Her use of the marine term made him smile. "Guilty."

"And two tours in Iraq."

"Didn't give Katie her leg back." He reached for the door handle, then turned back toward Maude. "I appreciate what you're trying to do."

"But you're too dad-gum stubborn to see it yourself," she shot back. "And that's the one thing you are guilty of, Matt Cavanaugh." She reached out a hand to shake his, her grip firm and direct. "I married a marine. Smartest move I ever made, so forgive an old lady for doing some matchmaking as opportunity arises."

"Yes, ma'am." He grinned, tipped his chin down and headed back into the rain, the bustle of people gone, the park round empty. He realized he'd half hoped Callie would still be here, which was downright silly because he'd see her back at the house in just a few minutes, right?

"Hey, marine."

He turned as her car rolled up alongside him, unable to fight back the smile of welcome. "Hey, yourself. You folks going the wrong way?"

Callie shook her head. "Just wanted to make sure everything was okay. I saw your truck parked here once I dragged Jake away from his buddies and…" She shrugged, pretending unconcern. "I didn't want you stuck or anything."

Add compassionate to her growing list of attributes, as if Matt needed more reasons to be attracted. He bent down, leaned in and grinned, pleased that she checked on him, staunchly refusing to examine why such a little thing felt so good.

Why did his smile make her heart feel stronger? Prettier? More desireable? Why did mere seconds in his company make her long for more?

You don't get it? Really?

Callie hushed the inner admonition. She *couldn't* get it, plain and simple. And since Matt understood the rules, they should do fine, right? "Then I'll see you at home and we can get started on the next group of windows, right?"

"Meaning you'll make food in the nice warm house while the rest of us install windows."

"And don't forget—" Jake began, excitement coloring his words.

"Christmas lights." Matt interrupted Jake with a grin and a wink. "And there's a great four o'clock game today." He gave his watch a pointed look.

"Reason enough for living right there," Callie drawled. "See you at home."

Her innocent phrase sparked something in Matt's eyes, a hint of longing that gave him a lost puppy look. The cool, crisp marine facade took over quickly, but Callie knew what she'd seen.

While not all soldiers bore physical wounds, all soldiers bore effects of service, good and bad. Life extracted nothing else.

But behind the wide smile, the patient hands, the warm embracing gaze, Matt's expression sought something. Yearning. Searching. Much like the face she saw in the mirror when no one was looking.

Pulling away, she refused to look back. Couldn't look back. Jake helped her out by pointing to the large sign at the front of the green. "Do you know how expensive those sleigh rides are, Mom?"

Callie shook her head.

"Way too pricey," Jake told her firmly. "And why would anybody need to go see Christmas lights when we can put up our own?"

Callie recognized the tactic and loved him for it. "You're right, of course. And we always take a drive to the neighborhoods and check out the lights, right?"

"For free."

A part of her wished that lack of money didn't govern every turn. Another part respected how Jake cared enough to accept certain things without haggle. "Free's a good thing these days. For a lot of people."

"And Shadow Jesus?"

She grinned, his innocence wiping away old thoughts of bad times. "After the lights. If not today, then one day this week after school."

"Good." They drove another minute forward before Jake twisted. A quick glance his way showed his concern. "Who was that guy yelling at Matt?"

Callie sighed. She'd hoped he'd missed that little confrontation on their first pass through town, but the kid was too smart for his own good. "That was Mr. Bascomb. I don't think he was yelling, honey. They were just talking."

Jake snorted. "He was mad, Mom. At Matt."

Conceding, she met him halfway. "He did look irritated."

"Ticked off." Jake shook his head. "I don't know why anybody would get mad at Matt. He's the best."

"He is." It wasn't bad to admit that, was it? Here in the privacy of their car, just her and Jake? "And if you want to help today, I'll have you work on window shims with us. The guys are coming by for a few hours to see if we can finish up."

"Cool." Jake swung open his door and turned Callie's way as they hurried toward the house. "And you don't have to pay me, Mom."

"Jake, people work to get paid. It's the norm. Blame our capitalistic society."

He grinned, held the door for her, then shrugged out of his jacket once they were on the porch. "I don't need money. You and Grandpa do. Really." He gazed up at her with earnest eyes, his expression firm. "I don't want you to pay me. I just want to help you and Grandpa."

Tears pricked her eyes.

"Aw, geez."

"You're such a good boy."

"Mom, get over it already." He ducked his head, shrugged under her arm and through the kitchen door, but sent her a teasing look over his shoulder, a look that reminded her of how Matt joked with her. Laughed with her.

"I'm getting changed for work."

Callie pegged her coat and headed upstairs behind him. "Me, too. And it looks like Grandpa's beat us over there with Buck and Jim, so we can get a quick start."

"I'm here, too." Tom's voice hailed her from down the stairs. "I'll meet you guys across the way. There's doughnuts on the table."

"Doughnuts! Thanks, Tom!"

Callie smiled, warmth seeking into her bones despite the cold rain.

Two weeks ago the future looked dim, Cobbled Creek looming like a dark abyss of failure.

Now?

She woke up excited each morning. To crew alongside the guys, watching these homes go together step by step... The entire process brightened her day, lightened her step.

She loved building. Creating. Operating power tools. Eyeing a square and a level, getting things just right. And not one of these men made her feel less feminine for her aptitude with a power hammer. So why had Dustin's rejection stung that much? That deep? Had she even loved him, or was their spontaneous marriage just a young lark gone bad?

She pulled on snug clothes, attached her tool belt to the air-channeled suspenders and headed across the street with Jake, humming a tune, then realized she was humming the tune Matt whistled all the time.

His truck pulled up alongside them. "I thought you were cooking today? Staying warm?"

His gruff tone revealed more than the cautionary words. She tapped her watch and continued toward the subdivision. "I've got two hours before I have to start the chili and the bread. I can do a lot in two hours, marine."

She didn't wait to hear his response, but knew she'd pleased him and refused to question herself on why that felt particularly good.

"See ya over there, Matt!"

"I'll be right behind you, bud."

Callie wasn't sure what jack-hammered her heart out of its easy rhythm—his voice or choice of words. But the smile on Jake's face showcased Matt's dual effect.

And when he's gone, her conscience niggled. *What then?*

Callie shoved that aside. Homes weren't constructed overnight, and if Phase One of Cobbled Creek sold in quick fashion, Matt might expand his efforts into Phase Two, a second grouping of homes moving up the slope. In the meantime she intended to enjoy doing what she loved most. Working side by side with family and friends, making dreams come true.

Chapter Eight

❧

"I've got this covered," Matt called down to Callie from the upper reaches of Hank's ladder late that afternoon, raising his voice above the rain. "It's not rocket science."

"Goes faster with two, especially in these conditions." Callie thumped the second ladder up against the house with military ease.

"Then send Buck out," Matt chastised, striving for patience. Wasn't this the day he wanted her to rest up? Stay warm and dry? She'd been working or cooking since they got home from church. Not exactly the R & R he'd envisioned.

"I would, but he's sound asleep in the recliner." She adjusted her ladder, drove in a couple of quick stakes to maintain the position and headed up the rungs, Christmas lights suspended from her shoulders.

"Nice necklace."

The rain blocked her grin, but he pictured her wide smile. Her reply only deepened the vision. "I wore it for you."

"And the boots?"

She laughed, and the bright sound eased the steady torment of being perpetually wet for nearly seventy-two hours. "Bloomingdale's. Like 'em?"

She waggled her foot off the edge of the ladder and he had a sudden urge to save and scold.

He quelled both. "Bloomingdale's carries army surplus? Sweet."

She began unwinding the lights from her neck, slipping the cord through the permanently affixed light hangers along the roofline, the long extension cord flagging in the wind and rain.

Matt worked her way until he had to shift his ladder. He climbed down, made his adjustment, then realized how close they were to being done as he headed back up. "I didn't realize this would go so fast."

"Dad put in the hangers years ago. And it takes exactly two strings minus eight inches, so when I get to the middle, we should meet up and be perfect."

Matt knew he should resist, but an opening like that was made to be used. "Nothing I haven't been saying right along, Cal."

"Ha, ha." She reached out, hooked a light, scrambled down the ladder way too quickly for his peace of mind and the wet conditions, moved it three feet toward center, applied her stakes and headed back up.

"You're quick," he observed, noting how much closer she was now. Touchable, actually.

"What I am is soaked," she shot back, deftly stringing the green wire through the last of the turned brackets. "And cold. Hence the speed."

"I'd feel sorry for you if you hadn't totally ignored instructions." Matt reached left as she finished the length of her light string and grabbed her hand as well as the cord. "I could have done this. I was already wet. And I wanted you to have one day to be comfortable. Warm. Dry."

"Well." She slanted him a smiling look, then swept their linked hands a glance. "This way I got you to hold my hand."

"Honey, you didn't need to climb a ladder in the rain for that. I'd have obliged under much more hospitable conditions."

She winked, wiggled her hand free, then watched him connect the two ends. "Someday when you're not my boss, we'll talk."

"Back to that." He climbed down the ladder as she did, stepped off and reached out, tugging her closer, her look of surprise and wonder saying more than words ever could. He held her gaze and her hand, the rain soaking through their hats, their neck warmers, their hoodies. "I can't even fire you for my own selfish purposes because you're too good at what you do, Callie."

A smile stole across her face, a look of pleasure that hinted more than humor. "Thank you for saying that."

He grinned, dropped her hand but wished he didn't have to, removed his ladder stakes and hers, then shooed her toward the house in a no-nonsense voice. "I only speak the truth, ma'am. Go inside. Sit by the fire. Get warm. I'll put the ladders away."

She looked about to argue, but then that hinted contentment invaded her features again, as if having someone watch over her was the most magnificent thing in the world. And that only made Matt want to do it more.

Except he couldn't. At least not right now.

Not ever, soldier. You think she'd be all doe-eyed and sweet-talkin' when she hears how you passed your teen years? Detoxing in a detention center after wreck-ing people's lives?

And yet, Katie hadn't looked wrecked that morning. She'd looked…wonderful. Content. Peaceful. And her spark of humor that earned them more than one scold-ing in junior high was evident in the grin she flashed the congregation as she challenged them with her fiddle.

What had Staff Sergeant Weckford told him years ago? "Never let a memory become stronger than a dream."

Matt thought he understood the inference, but re-locating to Jamison and Wellsville, seeing old haunts, old friends, new faces… His head accepted the practi-cality of moving on.

His heart longed for a do-over.

"Fire's nice and toasty," Hank greeted him as he came in. The warmth enveloped Matt, a comfort that came from more than the wood stove fire, although he wouldn't deny the welcome the DutchWest offered.

There was Jake, sprawled in front of the game, a bowl of popcorn to the side, maneuvering a team of soldiers through dense jungles of Pacific islands. Buck, head back, sound asleep in Hank's recliner, looking utterly content. And as Hank grabbed Matt's soaked hoodie and hung it near the fire to dry, Callie hustled down the stairs, a pair of fitted jeans replacing her loose working variety, while an aqua knit turtleneck hugged her like a second skin, the ribbed knit looking comfy-cozy while it showcased curves her work gear camou-flaged.

If Matt had a hard time getting her off his mind in flannels and hoodies, he'd jump straight to impossible now, the soft blue-green knit complementing her green eyes.

She looked absolutely beautiful and if Hank hadn't clapped him on the back as the home team scored on their opening drive, he probably would have stood and stared for who knows how long. Forever, maybe?

His family didn't do forever, not since Grandpa's time, but seeing Callie here, in the worn but genteel home setting, Matt began to realize that no one charted his destiny but him. Sure, he had a past.

Who didn't?

But maybe, just maybe, he'd be able to have a future, too. At that moment it seemed almost doable.

Jake spotted him and jumped up, a welcome interruption. "Are the lights hooked up?"

Appreciation for the boy's eagerness turned his serious thoughts to more youthful pastimes. "Yes. Once it gets dark, all you have to do is plug them in, bud."

"And it's getting dark earlier and earlier," Jake noted.

"Ah, to be the age when that was a joyous thing," Callie muttered to Matt. "And then tomorrow we'll put up the Holy Family."

"Not tonight?" A hint of whining drew Callie's gaze around.

"No. And no arguing. Everybody's been working hard all week. Tonight is rest time."

"Although I might be talked into a reenactment of our Aussie mates holding off a blitzkrieg on the carpet," Matt told him. "Once I get cleaned up."

Jake's brows shot up. "Really?"

"Jacob Henry."

Jake shot a quick glance to his mother. "If you're too tired, Matt, it's okay."

"Let me take care of this wet stuff." Matt made a face that had both Callie and Hank nodding agreement. "And then some of your mother's amazing chili."

"And her fresh bread," shot in Buck, awake just in time to publicly laud Callie's achievements.

"And that, of course." Matt let his eyes twinkle into Callie's, his thoughts only partially on food. "And then I'm yours, bud."

Callie moved closer, but kept her voice low. "You wanted to watch the game. It's okay to tell him 'no.' He'll survive. Promise."

Matt matched his voice to hers. "My way means I score points with the kid *and* his mother while Rodgers puts the offense over the top. Everybody wins."

The hint of color inspired by his banter made him long to touch her cheek. Feel the heat there. Maybe steal a kiss.

But a gentleman didn't toy with a lady's affections, especially a lady who'd been raked over the coals by someone not smart enough to realize how wonderful she was.

Exactly why he *couldn't* step out and act on his feelings. She didn't need more hurt or heartache, he was pretty sure of that. What she did need was money to cover basic things like food and shelter. One mess-up wouldn't only cost him great laborers, but it would also cost her the simple basics of life. Home. Heat. Groceries.

He'd cling to common sense. Help out quietly because he was living there. And try to think of a way to keep his distance, but seeing Callie in her everyday, nonconstruction clothes?

That image added a whole new level of difficulty to his task.

* * *

He noticed.

He noticed not.

He noticed...

Callie bit back a growl the next day, seriously disgruntled with herself, men in general, Matt in particular.

A convent would be so much easier.

"Callie, your level's off."

She jerked straight and eyed her bubble, chagrined. "Sorry, boss."

"No big deal. You feeling all right?"

Ignore the concern in his voice and the look on his face that says you matter. Trust me, you don't, except as a means to an end which is getting these roofs in place now that the rain has passed. "Fine. Just thinking."

"Stop that, okay?"

Eyes down, she nodded, knowing he was joking but unable to reciprocate. "Won't happen again."

He stopped nailing and whistling, the sudden silence making them seem like the only two people on Earth, but that was silly because her father, Jim and Buck were on the opposite side of the street installing underlayment over the plywood roofing on the last house.

"Hey." He moved closer and bent low. "You okay, Cal?"

"Yes, thanks for asking."

He didn't tease her back, didn't chuck her on the shoulder, didn't take the bait. "You sure?"

"Quite. And busy. How 'bout you?"

He touched a hand to her shoulder, a simple gesture of friendship, so why did it feel as if he was ready to lay down his jacket over the puddles in her life?

Too many puddles, not enough Carhartt.

Finch McGee's van pulled in, followed by Amanda Slaughter. Matt paused at the ladder and caught her eye. "It's almost worth not having coffee to avoid him."

"Tell me something I don't know." She waited one beat, then two, eyeing the ladder. "Are you waiting for me to go first?"

Matt shook his head, his gaze thoughtful, then inclined his gaze toward Finch's truck. "Does he ever bother you, Cal? I mean, *really* bother you?"

She hid the part of her that longed to bask in his concern because Callie knew what Matt meant by "bother." "Matt, I might have been army to your marine credentials, but I can usually take care of myself. I am trained in mortal combat, remember?"

"And I'd welcome a personal demonstration sometime," he quipped back, but the hand to her shoulder returned. "If anyone ever pesters you, I've got your back, okay?"

"It's not like they're lining up on the street, marine." She stepped onto the ladder in front of him and shot him a disbelieving look.

"A situation I haven't been able to figure out," he told her as he climbed down after her. "Guys down here aren't the sharpest tools in the shed."

"And here's a rope to prove it," Callie muttered as Finch approached. She beelined for the coffee, successfully side-stepping Finch, leaving Matt to deal with him.

Cowardly?

No.

Self-preservation at its finest. For some reason Finch McGee had set his sights on Callie either because she was in financial constraints and possibly an easy target, or he wanted to make a full one-eighty away from his blonde, petite ex-wife.

Either way, she wasn't interested, but he wasn't an easily discouraged guy.

She loved that about Matt.

It annoyed her with Finch.

"Things are really coming along." Amanda noted as she handed Callie an insulated cup. "You guys have done a great job and Jim said he's never worked with a better crew."

"Back at ya." Callie raised her cup, sniffed and smiled. "I love that you buy me girly coffee with flavored creamers. That makes my day. You know that, right?"

Amanda leaned alongside the truck and watched as Jim joined Matt and the building inspector. "We girls have to stick together. And protect our men from snakes in the grass."

Callie didn't have to follow her look to know it embraced McGee. "Except I don't have a man, so we'll join forces to protect yours."

Eyes forward, Amanda sipped her coffee and grinned. "You keep telling yourself that, honey. According to my husband, aka Mr. Obtuse, Matt Cavanaugh can't keep his eyes off you."

Callie stretched out her flannel covered arm. Worn, faded flannel at that. She swept her working attire a disparaging look. "Are ya kiddin' me?"

"Good men see beyond what we wear."

Callie made a face. "That sounds so wrong."

Amanda laughed. "It did, kind of, but you know what I mean. They see our heart. Our soul."

"You're watching that *Tender November* romance series on PBS, aren't you?"

Amanda didn't confess, but she did sigh. "Brontes. Austen. Alcott."

"No wonder you're twitterpated." Callie dipped her chin as the men headed their way. "Let's ix-nay the omance-ray, okay?"

"If you insist."

"Oh, I do." Callie straightened as Matt reached across for the coffee bearing his initials.

"Thanks, Amanda."

"You're welcome. Finch, I'm sorry, I'd have grabbed you a coffee if I'd known you were going to be here."

"Just had one, thanks." Finch's expression and tone eased up as he answered Amanda, then hardened again as he indicated his reason for stopping by. The one that *didn't* include checking out Callie. "I wanted to make sure those berms were re-covered with tarp and straw. Topsoil doesn't grow on trees."

"No, it doesn't," Amanda agreed.

Amanda's straight face only strengthened Callie's urge to laugh. Jake's school bus rumbled down the road, its caution lights flashing, a perfect diversion. "I'll be right back," she said to Matt with a wave toward Jake. "And I'll bring Jake over for cleanup."

She wasn't quite quick enough because Finch managed to fall into step beside her as she headed for the road. Figuring she'd lose him at his truck, a shot of dismay hit her when he didn't open the door and get in. No, he stayed alongside her, giving him ample opportunity to talk when the last thing she wanted to do was listen.

"I miss seeing you at the diner."

Face first, eyes forward. "I love what I'm doing here, though. If this could last forever, I'd be a happy girl."

"Lots of ways to find happiness, Callie."

Just when she thought she'd have to turn around and slug him in the solar plexus, Matt appeared alongside them. "Those notes for number seventeen are still on Hank's desk, right?"

Thank you, God. And thank you, Matt. "They are, yes. Would you like me to get them?" *Please say no. Please say you'll get them yourself and walk me to the house.*

"I'll grab them. I'm going to have the plumbing and electricity inspected before we apply the drywall, and I want to familiarize myself with the layout changes your dad made."

"Like the built-in bookshelves in each bedroom?"

"Exactly that. So, Mr. McGee? Is Wednesday good for you?"

Matt stopped along the road, his presence an obvious wrench in the other man's works.

Finch stopped, faltered, then nodded. "And you know I'm a stickler for code, right, Cavanaugh?"

The way Finch used Matt's last name, coupled with his caustic tone, made Callie want to give him a good, swift kick.

But nothing got inhabited without Finch's signature. Ticking off the building inspector who was also a zoning agent wouldn't be in anyone's best interest. He'd already shown disrespect for Matt, and that tweaked Callie's protective instincts because Finch had no cause. The people who moved into these sweet homes wouldn't have to worry that the builder cut corners. So why was Finch nailing Matt with a glare? Because of her?

Ridiculous.

"And I appreciate that, Mr. McGee." Matt kept his tone level, but there was no mistaking granite for anything else. He'd be polite because they were professionals, but his voice and stance said he didn't back down. Ever.

Finch drew a hint closer, just a smidge, as if trying to intimidate Matt. Not much intimidated a marine. Callie loved that.

"Mom!"

"Go get changed, Jake." Callie called across the two-lane road. "We're coming."

"Wednesday, Cavanaugh."

Matt nodded as if Finch weren't acting like a first-class bully, then headed toward the street with Callie.

"He was a jerk to you."

Matt glanced both ways before heading across. "Who cares?"

"I do."

"Aw." He slowed his step and shoulder-nudged her, an easy grin erasing the whispered pain she'd seen with Finch's tone. His words. But nothing bothered Matt, right?

"I knew you cared, Cal. Thanks for admitting it."

"I care about seeing a friend get rudely dismissed by a guy who shouldn't be washing your bootstraps."

"As I have done for others, so you should do." Matt settled a gentle look on her. "Christ washed the apostles' feet and told them to humble themselves. Humility isn't a bad thing."

"I don't think he was talking about Finch McGee."

Matt caught her arm just outside the door. "Sure he was. To a point." He shifted his gaze to Cobbled Creek

Lane where Finch waited for a car to pass before heading back toward Jamison. "His words can't hurt me, Callie. His actions can. And in the interest of time and funding, I'll let his rudeness slide. If we get this section done and sold and go on to Phase Two of the subdivision, then I'll ask to have Colby Dennis oversee our work."

He said "our work" like it was a given. Callie choked back a surge of anticipation because nothing was a given these days in home-building. Matt had taken a big risk by buying Cobbled Creek. She prayed daily that all would go well, although that hadn't come close to working in her father's case.

Oh, honey, I think the answer to your prayers is about eight inches from you, front and center.

Callie hushed her inner voice, but not before heat climbed to her face as they headed inside.

"You blushing, Cal?"

"Exertion."

A knowing grin set the laugh lines around Matt's gorgeous brown eyes a little deeper. "Coffee drinking is hard work." He took in her cup and her heated cheeks with a swift look of amusement. "So." He glanced around, the sound of Jake getting ready punctuated by things hitting the floor above them. "What did you come over here for?"

"To avoid Finch."

He burst out laughing and grabbed her in a hug, a spontaneous and wonderful two-arms-wrapped-around-you kind of hug that couldn't have been more perfect if he'd tried.

Until his laughter paused. His arms tightened, the grip different. Wonderfully different.

Should she look up at him?

Yes.

No.

But she did because there was no way she *couldn't* look up. Gaze into those coffee-no-cream eyes. See the look of gentle awareness there, the strength of a good man, a man who talked of washing feet and building homes, a man who walked with God and fellow soldiers.

"Callie…"

He whispered her name about the same time he feathered a kiss across her lips, the feel of strong, gentle and muscled arms tumbling her into a world of possibilities she hadn't dreamed feasible in a long time.

"Mom! Do you know where my thick socks are?"

Callie stepped back, joy and chagrin vying for emotional space. "Try the laundry basket in the hall."

"Got 'em!"

"Good."

"Very good." Matt whispered agreement and stroked one finger across the intensified heat in her cheeks. "I'd apologize, ma'am, but I'm not a bit sorry."

"No?"

"Oh, no." He stepped back as Jake's racing footfall announced his eager approach. "I had to know."

Know?

Oh, man.

"Ready, guys. I've got my stuff." Jake patted his waist where a smaller version of their belts held a boy-sized set of tools, his hard hat clutched tight in the other hand.

"You know you're on cleanup, right?" Callie sent his tool belt a hiked-brow look. "You probably won't need those today."

Jake's face fell. His lower lip hinted a quiver. "At all?"

"Not today, bud, but how about you work with me on Thanksgiving while Mom cooks?"

"Who said I'm cooking?" Callie drew herself up to her full height and met Matt's gaze straight on. "Why is it the girl gets elected to cook while the guys play with power tools?"

Matt's look of surprise said she got him. "I just thought—"

"You thought wrong." Callie waved a hand toward the kitchen behind them and figured they might as well get this straight. "I cook because I have to. I build because I can't *not* build. There's a difference, Matt."

"There is." He contemplated her, made a face and ran a hand across the back of his head. "But it *is* Thanksgiving, so someone has to cook, right? Maybe we can break it down? Do different jobs?"

She smiled, nodded and whacked his arm. "Now you're talkin', marine. And if we order pies from the bakery, that's one more thing I don't have to do."

Matt wasn't about to say that the very thought of homemade pies brought him to his knees. It had been a lot of years since he'd shared a holiday meal with anyone, so the anticipation of joining hands for Thanksgiving around the Marek table had painted a slightly different picture in his head.

Obviously the wrong one. Therefore… "I'm picking up the turkey tomorrow." He followed Callie and Jake out the door and down the porch stairs, The General loping alongside them, his shaggy ears keeping time. "We can pick up the pies Thursday morning."

"And make stuffing and sweet potatoes Wednesday night."

Now things were looking up. "Squash?"

Callie made a face.

"Okay, no squash. Jello?"

"I love Jello!" Jake fist-pumped that idea.

"One yes takes the prize on that one. Rolls?"

"Same bakery we get the pies from."

"Gravy?"

"Dad makes the best gravy known to humankind."

Matt ran the list through his head and nodded, surprised. "So we can actually all work on Thursday morning."

"Now you're getting it." Callie grinned up at him, her friendly smile ignoring the sweet kiss they'd just shared while his heart was counting the possible moments until they might share kiss number two.

His phone rang. McGee's number flashed in the display box, reminding Matt of why he couldn't pursue this delightful road with Callie while he let the call go to voice mail. Reason number one jogged ahead of them, the dog keeping pace.

Callie thought she knew him. She knew the improved version. No way would a strong, forthright woman like Callie want the old version around her kid. Her home. Her life.

Hank knew. Matt understood that.

But Callie didn't have a clue. That was evident in her easy manner. The calm, admiring looks she'd shift his way as the houses began to come together.

No doubt Hank was waiting for Matt to tell her. And he'd do that soon. Better to have this out in the open than let worry fritter away his heart, his soul. He had enough of that after seeing Katie, knowing he had to face her, another confrontation he needed to schedule.

Once the roofs were on and the windows in, he'd face his past with both women. Not wanting to do a job didn't get a man out of that job. Not a marine, anyway.

The houses should be sealed by the first Sunday of Advent. Then he'd switch gears and concentrate on completing the model, starting with the kitchen cabinets he hoped to put in on Thursday and Friday when they'd be low on help. By Saturday, Jim would be back to work, and Tom, too.

"Lost you, marine."

He sent her a quick look of apology. "Planning. Strategizing."

She nodded, having no clue that his plans might very well disrupt their working relationship. Once Callie realized the guy flirting with her had been a teenaged con, a whole lot of things would most likely change. The thoughts of that kiss, of seeking a different bond that went beyond work?

That would probably tank as well, but he'd be unfair to take this further without Callie's awareness, and Matt had vowed to never be unfair again.

Chapter Nine

"This is the coolest thing I've ever seen, bud." Matt finished positioning stakes meant to tether the wood-sculpted Holy Family into place on Wednesday night, then motioned Jake left. "Shall we turn on the spotlights, see what we've got?"

"Just make sure they're centered, or Mom will move 'em."

"Got it. See if anybody else wants to watch the lighting ceremony."

Jake dashed up the porch steps, calling for Hank and Callie while Matt stepped back, eyeing left, then right.

Centered.

Then he examined the spotlight positions, knowing that could slant the image.

Also centered.

He smiled. Callie liked things focused. Symmetrical.

So did he.

She loved building. Climbing ladders. Working rooftops.

Ditto.

As Callie and Hank crossed the yard with Jake, Matt

wondered what it would be like to be part of this family, a plan he'd never allowed himself. But at this moment, with these people, the vision seemed attainable.

Because you're living a lie.

Seeing Jake's grin and Callie's smile, he wouldn't think about that. Hank clapped him on the back as Jake flipped the switch, the colorful roofline lights adding nighttime wonder to the simply shadowed nativity scene below.

Matt's heart clenched, the reality of Bethlehem rubbing raw. They'd hobbled into town to find no room. No shelter, other than a cavelike barn. And a manger lined with coarse straw on a cold, winter's night. Little Jesus had been born there, in crude, meager conditions. Truly a child of the poor.

Like him.

"Hey." Callie moved alongside him, looking up as if he were the most wonderful thing in the world, all because he'd taken time to set up Jake's favorite Christmas decoration. "It's perfect."

"Centered properly?"

She laughed and hugged his arm. "Yes. Jake ratted me out, huh?"

"Nothing wrong with wanting things done correctly," Matt supposed. "And it saves a lot of work to do it right the first time."

Gazing forward, Hank's easy tone pondered Matt's pragmatic words. "But if we *do* mess up, God usually gives us chances to make amends. Embrace new ways."

His words targeted Matt. They both knew it. Matt breathed deep and shrugged, the thought of a baby born in less-than-perfect circumstances hitting home. One big difference pierced his heart like a three-penny nail.

Christ lived his life sacrificially; Matt had messed up repeatedly. "Not everything's fixable, Hank."

"True enough," Hank replied. "But I try to never second guess God's vantage point. Ours is limited. Omniscience gives God the advantage to see all. Heal all."

How Matt wished that were true. But he'd seen the horror on Katie's face, the shock, the realization that she was damaged beyond repair. A look he put there through careless, callous misdeeds.

"Thanks, Matt!" Jake launched himself at Matt, hugging him, his excitement over the decorations innocent and contagious. Matt could do nothing less than haul the boy into his arms, wondering again what kind of moron ignored a great kid like Jake.

"You're welcome, bud. Hey, it's getting cold out here. Shall we head inside? Start those sweet potatoes?"

"Got 'em done while you boys were doing this," Hank announced as they moved toward the steps. "The cookin' part anyway. I'll do the glaze in the morning, then all we have to do is heat 'em up to go with the turkey."

"And I cut up all the bread for the stuffing," Jake added as they pegged their jackets inside the door. "While Mom did the onions and celery."

"Teamwork." The idea of a family working together to produce a holiday meal was both alien and fun. Mostly fun. "Do I smell…?" Matt followed his nose toward the kitchen, then turned to see Callie watching him, waiting for his reaction. "You made pies?"

"I did. Not because I had to, mind you." She sent him a warning look and wagged her finger like The General wagged his ears. "Because I *wanted* to after you looked like a lost little boy when I said we'd buy them."

He pretended to scowl. "You weren't supposed to see that."

"Army training. And great peripheral vision. Anyway, what do you think?"

At that moment he thought she was the most remarkable, wonderful creature on Earth, but he couldn't say that out loud for a host of reasons. He cleared his throat and grabbed a fork from the table. "There's only one way to know for sure."

"Which will wait until tomorrow," she scolded, grabbing the fork. "But they smell great."

"Perfect."

She turned and met his smile, but the look on her face said she realized he was talking about more than the pies.

"Thanks, Callie."

"Well, you gave me plenty of time between the nativity scene and your book work."

"I hate keeping books," he admitted as he tugged off his shoes and set them by the fire. "And it's not even hard math, it's just tedious."

"Callie kept my books for me." Hank brought a plate of ham-melt sandwiches to the table, the quick supper a salute to Thursday's feast prep time. "And I can't say she didn't warn me we were skating thin ice a number of times."

"Everybody takes chances, Hank." Matt met his gaze candidly. "There are no givens. If you'd gotten this done before the housing bubble burst, you'd have been called a hero. But getting sick on top of rough financial circumstances." Matt shook his head. "Tough all around." He sat next to Jake, his attention on Callie. "But I'd be glad to pay you to take over my bookkeeping. Not much, of course," he added with a grin. "Are you familiar with QuickBooks?"

"I used it for Dad's records." She brought the coffee pot to the table and filled Hank's cup and his before topping off her own. "Which meant the bank could see there was no wrongdoing when things went bad. Just horrible timing."

"And overextending." Hank grimaced, then sighed. "But I've got to say, Matt, that having you here, working with you, seeing those houses take shape at last." Hank nodded his relief. "My dream is coming true, thanks to you."

"Thanks to us," Matt corrected smoothly. "And I've never worked with a better crew, including you, bud." He chucked Jake in the upper arm, making the boy grin. "So things worked out all around."

"And tomorrow..." Jake waved toward the front window, his mouth full, not waiting to swallow before reminding Matt of his promise.

Matt angled him a patient look. "Let's say grace. And yes, I remember. We're putting the kitchen in the model tomorrow and you're helping."

"Me, too," piped in Callie.

"Count me in," added Hank.

Matt waited as they joined hands, then lobbed a look around the table. "The whole family's rushing to get this kitchen done and the C of O signed?" He winked toward Jake. "Must be wearing out my welcome around here."

Callie squeezed his hand, her touch inciting sparks against his skin. "Oh, you're not so hard to take, marine. Kind of nice, actually. And you'll only be across the street. Easy visiting."

"Until the model sells," he added.

Her face shadowed.

Hank did his customary quick grace, and Callie let go of Matt's hand once done, but he had pretty good peripheral vision, too.

Was that a glimpse of misgiving because she'd put her heart and soul into that model?

Or because he'd move to town once the model sold?

But like it or not, he needed to get a couple of these houses contracted. And holiday time was the worst for selling homes. Most people avoided the time-consuming task of directing a building project until after New Year's. Which meant if the model caught someone's eye, he'd have to sell it and finish another home to occupy until spring.

"Wait on the Lord. Be of good courage and he shall strengthen thine heart. Wait, I say, on the Lord." The Psalm's sage advice had been his mainstay for a long time.

Patience. Perseverance. Persistence. Matt embraced these qualities as a marine, then again as a contractor, but with Cobbled Creek, a part of him longed to fast forward toward completion and the reason for that unusual impatience sat four short feet away, explaining why she'd chosen Golden Wheat stained maple for the Cape Cod's kitchen.

They'd passed the initial inspection today. Within a week or two the model should be deemed ready for occupancy. He'd listed the homes with local Realtor Mary Kay Hammond, but they both knew the score. December was a dead month in real estate sales.

And he should be fine financially as long as they contracted two of the houses before spring, then doubled that by summer.

"I'll have the turkey ready to go in at ten." Callie looked up from the list she was making. "So if we eat at four or so, that works out well, right?"

Matt propped his elbows on the table and leaned forward. "We could always take the day off like normal people do."

Three sets of eyes rounded on him like he'd sprouted an extra head.

"Why would we do that?" Callie asked.

"Yeah, why?" Jake echoed.

"I can't think of a thing to be more thankful for than seeing those houses cared for," added Hank. "If you're worried we'd rather have a day off, then you're sitting at the wrong table, son."

Their earnest desire eased Matt's conscience. "I can't imagine sitting at a finer table, sir."

Hank grinned. "Well, I do make a mean ham melt."

"And the coffee couldn't be better." Matt raised his cup toward Callie.

She ignored his grin and went back to her list. "Turkey at ten, potatoes and sweet potato casserole at three, rolls go in once the gravy's started."

"That way we catch the late game on TV," Jake added.

"With pie."

"And the day just keeps getting better and better." Matt hoisted his mug in salute. "To teamwork. And a beautiful Thanksgiving."

The house phone rang, interrupting the toast. Hank stood, picked it up, sent a quick glance Matt's way, then headed toward the back of the kitchen, his voice low.

"Who was that, Grandpa?" Jake asked when Hank returned to the table.

"Don."

"Is he coming tomorrow?"

The boy's innocent words caused a momentary discomfort. "Not this year."

"But—"

"He's busy, Jake."

"He's going somewhere else for supper?"

Hank was obviously no good at lying. "Well…"

"Jake, he's—"

Sensing the truth, Matt cleared his throat. "Hey, guys, it's fine if he comes. You know that, don't you?"

Hank exchanged a quiet look with Callie. "We'll leave things the way they are for now, I think."

"No, really, I…"

Callie shook her head and sent a swift cautionary look toward Jake. "Don's got plans already and it's not like we're going to be sitting around all afternoon chit-chatting, right?"

That made sense to Jake, but Matt felt like a first-class heel. "Listen, if…"

Hank interrupted him, obviously not wanting to say too much with little ears around. "Plenty of time for Don to stop by over the winter. He's staying in town this year, so it's not like it usually is, Jake."

"Oh." Jake nodded as if they were finally making sense. He turned Matt's way. "Don always has Thanks-giving dinner with us before he goes to Florida. He's known Grandpa a long time."

"He's staying here this year?" Matt directed the question to Hank, but Callie answered.

"Yes. He figured it was best all around. Going to Florida isn't cheap and there's no guarantee of work once you get there."

Did Matt sense a hint of something else in her words? He thought so, and the quiet look she exchanged with her father confirmed his gut instinct. And Don needed work. He'd mentioned that.

But Matt had plenty of help right now. More than enough. He pushed his chair back and stood, the perfect holiday now shaded with guilt.

His father needed help. Except he wasn't *really* his father. And he'd abandoned him long ago. And he had a drinking problem.

Matt didn't do drinking problems. He didn't do family. He didn't embrace the American dream that had emotionally thrashed him as a kid. Thinking of Don brought up thoughts of Neal Brennan and his mother's duplicity, the lies, the scandal, the family breakdown that left him pretty much on his own from age eight.

"When my father and mother forsake me, then the Lord shall take me up."

God had done that in the form of Grandpa Gus, but not before Matt realized that bad apples produce like fruit and the idea of love, marriage and sweet, dimpled babies should be someone else's dream.

His dream?

To love God, love his work and build beautiful, affordable homes that withstood the test of time.

And that's it? Home to an empty apartment every night? A cold stove?

Yes. Less risk for everyone.

Matt met Hank's troubled gaze. "I'm going to turn in early. Get a jump on tomorrow. If you hear me head over before dawn, don't feel like you have to rush. We've got all day."

"Sure, Matt!"

Jake's grin showed oblivion to the rising concern surrounding the table, and just as well. Little boys didn't need to be surrounded by old drama.

Whereas big boys didn't have much of a choice.

"Hey, bud, good job."

Callie and Hank exchanged a smile as Matt advised Jake the next afternoon, the boy's rapt attention the best kind of hero worship.

"Like this, Matt?"

"Exactly like that."

Matt let him read the level and Callie couldn't miss the delight in the boy's eye as he bent slightly. "Perfect."

"I couldn't have done better," Matt assured him. "And I'm real particular about installing cabinets. Finishing kitchens."

"Why?"

Callie suspected he slid a look her way, but pretended oblivion. "Kitchens make women happy. They like their kitchens just so, no matter how much they cook. Or don't cook, as the case may be."

Yup. Definitely targeting her. Such a guy thing to do. Teasing by innuendo. Kind of enchanting, actually.

"And a kitchen's called the heart of the home," Matt went on, abutting the next cabinet group to the first set they'd installed. "People are drawn to the kitchen. It brings back memories for lots of folks." Matt snapped his tape shut, and waved a hand around. "Your mom did a great job planning this one."

"She did." Hank agreed as he and Callie finished the lower bank of cabinets on the inside wall. "Pantry space, work space, and she picked out appliances that weren't top end but would last."

"Top end being ridiculously expensive," Callie added. "Unless you're a Food Network chef or planning a humongous family, a nice four-burner stove with a convection oven does everything I need it to do."

"Because you don't live to cook," Matt teased from across the room.

"You're a quick study, marine." She slanted him a look of approval as she and Hank marked space for the upper cabinets. "Eating is essential. Cooking isn't. Hence the impressive frozen food sections in today's grocery stores. And a fresh apple." She held up her half-eaten one as an example and grinned. "Lunch on the run."

"Because I've found myself inundated with crew members who tend to elongate their lunch hours rather than shorten them, let me just say I appreciate the difference more than most. The Marek family is amazing."

"Can't disagree." Hank stood, checked his watch and headed for the door. "I'm going across the street to check on the turkey and start the other stuff. No, General, you stay here." He waved the dog back into the front room. "I'll get the potatoes peeled and the table set. Then you guys come on over in an hour or so."

Another hour gave them time to finish those upper cabinets while Jake applied rustic-styled hardware to the lower ones. Callie nodded, balancing with one foot on the ladder, the other on the untopped cabinet unit below to get the best angle for drilling. "Sounds like a plan. Thanks, Dad."

Hank sent her a fond grin. "You're welcome."

"Like this, Matt?" Jake held out a burnished handle and lined it up with the holes Matt had drilled in the honey-toned maple doors.

"Yes." Matt crouched alongside the boy, looking like a proud father. Strong. Determined. Gentle. Stoic. "Now start the first screw just enough to hold things in place, then do the same with the second…" Matt paused while Jake followed instructions, his face a study in concentration while Matt looked on, smiling.

"You've got it."

"I did." Jake sent a grin Matt's way and high-fived him. "You can help Mom now. I've got this."

Callie bit back a laugh.

Matt straightened, patted Jake's shoulder and turned her way, his quiet look saying what they didn't dare say out loud.

The kid was outrageously cute, but at eight years old the last thing a sturdy boy like Jake wanted to hear was "cute."

Strong, yes. Tough? Most assuredly.

But cute?

Not so much.

Matt adjusted the cabinet jack below the first upper cabinet while Callie read the level. "We're good."

He handed her the drill and she did her best to ignore his proximity as she installed the holding screws, but that worked for all of two seconds.

Oops. Serious trouble. *When all else fails adopt a code of silence or go to inane conversation.*

Option two. It *was* a holiday. Silence seemed rude.

"You like this color for the cabinetry?"

Matt swept the kitchen a quick look. "It's great."

"I kept it light because even with south-facing windows, winter nights are long."

Matt nodded, agreeable. Maybe too agreeable. Which meant she might not want to talk about long winter nights. Cozy fires. Deer browsing for food beneath snow-swept hillsides.

"And I did the wall board in here myself," she continued as she settled the last screw into place on cabinet one.

"Lovely," he replied, but it only took one look to see the grin that said he wasn't just thinking about plaster board.

Maybe silence *was* a better choice.

"I like that you allowed space for built-in wall shelves flanking the fireplace in the living room," he told her.

"Dad's idea." Callie angled the drill until she felt the screw bite into the stud. "He said Mom begged for more storage space. Cupboards. Closets. Shelves. And of course, like the shoemaker's wife goes barefoot, she was still waiting for those extra cupboards when she died."

"Sorry." He sent her a look of sympathy that made her feel like what she said mattered. "When did she pass away?"

"I was ten." She made a face as she sidestepped to the next cabinet. "It was rough, but she was a great woman. And Dad loved her so much, the kind of love everyone wants to find, you know?"

"Reason enough to write fiction, I guess."

"Ooh. Cynical." She sent him an over-the-shoulder frown. "Nothing wrong with happily ever afters, is there?"

"If they existed, no."

"And on that note…" She sent him a "let's change the subject" look and quipped, "About the weather we're having lately…"

"Safe topic."

"Weather is what it is. Human relationships?" Callie flashed him a grin and shrugged. "Whole other box of tools."

The General stood, paced to the door and whined. "Jake, can you take The General out, please?"

"Okay."

Once Jake had pulled on his thick hoodie and dashed outside with the dog, Callie nudged Matt for his attention.

"Hmm?" He looked up, a pencil held tight in his teeth, his square positioned to mark the outside of the last wall cabinet on that side.

Callie jerked her head toward the door. "You did a great job working with him."

Matt shook it off. "No big deal."

Callie hesitated, then waded in. "It *was* a big deal to Jake. He loves learning the trade. Trying his hand at things. And when we were working steady two years ago, he was too small to be much help but he longed to learn." She settled a warm look on the work-in-progress kitchen. "This is what he's been waiting for. A chance to try his hand at things. Be the apprentice. I just wanted to say thank you when he wasn't around."

Her heartfelt words made Matt suck in a breath, and her sweet expression loosened a rusty internal clamp left over from his painful childhood. He glanced away, wondering how much to say, then shrugged, wondering where the shot of pain came from after all this time. He'd thought it erased, two decades of good negating one of bad.

Obviously it didn't work that way.

"My grandfather taught me a lot of what I know,"

he told her but didn't meet her gaze. "He was a lot like your dad. Strong. Kind. Straight-shooting. And he loved God, heart and soul."

"You miss him."

"Oh, yeah." Matt hauled in a breath, then swept the well-apportioned house a look of appreciation. "But mostly I want him proud. I want him watching me from heaven, knowing I stayed on the straight and narrow. Knowing I didn't stray. That I listened to everything he said and carried it with me."

"He knows."

"You think?" Matt faced her, hands out.

Callie smiled down at him, her look endearing. Engaging. "Oh, yes. I believe that utterly. When I've messed up, I can almost feel my mother's arm around me, saying, 'Well, then. Fix it.'"

Matt smiled. "Exactly." He hesitated, then waded into last night's dinner dilemma. "You know that Don's my stepfather."

Callie nodded as she applied the next screw. "Dad said as much. But that's all he said. And I couldn't wrestle information out of Buck either, so that's all I know."

"Neal Brennan was my father."

Callie stopped working and turned full about. "Jeff's father?"

"And Meredith's. Yes."

"Meredith was a year ahead of me in school," Callie mused. "Beautiful. Polished. Cheerleader. I didn't know her, but a part of me would have loved to be just like her."

"Kids hide a lot under an illusion of success."

"Did you?"

He snorted. "Not hardly. I went the other way."

Her expression said "Tell me more," but he wasn't about to spill everything here and now, when Jake would rejoin them at any moment.

"So Don married your mother..."

"If only it was that easy." Matt finished leveling the last cabinets, face forward. "My mother cheated on Don. She was a waitress, Neal was a customer. A rich customer. I was the result. No one knew until Neal made it public knowledge when I was eight years old. Don walked out, started drinking, and I never heard from him again. My mother began entertaining guy after guy, never happy. Never content. She died during my first tour in Iraq."

"Oh, Matt." Callie touched his arm, sympathetic. "I'm so sorry."

"Yeah, well." He shrugged one shoulder, and changed the subject, feeling like he'd shared enough darkness to shadow a blessed holiday. "We're good here."

Jake burst back through the door, scrubbing his hands together, the dog trotting alongside. "It got cold out there."

Matt knew that. And working in a house all day with no heat wasn't exactly comfortable, even with their layers. "One more cabinet and we'll call it a day. I've got to grab a few things at the lumber yard in the morning, so I'll head over first thing. They open at six."

"It's Black Friday," Callie reminded him.

He'd forgotten that.

"Most of the craziness will be at the big stores and the shopping areas in Olean, but..." she let her voice taper and shifted a brow up, "the lumber yard had an ad in today's paper, so they'll be busy."

He should have made the run yesterday, but he didn't and he hated standing in line.

"Shop-a-phobic?"

He grunted. "Not when there's a point to it. But Black Friday?"

"Want me to go instead?" she asked as she applied the last two mounting screws.

Matt shook his head as he and Jake gathered tools. "No. My bad. And if they have a quick lane open, I'll still be able to get in and out."

Callie's doubtful look said that wasn't going to happen, but Matt could hope, right?

"This is amazing, Hank." Matt walked into the dining area a short while later and swallowed a lumber-sized lump in his throat, the laden table set for four. "What can I do to help?"

Hank beamed. "Have a seat. We're all set except for mashing the potatoes and saying grace. Only thing is, Callie doesn't let me get away with quick grace on Thanksgiving, so I might hold off and do the potatoes after we pray."

"Funny, Dad."

Hank grinned her way, his pride and affection for Callie and Jake obvious, and as they finished drying their hands and settled in at the festive table, one of Matt's heart clamps loosened a little bit more.

He fit at this table. With this family.

He didn't dare make too much of that. He comprehended the darkness of past sins.

But it felt good to be here. Real good. And Matt hadn't sat at a family table to have a holiday dinner in fifteen years, so this…

Oh, this was nice.

They joined hands, heads bowed as Hank said the blessing, and while slightly longer than his usual, it wasn't overdone to the point of cold potatoes.

"You were right." Callie sent Matt a look of unsurpassed happiness a few minutes later. "This turkey is magnificent."

He grinned. "Told you so."

"Son, I haven't had a bird taste this good in a long time," Hank confessed. "We always buy the frozen ones they sell cheap in November. This—" he speared a piece of white meat and held it aloft "—reminds me of turkeys we had when I was a boy, when my parents would go to the farm and pick theirs out."

"Free range. Some mighty good eating right there."

"And even though I'm eating a feast," Callie confessed, "I'm already envisioning turkey sandwiches with cranberry sauce. Turkey and biscuits. Turkey and rice."

"And pie," Matt added with enthusiasm.

His tone of appreciation made her flush. "Now the pressure's on. What if they're not good?"

"They'll be wonderful."

"You used your mama's crust recipe, and crust makes the pie," Hank declared. "Now, Jake, if you'll hand me that dish of sweet potatoes, I think I've cleared a corner on this plate of mine."

Jake laughed and passed the bowl left, his eagerness for food warding off the urge to converse, unusual for Jake. But Matt understood the boy's attentiveness to a meal like this, and couldn't deny he felt the same way.

Warm. Fed. A place to belong.

Guilt niggled him out of nowhere.

Where was Don tonight? Did he catch Thanksgiving dinner with a friend? Or had this been his only option and Matt ruined it by being there?

Sizing up the amount of food they had, the twinge of guilt grew. There'd have been plenty of food for Don and leftovers.

Did he want his former stepfather hanging around? No.

But that gut feeling went against the grain of faith. Matt knew better. And if his original reason to work in southern Allegheny County was to mend old fences, he could have started with Don.

"Matt, you okay?" Jake asked when he'd been quiet too long.

"I'm fine, bud. Just thinking of how wonderful this is. How blessed I am to be here."

Hank met his look across the table. Read his mind. Matt saw it in a tiny flash of satisfaction that crinkled Hank's gaze.

He'd messed up by leaving Don out of this equation. But because Don was staying in town for the winter, Matt could find some way to fix it.

Add it to the list, his conscience scoffed. *And that list is getting a little long, don't you think?*

It was, but Thanksgiving night was a time for rejoicing. Eating pie. Watching football and the first Christmas specials.

"More stuffing, Matt?"

Callie offered the green-glazed bowl full of the most delicious stuffing he'd ever tasted, the bowl's color contrasting with the lighter green of her eyes. "Yes, please. It's the best I've ever had, Callie."

Gladness brightened her features, but she angled him

a warning look, sassy and spritely, total Callie. "Don't get used to it. I'd rather build, remember?"

"I won't likely forget. Nor would you let me."

But right then the thought of building together, eating together, grabbing frozen food together...

That seemed too good to be true, but for tonight, this night, he'd relax and enjoy the moment.

Chapter Ten

"Cavanaugh."

Matt cringed inside the next morning. Outwardly, he showed no emotion as Finch McGee sauntered his way, the lumber yard registers doing a brisk Black Friday business. "Mr. McGee. Did you have a nice Thanksgiving?"

McGee's glare contradicted his positive reply. "Fine." He scanned the box of hardware Matt held, the bite in his look unbecoming. "Not taking time off?"

"Time is money."

"It is." McGee drew closer. Too close. Matt resisted the urge to step back, the people behind him too close to allow room, and not wanting to give Finch the satisfaction of knowing he crowded him. But he also didn't want to pick a fight with the building inspector.

"And you know I'm watching you, right?"

Matt fought a sigh. McGee's attitude was growing tedious. And unless he missed his guess, the faint scent of hops meant Finch hadn't gone to bed sober last night. Great. "Any advice I get on finishing those homes is welcome."

"Oh, I'm not advising you." Finch leaned in closer, the rising volume of his voice drawing glances from nearby shoppers, strains of Christmas music blotted out by the building inspector's mounting tirade. "I'm hounding you. Watching. Waiting. Wondering when you're going to screw up again because I know you will. Your kind always does."

Should he set the hardware down and leave quietly, avoiding a scene?

The combined attention of the cashiers flanking them and the people in line said it was too late for that.

Change of subject?

One look at Finch's bloodshot eyes negated that option.

He'd punt the ball, figuratively. "Mr. McGee, what do you think of Councilman Gilroody's suggestion requiring all new housing to have metal roofs?"

McGee stepped back, confused.

Perfect.

"The one-time expense drives initial prices up," Matt continued as he moved closer to checking out and a much-needed escape, "but the home's value stays steady and gives banks less reason to refuse a mortgage, so the long-run offering is substantial."

"Gilroody's a good man."

Matt knew that. And the quick change of subject had gotten him to the cash register, so mission complete. "And the extended life warranty on those roofs is attractive."

Finch gathered his thoughts just long enough for the young woman to ring up Matt's purchases. He smiled at her, accepted the bag of hardware needed to finish off the kitchen in the Cape, then turned toward the door.

"Remember, Cavanaugh."

Matt headed out, saying nothing, unwilling to feed the other man's hungover angst.

Maybe Finch had a drinking problem. From the look of him, he shouldn't have been driving, and Matt could attest that he shouldn't have been talking either, his posture and words drawing attention from a crowd.

It was foolish behavior for a town official, but in Matt's experience, even a little power could turn a man's head. But Finch was in a position to cost Matt two things he couldn't afford to waste: money and time.

He needed Phase One complete before he requested Colby as his inspector. That good faith initiative went far in town government, and Matt was determined to make the grade, but Finch's attitude said this was far from over, and that didn't bode well.

He paused as he backed up the truck. He could return to Cobbled Creek and think about offering Don a job or he could man up and do it.

The clock told him it was early, but construction crews weren't much for sleeping in and Matt had looked up Don's address the night before. He had an apartment in Wellsville, five minutes from the lumber store.

Jesus had seized every opportunity to bring his lambs home. He'd gone hungry and thirsty to teach. He'd supped with sinners regularly, pressing the message that all were welcome at God's table.

Doing less felt wrong because it *was* wrong. Matt shoved the truck into drive and headed into Wellsville, hoping Don was awake. And sober.

"Matt?" Don scrubbed a hand to a lightly whiskered face and squinted at him in the doorway. "What are you doing here?"

"May I come in?"

"Sure." Don pushed the door open wider and let Matt into a threadbare apartment that smelled like coffee. "Want some coffee?"

"Please."

Don led him into the galley kitchen and filled two chipped mugs. "Got milk here."

"Black's fine."

"Sugar?"

Matt shook his head and figured they'd pretty much exhausted small talk. "You said you needed a job."

Don flushed, tentative. "I'm doing fine, actually. I've got some things lined up in Florida..."

"Except you're not going to Florida."

Don frowned. "Hank told you, huh?"

"Look, Don." Matt sat down in one of the two available chairs and pretended to be at ease. "I need a good drywall seamer. Hank says you're the best around."

"He's right."

"You've got to have steady hands to run seam."

"That's your way of saying no drinking." Don paused, glanced around, then met Matt's gaze. "I don't drink anymore, although there are days I want to. And the more I sit around, the harder that seems, but I don't want a job out of pity." He shifted forward, his gaze intent. "I did you wrong, Matt. I got mad at your mother for living a lie and I walked out, thinking biology made a man a father."

Matt gripped his coffee cup, unwilling to interrupt.

"I tossed eight years of loving you, being your dad, being so proud I could bust, into the trash over a cheating woman. It was a shameful thing to do. Between your mother and me, we did a lousy number on you and you ended up hanging with the wrong crowd, getting into all kinds of trouble. Considering that," Don hunched forward, his eyes clear, his expression guarded, "why would you offer me a job?"

"Because it's the right thing to do." Matt leaned forward as well, but not as far.

Regret shadowed Don's his features.

"I messed up big time," Matt continued. "But that was my fault as much as anybody's. I didn't hang with the wrong crowd, Don. I *was* the wrong crowd." He took one last long swig of coffee and stood. "I'm not good at all this talking stuff."

"Me neither."

"I need a seamer. I'd like us to get along. I can't have drinking around me, but if you're comfortable with that, I'd like to have you on board while the others work on sealing the remaining houses before the weather gets worse."

"Snow's forecast for next week."

"Which gives me just enough time if all goes well."

Don stretched out a hand, not a tremor in sight. "I'm in. And thank you, Matt."

A simple handshake between two construction guys. Why did it feel like so much more? "Head over once you're ready. I'll be in the model."

"Callie's house."

Don's easy remark made the words more real. The model reflected Callie in so many ways. Strong. Beautiful. Attentive to detail.

The idea of selling it made Matt feel guilty, but that was silly. She and Hank had designed the house with no intention of living there. Why should he feel bad?

He climbed into the truck and stared at his phone,

knowing Sunday loomed two days away. And Sunday meant church. And Katie, if he went to the White Church at the Bend again.

So he wouldn't. Why would he intentionally encroach on her life? So what that he felt at home the minute he walked in the door. That he'd eyed the structural problems of the old building, wondering what he could do to help.

He took Route 19 North and hung a right toward Jamison, taking the shortcut back to Cobbled Creek. As he followed the Park Round curve, Simon MacDaniel waved from the driveway of the church.

Matt slowed the truck and rolled down the window. "Hey, Si. What's up?"

Si pulled a worn but thick hoodie closer and grimaced. "I can't believe I'm hoping for snow, but this rain is wreaking havoc with our roof."

Matt thrust his chin toward the church and nodded. "I noticed that. And your interior damage will spread if it doesn't get fixed."

"And money's nonexistent with so many of the congregation heading south this time of year," Si told him. "We've gotten a couple of decent bequests and memoriam donations, but roofing is crazy expensive. We were hoping to hold off until next summer, but I don't think we can."

"I agree. But maybe we can patch the bad spot. Want me to have a look?"

Si stared at him. "You do roofing?"

Matt shrugged. "I own a construction company."

Happiness brightened Si's face. "Providence, right?"

Matt pulled into the drive, climbed out and met the other man's gaze. "You didn't know? Really?"

"Scout's honor," Si promised. "I was just out there, wondering what to do, praying and staring up while realizing I know nothing about constructing buildings..."

"But a fair piece about mending souls," Matt cut in.

"As nice as that sounds," Si replied, "it won't keep us dry when spring blasts us with torrential rains."

"True enough. You got a ladder, Si?"

"Back here."

They set the ladder against the lowest part of the church roof. Matt started up, then paused, looking back. "Thank you for not picking a church with a towering cathedral. Right now small and country seems a whole lot friendlier."

Hinted sadness darkened Si's eyes, passing almost quick enough for Matt to doubt his eyesight. But not quite. "I couldn't agree more." He ascended the ladder behind Matt and hung there while Matt surveyed the roof.

"You're frowning."

"Yup."

"In my experience, frowns equate expensive."

"Yeah. But the good news is, I think I can patch it," Matt told him. "Monday and Tuesday are both supposed to be clear. If I bring a couple of guys by, can we jump up here and get it done for you?"

"I'd be forever in your debt," Si declared.

Matt smiled as he climbed down. "No, you won't, but I wouldn't mind some extra prayers if you've got a mind to. They'd come in handy these next few weeks."

Si clamped a firm hand on his shoulder, his bright blue eyes meeting Matt's. "Consider it done, my friend."

Matt nodded, grateful, then pivoted to climb into the truck, only to stop dead.

Katie approached the two men, and there was no mistaking her look of surprise as she recognized Matt. "Matt, you're back."

He squirmed inside and out. "Katie."

"You're back and you haven't called," she corrected herself, her expression tart.

"I...um..."

"In nearly twenty years," she went on, moving closer, her stride smooth even with the driveway's upgrade. To see her move, he'd never suspect she was handicapped.

"You two know each other." Si offered the interpretation as though heading off trouble, but he needn't have bothered. The look on Katie's face said "storm front coming."

"I thought we did," Katie told Si, her voice signaling otherwise. "But friends don't desert each other when the chips are down. Friends don't abandon one another when things go wrong. Friends—"

"I get it." Matt faced her, feeling unprepared, but wasn't this what he came back for? To have it out with each and every person he'd wronged? Obviously it was Katie's turn.

"So that's it? You stumble across me here, shrug your shoulders and move on?"

He wouldn't do that. Couldn't do that. If God provided this unexpected opportunity, there was obviously a reason. "I have to get back to work right now, but I'd like to talk to you. See you."

Simon shifted beside him, as if wondering about Matt's intent.

"How about tonight?" he continued. "We could meet at that little coffee shop." He jutted his chin toward the café across the green, the artistic sign proclaiming great music, espresso and food beneath a bright yellow flower. "If you're free, that is."

She stared at him with little emotion, but her eyes…

Oh, those eyes said so much. Two decades of anger and disappointment deepened the pale gray to steel. But she nodded and took a broad step away from the truck. "Seven-thirty."

"All right." He turned back toward Simon. "And I'll be sure to come by either Monday or Tuesday with the guys. We'll get that patched up for you."

Simon didn't look quite as happy now, but Matt had enough on his plate. He climbed into the truck, eased it into reverse, and rolled down the driveway, carefully not looking left or right. He didn't need to see Katie's face to read the disappointment there, or Si's to acknowledge the look of question.

He gave up the idea of stopping for coffee, his gut advising him to wait, and headed toward the outskirts of town and Dunnymeade Hill, wondering why he hadn't taken the long way around in the first place.

He knew he had to talk to Katie. Apologize. Set things straight.

But he'd envisioned a more controlled approach. With considerable distance. A phone call, perhaps, or better yet, an email. That's how he'd imagined his first contact with Katie, just enough to give them both time to think. Ponder. Pray.

As he headed into Cobbled Creek, lights in the model told him the Mareks were already at work. The realization calmed him. He'd get through today, then face tonight. Either way, it would be over and done before his head hit a pillow, and he wasn't sure if that was a good thing or bad.

But he'd find out soon enough.

* * *

"Morning, boss," Callie called as Matt came through the side entrance of the model. His look appraised the work she'd gotten done. He whistled appreciation, the clean white primer pulling the kitchen's look together.

"You got here early, Cal."

She nodded, concentrating on cutting in along a cabinet's edge. "Couldn't sleep and I wanted this done before the countertop guys come on Monday. Then we can install the sink." She ducked low to do the baseboard, then asked, "What's your time frame on wallboard seaming?"

"Today."

"Want a suggestion?" She looked up at him, unsure of his reaction.

"Maybe."

Callie grinned. "Don's the best seamer around when he's sober and he's been sober for nearly a year."

He stared outside, then sighed. "I've already asked him. He's on his way."

"Really?"

He directed his gaze down to her.

"No argument, no convincing, no appealing to your sensibilities?"

"Yesterday did that."

"Perfect."

"Even when I'm not sure why I should feel guilty about anything concerning Don."

"Wanna talk some more?"

He pulled hardware out of the box and headed toward the living room. "No."

Okay, then.

He popped his head around a few seconds later.

"Sorry. Didn't mean to be short with you. None of this is your fault, and—"

"It's okay, Matt. Really."

He looked relieved by her reaction. Sympathy rose from within, a whisper of the little boy lost showing in his eyes.

Gorgeous brown velvet eyes. Deep. Soulful.

"Besides, the walls have ears around here," Matt added.

That was certainly true. "We could grab coffee later," Callie mused.

His look of chagrin said he was busy. Worse, that she'd caught him out. "Another time might be better, huh?" Callie asked, her mind going back to the message from Reenie.

Her voice must have said more than her words because Matt poked his head around the corner again. "I'm not dating anyone, Cal. And if you've got something to ask, darlin', just spit it out." He flashed that smile again, the one that said he'd read her hesitation and countered it. "And just to straighten things out, Reenie is the gal who does doll-up for me. She sweeps, mops, wipes things down, makes sure everything's pristine before buyers walk in the front door. She's in her fifties, married and has four grandchildren. Although her macadamia brownies *are* a temptation."

Callie sent him a scathing look, but he'd already ducked back to his side of the half wall. Just as well. She had work to do and conversation might pull her off-task.

"But I'd like to grab coffee with you," he called back, sounding more serious this time, "Talk about things. But not tonight. I, um…"

"Have plans." Callie filled in the blank without looking up.

"Yes."

The guy was entitled to a life, right? And what business was it of hers what he did on a cold, wet Friday night? "Let me know when. As long as Jake's taken care of, we're good."

"Thanks, Cal." Relief colored his tone which meant he didn't realize she was quietly stewing on the other side of the wall, a ridiculous fact because they both understood the boundaries they'd established.

Maybe she'd be better off returning to the diner. Working for Matt paid better, but dealing with these rising emotions put her at risk.

Why? Her conscience prodded. *You're here to do a job. You need money. And Matt's okay with the parameters, except when he's kissing you.*

That kiss. That one sweet, gentle kiss, a glimpse of what could be.

"Mom! I'm here!"

Reality pushed her wandering thoughts aside. Jake was her certainty. Matt understood and respected that. He'd said so. And God had blessed her in so many ways already. Even now, with losing the subdivision, they'd gained a friend and good employer in Matt Cavanaugh. Bad had turned into good. Callie was smart enough to recognize that.

"Hey, bud, can you keep going on those cabinet doors for me?" Matt called.

"Sure, Matt! Is it okay if The General comes in?"

"Jake. Wet dog." Callie scooted back and frowned. "Really?"

Matt's cell phone rang, a straightforward sound, no

fancy ring tones or songs. Callie liked that. He scanned the phone, frowned and headed to the garage, his look saying he wasn't getting a signal in the house, and the garage was a quieter choice as Hank and Jim's arrival added to the noise of doggie feet and Jake's excitement.

Besides, a guy was entitled to a little privacy. Callie refocused her attention on the walls, ignoring pinpricks of jealousy. She had a life. So did he. End of story.

Matt picked up the call in the garage and sighed relief when Mary Kay Hammond's voice came through loud and clear. "Mary Kay, good morning. You're working today?"

The Realtor laughed. "Make money when you can, I say. And while this never happens on a major holiday weekend, I got a call this morning from someone interested in Cobbled Creek. They're in town for the weekend, and they're coming by my office later to look at plans. They'd like to stop by tomorrow and see the model."

"They know it's not done, right?"

"They don't care. They're moving here from downstate and Cobbled Creek reminded them of the Catskills. They're enamored."

Matt laughed. "Enamored is good. What time tomorrow?"

"Ten-thirty. We're looking at a couple of existing homes as well, but these folks seem to prefer a new build."

Matt understood the difference. Some people cherished the feel of old wood, past times. Others? Nothing but new would do. And those were the ones he hoped to court with Cobbled Creek. "See you then. And they know we can upgrade any way they want, right?"

Mary Kay laughed. "I've got it covered, Matt. You build. I'll sell. And I won't promise them anything you can't deliver, okay? And we'll adjust the pricing accordingly."

"Excellent." Mary Kay's promise sounded light, but Matt had worked with salespeople who didn't have a clue what upgrades meant to the contractor's bottom line. Mary Kay? She got it, which is why she still had a business when others bellied-up with the housing downfall.

"I'll see you tomorrow, then."

"We'll be there."

Matt headed back inside, whistling softly. Callie looked up at him and smiled. "You look happier."

He shrugged, sheepish. "A prospective buyer coming tomorrow."

"Really?" Callie grinned, no hint of envy or remorse shading her features. "Matt, that's wonderful."

"It sure is," cut in Hank as he rounded the corner from the family room. "On a holiday weekend. And this time of year. I figured we wouldn't see anybody until February."

Matt had thought the same thing. He'd hoped for earlier, but knew it was unlikely.

"They interested in the model?" Hank asked.

Matt shook his head. "I don't know." He wanted to sneak a peek at Callie to see if that bothered her, but he'd already figured out that Callie was adept at painting on a game face as needed. "They're exploring their options."

"It would be wonderful to lock in a contract," Callie

said from the floor. She stretched to finish the last corner, and Matt thought how nice it was to have her there, keeping the bottom line in sight. Callie's pragmatism about getting a job done kept things focused. Balanced.

"I'll do a really good job on the doors," Jake promised.

Matt rubbed Jake's head as he went by. "Thanks, bud. Oh, and here's Don," he added as the aging car pulled into the drive. "He's going to start seaming today."

Hank slowed Matt's progress with a hand to his arm. The older man didn't say a word, but the approval in his eyes told Matt he'd done well.

But because flashes of the unresolved scene with Katie were fresh in his mind, Matt could only hope Hank was right.

Hank tipped his head toward the driveway. "This will be good for him. He's having a rough go right now."

"Due to?" Matt scrutinized Hank's calm look, then thought back. Don's pallor. His words. "He's sick?"

"I can't say more, but it's treatable. Still, a hard road when you're alone."

"Cancer."

Hank confirmed nothing, but Matt read his face. "Is he healthy enough to do this?"

"Best thing in the world for him. Purpose. Focus. He's never been much of one for leaning on God no matter how much I yammer at him."

Matt had no trouble envisioning that. "Thanks, Hank."

Hank sent him a cautionary look as he moved toward the stairs. "Between us, okay?"

"I hear ya."

Don pushed through the side entry and paused, inspecting what they'd done. "Nice." He turned and saw

Matt there, and the tentative smile punched another little hole into the hard core of Matt's heart. "This is beautiful, Matt."

"Thanks. Hank's upstairs." He jerked a thumb toward the stairway. "He can get you started."

Don headed up, looking more confident with a box of tools in his hand. What had Hank said? Purpose. Focus.

Matt hadn't realized what wonderful gifts they were, but seeing the quick difference in Don's gait? His expression?

That combination made Matt glad he'd manned up and stopped by Don's place. Now if only things went well with Katie.

But recalling the look on her face that morning, that didn't fall into the realm of likely.

Chapter Eleven

"You goin' out, Matt?" Jake asked as Matt descended the stairs that evening.

Matt shrugged into his jacket and nodded. "For a little while."

"Oh." The boy's chin dropped.

"What's up, bud?"

"Nothing." Jake shook his head and Callie wasn't sure whether to chastise him or kiss him for making Matt feel guilty. She'd decide that later. For right now she folded laundry while the dishwasher hummed and Jake gazed up at Matt with hero-worship eyes and a quivering jaw. "See ya."

Matt hesitated, torn.

Callie caved. "Jake, Matt spends lots of time with you. It's not nice to make him feel guilty for going out."

"Sorry, Matt."

Matt stooped low. "I'll be here tomorrow, bud. And we can wage war along the Pacific Rim if you want."

"I have to go to a birthday party tomorrow." Jake droned the words as if attendance was a fate worse than death.

Matt moved back, surprised. "Birthday parties rock. Ice cream. Cake. Games."

"For a girl."

"Oh."

"Yeah." Jake looked up, woebegone. "Mom said I have to go."

"Well…" Matt wavered, then nodded. "We've got to be polite."

"To girls?"

"Especially to girls."

"Jake, we've had this discussion," Callie cut in. "You're going, you will be polite, and Matt's going to be late for whatever it is he's doing tonight." And looking wonderful, Callie added silently, but then, this was Matt. He looked great no matter what, but tonight he was freshly shaved and had on a classy black leather bomber jacket.

Gorgeous.

"Be good tonight, okay?" Matt ruffled Jake's hair as he stood.

"I will."

"Good." He shifted his attention to Callie. "I don't know how long I'll be…"

"Grown-ups don't have curfews," Callie assured him, hoping her smile wasn't stretched too tight. "You have a life, Matt. It's okay to lead it."

He faced her across the table, his hands fisted.

She couldn't decipher the tense look in his eyes, or read the clench of his jaw, but instinct told her he might need help. She moved around the table slowly, holding his gaze, needing to reassure him. She stopped just short of him and reached up a hand to cup his cheek, his jaw. "If God is with us, who can be against us?"

His eyes softened. He leaned his cheek into her hand, just enough to send a message of gratitude, the feel of his skin warm beneath her palm. He smelled of pricey aftershave and clean leather, and when he smiled at her it was all she could do not to melt.

"Thanks, Cal."

"See ya."

He nodded, sent her mouth a look that said he wished they were alone, then moved toward the door.

He wasn't whistling. And she recognized the haunted look in his eyes, the stolid set of his face. She went to the door and gazed out, Matt's taillights growing smaller as he headed toward town. "God, bless him. Whatever this is, keep him safe. Sound. Peaceful. Help him bridge this gap, dear Lord. He's such a good, gentle man."

"Mom, can we start decorating inside tonight?"

Callie sighed and shook her head. "No, kid. I'm beat. But tomorrow, yes. However," she added, seeing his look of disappointment, "we can get the stuff out tonight and then we're ready for tomorrow. We can probably get a bunch of things done before the birthday party."

His smile uplifted her. Such a little thing to decorate for the holidays. And Jake's smile?

Totally a gift from God.

Matt paced the sidewalk in front of the café, half wishing Katie would stand him up.

She didn't. She headed his way from across the street, the village quiet, even on Black Friday. He stepped forward, not sure where to begin. Hello seemed appropriate. "Hey. Thanks for coming."

She studied his face as if looking for something, then shrugged. "I didn't want to."

"I know."

"But I had to," she went on as though he hadn't spoken. "Because *I* don't want to be the person who walks away and never looks back."

Matt felt the direct shot. He jerked his head toward the door. "Let's go in. If we're at a back table, we won't get overheard by too many."

A tiny smile flashed momentarily. "This is Jamison. All it takes is one."

True, but Matt wondered if that was such a bad thing. If a person chose honor and goodness, would they care what was said about them? Of course not.

Which meant small towns were fine as long as you behaved yourself. He glanced around once they were seated in the Green Room, surprised by the flurry of customers. "I thought it would be quiet."

"Not on weekend nights. People come in for the music," she trailed a look to a pair of guitar players settling in near the fireplace, "and the food. And the coffee is marvelous."

"Katie, hey." The taller guitarist moved their way, comfortable in the close-knit setting. "Did you bring your fiddle?"

She laughed. "It's at home, Cedric. It's not my night to play."

"Impromptu becomes you, Katie girl."

Katie leaned forward and gestured toward Matt. "Cedric MacDaniel, this is Matt Cavanaugh."

The man turned his way and extended his hand. "The builder."

"Yes."

"I'm Simon's brother. He told me you were coming by to patch his roof."

Matt nodded. "Hopefully we can get it taken care of this week."

"I roofed my way through college," Cedric told him. "If you need help, I'm available on weekends."

"Thanks."

Katie turned as Cedric headed back across the room. "He and Simon are fraternal twins."

"They're not from here."

"No." Katie shook her head, gave the waiter her order, paused while Matt did the same, then continued, "Simon took over the White Church ministry, then Cedric followed. Their parents were killed in the attack on the World Trade Center."

"Seriously?"

"Yeah." Katie nodded, rimmed her water glass with one finger, then sighed. "Simon was an associate pastor in Connecticut. Cedric was working in the financial district, but several blocks up."

"So he was right there." Matt couldn't fathom it, to be on hand and know your parents worked in the towers that came crashing down. "That's rough."

Katie turned her attention full back to him. "Rough stuff happens, Matt. To most of us. Then we pick up the pieces and move on, which you've obviously done."

Her tone didn't make it sound like a compliment. "I hope so." He paused, drew a breath and waded in. "I came back to apologize, Katie."

"And build houses."

Her cryptic tone said she wasn't buying his apology theory.

"That, too, but the reason I bought Cobbled Creek was to help make amends. To make something pretty out of threatened property."

"And make money."

"Let's hope." He met her gaze. "You don't stay in business if you don't make money."

"Or maybe," she said, leaning forward, her eyes locked on his, "you came back to show everyone how successful you are. How industrious. The bad boy returns and waves his success in the face of the people who wronged him."

"No one wronged me," he corrected her. "I was the one who messed up. I ruined a lot of things in my day, but the worst…" He shifted his attention away, then brought it back, reluctant. "The worst was what I did to you."

"Not calling me? Not coming to see me? Not writing?" She sat back, letting one rhythmic finger tap against the table top.

"Hurting you." He waved toward her leg. "Causing your injuries. Driving drunk and stupid."

"So seeing me is your reparation?"

Matt frowned. "Katie, it's…"

"Because, for your information, Matt Cavanaugh, totally ignoring me after the accident was way more painful than losing a limb ever thought of being."

"Katie—"

"Do you know how long I was in that hospital? In rehab? How I longed for a friendly face?"

"Your father wouldn't let anyone near you, Katie. You know that."

"Then you should have tried harder, Matt."

He scowled, wishing she was wrong.

"You let shame and guilt rule you. And you didn't even help the public defender when your court case came up. You could have pleaded down, you could have told the judge about your life, you could have helped yourself and maybe lessened your sentence…"

"I didn't deserve a lesser sentence. If anything, I should have served longer."

"Shut up."

He sat back, amazed.

"You." She half stood and shook a finger at him, her expression tough and tart. "You acted like a sacrificial lamb, like the whole thing was your fault, like Pete, Joe and I didn't have options. We had choices, Matt. We were stupid drunk just like you, and it was only by chance you were driving. The accident happened because four of us were stupid. Not one. And it was more hurtful to lose your friendship than to lose my leg, and if you think I'm not one-hundred-percent serious about that, then you don't know me."

Her words hit home, but was she right or sugar-coating a horrible circumstance? "I was driving."

"Only because Joe got sick," she reminded him. "Matt, listen." She edged forward again.

Matt leaned back. "Are you going to hit me?"

The tiny smile he glimpsed outside returned. "I'm tempted, but no. We were young. Stupid. We stole that car and went drinking and driving late at night, but each of us made a conscious choice to be there. We were just as wrong as you. But you…" she reached out and smoothed a hand to his face. "You took it on the chin for us."

"Katie, you lost your leg," he reminded her, hating that she felt sorry for him when he'd cost her so much. "I maimed you because I was reckless. I can't forgive myself for that."

"Well, then you're still stupid," she told him, but

her voice was softer. Gentler. "Because I forgave you a long time ago. And I forgave my father for being so tough and critical," she added, wrinkling her nose, an expression he remembered as though it was yesterday. "Although I try to avoid him as much as possible, and that's tough in a small town, but Matt," she bent farther forward, her tone strong but sincere, "our families were a piece of work for different reasons. God doesn't hold that against us. He knows kids make mistakes and need forgiveness. It's what we do as adults that counts. And did you ever stop to think the accident happened for a reason? That it might have been the wake-up call we needed?" She accepted her latte from the waiter and paused as Matt took his coffee.

"We were on the road to early graves," she continued. "That accident put the brakes on. Made us grow up. Now we've all got successful careers. Pete's got two beautiful kids and is a grocery manager at Tops. Joe's a mechanic at a big car dealership in Olean, and loves it."

"He always loved tinkering under a hood," Matt mused.

"And you've done well, Matt," she reminded him. "You've served your country, you've built a business, you're honest and upright."

"How do you know all this?"

She scoffed a laugh. "The web. I've watched you along the way, just checking to see if you were okay."

"I am." Saying the words out loud, Matt almost believed them. "I was nervous about meeting you."

"Me, too. But mostly mad," Katie added, grinning.

"I saw that, which might have been the source of my fear," Matt admitted. "You look wonderful."

"You, too. And I love that you've taken over Cobbled Creek," she added. "Not because I didn't want the Mareks successful," she hastened to add. "But just because they looked so sad that the whole thing fell apart. Callie is about one of the toughest, strongest gals I know…"

"She's incredible. I don't know what I'd do without her," Matt agreed. Something in his tone deepened Katie's smile.

"She is. And she works so hard at everything she does, and her little boy?" Katie lifted her shoulders. "He's wonderful even though his father walked out on him when he was a baby."

"A feeling I can relate to," Matt noted. "But Jake seems fine."

"He does," Katie agreed, "but it's got to bother him. Look back at you and me when we were young. There was a lot we didn't let show."

She was right. They'd hidden their emotional wounds, but things surfaced when they acted out as young teens. "I can't believe the dumb things we did."

"Me neither. And if I'm ever a mom," Katie continued, "I want to be a great one. With a wonderful husband who's committed to God and his family. And a good dog."

"You always loved dogs."

"Still do." Wistfulness softened her expression. "But I can't have one in my apartment in Wellsville and I'm never there anyway. I work as a nurse at Jones Memorial, play violin for the church and teach skiing on winter weekends."

Skiing? Matt didn't shield the surprise on his face quick enough and her finger waved again. "Don't make assumptions about what my life is like, Matt. You see me as broken, but I prefer to think of it as just another challenge. An extra mogul in the downhill slopes of life."

"You're incredible."

"Well." She patted her leg as the waiter brought a serving of spinach and artichoke dip with a side of pita chips. "Computerized prosthetics are a wonder these days. And they're using me to test new apparatus that responds to the brain."

"Your brain tells the leg what to do?"

"And the leg does it." She grinned and grabbed a chip. "Not quite as perfect as the real deal, but amazing, nonetheless. So yeah, I ski, I bike, I run, I play, I work." She reached out and held his hand, her fingers soft and warm. "I decided that I needed to work harder, better and longer to conquer those early demons. So I did. Same as you."

He gripped her hand, grateful for her forgiveness. Her friendship. "I'm proud of you, Katie."

"You, too." She lifted her chin and smiled as the first notes of Cedric's guitar sounded. "And being here with you on a Thanksgiving weekend? Laying all the old drama to rest?" She leaned forward and kissed his cheek. "Thank you, Matt. God bless you."

God had blessed him, Matt realized. In so many ways. He smiled and raised her fingers for a kiss. "You, too, Katie."

Jill Calhoun's Facebook pic shouldn't have hurt so much, but it did, and that only meant Callie'd been careless.

But the picture, sent from Jill's cell phone, showing Katie Bascomb kissing Matt, looking sweet, blonde and beautiful made Callie recognize her vulnerability. Obviously she'd misinterpreted Matt's looks, his words, that soul-searching kiss, but was that his fault or hers?

His, she decided. Men shouldn't toy with a woman's affections, and a single mom to boot? Shameful.

Her phone rang a short while later, Jill's number in the display. When she didn't pick up, a text appeared. "Is this the hunk working with you? No wonder you gave up your shifts at the diner! When opportunity knocks..." Jill had inserted a smiley face. "A smart girl's gotta be around to open the door."

Not so smart when the guy's off kissing someone else, Callie mused. She headed to bed, not wanting to be awake when Matt came home.

This isn't his home, her conscience stabbed. *It's a convenient place to stay. And that's it.*

The internal warning was just what Callie needed, a reminder to step back. Maintain distance. Being independent worked for her. She'd be foolish to forget that. Relationships meant risk, and her responsibility to Jake curtailed those opportunities. And because Matt was also her boss, and Dad's boss, well...

Time to revert back to what she'd known all along: Don't date the boss. Or flirt with him. Or daydream about forever afters in sweet stone-faced Capes with twinkle lights welcoming you home at Christmas.

She fell asleep with a headache. One that was her fault for letting herself get silly. She knew better, and she'd apply the brakes now. That was best all around.

Knowing that didn't help the headache, though.

Chapter Twelve

The smell of fresh coffee roused her early the next morning. She yawned, stretched, then remembered.

Katie and Matt. Kissing.

The headache re-erupted, full-blown.

Ibuprofen for breakfast in that case. She got dressed and headed downstairs, quiet.

"Hey." Matt's quick smile and pleased salute strengthened the headache's hold. Why had she let herself be so stupid?

"Morning." She crossed the room, poured coffee and fixed it in the kitchen, looking anywhere but at Matt.

"You okay, Cal?" His evident concern only strengthened the steel rod along her backbone.

"A little headache. Nothing major."

"Are you getting sick?" He stood and came her way, his closeness offsetting her planned evasive maneuvers.

A plan she was losing because he smelled marvelous. She took a broad step back. "I'm fine. Probably just slept funny."

"Do you want me to rub your shoulders? Your neck? Is your pillow too soft?"

Like she was about to discuss her pillow with Matt Cavanaugh. She shrugged him off, grabbed her lined flannel and headed for the door. "It'll work itself out. And I want to get the model cleared up before those buyers arrive. I'll see you over there."

His gaze followed her out the door, a marine's battlefield assessment. By the time he joined her in the model, she'd applied a finishing coat to the kitchen walls and was ready to hang kitchen lighting fixtures.

"Looks good."

Two words. That's all he said as he walked through, heading into the family room to apply trim. And his tone said they were words he'd have said to any worker, anytime, a casual compliment with nothing else implied, which was exactly what she wanted. So why did it feel so bad?

"Nice kitchen." Don came through the side door next. He examined the kitchen's layout and faced Callie. He smiled his appreciation. "You did a great job with this, Callie."

"Thanks, Don. Most of it was already in the plans."

He harrumphed. "I saw the original layout, remember? And the way you added the plate rack above, the spindles along the far edge, the double pantry...?" He took a contemplative sip of coffee. "Your mother would have loved this."

His words smoothed her prickled feelings, like extrafine sandpaper on wild-grained oak. "You think?"

"Oh, yeah. All this cupboard space, so neat and pretty? She'd have had a ball in a kitchen like this."

"Good." Callie finished the last strip along the upper edge and turned to step back onto the ladder. Her toe caught the lip of the cupboard fascia. She held a wet paintbrush in one hand and a can of paint in the other. No way was she about to spill paint on these new cupboards with people coming in two hours.

She tipped, knowing the fall was inevitable, wishing she'd stayed focused.

"I've got you."

Matt's strong arms braced her, holding her steady, his welcome words emotionally painful. He held on while she unhooked her foot, then asked, "Don, can you take the paint?"

"Sure."

Callie set the can in Don's hand, then the brush. She stepped back onto the ladder, feeling Matt's hand at her waist, wondering if he'd been this nice to Katie last night, wishing Jill never sent the photo.

But a part of her thanked God for the wake-up call. She'd promised herself no more missteps with men and romance. Falling for Matt?

Big mistake?

"Are you okay?"

Strong, rugged hands gripped her shoulders. And she thought she heard a slight tremor in his voice. *Don't look up.*

Too late. He released one shoulder and tipped her chin, scrutinizing her. "Did you pull anything? Sprain anything?"

"Besides my pride? No."

A soft smile brightened his worried features. "Pride goeth before the fall," he quipped.

She tried to ease back.

He didn't let go. And Don had disappeared upstairs, leaving them alone. "You scared me."

Yeah, well… "Glad you happened by, marine."

He studied her like he had before she left the house, then shrugged. "I'm confused. You're mad at me and I don't know why. We haven't seen each other since last night and you were fine when I left to meet Katie."

She flinched. An "aha" moment widened his eyes. "You're mad because I met Katie for coffee?"

She pulled back, harder this time. "Matt, it's like I told Jake last night. You have a life. You need to lead it. Living with us is a convenience, I get that, and we don't want to make you uncomfortable. Do what you've got to do and it will all work out."

She might have pulled back firmly, but her strength didn't come close to matching his, which made her gesture futile. "You're jealous."

"No."

He had the audacity to smile and that nearly got him taken out at the knees. "Yes, but I don't get why," he mused, not letting her go, almost enjoying this. One quick look at his face said there was no "almost" about it. "First Reenie. Now Katie. You got trust issues going on, Cal?"

She did, thanks to a cheating husband and a lousy self-image, but that was none of his concern. "I trust you for a paycheck, Matt. Nothing more. Got it?"

"Got it." He released her then, but the twinkle in his eye said more. Way more. "And I forgot how quickly information travels around here, so the next time I meet an old friend, I'll employ full disclosure up front, okay?"

"No need." She slapped the top on the paint can with more vigor than needed, droplets of paint spattering the subfloor. She growled, chagrined.

He leaned down, close. Very close. "You're awful cute when you're mad. You know that?"

Hank and Jake's arrival warded off her reply, and she spent the next two hours wiping, polishing, vacuuming and sweeping. When Mary Kay pulled in with the prospective buyers, the crew slipped out the back door. They aimed for the Marek house to give the Realtor time to show the people around. Matt hung back to meet the buyers, but he managed to catch Callie's arm as she left. She bit her lower lip, determined to say nothing. Silence seemed best at the moment.

Matt gestured to the cleaned-up model, his gaze teasing. He leaned in, dropped her a wink and drawled, "Reenie couldn't have done it better, Cal. Thank you."

"You're not funny."

"Oh, I am." He softened his grip on her arm and sent her mouth a wistful look. "But I'm sorry you misunderstood about Katie. I'll explain it soon, okay?" He glanced around the work space and shrugged. "I keep meaning to but we've been busy." He shifted his attention to the guys heading toward the Marek house. "And we're never alone."

That was certainly true.

"Soon. Promise." He smiled at her, his eyes sending a message her heart longed to hear, but was it the longing or the message that ruled the moment? Callie couldn't be sure, and until she was, she was safer maintaining distance.

The chatter of voices redirected her attention. "I'll head home. Make fresh coffee. Go schmooze these people with your charm and expertise."

"Expertise will get me further," Matt replied.

Not necessarily. He might be a first-class builder. She'd witnessed that. But his charm?

Off the charts. And that's what worried her most.

She gave the house one last look as the voices grew louder, hoping they'd love it, praying they'd see merit in her changes and upgrades, while a part of her hated to see it go. "Good luck."

"Thanks." Matt squeezed her arm and straightened his shoulders, heading back in. "I'll be over shortly."

"Or call if this takes longer than you expected. I'll fix you a cup and bring it over."

"Thanks, Callie."

She told herself she was just being nice, that she'd hope for anyone's success the same way, but the Marek–Cavanaugh building connection had her personally invested. Good or bad, they'd put heart and soul into this venture, and today's viewing could signal success or failure. She sent him a confident nod and turned toward home, wondering what they'd gotten themselves into. "Anytime, boss."

She doesn't want to sell the model.

The realization struck him as he closed the family room door.

Callie's personal investment in this house showed throughout, even though it wasn't quite done, and her quick look of longing?

That gripped his heart, but they'd built the model to sell, right? So why was this so hard?

"Matt, you're here." Mary Kay's warm greeting inspired his smile as she came through the garage entrance followed by a thirty-something couple. They looked nice. Normal. And as they stepped in, the woman grabbed her husband's arm, delighted. "Look at these maple cabinets, Ben. Aren't they gorgeous?"

"Very nice." He stuck out a hand to Matt. "Ben Wiseman. And this is my wife, Chloe, the woman who ignored my instructions about not showing how much you like the house because it drives the price up."

Matt laughed, shook his hand, and then Chloe's. "I've wired the walls to record conversation, actually. That way I can access every exclamation and adjust the price upward accordingly."

"Clever technology."

Matt grinned. "We do what we can."

Mary Kay linked her arm through his. "Matt is a marine. He did multiple tours overseas and when he got home he worked night and day to build this business. And by buying Cobbled Creek from the Marek family…"

The couple nodded, obviously up-to-date on the subdivision's history.

"Matt's been working *with* the Mareks to stay true to the original design and specifications."

"Isn't that tough?" Ben asked Matt. "Working with the family that lost this?"

Matt shook his head. "I'd have thought so, too, but no. It's been wonderful. And they live across the road, so they'll be your neighbors if you decide to live here. And you couldn't ask for better ones anywhere."

"Kids?" Chloe asked.

"A boy. Eight years old. His name's Jake."

"The same age as our Jordan." Chloe surveyed the kitchen. "And I love the ratio of cupboard and pantry space to work space in this kitchen."

"That's Callie Marek's doing," Matt told them. "She's got a great eye."

"We loved the layout of the neighborhood," Ben confessed. "And I probably shouldn't tell you that, but the minute we saw it, it reminded us of the vacation spot Chloe's parents had in the Catskills."

"The way you've nestled the homes into the hillside drew us," added Chloe.

Matt would have to thank Hank and Callie for their hard work. Sure, he'd come in at the last moment to pull things together, but money and timing couldn't fix poor initial planning, and the welcoming look of Cobbled Creek attested to that.

But now it was time to let Mary Kay do her job. Matt shook hands again and headed for the door, cell phone in hand. "If you need me, call, but I want to get out of your way so you feel free to examine things fully."

"Thanks, Matt." Mary Kay's nod said his timing was perfect, making him wish he could do that in all facets of his life.

Hah.

He headed toward the Marek house, his gaze drawn to the plywood Holy Family staked in the lawn. Simple. Austere. Poignant.

Callie and Hank didn't have much, but faith and love shined in everything they did. They took care of each other, the way a family should. Callie'd grown up with one parent. Jake was doing the same. Matt had been left virtually parentless at a young age, and for just a moment he wondered if the American dream of Mom, Dad and kids living together was an illusion. A shadow of reality, an old truth.

It doesn't have to be, son.

Grandpa's sage words washed over him.

It's all about choices. Good and bad. Every step of the way.

Grandpa was right. Eyeing the Marek house, Matt

recognized the growing feeling inside himself. The way his heart had stopped beating when Callie nearly fell. The way it ramped up pace when she smiled at him. How she managed to capture his heart by cupping his cheek.

He wanted to be her helper, her protector. Her knight in shining armor.

But that meant he had to set the record straight, and people would talk after seeing him with Katie last night. They'd reminisce and wonder out loud. Which meant he had to tell Callie first.

"Did they like the house, Matt?" Jake spouted the question the moment Matt stepped through the door.

Matt picked him up, tossed him into a fireman's hold and noogied the boy's head while Jake laughed in glee. "They seemed to, bud. But I had to get out of there and let Mary Kay do her job."

"What's that mean?"

"Schmooze 'em," explained Hank.

Jake frowned, confused.

"Mary Kay's job is to point out the good things about a house so people want to buy it."

"Although nothing about Cobbled Creek needs glossing over," declared Don.

"Absolutely not," exclaimed Buck, who must have joined the group after they'd walked to the Mareks'.

"It's beautiful just the way it is," threw in Jim roundly, adding his support.

"You sound like a bunch of pom-pom wavin' cheerleaders," Hank grumped, but his grin of appreciation showed his true feelings. "Matt, Buck brought bagels." He waved a hand toward the counter.

"Sounds good. Thanks, Buck." He turned toward Callie. "Weren't you and Jake going to start decorating?"

She nodded. "I figured now is the perfect time so those people can wander at will with Mary Kay, then I can work on the model this afternoon while Jake's at the birthday party."

"Good. I'll grab a couple of these," he took two bagels from the counter and wrapped them in a double paper towel, "and we can head back. Get some stuff done on number twenty-three."

Did he just glance wistfully at the stack of boxes? Like a little boy lost, gazing in a Christmas window?

No.

He headed toward the door, bagels in hand, almost hurrying, as if he couldn't wait to leave. *Or because he badly longed to stay.*

"Matt, can you help us?" Callie's voice stretched high, nerves showing.

"Really?" He turned, caught off guard, as if making sure he heard correctly.

"Sure, Matt!"

"I mean, if you're too busy…" Callie went on, offering him a way out. If he wanted one, that is.

"He's not, are you, Matt?" Jake implored. "Because you can work this afternoon when I'm at the party, right?"

"I can," Matt told him, his voice deep and easy. "Happy to do that, bud."

"Matt loved helping with Christmas when he was little," Don added.

A shot of pain darkened Matt's gaze, but Callie drew him forward, ready to fix old wrongs. Now was a time for hope. Happiness. Health. "Good, then you're experienced." She grinned at him and directed him to a spot on the couch. "You sit here and open these." She slid a pile of boxes to his left as the guys grabbed hats and gloves.

"The guys and I will start getting those plumbing lines laid in number twenty-three, Matt," Hank said smoothly, "because we can't finish those last two roofs until the weather clears. And then Don can head back to seaming the model once it's clear of people."

"I love plumbing," Buck announced. He headed for the door. "You sure it won't bother the folks looking around?"

Matt shook his head. "They know we have to work. And they've had more than a half hour already."

"And time's money," added Hank, but he winked Matt's way, "although we wouldn't mind nailing down that first contract."

"That would be wonderful," Matt agreed.

Chapter Thirteen

As the aging but earnest military crew trooped out, Matt turned, catching Callie's look. "A little obvious?"

Callie smiled. "Blatantly, but sweet."

Matt snorted as Jake dragged a box closer. "What soldier wants to be called sweet?" he asked, making a face.

Too late he realized his mistake as he caught Callie's look. "Present company excluded, of course."

"Uh-huh."

"So what's first?" He surveyed the boxes and let Callie take the lead.

"The manger scene goes on the painted chest alongside the fireplace."

"This box." Jake pulled a smaller one front and center. "And this one," he added, shifting another one forward.

"Great. Let me just grab a—"

"Gotcha covered, marine." Callie slipped alongside Matt and handed off a cup of coffee, fragrant and steaming hot, her thoughtfulness curling around his heart, the scent of coffee, Callie and a hint of wood smoke feeling like he'd come home to a greeting card Christmas. He leaned forward and bumped foreheads with her, ever so gently. "Thank you."

Her smile said so much. Too much? He hoped not. Prayed not. "You're welcome."

"So." He sat on the floor, balanced his coffee on a side table and opened the first box. "I'll unpack while you guys direct. Is that okay?"

"It's great, Matt!" Jake grinned in wide enthusiasm, his bright blue eyes different from his mother's jade green, but his gentle joy at grasping life? That was Callie all the way.

Matt reached into the first box and withdrew a rugged barnlike structure. "The stable."

"Which might have been a cave," Jake explained solemnly. "People aren't really sure, but we know they kept animals there."

"History lesson noted." Matt smiled up at him and handed him an unwrapped camel.

"These guys go over here," Jake continued, intent on detail. He moved the camel off to the side. "The wise men didn't get to see Jesus for a while, but we like to remember their visit at Christmas so we include them."

Matt angled a glance up to Callie. "Does he get his love of history from you?"

She sent him a dubious look. "Dad's been teaching him history since birth. And Jake eats it up. I'm lucky I remember breakfast."

"I get it." He unwrapped more figures and smiled as Jake set them carefully around the rough, wooden stable, frequently stepping back to see if they were placed just right. "The fussiness he gets from you," Matt observed, grinning, a few minutes later.

"I prefer to call it attention to detail," Callie shot back as she attempted to unravel a tangled set of twinkle lights. "Which is why that model kitchen might just sell a house for you."

"For us," Matt corrected.

She looked embarrassed but pleased to be included.

"I mean it, Cal. I couldn't have gotten this done without a great crew and having your family on hand. And the guys." Matt winked at Jake as he handed off a statue of Joseph. "Made all the difference in the world."

"We could just all work together forever," Jake announced, serious and cute. "That way we can build houses and everyone has a job."

"Jake."

"Great idea." Matt handed Jake a slightly chipped gray donkey and sent a lazy smile Callie's way. "We'll have to see how things go, okay?"

"Okay!" He grinned as Matt continued helping, the easy act of unwrapping history binding in its simplicity.

Callie finished unraveling the lights, plugged them in, then groaned.

Matt hid a chuckle behind a cough. "Might want to test 'em first the next time."

When she turned to scowl at him he tugged her down beside him, pointing to the second box. "Let's do these together. Then the lights. Is there garland for the mantel?"

"Yes."

"Lovely."

"And Mom always puts Christmas cards up there, and candles," Jake explained. "It's real pretty."

"Like your mom."

Jake turned, suspicious. "Are you guys getting mushy?"

"No," Callie said.

"Well…" Matt grinned at her, tweaked her nose, then handed Jake the next figure. She blushed, and in that heightened color Matt read the possibility of a future he'd denied himself, the thought of working with the Mareks, coming home to this family, a gift like no other. He watched Callie hand up a lamb to Jake, then asked, "How about if you and I do some shopping tonight?"

"Can I come?" Jake asked instantly.

"May I," Callie corrected. She shook her head, chin down, and continued to unwrap figures. "We probably shouldn't."

"Sure we should." Matt stretched across her and tugged the box of lights closer. "Jake can stay with Hank and you and I can get our Christmas shopping done."

"I'll be good," Jake wheedled.

"You'll be in bed," Matt corrected him mildly. He gave a lock of Callie's hair a tug. "What do you think? Good idea?"

Instinct had told her to say no after seeing Matt and Katie canoodling at a cozy table in the acoustic café. Shopping with Matt might possibly be the *worst* idea she'd ever heard, so why did she say yes?

Because you're a sucker for the little boy you see behind the rugged marine.

Either way, here they were at the mall later that night, the sweet glow of Christmas lights framing windows and doors, their bright presence climbing columns and archways. "This must look like fairyland to a kid like Jake," Matt mused as they walked through the food court surrounded by mouth-watering smells. Soft notes of Christmas music floated from a keyboard player centered amid the tables.

"You never came to the mall at Christmas when you were a kid?" Callie asked. One look at his face answered that. "Then I'm glad to be with you this time," she told him and hugged his arm.

"You think Jake's mad at us because we wouldn't let him come?"

Honesty was the best policy. *Most times.* "I think Jake has a wicked case of hero worship and thinks you're the best thing since sliced bread."

"No argument there." Matt grinned at her. "The boy's smart. So what are we shopping for?"

"Not much." She paused and faced him, determined to be up front, although admitting her limits made them seem more constraining. "My budget is small. Think miniscule. So is Dad's. Jake needs a new bike, so that's it. And some new socks and art supplies for school. Crayons, markers, cool pencils, tablets, et cetera."

Matt accepted what she said easily. "So if I got him some miniature cars and trucks, would that be okay?"

"He'd love that."

"And maybe his first power drill?"

"Matt—"

"And I could build him a workbench."

"Stop!" She put two fingers against his mouth to shush him, and tried unsuccessfully to ignore the feel of his face, his mouth against her skin. Right then she wished she had soft, feminine fingers, uncalloused, unworn, the silky-soft skin she saw advertised everywhere. And despite her attempts to heal the roughened skin with creams, her fingers showed the effects of working in cold, dry conditions on a steady basis.

Matt caught her hand, kissed it, smiled and said, "Okay, I'm a little excited. I've never shopped for a kid before. Maybe I should do the tool thing for him instead of cars."

"He does have some cars already," Callie agreed, trying to ignore the feel of her hand clasped in his and failing. "And we couldn't afford to get him a real tool kit of his own once everything went bad. He's got a few, but..."

"Tools it is," Matt decided. "And I'd like to get something for Jeff and Hannah. Besides what I'm getting for their wedding," he added. "And something for Dana Brennan and Helen Walker. Helen's always been good to me, and Dana, well..." He paused as though choosing his words, then said, "Dana has treated me kindly through thick and thin. She's one special lady."

"She is." Callie squeezed his hand. "And I'm delighted that Jeff and Hannah are having a New Year's wedding."

Matt bumped her arm. "That we're both attending."

"I—"

"I'll take that as a yes." He grinned, then tugged her along. "Already this is a productive night. I've got a Christmas plan *and* a date for the wedding."

"I didn't say yes," she retorted, shrugging her purse up her other arm. "And you didn't ask. You assumed."

"Will you go with me? Save me from a night of food, romance and music all alone?"

Callie flashed him a once-over. "I don't think you'd be all that lonely."

"Your presence ensures it." He paused outside the cookie and coffee shop. "Want a quick coffee? My treat."

"I'd love one." The piano notes paused as Matt ordered their coffees, then began again, different this time, as though…

Callie jumped as a voice rang out right next to her. Another voice joined in from across the way, followed by two, harmonizing, about eight tables back.

The piano danced along, the flow of voices joined by others as random people stood and sang around the center court.

"A flash mob," Callie breathed, gripping Matt's arm.

He shook his head, not understanding.

"Choral groups and dance troupes put these together and then randomly perform," Callie whispered. She squeezed his arm tighter. "I've always wanted to see one."

"Well, here you go." He smiled down at her as the far-flung choir offered a rousing Christmas medley, their voices blending harmony and praise. As the medley wound down, a lone man mounted a chair in the middle, his haggard appearance making him look cast-out. Wondering. Wandering. Slowly, note by note, he began singing "Joseph's Song," the poignant hymn expressing the awesome wonder and responsibility of guiding God's Son through life.

The lone man was singing to him. *Of him,* Matt decided as emotions grabbed hold and refused to let go.

The words filled Matt's heart, easing more of the angst. Simple piano notes balanced the strong tenor of the prayerful man, seeking God's will, a father's advice, wondering where a common man like him fit into such a wondrous plan.

The words, meant for Christ's earthly father, fit any man guiding a child not his own. A part of Matt wished

Don had felt this way, that he'd been strong enough to ask God's help and be part of Matt's life.

Another part envisioned Jake, another man's son, a child so sweet, so invested in life that Matt wondered if his presence would bless the boy's life. Could it?

Joseph was a simple carpenter.

Like Matt.

He accepted a child not his own.

A boy, like Jake, to father. Guide. Love. And Joseph embraced his wife despite questionable circumstances. He latched on to faith and clung to an angel's direction.

Could Matt be that strong? Could he embrace Callie and Jake, and be a father in the image of Joseph?

A tiny tear slipped down Callie's cheek, the spiritual words working womanly magic. Matt caught the tear and tugged her closer, holding her. Cherishing her. Wondering what he'd done to have this family put in his path, how this perfect timing had come about. No matter. She was here, and unless he messed up big time, her feelings for him reflected his for her.

Just right.

The song came to a whispered close, the soft chain of notes like a puff of wind.

"Here." Matt handed her a napkin, rolled his eyes and smiled. "Women. Always mushy."

"Like that didn't affect you?" she asked. She poked him with her elbow. "Seriously?"

"Oh, it did." He didn't dare tell her how much. "But the coffee's getting cold and the mall's open only three more hours."

"Then it's good we've got a short list," she told him.

He smiled and sipped his coffee, thinking the list might grow, whispers of promises and forever afters niggling his brain. But for now, they'd shop. Figure things out. Take this blessed night for what it was: a time to be together. Get to know one another away from the clatter and chatter that surrounded them at work. Tonight they were just a pair of shoppers, out to have a little fun.

He couldn't have asked for more.

Chapter Fourteen

Callie lifted her gaze to survey number thirty-seven's new roofline on Tuesday afternoon and put an arm around her father's waist. "It's beautiful, Dad."

"It is." Hank regarded the black architect shingles, then twisted to eye the homes leading up to this last one. "The neighborhood looks great."

"You do good work for an old soldier," she told him, basking in the gentle day, a rarity for early December. Snow was forecast for tomorrow, so getting these roofs complete, windows in, doors hung was imperative.

The gift of hard work, focus and God's hand with Mother Nature.

"Are you coming to work on the church roof?" Hank asked, rolling his shoulders to ease two straight days of shingling.

Callie shook her head. "You need only a few people. And Jake's bus will be here before the roof's done, so I'm going to finish painting the family room in the model. And the upstairs should be ready for paint soon, leaving us flooring and bathroom tiling to complete things."

"The countertop looks good, Callie," Hank told her

as they walked toward Matt's truck. "It has a rich look to it."

"Thanks." She waved toward the model as they drew closer. "The lighter cabinets let me go a little wild with the counter top. You don't think it's too dark?"

Matt came up alongside them, pulling off his hat and gloves. "The lighting offsets the dark tone," he assured her, smiling. "And I think we've had this conversation before."

Callie made a face. "I'm just wondering if that's why those people haven't made an offer, if maybe I messed up the balance and that put them off."

"They said they wanted time to consider their options and pray about it. Stop borrowing trouble." He bumped shoulders with her, then laughed at her scowl. "If they do move in, they'll probably be good neighbors. And with a kid Jake's age, that would be nice. A few days of waiting is worth it to get good neighbors."

"So it's not about the countertop?"

Matt raised his eyes heavenward and climbed into the truck. Hank took his place on the passenger side. "We've got just enough time to get this patched before dark, I think."

Matt nodded agreement, then waved as he backed the truck out of the driveway, the crunch of stones beneath the wheels a temporary sound. By spring Phase One would be complete, the road and driveways paved. Streetlights would brighten the nights, a torch-lit uphill path complementing the curving road.

They'd have a charming view out the front window, Callie mused as she entered the model. She adjusted the thermostat and smiled, the warmth of the new furnace a welcome presence. Painting a heated family room or working a crisp rooftop? She grinned and shed her gloves, knowing she'd gotten the easy end of this deal.

The front door opened as she rolled paint on the back wall. "Dad? Matt? That you?"

"It's me," said Finch as he strolled through the model, looking left and right, his gaze pinched.

"Hey, Finch." Callie nodded his way and continued working. "Matt's not here, but—"

"I know. That's the reason I came now. To see you."

Callie groaned inside, but kept her face affable. "Really? Why?"

"You and I need to talk," Finch declared. He stood still, folded his arms and braced his legs, battle ready. "It's time you knew a few things about your boss."

Cassie frowned, silent, deliberately obtuse. Rule one of battle: let the enemy state their position.

"You look around here," Finch waved a hand, exasperated, "and you see Matt Cavanaugh as a knight in shining armor. Well, he's not. Not even close."

Callie kept working but flicked a mild look over her shoulder. "Matt took an opportunity that came his way, then stepped in graciously. He's been nothing but a gentleman and a fine contractor. He doesn't cut corners, he doesn't do shoddy and he's generous to a fault."

"Fault is exactly what I'm talking about." Finch encroached on her space, determined and angry. "This guy waltzes into town and you follow him around like a love-struck puppy when you know nothing about him. Who he is, what he's done."

"First of all." Callie set the roller down, pivoted and met Finch's glare with one of her own. "Don't demean me. I'm perfectly capable of making my own decisions in all matters, so I don't need you to save me from myself. I have bills to pay and a child to raise, and working for Matt is a sensible way to do both affordably. Anything else is none of your business. Now if you're not here on town business, please leave."

"I make it town business when I'm keeping my eye on an ex-con."

Her face must have showed a reaction because Finch smirked and came forward again. "You didn't know that, did you? That the guy living in your house, teaching things to your little boy, is an ex-con with a record as long as my arm." He edged closer and tsk-tsked her. "You really should pay better attention to who comes through your front door, but then you've always been too trusting."

The best defense is a great offense. Callie strode forward and poked a finger into Finch's very surprised chest. "What is the matter with you, McGee? Why would you come in here trying to stir up trouble? You think I don't know Matt had problems?" She raised her voice and stood tall, straight and taut, a soldier's stance.

"When I was a child, I talked as a child," she summarized the wise verse from Corinthians. "And when I became a man I gave up childish ways." She leaned in, refusing to give ground, determined to have this out with Finch once and for all, hoping it wouldn't affect Matt's certificates of occupancy. "Everybody makes mistakes when they're kids, Finch, and sometimes when they're not kids. But grown-ups move forward and fix things. Do the right thing. So Matt made mistakes. Well, me, too. And I don't think that mirror you face every morning shows a man without scars, so how about we turn this around and figure out why you've been a jerk for two years."

Finch paled, but didn't back down.

"Your marriage failed. And I don't know anything about it, but I bet there's plenty of blame to go around. And you're mad at the world. That two-by-four chip on your shoulder's gotta feel pretty heavy by the end of the day, so why don't you wise up, take your troubles to God, go to church and make things right," Callie halved the narrow distance between them and tightened her gaze, "because I don't want you showing up here angry anymore unless there's something on site to be angry about. If you lay into Matt again about his work methods, or malign him in any way, I'll go to the town board myself and cite personal issues to have them put Colby in your place."

"You wouldn't."

"Would."

"But—"

"There are no buts," Callie told him. She squared her shoulders. "Stop living in the past, stop making trouble and do your job. I don't care what Matt Cavanaugh did before, what I care about is the future. And right now, Matt's work is the cornerstone of success for Cobbled Creek, and if you continue to try and thwart that, I'll…"

"I get it."

"Good." She nailed him with a glare, then sighed. "Finch, I don't pretend to understand what's going on with you, but you didn't used to be like this. Get a grip. Stop drinking, stop whining and move on."

Finch stared beyond her for a long moment, then shifted his attention back. "I've tried. Or thought I did. First it was Katie, way back when, but she didn't have eyes for anyone but Matt. Even after he crashed that car and crippled her, she longed for him. Talked about him. Wanted to help him, when all I wanted was a piece of him for being so stupid."

Matt had been driving the car the night of Katie's accident. Callie sighed inside, understanding how old wrongs could burn a hole deep into your soul. But only if you allowed it to happen. She swallowed hard, recognizing her own struggles, and couldn't help but wonder if two people with so many doubts could possibly be good for one another. But for now, she needed to set things straight with Finch.

"So this is about a two-decades-old romance gone bad?" Callie folded her arms and sighed. "Get over it already."

"And then there was you," Finch went on. "You knew I was interested."

"But I wasn't," Callie declared because her more subtle clues hadn't worked.

"I got that when I saw you get all goofy about Cavanaugh the first time I came by," Finch told her. "But then I saw him out with Katie and I wanted to punch someone."

"But you didn't." Callie sent him a look of sympathy. "That was good."

He growled and scrubbed a toe against the subflooring. "I miss my wife. I messed up big time. Not being home, being on time, helping with things, going to kid stuff. I got careless and she walked." He lifted his gaze to Callie's. "And now she's in Arizona with my kids, dating a land developer, and then Cavanaugh shows up here, playing the hero…"

Callie recognized the parallel. "You had a lot of buttons being pushed, Finch, but that wasn't Matt's fault."

"Katie's missing leg is Matt's fault," Finch declared, brows drawn. Then he sighed and acknowledged, "But that was twenty years ago."

"And she's obviously forgiven him," Callie added, remembering the picture.

"She never blamed him."

Callie could understand that. Katie's gentle nature reached out to others, nothing like her hypercritical father. "Katie's a sweetheart."

"She is."

"But Finch," Callie went on, determined to make her point. "You've got to stop spinning your wheels thinking you can determine the next steps. Let go and let God."

He grunted.

"I'm serious," Callie continued. "You said your marriage failed because you stopped paying attention to little things. I disagree. It failed because you missed the boat on one big thing: faith. If you'd grounded yourself in God's love, you wouldn't have messed up in the first place."

"You sound like my mother."

Callie grinned. "Your mother is a smart woman. Finch, you can fix this." She reached out a hand to his arm. "But there are no shortcuts, no quick inroads. And you shouldn't be concerning yourself with romance until you're on solid ground again. Restructure your priorities. God. Family. Country. Friends. And no more beer."

He hauled in a deep breath and exhaled slowly. "Is there a charge for this therapy session?"

Callie smiled and chucked him on the arm. "There will be if the paint on my roller gets tacky and I have to change it. That baby cost two-nineteen in the contractor's pack."

Finch flashed a sheepish grin as Callie picked up the roller. "Nothing but the best."

"Exactly." Callie tested the nubby surface and nodded, satisfied. "I'm glad you stopped by, Finch."

He made a face of disbelief. Callie caught it and smiled. "I mean it. It's better to clear the air than go on dodging bullets. And if you need help…"

"More therapy?"

"Exactly." She nodded, empathetic. "I've gone down your road. I had a husband walk out on me, so I know it's a tough go, but faith and family can get you through anything. But I'd be glad to talk to you more. As friends," she added, sending him a pointed look of amusement over her shoulder.

"Got it." He started to leave, then turned back. "Thanks, Callie. I hope Cavanaugh knows how lucky he is."

"He does," said Matt as he entered from the garage, his eyes sweeping the scene, his expression battlefield ready.

"Everything looks good," Finch told him, waving a hand.

Matt paused, weighing the words. "No problems?"

Finch sent a look of gratitude toward Callie. "None we haven't solved. Thanks again, Callie. I'll be back to check the electric and plumbing lines on the other houses whenever they're ready, Matt."

"I'll call."

"And don't worry about that two-day stuff either."

"You don't need quite that much time?" Matt asked. Callie kept working, but felt his gaze sweep her and Finch again.

"Work's slow," Finch admitted in a tone of voice that sounded like the guy she'd known years before. "Call anytime. I might even be able to come right out."

Matt smiled. "Thanks. Time's tight now with the weather and all."

"And time's money," Finch added. He nodded and headed for the door. "See you Sunday, Callie. If not before."

She smiled, satisfied. "Looking forward to it, Finch."

Matt was pretty certain he'd walked into an alternate universe.

Callie frowned up at him as she refilled her roller. "Why aren't you roofing at the church?"

"Buck, Jim and your dad have it under control, so I thought I'd come back here and help you." He moved closer and nodded approval, the new paint brightening the south-facing room. "This is beautiful, Cal."

"Isn't it?" She flashed him a smile that brightened the room even more. "I thought it might be too yellow, but it's not. It's just soft enough to reflect the light and keep things warm. Appealing."

"I agree," he said, but he aimed his look at her, not the wall.

"Matt."

"Callie." He moved forward and took the roller out of her hands, wondering when the smell of new paint became so wonderfully enticing. Or maybe it was the smudge on her cheek, the tiny roller spatters across her nose? He rubbed a gentle finger to make them disappear, and sighed, the feel of being close to her a new experience, sweet and good. Inviting. "You smell good."

She grinned and daubed a tiny bit of paint to his face with her finger. "I smell like paint."

He gave her a lazy smile and tightened his grip. "Then I must really like paint, because..." he let his kiss fill in the blank, the combination of Callie, fresh-sawn wood and new paint bringing all the factors of his world together in one pleasurable experience. He had no idea how long the kiss lasted, and really didn't care because he'd like for it to never end, but the rumble of the school bus engine interrupted way too soon. "Jake's home."

"Uh-huh."

He grinned down at her, glad he had a few inches on her in her work shoes, a height advantage that disappeared when she wore heels.

He didn't care. Tall, short, thin, wide, messy or dressed up, to him she was just Callie, the most delightful creature God could have put in his path. As the bus brakes squealed to a stop, he drew her forward. "Let's go meet the kid. I've got a surprise for us."

"A surprise?"

He smiled, set her roller down, then ushered her out the door.

The quick drop in temperature made the forecasted snow seem more real. Callie tugged her flannel tighter as she and Matt waited. Jake raced to see them, excitement showing in every step. "Hey, I got another A on my math paper, Mom!"

"Wonderful!" Callie high-fived him, then stepped back inside the warm house. "Seriously, Matt? It's freezing out there."

Matt and Jake followed her inside and Matt shut the door. "I know, it started dropping about the time we got on that roof."

"So we're patching it just in time," Callie noted.

"Yes." Matt ruffled Jake's hair and added, "Looks like snow tomorrow. And from then on, who knows?"

"I love snow!"

"Most kids do," Matt told him. He reached into his

back pocket and held up a flat rectangular piece of card stock. "And once it snows, we're taking a sleigh ride. If that's okay?" he asked Callie, raising his gaze to her as Jake attacked his legs.

"Matt, you shouldn't have…"

"Sure he should," Jake told her, astonished. "Because he knew I wanted to go and it's cheaper if three go, right? Because then we can each pay a third."

"Well, that's a mighty generous offer, bud," Matt drawled, making sure graciousness hid the laughter in his tone. "But I've got this one covered. Kind of a thank-you to you and your mom for all the hard work you do over here."

"But isn't that why you pay us?" Jake wondered out loud. "That's what Mom says anyway. You work hard and get paid for the work you do. She didn't say anything about a sleigh ride in the park with the lights."

"That's a fringe benefit, Jake," Matt explained, exchanging smiles with Callie. "When you work really hard, sometimes extra benefits go with the job."

His words drove up the heat in Callie's cheeks, and that delighted him.

"Then I like those fringe benefit things," Jake declared.

Matt sent a teasing look to Jake's mother. "Me, too."

"And on that note…" Callie headed back to the family room. "I need to get this finished. And our fire is probably out at home, so can you guys start one? And let The General out for a run?"

"Will do."

Jake headed out, but Matt lingered. "So, Finch's visit…" he trailed the words, an eyebrow arched.

"Something we'll talk about without little ears around," Callie told him.

Matt weighed the words and her expression. "He told you about my past."

"Yes. And I reminded him," Callie kept her voice even as she rolled the wall, "that everybody makes mistakes. And nothing's unfixable."

Matt clenched his hands, wishing that was true.

"Even Katie's leg," Callie went on. She met his gaze across the room and noted his hands with a glance. "We move on. We try harder. Stay strong. Everyone has a past, Matt."

"Even you?"

Her flush said yes. Her eyes said it wasn't a topic she was ready to explore which meant she'd buried the hurt, just like him. That only made him more determined to fix it. "Don't you have a fire to start?"

"I'm on it."

"Good. And Matt?"

He turned, the sound of her voice a sweeter draw than wood fire flames on a dark December night. "Yes?"

"Thank you."

"For?" He frowned, not understanding, then nodded and raised the ticket. "Oh. Of course. You're welcome."

Callie shook her head and met his look across the room, then waved a hand indicating the house, the road, the subdivision. Herself. "For all of it. Thank you."

He loved her. He knew it fully and truly, standing there, seeing her decked out in spattered work clothes, a day's labor behind her and still ready to do whatever it took to be a good mother. A fine daughter. And maybe, just maybe, something more.

He sighed, smiled and nodded, wishing he could

kick his heels in the air like Jake and the pooch. "You're welcome, Cal."

He headed across the field, whistling the "Marine's Hymn," keeping pace with the rhythm and the beat, his soul blessed, his heart… Well, full was the best way to describe that, and while it was an unfamiliar feeling, Matt decided he liked it. A lot.

He eyed the Quiltin' Bee as he passed through Jamison a couple of hours later, then parked the truck and headed inside, determined to make sure Callie had a great Christmas. He waited while Maude finished up with a customer, then frowned when she reached beneath the counter and withdrew a festively-wrapped box topped by a big red bow.

"This is?"

"Callie's quilt." She handed him a bill and added, "And if you don't have the money now, I'll wait."

"I've got it," Matt told her as he withdrew his wallet. "What I'm wondering is how you knew I'd be back."

She sent him a wizened grin. "At my age, there's less I don't know than I do. One look at you and Callie on the park round, well…" She softened the smile and shrugged. "Things just seemed to fit."

Matt couldn't disagree. He handed her his debit card, signed his name, then tucked the box carefully behind the seat of his truck, feeling like he was truly getting ready for the old-fashioned Christmas he'd dreamed of as a kid.

Chapter Fifteen

Callie watched Matt tuck the lap robe snug around Jake's legs a few nights later and tumbled right back into the danger zone she'd pledged to avoid. Matt's grin and Jake's answering broad smile made it seem less dangerous and more charming.

Matt climbed into the sleigh, slipped an arm around her shoulders and dropped a kiss to her hair.

If she hadn't tilted head over heels before, she did then, the feel of a strong, rugged marine taking charge, leading in ways of goodness and grace, here with her and Jake, fulfilling a little boy's dream. And maybe a big boy's as well, if the look on his face was any indication. She leaned closer. "I'm not sure which one of you is smiling more," she noted as they passed beneath a lighted arch made of naturally entwined tree branches and thousands of tiny twinkle lights.

"This is amazing."

"It is." Jake grinned up at Matt, his joy palpable. He wriggled beneath the blanket as they came upon an action scene of animatronic elves in Santa's workshop. "Mom, look! They're building a tool bench!"

Callie laughed out loud. "Those are my kind of elves, Jake. And see what Mrs. Santa's doing?" She pointed toward the left of the scene, where Mrs. Santa and a couple of girl elves fashioned baby dolls. "So sweet."

Jake snorted. "They're dolls."

Matt gave Callie's arm a gentle squeeze. "Did you like playing with dolls when you were little or were you always a tomboy?"

"Both," she told him, smiling. "I was never afraid to get dirty or run with the boys and play sports, but…" she slanted him a teasing look, "even then I cleaned up well."

He hugged her shoulder tighter, laughing. "Some things never change. Hey, do you see those reindeer?"

"A real Santa scene," breathed Jake as they drew closer, the horse hooves clip-clopping along the curved road. A well-dressed robust Santa groomed a small herd of reindeer, on loan from a local organic farm, and the picture added a dose of reality to the fantasyland surrounding them.

"Nice," Matt observed, his gaze roaming as if hungering for the next sight, the coming scene. They passed through a tree-lined path bathed in white twinkle lights, a Currier and Ives setting with the sleigh, the horse, the driver, the trees. A photographer snapped their photo as they emerged from the boughs, and Callie wondered if the photo would capture how perfect the moment felt.

Lighted scenes peppered the woods on both sides until they turned a corner that led them into the midst of a living nativity, spot-lit from all angles. Mary and Joseph hovered over a hay-filled manger, concern painting their features, while shepherds gathered in awe, chatting and exclaiming.

Sheep wandered the area, their thick woolly coats dusted with snow. A donkey stood to the right, placidly munching hay. Two well-dressed angels watched over the scene from above, their raised platforms hidden by dark draperies, while two more knelt below, paying homage to a newborn king, a child of the poor.

"Oh, Matt." Jake clenched Matt's arm and the sincerity in his young voice had Callie fighting tears. "They did it just right," Jake continued, awestruck. "The wise men aren't here, but the angels are gathering around. And the shepherds came back to see if the angels were right. And they were."

"Of course they were," Matt assured him.

Did his voice break a little? Callie peeked up, and the loving expression on his face made suppressing an overload of emotions impossible.

"Whenever I think of what Jesus did for us, I regret every time I whine or crab about anything. Born in a manger, hung on a cross." Matt shook his head and sighed. "And when I feel the most unworthy, I remember He did it for the least of us. And then I feel better."

Jake reached over Callie and hugged Matt. "I love you, Matt."

Fear and hope mixed like concrete and stone in Callie's gut. The thought of how bad this could be began to rise up, but then Jake leaned back and stared up into Matt's face. "If I had a dad, I'd want him to be like you. You're nice to kids like me and that's a good thing for a dad to do."

The look of love Matt settled on the boy was enhanced by the big, broad hand he laid against Jake's cheek. "You're right, bud. That's exactly what dads should do."

Jake matched and met Matt's smile, then sat back. "This is the most beautiful night I ever had."

Matt heard the boy's words and glimpsed Callie's tear-streaked face and realized he was in for the long haul. Only a rotter would back out now, and Matt had no intention of backing away from this family.

Callie fumbled for a tissue, wiped her eyes and blew her nose, then mock-scowled at him for sending a laughing glance her way. "It's cold out here."

"Uh-huh." He leaned closer, his mouth to her ear. "I think you're a sap, soldier. But pretty enough to be kissed." And he did that, right there, a sweet, gentle kiss feathering over her face, her mouth, not caring if Jake saw because Matt had every intention of establishing his very own family in Cobbled Creek.

If she'd have him, of course. But from the look on her face Matt was pretty sure nothing could get in their way.

"Hey, Matt. What's up?" Jeff Brennan pulled up next to Matt's car at a Wellsville gas station the next afternoon. "I keep meaning to get over to Cobbled Creek, but the factory's crazy busy. How are things going? Okay?"

Matt turned and shot a smile toward his half brother. *Brother,* he corrected himself, determined to mend every relationship he could, regardless of legality.

He nodded. "Amazing, actually. And you were right when you told me the Mareks are wonderful people. And I've got my stepdad doing drywall for me."

He hesitated saying that last bit, pretty sure Jeff would think it weird. As if their convoluted relationships could get any stranger than they already were.

"Awkward." Jeff sent Matt a look of understanding.

"But because that describes our family to a tee, it's a good place to start over."

"He's sick, too."

"Yeah?" Jeff's sympathetic expression said he empathized. "What's his prognosis?"

"Good. Just a road to travel. A rough go, alone."

"So it's nice he has you."

"I guess." At this moment Matt wasn't too sure what purpose he served anywhere, except with a hammer in his hands. Give him a toolbox and suddenly everything made sense. "Everybody's gotta have someone, right? How are the wedding plans coming?"

Jeff grinned. "Hannah and I put them in Mom's capable hands. She's happy, she's got Meredith to help her, and we're delighted to let things happen around us."

"Your mother's great," Matt told him. Jeff's mother had been the only person other than Grandpa Gus to visit Matt in juvie, and that was after Dana Brennan had her private life gossiped about in every home when the world discovered Matt was her husband's illegitimate son.

"She is. And you're coming over for Christmas, right?"

"Well…"

"Like you've got a better offer?" Jeff's teasing tone said he doubted that.

"I…um…"

"You *do* have a better offer," Jeff mused. His left eyebrow shifted up. "Which means the Marek family, because you've been holed up in Cobbled Creek for weeks."

"I might be spending it with them. Yes."

"With Callie, you mean."

Matt was hoping for that very thing, but... "Keep a spot at the table open for me. Just in case."

Jeff gave him a brotherly arm punch. "Will do. Although Mom likes nothing more than planning special events. So she'd be glad to jump in and help with anything you might need. You know that, don't you?"

Maybe he'd said too much. Or at least too soon. Matt leaned down. "Hey, about Christmas and the Mareks, don't say anything, okay?"

Jeff's grin spread wide. "You'll owe me."

Maybe having a brother wasn't such a great thing after all. "For?"

"Buying my silence."

Matt thought of how convoluted his life had just become and didn't hold back his sigh. "This one time, it will be worth it."

Jeff laughed and drove off, leaving Matt feeling like life was racing forward at break-neck speed and he'd forgotten how to apply the brakes. Except he didn't want to, not really. And he was surprised at how good that felt.

She should stay home, Callie decided, eyeing the storm and the clock on Saturday afternoon.

She moved toward the phone, then paused and studied her hands, strong and blunt. Weathered. Tough.

She should be working. Helping. The guys had been at it all day, with her at their side, until she took Jake to Cole's house to play.

And that was the difference, she realized. Jake was a little boy. Playtime was important for his growth and development. Hers?

Not so much.

She reached for the phone, but paused again, wondering. Was it so bad to take a little time for herself? Do something frivolous?

Not to mention pricey. With money scarce, why would she even consider seeing Matt's sister about something as useless as a manicure?

Hannah's arrival nixed the cancellation call. She grinned as Callie climbed in the passenger seat, then laughed at the look Callie shot her.

"Cal, seriously, it's not a firing squad. It's a manicure. And it's Meredith. We'll have a great time."

Callie indicated Cobbled Creek with a thrust of her jaw. "Do you know how many things I should be doing right now?"

Hannah laid a hand atop Callie's. "Listen, Martha…"

Callie smiled and groaned, the biblical analogy clear. Martha was the energetic, hardworking, get-'er-done sister of Lazarus. Mary was the quiet listener at God's feet.

"Every now and again, it's okay to take a little time off. Have some fun. And there's nothing wrong with taking care of yourself."

They pulled up to Dana Brennan's beautiful home, sprawling on a double village lot, a detached carriage house-style garage around the back. Callie sighed. "This is gorgeous."

"Isn't it?" Hannah headed for the side entrance. She pushed open the door, waved hello and turned back. "Callie, you remember Meredith, don't you?"

"I do."

One look at Meredith's flawless beauty, her stylish outfit, and Callie wished she'd opted out.

"Although high school was a long time ago." Callie reached out a hand, trying not to bumble, wondering if she should make a run for the door. "I was a year behind you."

"Callie." Meredith grabbed Callie's hands and drew her in, her smile infectious. "I'm so glad you came over. Hannah said Matt's been working you night and day, and you need a little pampering."

"No, oh, no." Callie shook her head in quick denial. She darted a troubled look at Hannah. "Matt wouldn't think of such a thing, I mean, he's always after me to slow down. Take time off. Relax a little."

Meredith shot Hannah a quick, knowing glance. "Whoa, spot-on. She's got it bad."

"Told ya."

"Hey." Callie frowned Hannah's way, but Hannah moved across the spacious kitchen, ignoring her.

"Come in here." Meredith tugged her forward, laughing, a feminine version of Matt's laugh. Warm. Enticing. Vibrant. "I was only kidding, but you totally took the bait, so there's no denying the spark going on between you and my brother."

"We work together," Callie insisted.

"Oh, we get it, honey." Hannah set out a box of fresh brownies. "I got these in case we needed to bribe you to talk, but as you can see," she waved a hand toward Callie but eyed Meredith, "totally unnecessary."

"Which means we can probe her for further information about Matt."

"All the good stuff." Hannah withdrew a brownie, grinning.

"Every little detail." Meredith half sang the words in anticipation.

Callie burst out laughing. "Stop. Both of you. I'm not

saying a thing. He'd be mortified to think we're talking about him like this."

"More like complimented beyond belief," Meredith argued in sister-like fashion. "But we'll shelve that for later." She took a seat alongside Callie and seized her hands, her fingers and eyes examining Callie's roughed-up skin. Seeing her hands against Meredith's more feminine version made Callie want to shrink back. Maybe run for her life, but then Meredith met Callie's eyes. "You wondered if I could help you, right?"

Self-conscious, Callie fidgeted. "Yes."

"Oh, honey." Meredith squeezed Callie's hands but leaned in, smiling. "I can work wonders on the skin and the nails, but what you've got here," she raised Callie's hands slightly, "are the hands of a woman unafraid to get the job done. And no matter what you might think up here," Meredith tapped her head with one tapered, manicured finger, "God has blessed you with beautiful hands to match a wonderful heart. I can create pretty-looking skin." She met Callie's look with a bright, knowing smile. "But only God can create amazing hands like yours."

"I—" Callie sat back, touched, pleased and not a little embarrassed.

"Having said that," Meredith grinned, stood, crossed the room and wheeled back a manicure tray, "let's have a little fun, shall we, girls?" She bent and plugged in a cord, then immersed Callie's hands in the small sink.

Jets of warm water soothed Callie's skin. Her hand muscles. Her fingertips, alternately chilled and dried by nature and job conditions. And as Meredith went through her usual routine of soaking, massaging, oiling and waxing, Callie's heart began to relax along with her skin. By the time Meredith put a finishing coat of clear polish on Callie's French manicure, Callie's hands felt nurtured. Cared for. Pampered.

Not that she'd be able to grow accustomed to this, but for once, to feel soft, feminine hands? Smooth-as-silk skin?

Delightful.

And by the time Meredith finished pampering her, Callie felt like she'd known the other woman forever. Meredith wasn't anything like Callie remembered from high school, but then, neither was she.

"Thank you." She reached out and gave Meredith a hug while Hannah gathered their scarves and gloves. "They feel wonderful."

"Aw, you're welcome." And when Callie tried to hand Meredith money, the other woman waved it off, smiling. "Family gets free perks."

"But I'm not family."

Meredith and Hannah exchanged smiles. "A simple matter of timing, honey." Meredith grinned at Callie's bemused expression and high-fived Hannah. "And having another girl around…"

"One who knows how to get things done," Hannah interjected.

"And puts a smile on Matt's face," Meredith added. "That's like the best Christmas present ever, right there."

Callie fought down the blush Meredith's words inspired, but felt the truth of them in her heart. Her soul.

Matt did like being with her. And seeing his sisters' joint approval?

That just made a season of miracles seem more possible than she'd ever considered before.

* * *

Five o'clock.

He was late and in danger of missing Jake's part in the Christmas Salute to Veterans concert at the elementary school, Matt realized as darkness fell that evening.

He finalized the wallboard contract for the remaining houses, rushed back to the Mareks' and jumped into uniform, wishing he'd had someone else swing south to pick up Don. Matt headed down Route 19 and turned west toward Don's apartment, impatient. He parked in the only available spot half-a-block down and dashed for Don's house, wishing he'd paid closer attention to the time.

Don's porch light clicked on. He pulled open the inner door, pivoted to shut it, then turned and stopped, staring at Matt as though he'd never seen him before.

The uniform, Matt realized.

"Ready?"

Don nodded. His gaze flicked up and down, then up again. "You look great."

"Well, thanks." Matt wore the formal uniform with pride, but he hadn't pulled it out since a funeral the previous year. He'd forgotten the reaction it drew from people. Don's was classic. "Sorry I'm late. Think we'll make it in time?"

Don put a hand to his arm, his expression tight. "I'm proud of you, Matt."

Part of Matt's heart churned. He'd have loved to hear those words twenty-five years ago. Now? Discomfort crept up his spine.

Now he just needed to get to Jake's concert in time to see the boy sing. He shrugged, embarrassed. "Let's go."

The overflowing parking lot said they'd gotten there

far too late to find Callie and Hank in the uniform-studded audience.

She found them instead, and that made Matt feel special. Beloved. Her waving hand beckoned from down front. He let Don precede him and followed, drawn by a sweet force that linked him to her. "Hey." He flashed a quick smile, grateful. "You saved us seats?"

"Yes."

"Thanks, Cal."

"You're looking good, marine."

He duffed the collar of her desert camo. "You, too."

She made a little face of disbelief, but Matt tucked a finger beneath her chin until she met his gaze. "You're absolutely beautiful, Cal. No matter what you're wearing."

Her eyes searched his, questioning. Wondering. He hoped his sincerity and intent showed in his answering look. Something must have telegraphed through because she ducked, blushing.

The blush. The smile. The averted gaze…

They had it bad, Matt realized anew. And he'd never imagined that having it bad could be so wonderfully good. But it was, right down to planning a future he'd refused to ponder, but being with Callie? Loving her? Anything seemed possible.

He sat beside her, her soft fingers clasped in his, ready to lay old doubts at God's feet, determined to grasp the life God offered, sweet and fulfilling. A life he didn't think he deserved, but he was finally learning not to question God's judgment.

Or Callie's embracing smile.

Maybe, just maybe, he could have it all.

Chapter Sixteen

Callie saw the message light flashing on the home phone as she made coffee for the crew on Monday afternoon, sweet memories of Jake's concert, Matt's presence and Christmas brightening the day. She listened to Mary Kay's excited news, then left the coffee to drip while she drove over to the subdivision. She burst into number seventeen, skirted an electrician running wire and cornered Matt in the great room. "They put an offer in on number twenty-three!"

Matt's brows shot up. "Really? How do you know this?"

"Your cell must be down. Mary Kay left a message on the home phone."

Matt grabbed her, spun her around and then just held her, the steady beat of his heart like music to her ears. "This is wonderful," he whispered.

"Yes." Oh, it was. To be held like this? Respected? Beyond wonderful.

"Good news?" Hank asked from above.

Matt fist pumped the air with one hand. "We've got our first sale."

Hank grinned and let his gaze linger on them. "Among other things."

Callie sidestepped Matt's arm. "Just celebrating success, Dad."

"We should do a special dinner tonight," Matt announced.

"As in?"

"We'll go to The Edge. Celebrate. The whole crew." The Edge was the area's acclaimed fine-dining experience.

Hank leaned over the roughed-in stairway. "Well, that gets mighty pricey. Let's save that meal for when we've got all nine sold. How 'bout for tonight we just throw some good steaks on the grill? It's snowing, but I don't mind cookin' in the snow."

"And we'll make baked potatoes," Callie offered.

"And cauliflower with cheese sauce," added Tom from a room away. "And rolls from the bakery."

"Then we need to shop." Callie glanced at her watch and frowned. Jake's bus would be along soon, but she hated to miss work time for errands.

"I've got to grab some things in town once I'm finished here," Matt told them. "I'll pick up the steaks, cauliflower and rolls."

"Excellent."

His grin reflected her feelings. It was good to have that first house sold, a done deal, long-awaited. "I ran over here to tell you before the coffee finished up, so when I'm back at the house I'm doing two things," Callie told him. "I'm calling to order the steaks because they might not have enough nice ones in the case this late in the day."

"Good idea."

"And I'm ordering a landline phone for the model," Callie continued. "And setting up a spare coffeepot there. It's silly to run across the road for coffee now."

"Go for it." He sent her a smile that made her heart feel like they were a team. "And don't bring coffee back for me. I'm going to finish this piece and get the errands done so we don't eat too late for Jake to enjoy it."

"As long as it includes ice cream, Jake'll love it," Hank told him. The smile of satisfaction lighting his face made Callie realize she hadn't seen her father look this at ease in years.

Darkness had descended by the time they'd washed up and gathered at the Marek house. Callie and Jake filled a big bowl with bright red punch, and as each man lumbered into the kitchen, Jake served him a fancy tiny-handled cup of the special concoction.

And not one of those big, burly guys laughed at the prissy glass cup they held.

Matt gave a short, sharp whistle. Conversation stopped as everyone turned his way. He raised his punch cup and surveyed the room, the glimmer of Christmas lights backlighting him. "Since none of us want those steaks to burn, I just want to thank all of you. To Hank and Callie," he met Hank's smile and matched it. "For your initial vision and hard work. And letting me bunk here. That proximity means the world to me." He smiled again and Callie hoped he meant proximity to more than the half-built houses.

"Buck, Tom, Jim and Amanda." He nodded to that group. "None of this would have been possible without you guys. You know that, don't you?"

They hemmed and hawed, embarrassed.

"And to Don." Matt turned to his stepfather deliberately and lofted the cup a little higher. "I've never seen better workmanship in drywall and that perfect finishing touch polishes the entire effect. Thank you. It's nice having family on board."

Don's face paled. His hand shook. He opened his mouth to say something, then paused, overcome, unable to speak. Amanda swiped a quick hand to her face when Matt and Don exchanged looks of understanding.

Matt veered his attention to Jake. "And to you, my young friend. I don't think there's ever been a better apprentice in this business and I mean that. Good job, bud."

Jake manned his glass cup of punch with all the seriousness an eight-year-old could muster. "Thanks, Matt."

"To us." Matt raised his cup higher. "To our continued good work and success. And let's not forget to thank God for that stretch of good weather, because—" Matt deadpanned a look outdoors, "—I think it was slated to be our last."

They sipped in unison, and Callie marveled at how quickly things had turned around. Six weeks before they'd been watching Cobbled Creek fade before their eyes. The view from her front window now embraced a lovely neighborhood, the hopes and dreams of two families coming together.

Matt gave Jake a quick hug and settled on the floor with him to play a quick round of checkers before dinner. Amanda came into the kitchen to help Callie. She swept Matt and Jake a smiling look. "Pretty nice scene, Cal."

"It is."

"The kind a girl could get used to," Amanda added.

"If the girl were one of those romance-loving gals

who believed in happily ever afters," Callie replied, although when she was around Matt Cavanaugh it was easier to dream. Hope. Believe.

"And that's the nice thing about life." Amanda trailed the words, her eyes laughing at Callie's attempt to maintain distance. "Things have a way of changing up when you least expect it."

"Steaks are done," Hank called out as he came back inside.

"Great." Matt stood, pulled Jake up beside him and surveyed the laden table, gratitude marking his expression. "Thanks for doing this, Callie, because you prefer a hammer to a stovetop."

"You know I make exceptions now and again." She sent him a smile across the table, and hoped he read the pride she felt. Working for him, seeing the homes progress, watching this plan come together at long last.

"I'm glad," Matt told her. His tone said he read her expression correctly.

Jake sat at a card table they set up in the living room with the two Slaughter kids. Once Amanda had them settled, the crew gathered around the table, the mixed scents of rich meat, tangy cheese and fresh-baked rolls teasing the senses. "God, you've blessed us with Matt Cavanaugh," Hank intoned as they clasped hands around the table. "You brought him to us and gathered us together. We thank you for that, and this food. Amen."

"Amen."

"Short and sweet." Buck nodded, affable. "Good job."

"Can't let the meat get cold," said Hank. "And I don't

want this to go to Matt's head. All this thankin' business."

"Wouldn't want that." Matt grinned at him, and took a bite of steak. "And right now I can tell you that no one on this planet cooks a better steak than you, Hank."

"Timing." Hank smiled as he savored his own first bite, but he let his eyes twinkle Matt's way. "It's all in the timing, son."

Matt read Hank's look and recognized the truth in the words. He turned toward Don. "Did I hear you say you've got a doctor's appointment tomorrow afternoon?"

"Yes."

"I'll go along."

Don started to shake his head, obviously uncomfortable, but Matt put him off. "No sense arguing. I know it's at the cancer clinic and that these guys all know about it, so we'll stop work around two and head over there, okay?"

Don's nod said he didn't trust himself to speak.

"And Matt," Buck cut in, jutting his chin toward the subdivision, "I'm putting the plow on my truck tomorrow so I'll keep the roadway into the houses cleaned out for us, okay?"

"Buck, that would be awesome. Thank you."

Buck shrugged that off. "Not too many weeks ago this was stretching to be a long, bad winter." He sipped from his tiny, glass cup and grinned at the looks the other guys shot him. "But now? Well, now," he raised his cup high in salute to Matt, the Mareks and Cobbled Creek, "things are looking up."

* * *

Hank had thanked God for him, Matt mused as he and Don headed toward the clinic in Wellsville the following afternoon. The idea that anyone placed stock in him both pleased and scared Matt, but with the Marek family? He'd go with mostly pleased.

He pulled up to the clinic's door, dropped Don off and proceeded to an open parking space at the back of the snowy lot. As he pushed through the entrance door, he spotted Don being led to a treatment room down a back corridor. Matt settled into an empty seat, picked up a sports magazine and started rifling the pages.

"Burdick? Joyce Burdick?"

"Here." An older woman stood slowly, a haze of pain creasing her features.

"Lean on me, Mom."

The older woman sent her son a fond look. "It's nice to have you home this weekend, Dustin."

"It's good to be here."

Dustin Burdick. Callie's ex-husband. Jake's dad. He was in town, but hadn't told Callie or asked to see his son.

Matt felt like he'd been punched in the gut. He had to hold himself back from having it out with the guy then and there.

"The treatment will take about an hour once we get her settled in," explained the nurse as an orderly helped Dustin's mother into a wheelchair. "So if you want to come back in about ninety minutes, that would be fine."

"Thanks." Dustin bent and kissed his mother's cheek, then headed for the door. "I'll get that Christmas stuff for you, Mom."

"Thanks, honey."

Honey?

The sweet endearment might mean something coming from Dustin Burdick's mother, but Matt found the irony too much to bear. He followed Dustin outside and called his name. Dustin turned, surprise and caution vying for his features. "Yes?"

"You're in town for the weekend?"

Dustin shifted left. "Do I know you?"

"No." Matt braced his feet and folded his arms, keeping his voice and expression taut. "But I know your ex-wife. And your son. And I'm just wondering what kind of guy walks out on a great kid like Jake and never calls. Never sends cards or gifts. Never visits his own flesh and blood. What kind of soldier were you when you can treat your own family like that?"

"Who are you? And what business is it of yours?" Dustin growled the words, his displeasure apparent.

"Callie works for me." *Lame, Cavanaugh, when Callie was so much more than an employee.* Still, he wasn't about to share their relationship with Dustin Burdick, a cheating spouse and deadbeat father. Matt had enough of that to last a lifetime. "And you didn't answer the question. How can you walk out on a kid like that? Just turn your back and go?"

Matt didn't try to fool himself that cornering Dustin in a public parking lot was the smartest thing he'd ever done, but good marines seize opportunities God sends their way. And today God put Dustin square in Matt's path.

Dustin sent him a cool look of appraisal. "I don't know who you are or what it matters to you, but I don't have to answer to anyone. I have a life. Callie has a life. We've both moved on. I suggest you do the same."

"You moved on while you were married to her." Matt kept his voice intentionally soft on purpose. More threatening that way. "You cheated on her, then walked out on your wife and infant son. You discredit the uniform."

Dustin took a step forward and hooked a thumb toward himself. "I hated the uniform. The rules. The time. The drills. The waiting around in hundred-and-ten-degree weather, half hoping something would happen. And there was Callie, kind of cute, working on the base. I'd known her in high school, so when we met up in Iraq…" He shrugged, nonchalant. "It gave me something to do."

Anger put a chokehold on Matt. Dustin married Callie for something to do?

The temptation to beat the stuffing out of this guy forced Matt back. He held up a hand. "You're not interested in being Jake's father? His dad?"

Dustin scowled. "I've got two kids. I'm lucky I can afford them. And don't have Callie try to garnish my wages again either. You can't take blood from a stone and she'll get nothing."

Matt appraised Dustin's leather coat and upscale jeans. "You hide your income so you don't have to support Jake."

Dustin's face said "Yes" as he shook his head. "I've got no income. Fresh out."

A flash of inspiration hit Matt, a possible way to emerge a winner from a bad confrontation. "Will you give up your rights to Jake?"

Dustin's scowl deepened. "Where do I sign?"

Matt really wanted to punch this guy. His fingers ached for wanting. But more than that, he wanted to be free to make Jake his own. If Callie would have him, that is. "If I have the papers sent to you, will you sign off as Jake's dad?"

"I don't have to worry about anybody coming after me for money ever again?"

No, dirtbag. Matt kept that feeling to himself, but it took effort. What he said out loud was, "Exactly. You'll be free and clear and I can adopt Jake."

A light sparked in Dustin's eyes. "This might be worth something to you, then?"

Matt took great pleasure in the spin move that put the other man's face up against the wall. "Don't even think about it, Burdick. Nobody," he gave Dustin's collar a slightly tightened shake to make his point stronger, "plays around with the value of a child like that, not in my presence. Got it?"

Dustin hadn't spent the last eight years staying in top form.

Matt had.

Whatever Dustin had been doing for money didn't pump up his triceps and biceps. His abs.

Building houses, hauling lumber, lifting windows and cabinets into place kept Matt on an Olympic-training regimen weekly. The reality of that knowledge shone in Dustin's nervous expression. He gave a quick nod, definitely in his best interest.

Good.

"And you'll sign the papers when you get them, and give them back to the courier who will then deliver them back here to Callie. Right?" He tightened Dustin's collar a smidge more, hoping he made his point.

Dustin nodded again. "Yes."

"Excellent." Matt loosened his hold but didn't back

off. "I love that kid. And I love his mother. And I didn't spend eight years in the marines *pretending* to be a man, so when those papers come, you open the envelope, sign where noted and send them back. Got it?"

"I said yes."

Matt angled his head slightly as Dustin faced him. "I heard you. I'm just making sure we understand each other."

Dustin blew out a breath. "If it gets me out of any more of her stupid court filings, we're good."

Matt had to take another step back. And nail his hands to his sides. And haul in a big breath. It had been a long time since the urge to pummel someone loomed with such ripe potential, but he pushed to keep his eye on the goal: making Jake his own. If Dustin signed off, Matt would be free to adopt Jake, if Callie gave her blessing.

Matt went back inside as Dustin strode off. He sat down, waiting for Don, his gut twisting. He couldn't make sense of walking out on a kid, maybe because it had happened to him. He'd lived the experience and suffered the fallout.

Why would God let that happen? Who watched out for little ones these days? Kids nudged aside by adult drama?

The strong words from the book of Joshua came back to him. "...then choose for yourselves this day who you shall serve...as for me and my house? We will serve the Lord."

That's what he wanted with Callie. The piece that had been missing from his growing years. Not just a home. Or a family. He longed for a family of faith, hope and love. God-abiding. Together. A tiny light flickered within as Matt realized how Dustin had used Callie for his own amusement. He'd never intended to stay, to be the husband Callie deserved and the father Jake needed.

Matt had every intention of doing just that.

And as Don turned the corner from the corridor leading to the treatment rooms, Matt comprehended something else. Life had sideswiped Don, just as it had him. Sure, Don was the adult. He should have and could have reacted better. Maybe with faith, he would have, but Don had been taken out at the knees when he learned he was living a lie, that his wife had cheated on him and passed off someone else's child as his.

He came toward Matt, his face tired. Worn. Matt moved down the hall and braced him with a soldier's arm.

"I'm okay." Don tried to shrug him off, but Matt held tight.

"Hey, can't a kid help his old man now and again?"

Don's feet shuffled to a stop. He turned. Met Matt's gaze. "I—"

"Do you need a wheelchair to the car?"

Don shook his head. "No. Just a little tired."

"Then lean on me, Dad. It's not that far."

Don looked up at him. His light-eyed gaze grew moist. Matt had to choke back a lump in his own throat, a knot of regret for so much time wasted.

But that was over. He braced the older man and started forward. "I know where there's a pot of stew waiting. Should be just about done. And some fresh, homemade biscuits."

"It sounds good," Don admitted.

"Then let's go. You need to make another appointment?"

Don shook his head. "Not for a while."

"Good, because we got a boatload of plasterboard delivered today, and you need to rest up. We're going to have one busy winter."

Don's shoulders straightened. His chin came up. His step seemed just a little bit stronger. More invigorated. He gave a quick swipe to his eyes and nodded back at Matt. "I'm looking forward to it, son."

An old smile crept up on Matt, the kind of smile he used to share with his father, back in the day. He squeezed Don's arm as he led the way to the snow-filled parking lot, pretty sure his personal life paths had been freshly plowed, and glad of it. "Me, too."

Chapter Seventeen

"**W**hat's this?" Matt studied the envelope he received the next afternoon and quizzed the courier standing on the doorstep of the Cape Cod model. "Is this a summons?"

"I need your signature, sir."

Foreboding made Matt hesitate, then he clenched his jaw, signed the form and waited as the courier separated a copy for Matt's records.

He stepped into the quiet and nearly complete home, tore open the envelope and pulled out a sheaf of legal-looking documents. He scanned the information, got the gist of the contents, then sat down hard on the second step to read more carefully.

"...because the rules of due process were not followed in Mr. Marek's case, and because his ownership rights may have been revoked without due cause and/or proper documentation, Wellingtown General Bank will pay you a sum as decided by the appraisal firm of Littinger and Littinger in Olean, New York, as reparation. Amount due will include but will not be limited to wages paid, materials secured and monies invested to buy the afore-named subdivision 'Cobbled Creek.'

"Wellington General regrets any and all difficulties this transaction may cause and sincerely extends its apologies while accepting no blame for the mistaken foreclosure involved."

Mistaken foreclosure?

Reparation?

Had he just lost Cobbled Creek?

Matt stared at the paper and swallowed hard.

They were taking Cobbled Creek away from him. Could they do that?

"No," said his lawyer firmly a few minutes later when Matt got through to him on the newly installed landline. "They can't just send you a letter that says 'Oops, we goofed, sorry. Let's have a do-over.' This is their first step in trying to rectify a big mistake. They're hoping you'll give in gracefully so they don't look bad or careless, which is exactly what they were in this case and many others, using people to robo-sign documents."

"Robo-sign?"

The lawyer sighed. "Instead of having bank professionals read each document the way they're supposed to, some banks hired new graduates to handle the influx of foreclosure documentation the past couple of years. Their job was to count the pages, make sure they were all there, then sign off as the bank's representative."

"You're kidding."

"I wish I was. And none of this was obvious last month when we closed. Then the scandal broke and banks started scrambling to put their houses in order."

"So I don't lose Cobbled Creek? Is that what you're saying?"

"We have to fight it, but yes, you will be able to keep the subdivision because it's their fault. Not yours. And then it's up to them to pay Hank Marek some sort of compensation for taking it over illegally. And making restitution for his loss of income."

"And his daughter's loss of income for those two years? Do they cover that?"

"No, that would be an indirect consequence unless she's listed as co-owner, but that wasn't the case."

How could he grasp this? Make sense of it? Half an hour ago he had his life mapped out before him, and it looked good. Sweet. Inviting.

Now?

One piece of mail and a bank's overeagerness to seize property put it all in jeopardy. "I need time to think, Jon. To figure this all out."

"There's no hurry," Jon told him, "but Hank Marek has most likely been notified at the same time you were. Just so you're prepared. He may pay you a visit."

"I'm living with him."

"You're what?"

It sounded weird considering this turn of events. "They let me stay in an extra room in their home because it adjoins the subdivision. And they've been working for me from the beginning."

"That's not a good situation to be in right now," the lawyer explained in a no-nonsense voice. "It's a conflict of interest at best and being professionally involved with a family you may bring litigation against could color your judgment."

"I thought it would be against the bank." Matt gripped the phone tighter. "You mean I might have to sue Hank?"

"Depending on how this plays out, yes. It's a numbers game, Matt. And a power play. But we've got the power because we have ownership."

"Illegally."

"Not on our end," the lawyer said roundly. "We had no information that led us to believe any of this had occurred. This is the bank's error. Not ours. They're just hoping you bow out gracefully."

Bow out gracefully? How about run screaming? "I've got to go, Jon. Think this through. Pray."

"Don't think too long. Wellington General is no slouch in the money department, and they'll cough up a nice piece of change, but we need to respond quickly."

A nice piece of change.

Is that what his hopes and dreams came down to? His attempt to come back home and make amends? Was he here to gain a "nice piece of change" at Hank's expense? At Callie's expense?

Callie.

His gut clenched as realization hit.

What would people think if he courted Callie now? If Hank regained ownership of Cobbled Creek? They would assume he was looking out for number one. People would see it as a ploy to maintain a Cavanaugh Construction interest in a lucrative business venture.

What should he do? What could he do? Sue the bank? That meant suing Hank's interest in Cobbled Creek as well.

What would Grandpa Gus do?

He'd pray, Matt realized. He'd pray hard, then man up and do the right thing, an upright man in all regards.

Matt climbed into his truck and drove north, away from the dream that just evaporated around him, knowing if he fought Hank on this, the entire lower half of the county would see what they'd come to believe twenty years before. A guy who put himself first, all the time.

He found a small church open in the college town of Houghton. He crept in the back door and found a quiet corner, a place to talk to God. Examine his options. And by the time he stood to leave a long while later, he knew exactly what he had to do, but didn't pretend acceptance. He'd be giving up his dream of a home with Callie. Of adopting Jake. Of being the father he'd never had, an upright man in all regards.

Keeping Cobbled Creek when Hank had been grievously wronged could never be considered right.

And the swirl of malicious gossip that would circle around Callie and Jake if he stayed in the picture was the very world he'd come back to fix. Not reinstigate. He wasn't a gold digger. Or a user. But marrying Callie would look that way, and Matt knew firsthand how tongues would wag, mostly because he was involved and he hadn't been in town long enough to prove his worth.

Lousy timing, all told, not unlike what happened to Hank Marek a few years before.

He headed back toward Jamison and the life he thought he'd have, now gone, and couldn't act as if the journey didn't break his heart.

"You worked late, Dad," Callie observed as her father pushed through the side door that evening. "I'll start the burgers when Matt pulls in," she added, then nodded Jake's way. "And this guy's teacher says he's doing great, he's hardworking and focused and she's pleased with his progress. So we'll celebrate that with cupcakes later." She pulled a broiler pan from the lower cupboard, then turned toward her father more fully. His expression said something had gone wrong. Very wrong. "What's happened?"

Face set, Hank settled into a chair.

"Are you okay?"

He scowled and thumped the table with his fist. "Matt's gone."

"Matt's…" Callie worked her brain around her father's appearance, his accelerated breathing, his heightened color and…

Nope. Couldn't do it. She sat next to him and was surprised to see a sheen of moisture in his eyes. Army men didn't cry. Ever. "Dad, you're scaring me." She leaned closer, keeping her voice low. "What do you mean 'Matt's gone'?"

"He left. This afternoon. Packed up his stuff, signed Cobbled Creek back over to me and took off."

None of this was making any sense. "He signed Cobbled Creek over to you? What does that mean?"

Her father withdrew a bundle of papers from inside his jacket. "The bank messed up. They seized Cobbled Creek illegally. And now they want to fix things, which means they'll pay Matt to give it up."

"Illegally? How?"

"Not following procedures. So they notified Matt and me today and Matt got it in his head that he'd be better off bowing out and letting me take it back."

"But—"

"I know." Hank lifted his gaze to Callie's. "He *belongs* here. I felt it. You felt it. For pity's sake, *he* felt it, but then this." Hank grabbed the papers and lofted them into the air. "This happens and everything gets messed up."

"He left."

"Yes."

Without saying goodbye. Because that was the story of her life, it shouldn't come as any big surprise.

Callie stood, her legs wooden, her jaw tight. Suddenly the act of flipping burgers seemed like too much work.

But there was Jake to think of. What would he think when he found out Matt had left? How would he react?

She moved back to the kitchen, her head spinning, trying to make sense of things and failing, but she knew one thing. She'd stepped out of her comfort zone and trusted a man whose heart seemed to match hers. Kind. Caring. Loving to build, to see beautiful things rise from the ground, take shape against a God-given sky.

She'd been stupid. Again.

Old doubts consumed her. How needy was she that Matt's bright smile and sweet compliments won her over so quickly? Hadn't she wondered from the beginning?

Yes.

But she'd let foolish hopes and dreams color her judgment, pull her off task. Make her think Matt really cared about her. About Jake.

Jake.

He'd be brokenhearted, and it was all her fault.

Regret warred with anger and sadness, a sorry threesome. Simple math filled in the rest. Matt would get bank money for Cobbled Creek and her father would have his business back. For a win-win situation, this felt like a total loss.

She swallowed tears around a lump the size of a stair

runner and slapped ground beef together with way more power than necessary, but better to take her anger out on meat than on her father. Or her son. Or…

No, that's right, Matt wouldn't be around anymore. At all. Ever. And just like that her hopes and dreams disappeared in the blink of an eye. Just as well, really. Better to count on herself. She knew that. And she'd be fine. Just fine.

"Can we play Christmas music, Mom?" Jake poked his head up from an internet site about the battle at Midway. "And did Grandpa forget to turn on the Christmas lights?"

"I did." Hank pushed to his feet, looking anything but festive. "I'll see to it right now."

"When's Matt coming?" Jake continued. "I'm starved."

Callie ignored the first question by zeroing in on the second. "I'll make the burgers. They can always be warmed up later."

"Okay."

She wanted to shout that Matt wasn't coming back. That he'd moved out. Moved on. He had his money and he'd taken the quickest path north. But she couldn't say any of that, couldn't even think it without wanting to bawl her eyes out. Except soldiers don't do that. They keep on keepin' on.

By the time Jake went to bed, Callie felt numb. Numb from pretending, numb from fielding questions, from avoiding the looks of concern her father shot her.

Mind-bending numb, but nothing an all-night crying jag wouldn't cure. And she was headed that way when her father stopped her. "So, what are you going to do?"

"Do?" She raised her shoulders, dropped them and shook her head. "About?"

"Matt."

"Matt's gone, Dad. End of story."

Hank stared at her, then swiped a hand across his face. "You're not getting this, are you?"

"That Matt needs distance, he's got his money and he booked out of here like a race car driver? I'm getting it just fine, Dad."

"No." Hank settled his hands on her shoulders and met her anger with compassion. "He didn't leave because he didn't want to be with you. With us."

"Um, right." Callie sent him a look of disbelief and when he smiled, she had to remember why it was wrong to fight with your father.

"He left because he thinks it's the *right* thing to do."

"That makes no sense."

"It makes perfect sense," Hank countered. "Matt came here and helped our dream come true, but when that letter came today he realized we'd been wronged. That the bank acted too quickly. And that wasn't fair."

"So he left without saying goodbye to me or Jake? Right. Thanks for the pep talk, Dad."

She moved to step away, but Hank wouldn't let her. "He loves you."

Callie snorted. Very unfeminine, but then that was the story of her life. Unloved. Unfeminine. Uncherished.

"He does," her father insisted, "but think about this from his perspective. Either he loses Cobbled Creek or he fights us for it. Matt cares for us and doesn't want to hurt us."

"Very altruistic of him. But he still fled for places

unknown without saying goodbye, therefore final chapter. End of story."

"It's nothing of the sort, and you've got your mother's stubbornness," Hank replied. "How will it look to people if Matt starts showing interest in you after he's had to relinquish the subdivision?"

"I—"

"Like he's a gold digger. Like he's trying to hang on. People talk, Callie."

"I don't care what people say," she told him, but a sheen of reality started to seep through. "Why would Matt?"

"Because Matt was talked about for years," her father reminded her. "And he came back here to fix things, not stir them up. He'd never want you and Jake to be targeted by gossip."

"You mean…"

"People might think he was after you to maintain his interest in Cobbled Creek."

"But that's ridiculous."

Hank's arched brow said it wasn't ridiculous. It was quite possible, actually, the way some small-town tongues wagged. "You're sure, Dad? Because I'm not a big risk-taker anymore."

Hank leaned closer. "I'm one-hundred-percent sure. I asked Maude to make a blanket for you a bunch of years back. A quilt that reminded me of your mother. All flowery and pretty, like spring."

Callie nodded, unsure where this was going.

"Then things went bad and I couldn't pay for the blanket. Maude hung on to it, and I went into town the other day to buy it."

"What's this got to do with—"

"It was gone," Hank continued as if she hadn't spoken. "Matt bought it for you. Maude said she wrapped it up real pretty. Said she knew he was smitten weeks ago and told him about the quilt, and he told her he was going to make sure Callie had the best Christmas ever."

Tears pricked her eyes, but they were different tears. Tears of anticipation and hope, not anger. "He bought it for me?"

"Yes, but probably has no clue how to fix this whole mess because of a stupid bank mistake. Do you love him?" Hank's direct question put it all on the line.

"Yes." Callie met her father's gaze. "Oh, yes."

"Then show him."

Callie's mind spun with this new assortment of facts, but she recognized one thing: Her father was right. If this was going to get fixed, Callie needed to be the one to do it because while Matt might be handy with tools, he was a proud marine, first and last. And a marine would never shackle those he loved with rumor and speculation. It was up to her to show him the way to the family he never had. If the guy wasn't too proud and stubborn to see what God had laid before him, that is. "I will, Dad, but I'll need your help. Can you call him? Get him to come back here tomorrow evening? And meet you at the model home?"

Hank grinned. "Will do. And Callie?"

She turned from the stairs and met his gaze.

"I'm proud of you, honey."

And she felt it, right to her toes. She met his smile and returned it. "Thank you, Dad."

Chapter Eighteen

Matt saw Hank's caller I.D. and hated to answer the phone, but he did. "Hello."

"Matt?"

"Yes, Hank. What's up?"

A slight pause tempted Matt to ask about Callie. About Jake. How things were going. It had been one whole day, after all.

Pathetic, Cavanaugh.

"Can you meet me at the model house later today?"

The house Callie loved? "How about we meet in town instead? I'm staying at my brother's place in Wellsville while we get things resituated."

"I'm tied up all day." Apology laced Hank's tone. "And I need to go over a few things with you about the model and the house that's sold. I'd do it here, but…"

Matt understood. Callie would be there. So would Jake. And he wasn't in any shape to see them right now, to witness his sacrifice firsthand.

You don't have to give up anything, son.

Grandpa Gus's wisdom poked him from within.

God's offered you a wonderful chance, the chance to love. Grab it. Run with it. Embrace it.

Right. And have the whole town think he was scrambling to hang on to Cobbled Creek through Callie? Honor first, and that meant Callie first, in this instance. Subjecting Jake and Callie to the gossip mill he'd lived with all his life? Wasn't gonna happen. Not on his watch.

Pride and dismay clenched his gut as he angled the truck down Cobbled Creek Lane that evening. He didn't look toward the Marek house to see their tree winking softly in the side window, or the string of lights he'd helped Callie hang in the rain. Or Shadow Jesus.

The memory of Jake's upturned face C-clamped Matt's heart, his earnest explanations about Bethlehem. Mary and Joseph and a child born to the poor. The little guy paid such close attention to detail, a rare trait, Matt thought; but then, Jake was no ordinary child. He was Callie's son.

The clamp tightened its screw hold on Matt's heart as he approached the model home, the pretty walkway welcoming him.

Should he ring the bell? Walk in?

Swallowing frustration, he pushed open the door and called Hank's name.

"Dad's not here."

Callie.

His heart jumped, then sank. "He was supposed to meet me."

She came forward, looking absolutely wonderful, but then he felt that way when she donned triple layers and flannels to work side by side with him. But tonight the one-shoulder top over fitted jeans left no doubt that Callie Marek was in good shape.

And breathtakingly beautiful.

Matt scrubbed a hand to his neck and looked around. Her presence made his determination to stay away seem somewhat dumb. And maybe impossible. But he was doing it for her, he reminded himself as she drew closer.

"You left."

He nodded, holding himself arm's length away when what he longed to do was reach out and touch her. Slide that curl tickling her cheek back behind her ear.

"It seemed best."

"For whom?"

He waved a hand. "Everyone."

She encroached a little more. "Really?"

"Yes." He thought so at the time anyway, but right now, with Callie so near, smelling Christmas-cookie sweet, he wasn't so sure. Which meant he should take a step back. He did.

Callie followed.

"Cal, listen…"

"No, you listen, marine." She closed the distance between them and gave him a very unromantic thwack on the arm. "What on earth are you doing, Matt Cavanaugh?"

"Trying to find your father and settle our affairs."

She sighed out loud. "Not with him. With me." She waved a hand between them. "Us. Because here's how I see things, and let me just add, it's pretty obvious that you and my father need a woman around and you should be thanking God I'm available."

Available as in…

"First of all—" he didn't think it was possible for her

to move closer, and yet she did, wagging her pointer finger in the air "—you love me."

Honor, integrity and honesty disallowed a lie. "Yes."

Callie rolled her eyes. "You could try to sound a little happier about it."

"Callie—"

"Ah." She put two sweet-smelling fingers to his mouth to shush him, the feel and scent reminding him of those shared kisses. The hopes and dreams he'd thought possible the past weeks. "Still my turn. And you love Jake."

"Who couldn't?"

She smiled up at him, and he realized she wasn't wearing heels. She was, in fact, just wearing socks, looking way too cozy and at home, but then, this house fit her as if...

"Here's my proposal," she went on as if sealing a business deal. "You get all this nonsense about what people will think, about giving up your dream and handing over Cobbled Creek to my dad out of your head."

"But—"

"In lieu of that we form a partnership of sorts."

Her slanted smile released the clamp on Matt's heart a bit more. "Are you suggesting a merger?"

Her smile deepened. She poked him in the chest. "Exactly that." She couldn't get any closer without touching him, so she did, letting her hair riffle against his chin, his neck. Then she squared her shoulders. "Of course there are terms to negotiate."

"I'm a great negotiator."

"I don't doubt it for a minute," she agreed amicably, as if they weren't discussing very serious things like weddings. Babies.

Unless he misunderstood her.

One look into those pretty green eyes nixed that. "You know I was no choirboy, Cal." Despite the lure, the attraction, the love, he didn't want Callie blindsided ever again. About anything. "My past might trip us up from time to time."

She met his gaze straight on. "It could, but I'm going to trust God to get us through whatever happens. Once I get it through that thick head of yours that it's okay to love us." She reached up and feathered a soft kiss to his jaw.

"Stop." He put up a hand and stepped back. Confusion swam in her eyes until he dropped to one knee and grasped her hand. "If we're going to do this, we're going to do it right."

Her mouth formed a perfect O, and then she smiled, delighted. "Please do."

He squeezed her fingers and held her gaze, wishing she could see his heart. His soul. "Callie, you are the most incredible and beautiful woman I've ever known. You have a heart of gold and you're really good with power tools."

A bubble of laughter mixed with the sheen of tears in her eyes.

"Will you marry me? Share your life and son with me? Grow old with me, building houses?"

"Homes," she corrected, and drew him up. "Not houses, Matt. Homes. And yes, I'll marry you. Have your babies. And work beside you all my days."

Matt lost himself in the feel of Callie's arms, her kiss, her presence, feeling like he'd come back to a home he'd never really had.

Lights burst on around them. Twinkle lights. They lined the windows of the first floor, and a tree, a real Christmas tree, lit up the soft yellow great room at the back of the house. Matt hugged Callie and grinned as Hank and the guys tried unsuccessfully to slip quietly out the back.

"Jake."

The boy broke ranks with the older men and raced back into the house. He barreled into Callie and Matt and Matt tipped the boy's chin up to hold his gaze. "Jake, I'd like your permission to marry your mother. I love her and I love you and I think we'd make a great family together. What do you think?"

Jake's face beamed as bright as the Bethlehem star, a symbol of a new beginning. A new hope. "I say yes."

"And," Matt shifted his gaze to the pretty woman in his left arm, a woman who'd known pain and abandonment but was wise enough to let God guide her through it all, step by step, "I think we should live here."

"Here?" Callie swept the model with the wistful look she'd tried to contain weeks before.

"Right here. If we're going to forge a family business, we need proximity. Affordability. And," he let his eyes twinkle into hers, "it's a four bedroom which means growth potential."

Callie blushed.

Jake laughed and fist pumped the air. "And I get to help you and Grandpa build, Matt!"

Matt ruffled a hand through Jake's hair and dropped another kiss to Callie's smiling mouth, wondering how he'd ever considered walking away. "You sure do, son. You sure do."

Epilogue

"Oh, look." Callie pointed to the left of the auditorium stage the following December and gave a momlike wave. "There's Jake. Right next to Jordan."

Chloe Wiseman leaned across her husband. "They're peas in a pod, those two. Have I mentioned often enough how happy we are to live in Cobbled Creek? Near you guys? To have such a nice friend for Jordan, so close?"

Callie laughed and squeezed the other woman's hand. "I feel the same way. And we've got a great bunch of neighbors with Phase One complete."

A tiny noise erupted from Callie's left. "Dad, you okay over there?"

Hank rearranged the pink-swaddled bundle in his arms and gave a sage nod. "Nothing a bottle and a burp won't cure. But I'm still not loving the pink camo."

"It's adorable," Callie protested.

"It's pink," Hank argued. "Camo should never be pink."

"Well, she is a girl," Matt reminded him. He shrugged and met Hank's grin. "Pink goes with the territory. Doesn't it, Morgan?" Matt leaned in and ran a finger along the tiny girl's soft-as-down cheek.

"Dresses, fine." Hank kept his voice army-gruff, but his eyes twinkled as the newborn accepted the bottle with fisted hands and greedy tugs. "But army gear should be army gear. Never the twain shall meet."

Matt leaned closer to Callie. "What's he going to think of the pink leopard print stuff Hannah gave us?"

Callie laughed, Hank made a face and Matt watched with pride as Jake *Cavanaugh* stepped up to the microphone to welcome people to the eighteenth annual Christmas Concert for Veterans. And when Jake found them in the crowd and sent a grin their way, Matt felt like Grandpa Gus just clapped him on the back, showing his full approval.

And it felt good.

* * * * *

REUNITED AT CHRISTMAS

Belle Calhoune

For my father, Fred C. Bell,
who always worked hard to make Christmas
a wonderful time for his children.
And for paying all of my outrageous library fines
I accrued over the years.

Acknowledgments

For my family… Thanks for always listening to
all my story ideas and giving me a thumbs-up.

For all the readers who have been asking for
more stories set in Love, Alaska. Thank you
for embracing the Alaskan Grooms series.

For my editor, Emily Rodmell,
for all of your support and enthusiasm
for Liam and Ruby's love story.

Beareth all things, believeth all things,
hopeth all things, endureth all things.
—*1 Corinthians* 13:7

Chapter One

Dr. Liam Prescott had always loved Christmas. When it came right down to it, there was no place he would rather be celebrating the holiday than in his hometown of Love, Alaska. Candy canes. Twinkling lights. Peppermint hot chocolate at the Moose Café. Pine trees at the ready for decorating. Caroling from door to door. Normally there wasn't a single thing about it he didn't enjoy.

He'd been putting up a brave front these past few weeks, but he still felt as if he had a huge hole in the middle of his heart. It was especially hard over the holidays to deal with the loss of a loved one.

This year he would focus on Aidan. It would serve as a distraction from everything they had lost two years ago. The sound of his four-year-old son's tinkling laughter as he enjoyed the spirit of the season would be the highlight. To see it unfold through Aidan's eyes would be wonderful. Despite the fact they were still grieving, he wanted to give his son the most memorable Christmas ever. Although he would try his best to enjoy the festive season, it was still incredibly difficult. The loss of his wife in an avalanche search-and-rescue mission two years ago continued to sit heavily on his chest like an anchor.

Liam walked down Jarvis Street, pausing to peer through the window of the five-and-dime so he could check out the toys on display. So far he had a few items stashed away for Aidan, but nothing that would knock his socks off. He needed something fantastic that Aidan could rip open on Christmas morning and feel ecstatic about. Maybe if he focused on his son's joy he wouldn't have to deal with his own pain.

He regarded the red toboggan with a critical eye. Red was Aidan's favorite color. His son was getting to the age where he wanted to fly down the smaller hills in town without his father cramping his style. *I'm a big boy, Daddy.* Aidan's words buzzed in his ears. His pluck and grit made him smile.

Every day Aidan was growing, both physically and emotionally. He was starting to ask questions about his mother and the tragedy that had befallen her and irre-vocably changed both their lives. Liam always tried to be as honest as possible, while still protecting his son's innocence. He wished that he could tell Aidan that he himself understood why Ruby had been taken from them. But he didn't understand. Not one little bit.

People often said losing a loved one was like navi-gating a treacherous, winding river. As far as he was concerned, it was much worse. He knew he should have pushed past the initial overwhelming grief stage, but every time he thought about his sweet, beautiful Ruby, he found himself floundering in a tidal wave of loss.

How did a person ever make peace with losing the love of a lifetime? He still hadn't found an answer to that question. Liam had come to terms with the idea that he had to move forward with his life, but he still ached for Ruby. He still agonized about the things he could have done differently. He continued to ask God why He hadn't spared her.

The insistent buzz of his cell phone had him digging in his coat pocket. A quick glance at the screen displayed his brother Boone's number at the sheriff's office.

He tapped the phone with his finger. "Hey, Boone," he answered as he took the call "What's going on?"

"Where have you been? I've been calling you for the last hour." Boone's voice had a frantic quality.

"I'm right here on Jarvis Street, heading back to the clinic," Liam explained. "I just finished eating a few minutes ago."

Liam had stopped in to eat lunch at his other brother's coffee bar, the Moose Café. No doubt the din inside had prevented him from hearing his phone ring.

"Can you come by the sheriff's office right away? It's important." He hadn't imagined it. Boone's voice sounded tight with strain.

"What happened? Is it Jasper?" Liam asked, inquiring about their grandfather, Mayor Jasper Prescott. His pulse began to race wildly. As patriarch of the Prescott family, Jasper was well loved. At times irascible and feisty, he could also be tender and wise. And due to his heart problems, they had almost lost him not too long ago. His health was a constant source of worry.

"No, it's not Jasper. You have to prepare yourself—" The line crackled. Boone's voice was swallowed up by static.

"Boone! Boone!" he called out. "I can't hear you. The call is breaking up."

"Urgent. Need to tell you—" A crackling sound came across the line. Suddenly the call dropped.

Something was wrong. Liam had heard it in his older brother's voice. The sheriff's office was only a few minutes away. Rather than call Boone back, Liam decided to head straight over to his office. *Please, Lord. Let my family be safe and sound. We already dealt with the worst when we lost Ruby! Don't let anything take us down that road again.*

Liam raced down the street, barely pausing to say hello to passersby as they greeted him. As a doctor here in town, he had a lot of clients who loved to stop him for a chat whenever he passed by. There was no time for that today. There had been something strained in his brother's tone that Liam had found alarming. He pushed open the door to the sheriff's office and rushed inside. Shelly, Boone's receptionist, stared at him with wide eyes. Fear skittered through him. Normally she greeted him effusively.

What in the world is going on?

Shelly pointed toward Boone's office without saying a single word. With his heart in his throat, Liam thrust the door open without even knocking. Boone was standing in front of his desk, his head bowed. There was a woman seated in the chair facing his desk. All Liam could see was the back of her head and shoulders.

"Sorry to interrupt your meeting. The call cut out, so I headed straight over here." The words tumbled from Liam's lips. His chest was rising and falling rapidly. He felt almost breathless.

Boone held up his hands. "Liam. Let's go in the next

room. I need to talk to you." His face had a gray tinge. His jaw was tightly clenched.

Just as Boone stepped toward him, the woman turned her head around, allowing him to see her face head-on. It was a face that had been seared to his heart, mind and soul for eight years. Long, dark brown hair. Brown eyes flecked with caramel. Café-au-lait-colored skin. A heart-shaped face.

Liam let out a guttural cry. He felt a falling sensation, as if someone had pushed him off the highest branches of a mighty oak tree. For a moment he couldn't get a breath. There was no way he could utter a single word.

"Steady!" Boone said, grabbing hold of his arms as his knees buckled underneath him.

The room began to spin. He pressed his eyes closed. What was happening to him? Nothing was making sense at the moment. Everything in his world had turned upside down.

When he opened his eyes again, she was still sitting there, regarding him with a shuttered expression on her face. Ruby. His wife. The only woman he had ever loved.

Although she had been declared dead approximately two years ago in a failed search-and-rescue mission in Colorado, she was now sitting in Boone's mahogany chair, looking very much alive and well.

Ruby stood from her chair, wanting to be on the same level as the sheriff and the man he'd referred to as Liam. It already seemed as if she was at a distinct disadvantage in this situation. Having amnesia meant she had no tangible memories of this fishing village in Alaska, nor did she recognize the man named Liam who looked as if his legs might buckle underneath him. She was still getting used to the name Ruby. For the first year after her accident she'd called herself Kit until she had remembered her real name.

Sheriff Prescott hadn't told her who he had been on the phone with earlier, although she had heard him speak in an urgent tone. Next thing she knew, Liam had crashed into the room like a man on a mission.

All she felt at the moment was an overwhelming sense of fear. It was the same emotion she'd been battling for the last two years. Her legs were shaking like crazy. Coming to Love, Alaska, had been an act of pure bravery on her part. She had wanted to face her nebulous past so she could move forward with her life. And now, caught in this uncomfortable moment, she found herself wishing she had stayed back home in Colorado.

Home? That was a misnomer. She hadn't yet found a place to call home. Perhaps she never would. After seeing a story on the news about a matchmaking program called Operation Love, she had experienced a strong feeling of connection with the town featured in the report—Love, Alaska. As a result, she had ventured all the way there in the hope of getting answers. And standing here before her was a man who might be able to provide them for her.

Her entire body froze. There was so much emotion etched on the man named Liam's face. The way he was looking at her caused something to tighten in her chest. There had been a look of absolute shock, followed by an expression of such joy that it made her want to sob. The sheriff hadn't told her anything about who this man was, but she knew instinctively that he had been a huge part of her life. His reaction to her presence spoke volumes.

"Ruby!" Liam's voice sounded raspy and filled with surprise. He moved toward her with his arms open. She took a step backward, overwhelmed by the thought of being touched by a stranger. The sheriff held him back, and Ruby heard him say, "She doesn't remember you, Liam."

Liam let out a strangled sound that caused her to flinch. It was infused with pain.

Liam. It was a nice name. Strong. Solid. He was good-looking. Rugged. He had dark brown, chin-length hair. His warm, blue eyes radiated an intensity that unnerved her. He was tall, with a rangy build. And he couldn't seem to take his eyes off her.

She shifted from one foot to the other, feeling the heat from his intense gaze, folded her arms across her chest and watched the interaction between the two men. She was good at picking up on cues. It was a skill she had honed ever since her amnesia diagnosis. These men were close. Brothers or best friends, she imagined.

Liam ran a shaky hand over his face. "W-what are you talking about, Boone?"

The sheriff still had a hold on Liam. They were face-to-face, staring each other down. Electricity crackled in the room. What had Sheriff Prescott told Liam over the phone?

"She showed up here looking for any information we could provide about her past or family connections. From what I've been able to piece together, she sustained a head injury that led to amnesia. She was living in a remote area of Colorado until a recent move to Denver." Boone let out a sigh. "I couldn't believe it when she walked into my office."

Liam shook his head as if in disbelief. His face held

a dazed expression. He swung his eyes back to her. "Ruby," he said, brushing off the sheriff's grip. He took two steps toward her. She held her ground without retreating. "I can't believe it's you. I feel like I'm dreaming. You're back!"

"I don't remember you. Or this town," Ruby blurted. She tilted her chin up, locking gazes with him. "I'm sorry," she said in a brusque voice. "But you need to know that before you get your hopes up."

His face fell. It made her want to cry to see him so torn up inside. And to know that it was due to her. But she wasn't going to mince words. Raising his hopes would be cruel.

"What do you remember?" he asked, his voice sounding ragged.

"Flashes. Moments. Bits and pieces. Something about this town feels familiar. My name," Ruby said. "Although for a long time I couldn't remember it, so I came up with another name for myself."

The sheriff moved forward. "Her doctors said it's retrograde amnesia."

"Retrograde amnesia," Liam mumbled. He appeared to be a bit dazed. "I—I don't understand."

"In my case they theorized that due to a head trauma I lost all my memories from before the accident," Ruby explained. "I get flashes from time to time, but they're disconnected and not grounded to anything solid. Sometimes it feels like a really fast slide show."

Liam met her gaze. "Will the memories eventually come back?"

Ruby shrugged. "Some people do recover their memories, but the doctors have told me there's no way of knowing whether mine will return."

"So you don't remember marrying me? Or being my wife?" Liam asked. His jaw trembled.

"A-are you really my husband?" she asked. She jutted her chin in Boone's direction. "He wouldn't tell me anything when he called you. He wouldn't even tell me who he was on the phone with. Needless to say, I don't like being kept in the dark. It's pretty much been the story of my life for the last few years."

"My name is Liam Prescott. I'm Sheriff Prescott's brother. And, yes, you're my wife," Liam said. Tears misted in his eyes. He ran his hand over his face. "I'm so sorry, Ruby, that you don't remember any of this."

Although on some level she knew there was a possibility this man was her husband, just hearing the words come out of his mouth served as a jolt.

Ruby couldn't help but let out a gasp. The news made her feel wobbly. She should have been prepared for this since the slight indentation on her ring finger had caused her to question whether she was a married woman. But where was her ring? Had she lost it during whatever traumatic incident had caused her amnesia?

And why else would the sheriff have called Liam down here? Liam's emotional reaction made perfect sense now. He was a man whose wife had been presumed dead for several years. And now she was back with no warning and nothing to prepare him for the startling sight of her.

"If you're my husband, then who is Aidan?" she whispered. It was staggering to find out that this gorgeous, emotional and rugged man belonged to her. Although she had always had a niggling sensation of having been married, there had been no flashes of this man or events from their life together.

Liam's blue eyes lit up. Relief swept across his features. "So you do remember something? You remember Aidan?"

She shook her head, her long hair swirling about her shoulders. "No, I don't. I've been wearing this. At first I thought it might be my name even though it sounded masculine." She held up the necklace that had been hidden from sight under her winter coat. The name Aidan had been etched on the gold pendant in flowery script.

Emotion flickered in his eyes. "I gave that to you as a birthday gift. You wore it every day without fail."

"What does it mean? Who is Aidan?" she asked, voicing the question she'd been asking herself for two years. The necklace had become important to her—it had been the only tangible thing tying her to the life she couldn't remember.

Liam seemed to be searching her eyes for clues. "He's our child, Ruby. Yours and mine."

Child. Hearing that single word served as a kick in the gut. She had often wondered if she was a mother. If she was being completely honest with herself, she had known deep down in her soul that she was somebody's mama. She remembered bits and pieces. Nothing more than fragments.

The smell of talcum powder. Cradling a newborn in her arms. Singing a soothing lullaby. A tuft of dark hair.

She sank back down into the chair, overwhelmed by the knowledge that Aidan was her son. "How old is he?" she asked, her voice a notch above a whisper. It felt strange asking questions about her own child. But she wanted to know. She needed answers.

"He'll be five in a few weeks," Liam said. A hint of a smile played around his lips.

"Five," she said with a nod. "That's a great age." Why had she just blurted that out? What did she know about five-year-olds?

"He's a wonderful boy. You'd be proud of him," Liam said. "You two used to be inseparable."

Ruby had no idea what to say to that. It hurt terribly to know that she couldn't remember precious moments with her own flesh and blood. A child she had carried in her womb and given birth to and nurtured. A boy who had been emotionally tied to her. Pain unlike any she'd ever felt before ricocheted through her. She had felt lost ever since she'd woken up in Colorado with no memories of who she was or where she belonged. Although she hadn't thought it possible to feel more agony, finding out about her son and husband filled her with a sense of yearning to fill all the holes in her memory.

They must have loved her, and in return, she must have loved them back.

Lord, please help me. I've been stumbling around in the dark for so long. But now a big bright light is being shined on my past and yet I feel nothing but confusion. I'm still uncertain about who I am and where I'm going. I'm a mother and a wife, but I'm not sure I know how to be either of those things.

Liam shoved his hand through his hair. He let out a huff of air and exchanged a look filled with hidden meaning with the sheriff. "Aidan. I have to bring you to see him, Ruby. He prays for you every night."

Ruby raised her hand to her trembling lips. Just thinking about a little boy uttering prayers for her was enough to make her come undone. *He's not just any little boy*, her voice buzzed in her head. *He's your son. Your flesh and blood.* That raised the stakes even higher.

She shook her head as a tidal wave of emotions rolled over her. Trudy and Ezra had been concerned about this very thing happening. They had wanted to make the trip with her, but after two years of being under their wing, she had needed to do something without their sheltering arms.

But everything was rushing at her now, like a freight train at maximum speed. Suddenly she started taking rapid breaths of air. It felt like she couldn't breathe. She folded her arms around her stomach and began deeply breathing in and out.

"Ruby! Are you all right?" Liam took the final few steps toward her, quickly swallowing up the distance between them. She felt his hands touching her. There was something comforting about his hands resting on her shoulders. It was the oddest thing, since he was technically a stranger to her, and she always felt wary of people she didn't know.

"It might be a good idea to give her some space," Boone said to Liam. "This could be very overwhelming for her," he explained, casting Ruby a concerned glance.

With a begrudging look on his face, Liam took a few steps back. Boone followed suit.

"If you're not feeling well, I can get you something to drink or take you to my clinic," Liam said. "I'm a doctor here in town."

Liam was a doctor? She shouldn't be surprised by the news. He exuded a kind and authoritative air. It wasn't hard to imagine him treating patients or calming a distraught child who needed shots. Ruby didn't know whether there was a part of her that was remembering something from the past or whether it was strictly her imagination, but a picture of Liam outfitted in a white lab coat, a stethoscope hanging around his neck, flashed before her eyes.

"I'm fine," Ruby said. "I think everything is just catching up to me." She rubbed the back of her neck. "The plane ride. Being back here. I know you're saying this is where I'm from, but I feel like a newborn filly finding its legs."

"Ruby, I know this can't be easy for you, but this is a blessing for our family. God answered our prayers." He locked eyes with her. "And now I need to bring you back home where you belong so you can reunite with Aidan."

Oh, no! She didn't think she was quite ready for that. Ruby wanted to see her child, but she was terrified. What would she say to him? Would he expect her to be a certain way or hold him in a special manner? She didn't know a single thing about being a mother.

"I hadn't planned on anything like this," she said lamely. "I—I don't know what I would say to him. How do I explain that I don't remember him?"

"If you don't face this, you might never really be able to move forward." Liam's voice held an intensity that reverberated throughout the room. "Part of that is meeting your son."

Ruby bit her lip. A feeling of anxiety swept over her. Had coming to Love been a huge mistake? Everything was happening so quickly. In a matter of minutes her life had dramatically changed, so much so that she wasn't sure she could keep up with all the shifts.

"Can Ruby and I have a moment alone?" Liam asked, looking over at the sheriff, who nodded before stepping out of the room.

Once they were alone, Ruby felt a sudden shyness take over. This tall, good-looking man with the soulful, intense eyes was her husband. He belonged to her. And she to him. The weight of it settled over her like a warm blanket. Even though she couldn't remember him or any specific details about their life together, she felt a tremendous pull in his direction that shook her to her very core. She fought against a sudden impulse to run all the way back to Colorado where she'd been safe from this gorgeous, rugged man who seemed to want the world from her.

Chapter Two

Once they were alone, Liam took a moment to simply gaze at his wife. She was even more beautiful than before, he realized. If that was even remotely possible. Since the very first time he had laid eyes on her, he'd believed that Ruby was the loveliest woman in the world. She had the type of beauty that turned heads. Her warm brown eyes had always showed him her truths. Now, he couldn't see anything radiating from their russet depths but fear.

And it killed him that instead of making her feel safe, his presence brought her anxiety. Hadn't Ruby always sought him out for love and protection? At least she had until the last few weeks before the accident in Colorado. He'd never admitted it to a single person, but his marriage had been coming apart at the seams. They had fought over the dangers of her occupation and Liam's desire to have her close to home rather than flying out on rescue missions. Now, with Ruby's memory loss, he was still the only person who knew she had asked for a separation before heading to Colorado.

"You can trust me, Ruby. I'm not going to do anything to hurt you," he said, moving toward her slowly so as not to startle her. At the moment she resembled a deer caught in the headlights. His insides twisted painfully at the sight of her discomfort. He could only imagine how difficult it would be to come face-to-face with a past you couldn't remember.

"That's not what I'm worried about. I don't want to hurt Aidan." She twisted her fingers together and bowed her head.

His heart leaped at the sight of it. It had been a tic of Ruby's whenever she was nervous. It was reassuring to know that she had still retained something about herself that he recognized. Even though she couldn't remember him or their life together, this was still Ruby, despite the obvious changes in her demeanor. His wife. The woman he had vowed to love for a lifetime.

Something told him he might be repeating this mantra over and over again in the weeks and months to come.

"Hurt him?" Liam asked. "That's not possible. He's going to be over the moon to have his mother back."

She lifted her head up and looked at him, her expression mournful. "But I won't be the same mother who raised him. I'm a different person now, and I know that must be confusing and heartbreaking to you, but the accident changed all that."

Her words popped his euphoria like the bursting of a balloon. This wasn't nearly as straightforward as he would like to believe. The woman standing before him wasn't his Ruby.

"What happened to you?" he blurted. He had so many questions about where Ruby had been for the last few years and how she had lived. Ever since he had walked into Boone's office they had been churning inside him like acid.

A sigh slipped past her lips. "I was in an accident, I think. I've had CT scans on my head, and it's pretty apparent that I suffered a traumatic brain injury. I don't know exactly what happened, but when I woke up I was in a remote, wooded area." She shook her head. "I must have wandered there in a daze from the mountain. God must have been watching out for me."

"You were in Colorado doing a search-and-rescue operation." He smiled at her. "That was your job. You were really great at it, too. You were caught up in an avalanche when you were doing a mountain rescue."

Ruby's jaw dropped. "Search and rescue? I had no idea. The reason I came to Love was because of a news story I watched on television about the Operation Love program. It basically detailed how the town mayor was matching single bachelors from here in town with women from all over the country." She furrowed her brow. "There was something so familiar about the town. And I couldn't get it out of my mind for days and days after I watched the segment. It gnawed at me. Call it a gut feeling, but I knew there was some connection between this quaint village and my old life. So I made the decision to fly out here and do some digging. I hit pay dirt the moment I entered your brother's office. He practically hit the floor the moment he laid eyes on me."

"Can't say I blame him," Liam murmured. "I had the same reaction."

"It's understandable. It's been two years since the accident."

"My dad was there that day in Colorado, helping out with the operation. He's search and rescue like yourself.

He saw you get swallowed up by the snow-slip, along with three others who were standing on that mountain ledge." Just recalling it sent shivers through his body. It had been the darkest day of his life.

Ruby's brown eyes widened. "Did they make it?"

"No," he said somberly. "Only one body was recovered. All three of you were presumed dead."

Tears pooled in Ruby's eyes. "I have no idea how I survived that. All I know is that I was discovered by a couple who live in a remote area, miles away from the mountain. I don't have a clue as to how I got there, but my friend Trudy spotted me wandering aimlessly near their cabin. When she brought me inside she said I was disoriented and couldn't even remember my name. For the first few months she and her husband called me Kit. Then I remembered my name. It just came to me out of the blue."

Liam felt a burst of anger toward the couple who had taken Ruby in. He clenched his teeth and reminded himself to count to ten so he didn't vent. "How in the world didn't they connect you to the rescue operation on the mountain? It was in all the papers and on the internet."

Ruby quirked her mouth. "The couple who rescued me lives off the grid. Their lifestyle is very humble. They don't have television or internet. And they were very protective of me. They brought in a doctor who examined me at their home since I was too afraid to leave. There was a bump on the back of my head, along with bruised ribs and some contusions. He wanted me to come in for additional testing, but I refused any further medical intervention."

"You're incredibly fortunate there wasn't bleeding on the brain or anything else that might have been fatal."

Liam hated sounding like a medical know-it-all, but he couldn't help but see this from a doctor's vantage point. Not seeking medical attention at a hospital had been foolish. And risky.

Ruby sent him a sheepish look. "Not too smart of me, I know. I was a wreck for months and months. I jumped at the slightest sound, and I refused to do anything outside of my narrow comfort zone. It wasn't until I went to Denver that I began to get connected with modern-day living. That's when I finally had medical tests to get a firm diagnosis."

"I'm amazed that you went so long without medical attention," Liam said with a shake of his head. "But I understand that your circumstances were extreme. Having no memories must have been terrifying."

"It was," Ruby said with a sigh. "I don't want to say I'm used to it now, but nothing is as bad as those first few days and weeks when nothing made sense. Lately I've experienced more flashes of memory. I'm grateful that I remembered my name and this town...even though I have to admit it's not easy being here."

Liam observed the worry lines and strain etched on her face. He wanted to reach out and take away all her fears and worries. Back when things were good between them he would have reached out and swept a kiss across her brow and soothed Ruby the way he knew best. If only he could. Those days felt like a million years ago.

He smiled at her. "I feel very grateful that those flashes led you back home."

"Home." She wrinkled her nose as she said the word. "I don't want to hurt your feelings, because you seem like a very nice man, but home isn't something I've ever known. Not really. The home we shared… I wish that I could remember it, but I can't."

Liam's heart lurched at the look of utter defeat etched on Ruby's face. The woman he knew was a fighter. She had never given up on anything. Not a single time. Not ever.

"I know everything is coming at you fast and furiously. But I need you to know that when I married you I took our wedding vows very seriously…we both did. We're still married, Ruby. My home is your home."

"Liam," she protested, "what you're saying is very sweet, but I don't—"

"I know you don't remember us and our life together, but I remember you," Liam interrupted. "The food you like. What makes you laugh. Your favorite color. The way your cheeks flush when you get angry."

A vein began thrumming above her eye. "Those things may have changed. I've done a lot of research on my condition. Tastes can become altered after a brain injury. For instance, I love apples. I may not have before."

Liam grinned. It made him happy to know that she hadn't changed completely, despite the differences he noticed in her demeanor and personality. "You've always loved apples," he said. "Ever since I've known you."

"That's good to know," she said. A hint of a smile played around her lips. For a moment she looked less somber. Almost lighthearted. Within seconds, a shadow crossed her face. "I'm not sure about meeting Aidan. I don't know how to act, what to say to him."

Liam had to stop himself from reaching out and caressing her cheek. She looked so vulnerable right now.

"You're his mother, Ruby. For him, that's going to trump everything else. Remember, he's only four years old. He's at the age where he accepts things at face value for the most part. Unless, of course, you're trying to get him to eat his vegetables." Liam let out a chuckle. "Aidan and broccoli have been having a tough time of it lately."

Ruby scrunched up her face. "Broccoli? Yuck. The kid has good taste. I like him already." She let out a sweet laugh.

"And I'm not an expert on amnesia, but as a physician, I know that certain things can trigger memories. Maybe seeing Aidan will cause you to remember something solid about your life before the head trauma," he said. "Something that can ground you in the here and now."

She chewed her lip for a moment. It seemed as if she was soaking in everything he had explained to her. "You're right," she said with a nod. "I owe him a shot at remembering. He's mine, whether I remember him or not. I'm not sure if I know how to be his mother, Liam, but I know it's not right to walk away from this. At least not without seeing him first."

"I'm not asking for the moon, Ruby. I just want you to meet him, to see him face-to-face. We'll cross the bridges as they come."

"I'll do it," Ruby said with an emphatic nod of her head. "I want to see our son."

Liam felt a tightening sensation in his chest. Aidan was going to be reunited with his mother! It was almost as wonderful as the moment the knowledge had seeped in that Ruby was alive. For the last two years he had been walking around like a man with half a heart. Now, for the first time in forever, he felt as if he had hope.

Although he knew the odds might be stacked against Ruby getting her memory back, he couldn't help but feel optimistic about their lives returning to normal. And, above all else, Aidan getting his mother back.

With Ruby back in their world, God had just presented him and his son with the best Christmas gift ever.

Ruby sat in the passenger seat of the big, midnight-blue truck and gazed in wonder at her surroundings. She almost felt like a little kid as she swung her eyes in every direction. Everything in this village was so beautiful. It resembled an old-fashioned postcard. Jarvis Street—the main area in town—had quaint shops lit up with sparkly Christmas lights and charming lampposts decorated in red and white.

A huge pine tree sat on the town green, adorned with colored lights and an abundance of ornaments. Couples were walking hand in hand down the street while a group of children had their noses pressed against one of the shop windows. A big sign with the words Operation Love hung on a shop door. Her attention was drawn to an establishment called the Moose Café. It looked festive and fun, judging by the moose logo above the door and the customers who sailed out the door with contented smiles on their faces.

"That's my brother Cameron's place." Liam glanced over at her, as if waiting for her to react to the name he'd tossed out. It hadn't registered at all. She felt a little dip in her stomach. It felt as if she might be disappointing him by not remembering names and places and this glorious town. But she could never pretend about her memories just to make someone happy—they were sacred.

"It started as a coffee bar, but it's morphed into a pretty good restaurant," Liam explained. "He serves up a mighty good mochaccino and a whole assortment of other fancy coffee drinks."

"It seems like a great place," she said, admiring the soft glow emanating from inside. It looked like the sort of establishment where friends gathered to share food, good conversation and fellowship. Who had her friends been in this small fishing village? Had they mourned her passing? Had they missed her?

"He built that place out of sheer grit and determination. You used to always say that Cameron could do anything he set his mind to." A ring of satisfaction laced his tone.

"I guess I was right," she murmured. "That's quite commendable of him. How many siblings do you have?"

"Three. There's Boone, who you just met. He's the oldest. Cameron, who owns the Moose Café. And last but not least, is my sister, Honor. She's the baby of the family." He quirked his mouth. "I don't want to make you feel any pressure, but my little sister always thought you hung the moon. She's at the house now, watching Aidan, so she's going to be very emotional about your return. I sent Boone ahead of us so he could tell her. Be prepared for a few waterworks. That one wears her heart on her sleeve."

Ruby was thankful for the heads-up. There was nothing worse than being blindsided. She wondered if that's how Liam felt about her showing up in Love without even the slightest warning.

He must be a strong person, she realized. Liam seemed to be handling the news incredibly well, much better than she was. Her own emotions were all over the place. She could feel something bubbling up inside her and threatening to overflow. She had been so used to stuffing her feelings down in an effort to minimize the pain of not knowing her identity. It was as if someone had pulled back her layers and exposed her core. All her nerve endings were tingling.

She bit her lip. Ruby turned toward him, admiring how good-looking he was in profile. "What about me? Do I have any brothers or sisters? And what about my parents? Shouldn't you call them?"

Liam's hands tightened on the steering wheel. "Your parents are both gone, Ruby. But you do have a brother, Kyle. You raised him after your parents died in a car accident. He lives in Alaska, but not here in Love. He's a volunteer fireman. I'll call him once we get home and see Aidan."

"Were we close?" she asked. Her pulse began to race at the idea that she had a blood relative she had loved dearly enough to raise on her own.

Liam turned to her, a sheen of moisture in his eyes. "Very close. He was inspired to become a fireman after watching the work you did with search-and-rescue operations."

Ruby felt a big smile take over her face. "That's nice. It makes me feel good to know that I worked in a meaningful profession and that I impacted people's lives."

"You saved a lot of lives, Ruby. Even on that terrible day on the mountain, you rescued people. Pretty amazing, isn't it?" Liam's voice radiated a deep respect. "You were a hero."

It was fairly wonderful, Ruby thought. A feeling of pride rose inside her. There wasn't much in her day-to-day life to feel accomplished about. Back in Denver she worked at a restaurant as a waitress. It was a low-paying, boring position that left her feeling as if there had to be more to life than her current situation reflected. But with no past, no degrees to put on a résumé and no known skills, making a living had been difficult. Her boss paid her under the table and hadn't pressed her for a social security number after she'd explained her circumstances. She was thankful she was able to live a modest life on her salary, but the work didn't fulfill her in any way.

As Moose Crossing signs appeared on the road ahead and a magnificent mountain loomed in the distance, majestic and proud, the enormity of the situation crashed over her in unrelenting waves. She had stepped out on a leap of faith by making the trip to this lovely Alaskan hamlet. Leaving Colorado had pulled her out of the comfort zone she had established for herself in Denver. Despite her fears, Ruby couldn't remember ever having felt this wonderfully alive and present.

With every passing moment she was realizing that her being here in Love came with a host of complications. She had only brought a few days' worth of clothes with her. Somehow in her mind she had imagined coming to Alaska and doing a little bit of digging around, then heading back to Colorado to continue with her life. Closure had been her objective. Finding out about her son and Liam had added a huge wrinkle to her plan. She had meaningful ties in this town. And there was nothing about Liam Prescott that made her believe he would sign divorce papers and send her on her merry way.

Truthfully, she wasn't certain that she was fully prepared to greet her old life head-on. A husband and a child? A brother? Family and friends? She wasn't sure she could handle all of these new connections without coming apart at the seams.

Liam shot a quick glance her direction. He reached out and touched her hand. She jerked it away, feeling uncomfortable at the tender gesture. Despite the circumstances, it was too intimate. She didn't know him like that.

"I'm sorry. I didn't mean to startle you," Liam said. "You looked so nervous I just wanted to reassure you. Everything will be fine."

Ruby turned her head away and glanced out the passenger-side window. *Everything will be fine.* She wasn't sure she truly believed that. Liam couldn't possibly understand her journey as an amnesia victim. He didn't know the twisted road she walked each and every day. The fear. The anxiety and stress. The frustration over not being able to access her own memories from her mind. And now she was going to have to face her four-year-old son and deal with questions she wasn't sure she was prepared to answer.

Look up, she reminded herself. It served to remind her that when things in life became jumbled or stressful, to look for God. He was always there for her. Ever present. Always faithful. Ruby didn't know where her faith had come from, but she was grateful for it at moments like this when her fear felt like a living, breathing thing that might consume her.

"We're here," Liam announced as he turned off the road and down a private, tree-lined driveway. Ruby peered out the window. Her surroundings resembled a winter wonderland. Spruce trees were everywhere. She recognized them from Colorado. They were beautiful, with full branches covered in a blanket of white.

The tires crunched noisily on the ice and snow in the driveway.

Fear skittered through her. *What have I gotten myself into by agreeing to come here?* She took a deep, fortifying breath to calm her nerves.

Liam had been right about her meeting with Aidan. What he was asking of her wasn't a lot, considering he'd been doing it alone for two years and raising their son by himself. Something was pushing and prodding at her. A feeling deep down inside her that she'd been stuffing away for months. She ached to hold her child in her arms, to give him back the mother he'd lost. It felt instinctual, but it was terrifying to imagine how she might feel if he rejected her. What if after all this time she wasn't enough?

All of a sudden everything buzzing in her head hushed and stilled as Liam's house came into view. It resembled something out of a fairy tale. Nestled in the woods and surrounded by snowcapped trees sat a small log cabin that brought to mind a rustic lifestyle. A fat, plastic snowman gave the front porch a festive air. A green pine wreath with red ribbons adorned the front door. A smattering of icicles hung from the eaves.

A sigh slipped past her lips. It was a delightful house. Perfect for raising a family and happily-ever-afters.

Had she been happy in this cozy, eye-catching home? Had all her dreams come true when she had married Liam and given birth to their baby boy? From all appearances, Ruby Prescott had been living the dream.

"We built this house from the ground up. It was your dream, Ruby, ever since you were a little girl, to live in a log-cabin home in the woods," Liam said, his eyes moistening.

"Thank you," she blurted.

Liam frowned. "For what?"

"For giving me that…the home I always wanted. It must have meant the world to me," she said, feeling a pang in the region of her heart. To have been so loved by her husband that he had made it a priority for her to have her log cabin in the woods was a wonderful thing. It spoke of devotion.

Had our life together really been so idyllic?

She felt a wave of sadness pass over her. To have lost so much—a loving husband, a dear son and a wonderful home built straight from her imagination was painful. And although Liam's home was unbelievable, she still didn't feel any sort of connection to it. Nothing had been stoked inside her except sheer admiration.

"You don't need to thank me, Ruby. Anything I ever did was based on love. And you returned those blessings wholeheartedly and without reservation." They locked gazes for a moment. Something simmered in the air between them that caused her to turn her eyes away. It was hard to wrap her head around discussing love with someone she had just met.

Liam turned off the engine and made his way to her side of the truck before she knew what was happening. He opened the door and reached for her hand, reminding her to watch her footing on the slippery ground. Knowing her boots had already caused her to slide several times that morning, she clutched Liam's elbow as she felt her foot slipping. Liam didn't flinch as her full weight leaned on him. "Sorry," she said in a low voice. "You would think I'm used to this because of all the snow we get in Colorado."

"No worries. I've got you," he drawled, causing tiny

butterflies to do somersaults in her tummy. He led her the rest of the way to the porch steps, easing his stride so as not to rush her. The gesture spoke volumes to Ruby about Liam. Considerate. Caring. A true gentleman. She felt as if she was slowly but surely piecing together the clues as to what kind of man Liam Prescott was. So far he seemed like an incredible human being. She could very well imagine women tripping all over themselves to be with a guy like Dr. Liam Prescott.

Before they had even reached the top step, the front door sprung open. A young woman with long, chestnut-colored hair and gentle features stood there, her gray-blue eyes awash with tears. She looked Ruby up and down, her expression incredulous.

"Honor," Liam said in a warning voice. "Take it easy. We don't want to overwhelm her. She's just getting her bearings."

Before Ruby knew it, she found herself enveloped in an enthusiastic bear hug, the likes of which she had never before experienced. At least not that she could recall. Honor's arms were squeezing her so tightly that for a moment it felt overwhelming. She watched as Liam untangled his sister's arms from around her and gently pushed her away.

"I'm sorry. Boone said to go easy, but I couldn't help myself." She sniffed back tears, her stare never wavering from Ruby. "I'm so happy!"

Ruby sent Honor the warmest smile she could muster. This young woman seemed so sincere and good-hearted. It made her feel all warm and fuzzy inside to know that she had fostered a tight relationship with her sister-in-law. She could feel the love radiating from Honor.

Once Liam ushered her inside the house, Ruby stood in the foyer and looked around at her surroundings. The décor was warm and cozy. Cream-colored walls provided a soothing vibe while family photos on the front table provided a personal touch. She spotted a picture of herself and Liam. It was an odd sensation to see a photo she didn't remember posing for. She was gazing up at Liam adoringly. He was holding a baby boy in his arms. Most likely it was their son.

"I just can't believe it! Ruby's back. You have your family back, Liam. All of our prayers have been answered." Honor gushed as she threw herself against Liam's chest. As Ruby stood and regarded the heart-warming scene unfolding before her, she couldn't help but fret over the very real possibility of letting everyone down. Especially Aidan. She had traveled to Love to get answers her own mind couldn't provide. She hadn't even been certain that she'd been on the right path. The thought of staying there in town hadn't ever crossed her mind.

Dear Lord. Please provide some clarity. I need You now more than I ever have before. How do I embrace these people who care about me without raising false hopes about my return? My name may be Ruby Prescott, but I don't remember who that is or how to be her.

Chapter Three

Liam felt Ruby's eyes on him as he cradled Honor against his chest. He felt a spurt of sympathy for her. She looked a tad overwhelmed. There was a tight look to her expression, as if one little thing might cause her to shatter into pieces. Although he loved his baby sister to no end, she veered toward the dramatic. Ever since she was a little girl, she'd shouted her feelings from rooftops. As her big brother, Liam had always wished he could protect her from the slings and arrows of life, but he had learned through trial and error that it just wasn't possible.

He felt relieved about his decision to have Boone break the news to Honor about Ruby. There was no way he had wanted to have that conversation over the phone with his baby sister, nor had he thought it wise to simply show up with Ruby in tow. It would have been too much of a shock for Honor. As it was, she had practically strangled Ruby with her enthusiastic embrace.

Ruby hadn't seemed to remember his sister at all. There hadn't even been a glimmer of recognition on her face.

Retrograde amnesia? Liam had heard the term, but had never dealt with a patient who suffered from the condition. As far as he knew, it was incredibly rare, which made the situation even more baffling. And he felt a little guilty about the fact that her memory loss prevented her from remembering the pitiful state of their marriage prior to the accident.

Was it right to allow her to believe things had been wonderful between them? He himself wasn't under any illusions about that, but he owed it to Aidan to try to patch their family up. There was nothing Aidan wanted more than a family of his own.

Earlier, Boone had promised that he would keep Aidan occupied until Liam could speak to him in private about his mother's return. A quick glance around confirmed that his son was nowhere in sight.

Honor moved out of his arms and wearily ran a hand across her eyes. She appeared emotionally drained.

"Where's Aidan?" he asked, knowing he had to get down to the business of talking to his son.

"Boone is keeping him occupied in his room," Honor said. "He was super excited that Uncle Boone showed up out of the blue. I bet they're playing cops and robbers."

"I better go talk to him," Liam said, addressing Ruby. "Boone can only keep him in there for so long."

"Do you know what you're going to say?" Ruby asked in a tentative voice.

Liam shrugged. "Honestly, I'm going to wing it a little bit. There's really no script to follow here. I'll be sensitive and caring, and try to help him understand it as much as any kid his age possibly could."

Ruby bit her lip. "Could you make sure to tell him

that I didn't stay away by choice…that I was sick and couldn't find my way back home."

"Of course I will," he said, emotion clogging his voice, turning it raspy. Just the thought that Ruby had been out there this whole time and living in Colorado unbeknownst to him, frustrated him to no end. But he was going to focus on what today had brought him and his family. Psalm 30:5 rolled through his mind like thunder. "Weeping may endure for a night, but joy cometh in the morning."

Ruby's return had brought him immense joy. Mixed with that joy was trepidation. The road ahead wasn't going to be easy. He knew it with deep certainty.

Liam turned and walked down the hall to Aidan's bedroom. He paused for a moment to collect his thoughts, then turned the knob and stood in the doorway. Aidan and Boone were both stretched out on the floor playing checkers. It was Aidan's favorite game. He watched the two of them, a feeling of deep love welling up inside him at the sight of his big brother bonding with his son. After the sorrow that had invaded their lives over the past few years, he felt so very blessed at this moment.

He stepped into the room, causing Aidan to look up from his game. His brown eyes lit with happiness at the sight of him.

"Daddy! I've been waiting for you to come home."

"What have you been up to, A-man?" Liam bent and tousled his son's dark curls.

"I been playing with Uncle Boone." Aidan grinned.

"Running circles around me is more like it," Boone muttered.

Aidan giggled and covered his mouth.

"Hey, little man. I need to have a big-boy talk with you about something," Liam said, trying to keep his voice casual.

Aidan's eyes bulged. "Uh-oh. Did Auntie Honor tell you about the snowball?"

Snowball? "No," Liam said with a raised eyebrow. "Is there something you need to tell me?"

Aidan gulped. "You go first."

Boone and Liam exchanged a glance. Neither of them could resist grinning at Aidan's comment. For a four-year-old, he was pretty fast on his feet.

Boone sprung up from the floor and said, "I'll give you guys some time alone."

As he walked toward the door, Boone reached out and squeezed Liam's shoulder. "Let me know if you need anything," he said with a nod.

As always, his brother was proving he was a strong support system to lean on during tough times. Once Boone had closed the door behind him, Liam went and sat on Aidan's bed. He patted the spot beside him and said, "Come on over and sit down, A-man. We need to talk something out."

Aidan joined him on the bed and peered up at him, a curious expression etched on his face. "What is it, Daddy? Did I do something wrong?"

"Absolutely not," Liam said, reaching out and tweaking his nose. "You're the bee's knees as far as I'm concerned. You're the best son on the planet."

"The planet? Whoa!" Aidan said in a raised voice. "That's cool."

"You're my best buddy. We've been through a lot since we lost your mother."

Aidan made a sad face. He let out a little sigh and bowed his head.

"I know it's been hard not having a mom." Liam placed his arm around Aidan's shoulder and squeezed.

"I wish I could remember her more," Aidan said in a soft voice. "I like looking at her face in the album. It helps me make a picture of her in my mind."

Aidan's words went straight to his heart, as they always did whenever he talked about his mother. How would he ever find the right words to tell him she was alive? How could a little boy even begin to process the information?

"Aidan. Something has happened. It changes everything for us." Aidan looked up at him with wide eyes. "It's something good. Spectacular, really."

Aidan rubbed his hands together. "Oh, I love great surprises."

"Do you remember what I told you happened to Mommy? On the mountain?"

"Yes," Aidan said in a solemn voice. "She was being a hero and snow came and swallowed her up."

"Pretty much," Liam said, biting back a smirk. "Sometimes things aren't what they seem. We thought Mommy died on that mountain, A-man. But I found out today that she didn't."

"She didn't?" Aidan asked, his mouth hanging open in shock.

"No, she didn't," he answered, blinking away the tears blurring his vision. "She hit her head and she was really sick for a long time. And she's here, right out there in the living room."

"No way!" Aidan said, jumping up from the bed. "Can I see her? Can I? Can I?"

Liam couldn't help but grin at Aidan's unbridled en-thusiasm. Even though things were far from perfect with regard to Ruby's return, his son's innocent take on the situation made him feel on top of the world. He had received the news just as Liam had prayed he would...joyfully.

"There's something else I have to tell you before you see her... When she hit her head, she lost her memory. So, she's still the same mommy, but she's going to have to get to know us all over again," Liam explained.

Aidan's face fell. He stuck his lip out. Tears welled in his eyes.

"Hey, buddy. What's wrong? Just smiles today. No tears, okay?"

"I just feel sad that she lost her memories," Aidan said. "That means she doesn't remember the day I was born or getting married to you. And she won't know my favorite color or the foods I like to eat." He bowed his head and focused on the carpet.

Liam reached out and lifted Aidan's chin. "But here's the thing. Since you're getting to be such a big boy, I have a huge job for you. I'm counting on you to tell your mother all about the things that matter most to you. The name of your turtle. Your favorite toy. How you like reindeer pizza better than anything else in this world." He held out his hand. "If you're up to the mis-sion, let's shake on it."

Aidan shook his father's hand. "I can do it. I'm going to be five soon. That means I'm getting so big."

His chest was almost about to explode with love for this boy. There were certain moments he wished he could just capture in a bottle for all time. This was one of them.

It was time to make new memories. With Ruby. "How about we go out there and get you reacquainted with your mom?"

Aidan nodded his head enthusiastically. Before Liam could stop him, he raced toward the door and pulled it open. His son tended to lead with his heart in all things. A part of him wanted to wrap Aidan up in his arms to protect him from the inevitable hurts life would bring him.

Liam took a deep breath. He knew instinctively that the road ahead was going to be difficult. God had blessed his family today with the return of Ruby. But there were still so many unanswered questions, so many potential roadblocks in the future. This wasn't going to be a cakewalk by any means. He bent his head and prayed.

Dear Lord. Sustain me with Your wisdom and guidance. Help me put my family back together. Please allow Aidan to get the Christmas gift he wants most—a mother.

Ruby sat in the brightly lit, all-white kitchen with Boone, his wife, Grace and Honor while Liam was having his private talk with Aidan. Grace had just showed up at the house a few minutes ago. With her jet-black hair and blue eyes, she was stunning. Her petite frame couldn't hide the fact that she was heavily pregnant. Ruby imagined she was set to deliver any day now.

The moment she introduced herself to Ruby, Grace had put her at ease by saying, "This is the first time we've met, so no worries about not remembering me."

Ruby had heaved a giant sigh of relief. It was one less person she had to worry about feeling awkward around.

Everything in the room was pleasing to the eye, from the granite countertops to the copper pans hanging from the rack. She couldn't help herself from gazing around with a deep appreciation for the setup. Ruby nearly fell off her chair when Honor told her she had been the one to lay out the plans for the kitchen design. Everything had been done to her specifications. Dream house. Dream kitchen. From everything she had seen, her life had been fairly wonderful. She hoped the old Ruby had been thankful for her blessings.

At the moment she was about as nervous as she'd ever been, even counting earlier this afternoon when she had walked into the sheriff's office. This was all starting to feel surreal. A husband. A kid. A town full of people who knew her.

What did she know about being somebody's wife or mother? What could she possibly achieve in this situation? Having no memories of the past was a severe limitation. It didn't allow her to have any sort of frame of reference with them. The harsh reality was that they were all strangers to her. And she was sitting here among them not knowing what to say to fill the silence.

"Would you like some more tea?" Honor asked. They were sitting at the kitchen table, sipping tea, eating chocolate-chip cookies and making polite conversation. Both Boone and Honor seemed to be avoiding any topics that might get sticky. Neither one mentioned her amnesia.

"No, thanks. This green tea is delicious, though," she said, raising the cup to her lips for another sip.

"It was always your favorite," Honor said. She placed her hand over her mouth. "Oops. I hope it was okay to say that."

Ruby reached out and squeezed Honor's hand. Her wanting to touch her sister-in-law surprised her. She wasn't really comfortable having physical contact with strangers. There was something so sweet and genuine about Liam's sister. She radiated goodness, which put her at ease.

"You don't have to walk on eggshells with me, Honor. This is a very unusual set of circumstances we find ourselves in. If you have any questions, feel free to ask me. I'll try to be as forthright as I can."

Boone let out a groan. He shook his head. "You have no idea what you just got yourself into."

Honor playfully swatted him with her hand. She turned back toward Ruby. "Do you remember anything? Smells? Sights? Liam's voice?"

She thought for a moment before answering. "Yes. I do. Fragments, I call them. I remember cradling a baby. And that feeling of loving him with all my heart. But I suppose I never connected that baby to myself because I had no memory of giving birth. And I'm very eager to go to the Moose Café, because the smell of coffee always reminds me of snow." She let out a giggle. "I have no idea why, but the brain is a funny thing."

"Hello."

Ruby heard the voice before she laid eyes on Aidan himself. He was standing in the doorway of the kitchen, all sweet brown eyes and chubby cheeks. His dark curls framed a handsome little face that closely resembled his father. Something twisted inside her chest.

Ruby stood from her chair and walked toward her son. Her palms were slick with moisture. Her tongue was all twisted up and useless. For the life of her she couldn't think of what to say at this monumental moment.

By this time Liam was standing in the doorway, quietly observing the reunion.

"Hi, Aidan. How are you doing?" She pushed the words out of her mouth.

Aidan seemed to be studying her. His face was scrunched up. He was deep in thought. "You're pretty. Daddy always said you were the prettiest girl he'd ever seen," he said. "And you look just like the pictures we have."

"Why, thank you. You're just about the cutest boy I've ever seen." Ruby wasn't exaggerating due to the fact that he was her child. With his jet-black lashes and striking features, Aidan was sure to stand out in any crowd.

"That's what Auntie Honor says," Aidan cried, seeming thrilled at the compliment.

"Do you have anything you'd like to ask me?" Ruby asked, wanting to make sure he was comfortable.

Aidan nodded slowly. "Yes. I do."

"Go for it," Ruby said.

"When the snow swallowed you up on the mountain, did it hurt?" Aidan looked at her with an awed expression.

Ruby could feel the corners of her mouth twitching with merriment. Aidan's expression was so earnest. She didn't want to hurt his feelings by laughing at his question.

"Just a teensy bit," she said, holding up her thumb and forefinger to demonstrate. "But I tried to be very brave."

Aidan cast a quick glance at Liam. "Daddy always tells me that you're a hero."

She felt her chest tightly constrict as if someone was

inside squeezing her heart. This little boy was sweet and endearing and wonderful. "I... I don't know," she said in a halting voice. "I wish I could remember that, but I don't."

Suddenly a crashing sound rang out in the house. Footsteps echoed on the hardwood floors.

"Liam! Where are you?" a deep voice boomed. "I need to speak with you."

Liam let out a groan and moved further into the kitchen. "Oh, no! Who told him?" he asked with a frown, his gaze shifting between Boone and Honor.

Boone held up his hands. "Don't ask me. I haven't even had time to tell Gracie yet, never mind blabbing to Jasper."

"I haven't spoken to Jasper in days," Honor said with a fierce nod. "It wasn't me."

"Who's Jasper?" Ruby asked, wondering why everyone was acting so strangely.

A man with silver-white hair and whiskers strode into the kitchen, his face appearing more animated than a cartoon character's. "Liam! I'm glad that I caught up with you. I heard the strangest rumor a little while ago that I'm determined to clear up." He shook his fist in the air. "And whoever spread this vicious rumor better run for cover. By the time I get through with them, they're going to wish they'd never let the name Prescott come out of their mouth."

"Settle down, Jasper," Liam instructed. "You know you're not supposed to let your blood pressure skyrocket."

Jasper! Mayor Jasper Prescott. She recognized the name from some searches she had done on the internet about Love, Alaska. He was the town mayor and the creator of the Operation Love campaign, the program that brought single ladies to town to match them up with single bachelors. It seemed this town had a female shortage. And women from all over the United States were flocking to this fishing village to find themselves an Alaskan groom.

If she wasn't mistaken, Jasper was Liam's grandfather.

"Liam's right," Boone said with a frown. "Calm down before you blow a gasket."

"I will do no such thing," Jasper roared. "If you knew the heinousness of this particular rumor, you'd want to run this person out of town on a rail." Jasper wiggled his eyebrows at Liam.

"Jasper, I need to tell you something," Liam said.

Before Liam could get a word out, Jasper swiveled his eyes in her direction.

He let out a guttural cry then raised his hand over his heart. "I'm seeing things. I must be having a stroke. Call a doctor."

"I am a doctor," Liam drawled. "And you're not having a stroke."

"Grandpa, it's okay," Honor said, tugging on Jasper's arm. "She's real. It's not a vicious rumor."

Jasper pressed his eyes closed and began taking deep breaths. When he opened them, he glared at his family members. "What are you trying to do to me? Send me to my grave well before my time?"

Boone snapped his fingers. "Bravo. You've stumbled upon our diabolical plan."

Jasper rolled his eyes at Boone then took a halting step in Ruby's direction. He stuck out a finger and poked her. Ruby let out a little squeak. "You are real.

Ruby! Oh, Ruby. You're back. I could almost sob with happiness."

Liam tugged at his arm. "There's something you need to know about Ruby."

"She's got a problem with her brain," Aidan explained in a chirpy voice. "It won't let her memorize stuff."

"Huh? What in the world are you going on about? That's the craziest thing I've ever heard," Jasper grumbled. He stared at Ruby with wide eyes.

"It's completely true, though," Ruby said. She stuck out her hand. "Jasper, I presume. I'm Ruby. I wish that I could say I remember you, but I don't. And you seem very memorable, by the way."

Jasper stared at her hand for a moment, his expression shuttered. Laser-sharp blue eyes roamed all over her face before settling on her eyes. "Since you don't remember me, let's get one thing straight. I don't do handshakes with pretty girls." He winked at her. "The first hug is free of charge."

For the second time in the span of an hour, Ruby found herself being enveloped in the world's tightest hug. Jasper smelled like nutmeg and coffee beans. His embrace made her feel as if she was greeting an old friend. His sincerity was palpable. Strangely enough, she didn't want the embrace to end. It felt like a safe harbor.

When they broke apart, she noticed tears sliding down his face. He wiped them away with his palm. "Whether you remember me or not, I'm feeling mighty blessed to welcome you back into the fold," Jasper said, reaching out and grasping her hand. "We've missed you."

Ruby wasn't sure how to describe what she was feeling. She felt all tingly inside, and her chest tightened with a groundswell of emotion. Although there was a wealth of information that eluded her about her life in Love, Alaska, she knew for certain that Ruby Prescott had been well loved.

"Why don't we put the kettle back on and have some hot cocoa?" Honor suggested.

Aidan clapped his hands enthusiastically. Auntie Honor knew the exact thing to say to get her nephew's attention.

As everyone settled around the kitchen table, Liam gently pulled Ruby aside. He shook his head as a feeling of mortification slid through him. "Sorry about Jasper's over-the-top behavior. He takes some getting used to. Sort of like sushi. He's an acquired taste."

"Not from where I'm standing." Ruby smiled. "I think he's pretty amazing from what I've seen so far. He exudes such a positive vibe. And he seems to be a true original. I like that. And I get the feeling one always knows where things stand with Jasper. He doesn't seem the type to mince words."

Liam ducked his head and laughed.

"What's so funny?" she asked.

"You always were partial to Jasper. He was like the grandfather you never had. Or so you said," Liam answered. "You always took his side against me."

"Sorry about that," Ruby said in a light voice.

"It's okay," Liam conceded. "Watching the two of you getting along like a house on fire was always enjoyable."

Ruby shrugged. "I don't want to sound like a broken record, but I don't remember that…or Jasper. Although—" Ruby frowned.

"What is it?" Liam asked. Had more flashes of memory occurred?

"Ever since I've been back I've felt this overwhelming sense of familiarity. I can't put my finger on anything in particular—but it's there, right under the surface."

Liam felt his heart pound like crazy inside his chest. His feelings about Ruby's memories were so conflicted. He desperately wanted her to get her remembrances back, but at the same time he dreaded what she might remember about the state of their marriage. It was a selfish thought, he realized, considering all Aidan stood to gain if Ruby was whole again.

"Where are you staying tonight? If you like, I can put you in our guest room," Liam offered.

"I have a reservation at the B and B on Jarvis Street." She twiddled her fingers and looked down. "I'll only be staying there for two nights, Liam. Then I've got to catch my flight back home."

Home? What was Ruby talking about? Love, Alaska, was her home, whether she realized it or not yet. He believed that with a deep certainty, despite his doubts about his relationship with his wife.

"Why don't you let me cancel your reservation?" he suggested. "Stay here with us. You'll be able to spend more quality time with Aidan in his element."

Ruby regarded him solemnly and then nodded her agreement. "I know that I only just met him, but he's everything you said he was." She glanced over at their son. "I don't need my memory back to tell me that he's the best thing I've ever done in this world."

"I feel the same way," he said as a feeling of pride swept over him.

Aidan patted the seat next to him then beckoned Ruby with his other hand. "Come sit with me," he called out, clearly wanting to be near and dear with his mother.

As he watched her settle next to Aidan at the table, Liam's thoughts were focused on his son's quality of life. Aidan needed his mother. His son's world would be so much richer with her in it. How many times had Aidan cried himself to sleep because he didn't have a mother? Or asked him dozens of questions about Ruby? There were so many things that only a woman could provide for a young boy. A tender touch. A lullaby to put him to sleep. A soft place to fall when he needed it.

This was all about Aidan. For the moment Liam wasn't even putting himself in the equation. His own heart had been a little bit broken when Ruby had taken off her rings and headed to Colorado on the rescue mission. And even though he was ecstatic about her return, he still felt as if he was walking on a tightrope. What if Ruby remembered that she had asked for a separation? What if he did what he had always done with Ruby and followed his heart, only to have it smashed to pieces again?

No, he wasn't going down that road. His one and only goal would be to give his son his most fervent Christmas wish. The best gift God could ever bestow on him. A mother of his own.

Chapter Four

Ruby woke the next morning with the smell of bacon wafting under her nose. She sat up in bed and cast a quick glance around her. She had been so exhausted last night after all the Prescotts had left the house that she'd barely had time to take in her surroundings.

The guest bedroom had a quaint, cozy vibe. An oil painting of the Alaskan tundra hung from the wall. A big, fluffy, eiderdown comforter had kept her warm and cozy all night. The bed frame was made of cedar wood. She had no idea how she recognized the wood, but she did. She reached out and touched its smooth surface as a feeling of familiarity ran through her. Someone had made this for them! A man. One she dearly loved. A face flashed before her eyes—warm brown eyes and a cocoa complexion. An endearing smile and a hearty laugh. Her brother?

Before she had turned in, Aidan had peeked into her room and wished her good-night. He had been a little shy but filled with curiosity about her. She was so worried about disappointing him. Ruby fretted that in his mind she was a super hero. That would be a tough act to follow.

She quickly got dressed and checked her appearance in the mirror above the dresser. In her baby blue sweater and jeans, she appeared casual and not half as serious as she felt. A slight case of nerves overtook her. For all intents and purposes, she was a stranger in her own home. Aidan and Liam were blank slates for her. Yet every time she looked at her son she felt a tugging sensation in the region of her heart. Try as she might to convince herself that he was a stranger to her, he made her feel things she hadn't ever felt before. Or at least not since she'd woken up as an amnesiac.

Once she left the bedroom, the delectable aromas of breakfast food emanating from the kitchen were even more enticing. Before she had even managed to take a step, Aidan stood from his spot on the floor outside her door. Right next to him was a fire engine set he'd been playing with as he'd waited. He sent her a smile that made her heart do flip-flops.

"Daddy said I should let you sleep."

"That was mighty nice of him," Ruby said, stuffing her hands into the pockets of her jeans.

Big brown eyes that looked a lot like her own gazed up at her. "Are you hungry? We're having bacon and flapjacks."

She rubbed her tummy and let out a contented sigh. "Bacon. I love bacon."

"Me, too," he said, his voice ripe with enthusiasm.

She winked at her son. "And flapjacks ain't so bad, either."

"Daddy made them specially for you. And I helped stir the batter."

"That's wonderful. I always say it's all in the stirring." She smiled at him, noticing the way he was staring at her with a hopeful expression on his face. She felt a burst of sympathy for him. He was so little. Way too young to wrap his head around his mother unceremoniously showing up in his life after having been presumed dead for two years. She wished there was a manual for how to deal with this situation with grace and wisdom. As it was, she felt scared to death about saying or doing the wrong thing.

She bent at the waist and peered into his perfect little face. "Is there anything you want to ask me?"

Aidan shifted from one foot to the other. "How can you be my mother if you don't remember me?" His lips quivered.

Aw. It was a sucker punch straight to the gut.

She swallowed past the lump in her throat. "Well, unfortunately, due to my accident, there are lots of memories I can't access. And I may not remember everything about you, but I do recall certain things."

His eyes widened. "You do? Like what?"

"Smells. I can't be around talcum powder without thinking about holding a baby in my arms. One who had dark hair and chubby little legs. That was you, Aidan."

His jaw dropped. "Wow. That's so cool. Daddy showed me a picture once of you holding me like that when I was a baby. Maybe he can find it so I can show you. It might help you remember more things."

Tears misted her eyes. His voice was filled with such hope and innocence. She prayed he didn't get hurt in all of this. There was still so much to sort out. How would Aidan react when she left to go back to Colorado? Was he imagining that his parents would reunite and live happily-ever-after? As an almost-five-year-old it was entirely possible.

"I'd like that very much," she murmured, overcome with emotion.

"After we eat, can I show you my Christmas list I made for Santa?"

She reached out and palmed his cheek, shocking herself by the intimate gesture. "Sure, Aidan. That would be great."

"Let's eat before the flapjacks get cold." He reached for her hand and tugged her down the hall into the kitchen. Once she crossed the threshold, she stopped in her tracks. Liam was standing at the stove, looking impossibly handsome in a pair of dark jeans and a long-sleeved, oatmeal-colored shirt. Although she had noted her husband's good looks immediately upon meeting him, she couldn't help but notice that he looked even more handsome today. With his dark brown hair, rugged physique and ice-blue eyes, he was a looker. It was no small wonder she had fallen in love with him and sealed the deal with a ring and a wedding. He was definitely an Alaskan hottie.

"Good morning," he said, spatula in hand as he flipped the flapjacks on the griddle. "I hope you had a good night's rest."

"I slept like a log," Ruby admitted. "It must be the Alaskan air."

Liam nodded. "I was born and bred in Love, so I'm a little biased about the benefits of this little town."

She shifted from one foot to the other then jammed her hands into the back pockets of her jeans. "Is there anything I can do to help?"

"Not a thing. I'm just about done. Why don't you

and Aidan sit down at the table?" Liam nodded in Aidan's direction. "Put some napkins by each place setting, okay?"

Aidan quickly placed the napkins on the table and beamed as if he knew he'd done a good job. Liam walked over and placed platters of flapjacks, bacon and eggs on the table.

As they dug into the breakfast Liam had prepared, Ruby found herself surprised by the lack of awkwardness between the three of them. Strangely enough, she didn't feel nearly as uncomfortable as she usually did in the presence of people. Aidan entertained them with stories about his friends and a little girl down the road who wanted to marry him.

Liam and Ruby exchanged a smile as Aidan explained very solemnly that he didn't have any plans to settle down until he was a grown-up. As soon as he finished eating, Aidan asked to be excused, then jumped up from the table, placed his plate in the sink and ran toward his bedroom.

Liam shook his head, his gaze trailing after their son. "If I had half his energy, I'd be over the moon." The sound of Liam's laughter washed over her like a warm blanket. It tugged at something deep inside her. She knew his laugh. The deep, throaty sound of it was familiar. It was as if she'd always known it.

She couldn't escape the fact that being back here in Love was stirring up her memories. It hadn't even been a full twenty-four hours and she'd remembered several meaningful things. Perhaps being here was the healing balm she needed.

"I remembered something...or someone," she blurted. "It happened this morning when I woke up."

"You did?" Liam asked, his handsome face lit with surprise.

"Yes," she said with a nod. "This might sound like an odd question, but did someone close to us make the bed in the guest room?"

Liam chuckled. "Someone very near and dear to your heart. Your brother. In addition to being a volunteer fireman, he's also a very skilled woodworker. He made that for us when we moved into this house. It was his creative way of presenting us with a housewarming gift."

Ruby clapped her hands together. "I knew it! His face came to mind, and it was such a vivid recollection. He had this huge smile and it gave me such a good feeling about him."

"Being here seems to have triggered your memories."

"It's pretty staggering, but I would have to agree with you," Ruby said. "As we were flying over Kachemak Bay, this feeling of familiarity began to gnaw at me. The moment the seaplane landed in Love, I got goose bumps." She shivered at the recollection then wrapped her arms around her middle. "There was this feeling of déjà vu. I knew I'd been here before even though I didn't have specific memories to ground me. It was palpable."

Liam stared at her, his eyes assessing. "I know you hadn't planned on staying in Love, but now that you know about Aidan...would you consider staying in town for a while so the two of you can work on rebuilding your relationship?"

Even though it was the last thing she'd expected to hear, a feeling of calm settled over her. Love, Alaska, was so lovely and quaint and unlike anything she'd known in Denver. Was it possible that she might find roots in this quaint fishing village? In coming here, her sole goal had been to discover her identity. Na- ively, she had imagined that once she dug up her past she would return to Denver. Finding out about her fam- ily had changed everything. God had other plans for her. She knew He had planted her exactly where she needed to be.

Aidan belonged to her. And for the last two years, there hadn't been a single person or place she'd felt this way about. It was love—primal, gut-wrenching love that emanated from her very core. What she felt for her son surpassed anything else she might feel about the situation. It was still nerve-racking, and she was still afraid, but she wanted to see things through in Love. Ruby wanted to build relationships rather than fumble through life without any meaningful connections.

There were still a few questions rattling around in- side her head. "How would that work, Liam? What about my job?" Even though her waitressing gig was no great shakes, she depended on it for income.

"If you're worried about money, I'll write you a check for the money that was in your savings account. After you were officially declared deceased, the monies were transferred over to my account." He scratched his jaw. For the first time she noticed a slight five-o'clock shadow. It only served to make him more ruggedly at- tractive. "And I've been holding on to the majority of your personal belongings—clothes, jewelry, toiletries." He made a face. "The thought of getting rid of every- thing seemed too final."

"That's understandable. It would have made it too final, I imagine." Sadness swept over her at the thought of Liam having to perform that solemn duty. He seemed like such a strong man, but it spoke volumes about his grief that two years in and he hadn't been able to dispose of her belongings.

"We're going to have to contact the authorities so they can reverse their declaration about your status. That way you can get an Alaskan driver's license and credit cards with your name on them."

"I have a Colorado driver's license. When I lived with Trudy and Ezra they let me tool around with their car. I figured out pretty quickly that I knew how to drive."

"You learned to drive at fifteen," Liam explained. "An accomplishment that you were quite proud of. Your father showed you the ropes."

Her father. Other than a feeling of happiness when she thought of her childhood, there still wasn't much of a memory of him. Or her mother. It saddened her, particularly since they were no longer living. She would never have the opportunity to see them again or share her life with them.

"So, if I decide to stay in Love for a period of time, how would it play out between us?" She fumbled with how to express herself. "I know we're still married, so I'm just wondering."

She wasn't sure if he would expect her to work on their relationship, as well. After all, they were husband and wife. Did he still love her? Would her feelings for Liam come back to her in one fell swoop?

"I don't have any more answers about our marriage than you do, if that's what you're asking. There'll be plenty of time in the future to figure that out. For now, Aidan comes first. That's where our focus should be."

She let out a relieved breath. Working on a marriage

when she didn't remember her husband would have been extremely difficult. Not to mention awkward. Now if she could just stop staring at the little cleft in his chin and his wide shoulders.

"I know it might not be easy to leave your job and friends behind for an extended period, but I think we can both agree that our son's needs should come before anything else."

Ruby shrugged. "My life in Denver is…small. I don't have a large circle of friends. And my job…well, let's just say that I'm not saving lives the way you do. It's not the stuff of which dreams are made." She bowed her head, feeling embarrassed at what she'd just revealed.

Before she knew it, Liam's fingers were at her chin, lifting it so that their eyes were level. Compassion flared in his eyes. "Hey. Don't down yourself. You've been on a torturous journey these last few years. I can't even imagine how difficult your life has been. And it strikes me that you're just as brave as you've always been. You may not have been saving lives on rescue missions for the past two years, but you've been putting one foot in front of the other and surviving. That's huge."

They looked into each other's eyes as an electric pulse crackled in the air around them. Her eyes shifted to his lips. They were full and perfectly shaped. What would it be like to be kissed by this tender, giving man? It was sad that she couldn't remember what it felt like to be kissed. Or to be held by someone who loved her. She let out a sigh. Sometimes it felt as if those days were behind her.

"I want Aidan to have a mother," Liam said in a strangled voice.

She fiddled with her fingers. "I do, too, but I don't

know how to be that. I'm going to have to learn how all over again." Even though the thought of it was terrifying, it was also invigorating. Heartwarming. Being someone's mother gave her a purpose in life outside of herself. For the last two years there hadn't been anything that inspired or motivated her. She had basically been putting one foot in front of the other and trudging through life. That wasn't living! It was merely existing.

"I promise to help you, Ruby. Can we work something out that doesn't involve you going back to Colorado, at least not yet? Give Love a chance. Maybe you'll find you like it here." The look on Liam's face could only be described as intense. "Please? For Aidan?"

She ran a shaky hand through her long brown tresses. Staring into his eyes for too long made her feel nervous. It seemed impossible to resist his plea when he appeared to be motivated by love and concern for Aidan.

"Where would I live?" she asked. She couldn't imagine herself living all by her lonesome in strange surroundings. One thing she had learned about herself since the accident was that she didn't thrive well in solitary settings. She needed human contact.

Liam gestured around him with his hands. "I'd like it if you would stay here with us. There's plenty of room. Honor was staying with us, but she just moved to live out at the wildlife center. I think it's the perfect venue for you to bond with Aidan and get your bearings."

The idea of living with Liam and Aidan in this fairy-tale house nestled in the Alaskan woods was appealing. It was far nicer than anything she'd experienced in the last few years. She could put her cooking skills to use in this airy, fantastic kitchen. And she would be close to her son…and Liam, too. The idea of spending time around her husband was a bit nerve-racking. She didn't want to get pulled under by the sheer force of his magnetism. There was so much to figure out and process. Would he expect her to fall into old, familiar rhythms she didn't even remember? Was he hoping to get his partner back?

"I think being here is helping me to recover my lost memories, which is why I came here in the first place. Sticking around for my son is a no-brainer. There's really no way I can say no."

Liam let out a huge sigh that sounded like relief. He reached out and placed his hand over hers. He gently squeezed it. Ruby felt a spark in response. Liam's eyes widened as if he had also felt a connection. Judging by his expression, he was just as surprised as she was by it.

Just then Aidan darted into the room. His hair appeared less rumpled, and he had changed out of his pajamas into a pair of corduroys and a festive sweater. "Hey, Dad. Remember you said we were going to pick out our tree today."

Liam let out a groan. "It's amazing how you can remember all of my promises, yet you keep forgetting to brush your teeth before bed."

Ruby giggled at the sight of Aidan jumping up and down with excitement. She hoped she would be able to keep up with him and his unbridled enthusiasm and energy.

"Hey, buddy, I'm on call today, so I have to be ready to run to the clinic if anyone needs me. You know the drill, right?"

Aidan nodded his head. "Yep. You made a sacred oath to help people."

"That's my boy," Liam said, his tone full of pride.

Aidan walked over to his dad and tugged at his sleeve. He gestured for him to lean down. Aidan cupped his hands around his mouth and began whispering loudly in his father's ear. Ruby couldn't hear every word, but she managed to overhear the words "tree" and "please" and "ask." Suddenly, two pairs of eyes were focused on her.

"Ask her," Aidan urged in a loud whisper. He put his finger in his mouth and began to nibble.

"How about it, Ruby?" Liam asked. "Do you want to come with us into town and go shopping for an Alaskan Christmas tree?"

Watching Ruby getting along with Aidan like a house on fire warmed Liam's insides like nothing else ever could. They had driven into town and parked on Jarvis Street, then made their way to the town green where Alan Pendergast's tree stand had been set up. Liam's family had been buying trees from Mr. Pendergast ever since he could remember. Now, he was passing the tradition down to his own son.

This moment was almost surreal. If anyone had told him two days ago that he'd be picking out a Christmas tree with Ruby and his son today, he would have called them all kinds of crazy. God was good! He had given his family back the person who had always been at the core of it with her huge heart and unwavering kindness.

A tight feeling seized his chest as he studied the familiar, graceful slope of Ruby's neck and the long strands of mahogany hair that trailed down past her shoulders. A hint of a smile played around her lips. She was patiently listening to Aidan and nodding her head in response to his comments.

Was the woman he loved still in there somewhere? Was she still his Ruby? Or had all that changed forever as a result of her head trauma?

Ruby had always been the love of his life. They had planned on being each other's forever. He fought against a feeling of sadness that crept over him. So much had changed between them. Ruby didn't even remember him, which he was trying not to take personally. She remembered Aidan and Kyle and the town of Love, as well as a host of other important things. But not him. Not a single memory of him or all the happy times they had shared. It played into every insecurity he had about his relationship with his wife. And even though he dreaded her remembering the rocky state of their marriage at the time of her accident, he still ached to have her remember the sweet and tender moments— their wedding, Aidan's birth, their very first Christmas together as man and wife.

He stuffed down the feelings of hurt. This wasn't about him. Aidan was the focus here. Sooner or later he and Ruby would have to figure out where they were headed, but for now it was all about restoring Aidan's relationship with Ruby. It would be the ultimate Christmas gift.

As he watched Aidan, Liam had the sneaking suspicion his son's face might crack under the weight of his huge grin. Liam felt as if his heart had expanded to ten times its normal size just watching his joy. It pulsed and hummed in the frigid December air. Aidan was on top of the world as he walked hand in hand with Ruby. Every time he saw an appealing tree, he would begin circling it and eyeing it up and down.

Although word had gotten around about Ruby's return, there was still a good amount of heads turning in their direction, as well as astonished faces. Thankfully, the place was fairly deserted. Otherwise it would have been overwhelming for Ruby. And Liam was a little tired of explaining the situation to the few townsfolk who pulled him aside and asked. He didn't blame them for being shocked, but he simply wanted to savor this moment with his family. Liam felt fairly certain his grandfather might have to call a town meeting simply to announce the incredible news.

His family. He still couldn't believe it. Tears misted his eyes. He blinked them away before Aidan or Ruby could see them.

"This one!" Aidan said triumphantly as he pointed at a large pine tree. "Isn't it great, Dad?"

Liam walked over and looked the tree up and down. He turned toward Ruby, who had a bemused expression on her face. "It's pretty impressive. What do you think?"

"I think it's a keeper," Ruby said, holding her palm up so Aidan could give her a high-five. He jumped up and slapped her hand, letting out an enthusiastic cry that sounded a lot like triumph.

"If you're sure, I can go pay Mr. Pendergast," Liam said. Aidan gave him a thumbs-up sign.

Liam paid for the tree and helped Al carry it over to his truck where they strapped it down with rope.

Once the tree was secure, Aidan seized the moment. "Can we go to the Moose Café for hot chocolate? I want to show my m…" His voice trailed off after he stumbled with the words.

Ruby bent and tweaked his nose. "It's all right to call me Mom. If you want to," she said. She glanced over at Liam with a questioning look in her eyes.

Liam sent her an encouraging nod. He hadn't thought to bring up this topic before. Calling her Mom would be natural, but perhaps it would be too much too soon for Aidan.

"I don't want to hurt your feelings," Aidan said, his eyes focused on the snowy ground, "but it might take a while to get used to. So I might wait a while. If that's okay with you?" He didn't look up at Ruby but began to push the snow around with the tip of his boot.

"Of course it is," Ruby said in a gentle voice. "I'm sort of relieved that you said that because, if I'm being completely honest with you, Aidan, it's going to take a little bit for me to get used to being your mother. And I hope that doesn't hurt your feelings, because as far as I can see, you're the most awesome almost-five-year-old on the planet."

Aidan tried to keep it together but his grin was effusive. Liam let out a sigh of relief. There were bound to be bumps and hiccups on the road ahead, but it was comforting to know that Ruby and Aidan had worked this one out on their own. There would be plenty of time for Aidan to get used to his mother on his own terms and at a pace that felt comfortable to him.

"How does hot chocolate sound?" Liam asked with a glance in Ruby's direction.

Ruby bobbed her head. "It sounds perfect." She held up her mittened hands. "My fingers are beginning to tingle. This material is no match for Alaska cold. I need to invest in a new pair of mittens."

"There's also lattes and mochaccinos and tea and lots of other types of coffee drinks." Aidan practically chirped. "This place aims to please."

"Wow," Ruby said. "You're good! You could be a great advertisement for the Moose Café."

"Cameron has been training him well," Liam teased, patting Aidan on top of his hat-covered head.

They all chuckled, with Aidan laughing louder than either of them. As they walked down Jarvis Street, pausing to admire the festively decorated store windows, Liam wondered if anything felt familiar to Ruby. He stopped himself from asking her, realizing that it might get tiresome to have to continually answer questions about her memories.

Before he knew it, they were standing in front of his brother's establishment. The bronze, embellished sign welcomed them to the Moose Café, Love's most happening coffee bar. "We might as well bite the bullet and go inside," Liam said. He sucked in a strengthening breath of air.

"Is it going to be that bad?" Ruby fretted.

Liam made a face. "Um, how should I put this? You were beloved in this town. Still are."

She raised an eyebrow. "Which is a good thing," Ruby said. "Right?"

"Yes. But that means that there are dozens and dozens of villagers who are going to go a little bit crazy when they see you. Not to mention all the members of my family who are going to swarm all over you, like Cameron and Paige…and then there's Hazel, and Declan and his new wife, Annie. Not to mention Sophie and Myrtle."

Ruby's eyes bulged. She made a gulping sound. "Wow. Sounds like I had a lot of friends."

"Sophie and Annie are new to town. They both came as part of the Operation Love program. But everybody who knew you, loved you." Liam's statement hung in the air, dangling like a fully inflated balloon. *Especially me*. He almost blurted it out but he stopped himself. It wasn't the time or the place to go down that road. At the moment it would only serve to muddy the waters.

"No matter how crazy it gets, don't forget I'm here. I've got your back," Liam said.

He opened the door to the café, allowing Aidan to sail through as if he owned the place. Try as he might, Liam couldn't stop himself from wanting to protect his wife. He placed his hand on her lower back and ushered her inside, all the while praying she would be able to handle her re-entry into Love society.

Chapter Five

The moment Ruby stepped inside the Moose Café, delectable aromas assailed her senses. Aidan ran off toward the kitchen as if his sneakers were on fire. Waitresses with cartoon moose emblazoned on their T-shirts hustled to and fro, serving customers and taking orders. There was a loud din emanating from the robust crowd. Perhaps it served as an indication of the popularity of this particular establishment. It was filled to capacity. A roasting fire roared in the dining area, lending a rustic, warm atmosphere to the eatery. Antlers hung on the wall above the fireplace.

She heard several people call out to Liam. "Hey, Dr. Prescott" and "I need to see you about my gout."

The place oozed charm. It seemed like the sort of eatery where you could settle in for a refreshing coffee and good conversation while enjoying a pleasant ambience.

"Liam!" a boisterous voice called out. Ruby turned to see a tall, good-looking man with dark hair and an easy stride making his way toward them. He exuded a great deal of confidence. He flashed them a pearly smile.

"Welcome to the Moose Café, Ruby. Let me show

you to a place of honor at my best table over here." He held out his elbow so she could place her arm through it. The gentlemanly gesture made her want to chuckle. He was treating her like a fragile piece of china.

Liam glared at the man. "Cameron. Take it down a few notches, okay?"

"Sorry," Cameron said in a less animated voice. He reached out and grabbed Ruby by the hand. He raised her hand to his lips and pressed a kiss against her knuckles. "I can't tell you how overjoyed we all are that you've come back to us."

Aw. He was a sweetheart in addition to being almost as gorgeous as Liam. This town sure had its fair share of attractive men. No wonder the media was in a frenzy over this town's matchmaking program. It was just the type of human interest story that you read about in glossy magazines.

"In case you haven't figured it out yet, this is my brother, Cameron. He's the owner of this place," Liam explained.

"Nice to see you, Cameron. Your café is gorgeous," Ruby said. "And if the aroma is any indication, I know I'm going to enjoy the food here."

"Thanks. My wife, Paige, helped me redecorate it. Let's just say it was a little masculine in its décor. That's what happens when you have a town full of men."

"Ruby." A sweet, feminine voice washed over them. A tall, regal woman with blond hair and a stunning face took faltering steps toward her. She stopped short, seeming to be wary of crossing any boundaries. "I know you don't remember us, but I'm Paige. We were best friends."

"Hi, Paige," Ruby said, wishing she could remember

this woman who had clearly been an important part of her life. A sudden sound caused her to look down. A beautiful little girl who looked a lot like Cameron stood clutching her mother's leg. She looked up at Ruby with curious, almond-shaped eyes. Then she gifted her with a toothy grin that melted Ruby's heart.

By this time all the patrons were staring and whispering. It made her feel uncomfortable. Ruby moved closer to Liam. It felt awkward to be the topic of everyone's conversation, especially when none of the faces were even remotely familiar. Why had she agreed to come inside the café in the first place? She felt completely outside her comfort zone.

"As I live and breathe!" A tall, broad-shouldered woman with graying hair stepped into their circle. An apron decorated with dancing moose let Ruby know she was one of Cameron's employees. Tears streamed down her face and she wiped them away with the back of her hand. "Jasper told me you were among the living, but a part of me couldn't wrap my head around it. Ruby Prescott, you're a sight for sore eyes. Come over here and give me some sugar." The woman held her arms open wide and motioned for Ruby to step toward her. When Ruby hesitantly approached her, she felt strong arms envelop her. Helpless to extricate herself, Ruby sank into the embrace.

All of a sudden, a sharp, high-pitched whistle brought silence to the room. Ruby found herself being tugged away from the embrace. Mayor Jasper Prescott was standing there with an irate expression stamped on his craggy face. His cheeks were rosy, although Ruby wasn't certain if it was from the frigid temperatures outside or his ire.

"Hazel, give the gal some breathing room!" Jasper barked. "You're going to suffocate her with all that mothering you're doing."

"Oh, give it a rest, Jasper," Hazel fumed. "We were having a moment until you came barreling in here like an out-of-control tornado."

"If you'd have hugged her any tighter she might have snapped in two." Jasper huffed. "Let the girl get acclimated before you start squeezing the life out of her."

Hazel let out a harrumphing sound and turned her back on Jasper. "Neanderthal," she muttered. She turned all of her attention back to Ruby. "Welcome back, darling," Hazel said, wiping away tears from her face. "I know you don't remember me, but we were almost like family. Before you married your honey here, you lived out at my Black Bear cabins. Those sure were some good times. I'm looking forward to making new memories with you."

All Ruby could do was smile. Her face felt a little stiff from grinning. She didn't know what else to do in response to all the love the townsfolk were showing her. Her head was beginning to spin. She now knew what Liam had been referring to earlier when he'd been hesitant to enter the café. She would never have imagined that a tiny fishing village could have so much of a social component. Granted it was almost lunchtime, but the Moose Café was a real whirlwind. People were coming out of the woodwork.

She could feel the heat of Liam's gaze. He narrowed his eyes and studied her then leaned in toward her. "Are you all right?" he asked in a tender voice. "Just say the word and we can blow this Popsicle stand."

"I'll be fine once we sit down and order a hot cocoa," she said in a low voice. "I'd like to get off my feet."

Liam turned toward Hazel. "Hey, can you find us a table?"

"Why don't you sit down at this table right here and I'll make you the best hot chocolate known to mankind," Hazel suggested. Her eyes radiated kindness. "Aidan is in the back with Sophie, by the way. She's showing him how to make frozen hot chocolate."

"While you're back there, make me one of those caramel lattes with the cinnamon sprinkled on top," Jasper requested.

Hazel let out a snort. "Coming right up, Your Highness. One caramel latte sprinkled with arsenic flavoring."

As she stomped away, Jasper frowned at her retreating figure. He shook his head. "You heard that, right? Threatening the life of a beloved town leader."

"Jasper, be nice," Paige cautioned. "You've really been sniping at Hazel lately. A woman can only take so much." She bent and picked up her daughter, then handed her to Cameron.

Jasper sputtered. "That right there is a perfect example of why I'm not putting a ring on it." He began muttering under his breath. "Plenty of women would be mighty glad to have a boyfriend like me."

"Yeah," Cameron said. "Those Operation Love gals are just lining up outside the mayor's office in droves, aren't they?"

Liam rolled his eyes. "Don't mind Hazel and Jasper. They have a love tiff at least once a week." He pulled out the chair so Ruby could sit.

"I figured they might be romantically involved by the

way they were bantering. They're both pretty feisty," Ruby remarked. "For a moment I thought we might have to take cover."

"Just so you know, you and Liam weren't like that," Cameron interjected. "I promise. You were the perfect couple as far as this town was concerned. Ruby and Liam forever."

Liam jabbed his brother in the side. Cameron made a grunting sound then shot Liam a dirty look.

Perfect couple? Just hearing that phrase made Ruby feel she had a lot to live up to. The word "perfect" rubbed her the wrong way. And although she knew Cameron was only trying to be complimentary, it made her feel that there was no way she could ever be half as wonderful as the Ruby she'd once been. It wasn't possible. She was no longer that woman. And even if she got her memory back, she'd be a different woman than the one who had left this town two years ago. Suddenly it felt like she would be trying to fit into a life that no longer existed as it once had been.

"Attention, please. Attention." Jasper scrambled up on a chair and let loose with another whistle to get everyone's attention. He was wildly waving his arms around.

"Unbelievable!" Liam muttered as he folded his arms across his chest and sat back in his chair.

"If he breaks that chair, he's paying for it," Cameron grumbled. "There's no family discount for destroying the property around here."

As soon as all eyes were focused on Jasper, he began to speak. "I'd like to make an announcement. I'm sure most of you are pretty confused about what's been happening here today. The Prescott family is delighted to announce that reports of Ruby Prescott's death were greatly exaggerated." He let out a chuckle. "Not that it's anything to make light of, but we're just so thankful to have her back in the fold."

Loud gasps and murmurs rippled through the café. Customers turned toward her to gape at her. Ruby ducked her head. She didn't want to make eye contact with anyone. Awkward didn't even begin to describe this experience. She might have liked some warning about Jasper's announcement, but one look at Liam's face told her he'd been caught off guard, as well.

"Ruby has amnesia, but God has shown Ruby the way home after two years. She was in an accident that day in Colorado when she was saving lives. As a result, she's lost most of her memory of life before that day. That means that in all likelihood she won't remember you. It also means that we're going to help her in any way that we can. With patience. And kindness. And good, old-fashioned Alaskan hospitality. She still has healing to do on her road to recovery. This town has always supported our own and this won't be any different."

"Hear! Hear! Mayor Prescott!" Hazel stood nearby, clapping and cheering. Ruby spotted Aidan standing nearby, beaming from ear to ear. A stunning redhead— presumably Sophie—had her arm around his shoulder. Hazel stepped forward and helped Jasper down from the chair, then reached out and grazed her palm along his cheek. "That's the Jasper I know and love," she cooed.

"And don't you forget it, woman," Jasper said as he reached for Hazel and placed his arms around her waist, then dipped her backward as he planted a kiss on her lips.

"Close your eyes, Emma," Cameron said to his baby

daughter as he placed his hand over her eyes. "You really don't need to see this."

Paige reached over and removed his hand from their daughter's eyes. She shook her head at her husband and made a tutting sound.

Everyone in the Moose Café began clapping and hooting. Liam threw back his head and laughed. It was nice to see him so relaxed and lighthearted, Ruby realized. It suited him well.

Ruby felt shame almost eat her up inside as she watched Hazel and Jasper's display of affection. When the town mayor had first begun to speak, she'd wanted to sink into her seat. She had felt embarrassed and slightly annoyed. Jasper's words had surprised her. They'd been heartwarming and beautiful, leaving her feeling choked-up. Since she was struggling to discover what her place was in this Alaskan town, it meant the world to her to know that she had his support and friendship.

God had led her back here to Love. Of that she felt certain. Now if she could only figure out her role in the grand scheme of things.

Aidan's mother. Liam's wife. Friend to all.

Those things were meaningful, but were they enough to keep her in this town for the long haul when she still didn't remember much of anything about her former life?

Not long after Aidan joined them for hot chocolate at the table, Liam could detect fatigue etched on Ruby's face. Her warm brown skin seemed a bit washed out, and her eyes no longer sparkled. She appeared a bit worn down. He chided himself for indulging Aidan in his desire to have hot chocolate at the Moose Café. He feared it had been too overwhelming an experience for Ruby. Between Jasper, Cameron, Paige and Hazel, not to mention a handful of villagers who had approached Ruby with well wishes, it had turned into a lot more than a casual outing. He imagined Ruby felt as if she was being pulled in a dozen different directions.

After saying their goodbyes, Liam drove them back to the house. Ruby was very quiet during the ride. He tried to lighten the mood by turning the radio on and blasting festive holiday songs. Aidan played along, singing his favorites at the top of his lungs. Although he saw Ruby tapping along to the beat a few times, she remained somber. From this point forward he vowed to do a better job of protecting Ruby from situations that were too much for her to handle.

As he navigated the lane and pulled into the driveway, a familiar physique standing at their doorstep immediately captured his attention.

"Oh, no. Not now of all times," he muttered.

Ruby turned toward him, her brown eyes full of concern. "What is it? Is something wrong?"

"It's Uncle Kyle," Aidan shouted. As soon as the truck came to a stop, he quickly unbuckled his seat belt and wrenched open the door.

"Kyle? Isn't that my brother's name?" Ruby asked. Her pretty features were creased with worry. "Is that him?"

"Yes," Liam said in a clipped tone. Frustration speared through him. Already, Ruby was feeling overwhelmed by the events of this afternoon. He'd told Kyle to call him so they could arrange a time for him to come visit Ruby. Clearly, Kyle had decided to just fly to Love from Homer.

Ruby bit her lip. "He's a big guy. If the fireman thing doesn't work out, he may have a future in professional wrestling."

Ruby's comment made Liam grin. At six-three and two hundred and twenty-five pounds, Kyle was known as a gentle giant. Well-mannered and kind, he was a favorite among the townsfolk here in Love whenever he visited. Aidan thought he was the very definition of cool.

Liam and Ruby emerged from the vehicle and headed toward the house. Kyle was holding Aidan in his arms, but his stare was intently focused on Ruby. Tears welled in his eyes. He slowly lowered Aidan to the ground.

Before Liam could say a word, Kyle stepped toward Ruby. "I know you're not expecting me, but I couldn't stay away. I've been missing you for two long years, and not seeing you for another single day felt like torture."

"I understand," Ruby said in a low voice. She was gazing at her brother with such intensity it seemed almost as if she was trying to memorize his facial features.

"I know you don't remember me—" Kyle began.

"That's not true," Ruby said with a vehement shake of her head. "I do remember you. Your face. Your warm brown eyes. A smile like no other. I have a distinct recollection of you crafting that bed in the guest room for us. And jelly beans."

Tears slid down Kyle's face. "You do remember me."

Ruby reached up and wrapped her arms around Kyle. She placed her head against his chest and closed her eyes.

Jelly Bean was the nickname Ruby had given Kyle when he was a kid, due to his effusive love for jelly beans.

Liam didn't know if he'd ever felt as jealous before in his life than he did at this very moment. Ruby had

distinct memories of Kyle! And she had reached out
to him with an embrace. He swallowed past the huge
lump in his throat. It wasn't a contest, but knowing that
she still had no recollection of him or their life together
burned like acid.

It served as a huge reminder that the love Ruby had
once felt for him had in all likelihood died even before
she'd tumbled off the Colorado mountain.

Liam and Kyle took the tree down from the top of the
truck and carried it into the house. All the while Aidan
was shouting out directions. Ruby trailed after them,
excited at the idea of an honest-to-goodness, live pine
tree for Christmas. Last year she'd put up a little plastic tree that had resembled something out of a cartoon.
Things were definitely looking up!

"Where would you like it, Ruby?" Liam asked. "It's
your choice."

Ruby looked around the living room. There was a
great spot right in front of the window that would be
perfect. "Right there by the window," she said, pointing over at it. "That way anyone who comes to visit can
see the tree all lit up from the outside."

She didn't know where that idea had come from. It
had just popped into her head. She could see it all in her
mind—the tree fully adorned with strings of lights and
popcorn and cranberries. Precious ornaments handed
down from family members would hang gracefully
from the branches. A gold star shimmering brightly
from the top.

Aidan grabbed the Christmas tree stand and placed
it on the floor directly in front of the huge bay window.

Kyle lifted the tree and placed it into the hold while Liam got down on the floor and began tightening the screws so the tree would stay up.

"There we go," Liam said as he scrambled to his feet and eyed the tree. "It looks straight, right?"

"As straight as an arrow," Ruby remarked. "It looks wonderful."

"I can't wait to decorate it," Aidan shouted, jumping up and down with excitement. "This year Daddy said he's going to lift me up so I can put the star on top."

The sound of a cell phone buzzing caused Liam to dig around in his pockets. He pulled out the phone and said, "I've got to take this. It's the answering service for the clinic." He strode out of the room and walked in the direction of the kitchen.

"Uncle Kyle, wait right here. I need to go get my new fireman truck so I can show you." Like a flash, Aidan disappeared right before their eyes.

Suddenly it was just the two of them standing there looking at each other as if neither knew how to bridge the gap.

"Would you like something to drink? A snack?" Ruby asked, feeling desperate to fill the silence.

"I'm good. The question is…how are you doing? Really?" He leaned toward her and reached for her hand. Kyle squeezed it gently.

It felt like being supported by a strong oak tree.

She gestured toward the sofa. "Why don't we sit down so we're more comfortable?" Ruby suggested. She sank onto the couch and watched as Kyle sat next to her.

"I'm doing well. Or as well as can be expected. I didn't expect all this when I came to town." She let out a laugh. "I guess I was naive to think that I was going to stroll into town, find my family connections and then just sail out of town back to Denver."

"So how are you handling it all? Aidan and Liam? And all the Prescotts? They can be an intense bunch."

"Everything is coming at me kind of fast right now. I just came from town. We stopped into Cameron's café after picking out our tree. The hustle and bustle and the people quickly became overwhelming." Tears stung her eyes. "I want to be strong enough to face this, but I have to admit, I just wanted to bury my head under my covers."

"And here I just show up unannounced on your doorstep to add to your troubles." Kyle groaned. He slapped his palm on his forehead.

"It's fine," Ruby said. "To tell you the truth, I don't feel overwhelmed at all sitting here with you one-on-one like this. I think the sheer number of people makes me a little uncomfortable."

Kyle nodded, his expression infused with sympathy. "You were a people person. A social butterfly. Ever since you were little, people have been drawn to you. So of course they're flocking to you now, because they all shared a connection with you in the past. And I'm sure that must feel intense to you since all you have is a blank slate."

She sighed with relief. "Yes. You understand it perfectly. And Liam has been fantastic, but it's strange knowing we're husband and wife. Be honest with me, Kyle. How were we as a couple? Liam and I? Were we head-over-heels in love? Was I a good mother?"

These questions had been plaguing her ever since her arrival. She had left her toddler son at home to go on a dangerous search-and-rescue mission in another state. It worried her that perhaps she had been one of those mothers who put her career before her husband and child. If that was the case, she would feel ashamed of her choices.

"First of all, you were a fantastic, engaged mom. From the time Aidan was born, both you and Liam doted on him. First steps. First words. You were both over the moon about him." He let out a ragged breath. "From the moment you met Liam, it was a love story. You fell for each other pretty fast, then got engaged and tied the knot shortly thereafter. Everyone in Love held you up as the gold standard." Kyle held up his hands. "No pressure, though."

Ruby let out a sigh. "That's the problem. I do feel that pressure to be something I can't even begin to wrap my head around. And, of course, Liam is this dreamy doctor with soulful eyes and a good heart, but it's not like I'm in love with him or anything."

A loud crash startled both of them.

Aidan was standing there in the doorway, his red fire truck on its side on the floor. His cheeks were blotchy, fists clenched at his sides. He was huffing and puffing like a fire-breathing dragon. "You don't love my dad? That's awful. Maybe you should just go back to Colorado where you belong!"

Chapter Six

Just as Liam ended his call, the sound of a loud crash drew him back toward the living room. He saw Aidan run down the hall into his bedroom, followed by a loud slam of his door.

"What in the world just happened here?" Liam asked, looking back and forth at Ruby and Kyle. Aidan wasn't a perfect kid by any means, but it wasn't like him to throw temper tantrums.

He spotted the fire truck on the floor in disarray. One of the ladders had broken off, along with a tire.

"Did he do this?" he asked. Aidan knew better than to treat his belongings so frivolously. Jasper had just purchased the fire truck for him.

"Yes, but he was upset about something he overheard. It's all my fault, Liam," Ruby said tearfully.

Kyle patted her on the shoulder. "Just chalk it up to the extraordinary circumstances of the last few days. It's perfectly normal that he's acting out."

"Let me go talk to him and straighten him out," Liam said in a fierce tone.

Ruby jumped up from the sofa. "No, Liam! Please.

Let me do it. I'm the one he's angry at. I need to smooth things over so there isn't any awkwardness moving forward."

"Are you sure? He can be a handful when he's riled up," Liam warned.

"If I'm going to get back in the swing of things with my son, I can't avoid the hard stuff."

"Care to tell me what this was all about?" he asked, studying the frantic expression on her face. Something big must have gone down to lead to Aidan's meltdown and the look of distress etched on Ruby's face.

"Later. After I talk to Aidan," she promised. He nodded as she walked down the hall in search of their son.

Once Ruby was safely out of hearing distance, Kyle leaned back into the sofa and let out a massive sigh. "This is a really complicated situation, Liam. It could really explode if you don't tread carefully."

Liam stiffened. He didn't need to be lectured by his brother-in-law. Kyle had no clue how difficult this situation was to navigate. As confused as he was about his new reality, he had to stay positive. "It'll all work out. We're only two days in, Kyle. We need time to adjust as a family."

Kyle's expression hardened. "I'm not sure how long I can keep Ruby in the dark."

Liam crossed his arms over his chest. "About what?"

A sigh slipped past Kyle's lips. "Come on, Liam. We both know that when Ruby left for that rescue mission the two of you were at odds with one another. You were talking separation. She told me everything."

"Marriages go through rough times and people ride them out." He frowned at his brother-in-law. "And after everything that's happened, how would it serve Ruby to have that information?"

Kyle shrugged. "I don't know. But I do know that my sister and I never kept secrets from one another. And this feels like a big, dark secret to me." Kyle's brows were knitted together, his caramel-brown eyes appeared troubled. "Maybe she should know so she can make informed decisions."

"I would never ask you to be dishonest, Kyle. But with Ruby having suffered amnesia and trying to get her bearings here in Love, I just don't think it would be wise to bring up things that might cause distress."

"For Ruby? Or for you?"

Tension hummed in the air between them.

Liam clenched his jaw. He had always gotten along well with Kyle, who was a kind and loyal guy. But he wasn't about to condone his brother-in-law throwing a keg of dynamite on an already explosive situation. He couldn't risk the hurt Aidan would feel if everything fell apart. Or the pain Ruby might feel. Everything may have changed in his world, but he would never stop being his family's protector.

"I've never given you reason to question my motives before, Kyle. My main concern about telling your sister is Aidan. He's over the moon to have his mother back. Let's give them an opportunity to bond without throwing a monkey wrench in the mix."

Kyle nodded. "I'm sorry if I sounded curt or if it appears that I'm sticking my nose where it doesn't belong. I just don't want this to blow up in everybody's faces."

"Neither do I. I promise you that I'm doing everything in my power to make sure Ruby is safe and protected and loved."

Kyle knitted his brows together. "I believe you, but what if she remembers everything, Liam?"

He felt torn about Kyle's question. On one hand, it would be a dream come true. But, if Ruby had total recall, she might decide their marriage had died two years ago. She would realize he hadn't been completely on the up-and-up with her. Although he had done a good job of convincing himself this was mainly about Aidan, he couldn't deny his marriage hung in the balance.

Either way, this was his marriage and he wasn't going to let anyone else determine its fate. "I'll cross that bridge when I come to it," he said, a slight edge to his voice.

"Just make sure that you protect Ruby in the process," Kyle said.

Cold, harsh anger flared inside him. "She's my wife, Kyle. I've always had her best interests at heart. Since the day we pledged our lives to one another, I've always kept that vow. That's never going to change."

For a moment they stared each other down. The tension between them palpable.

All of a sudden Kyle broke the tension by sticking out his hand. Liam reached out and clasped it. Kyle pulled him in for a hug.

"You're a good man, Liam," Kyle said. "And I've always admired you as a husband and father. I just don't want Ruby hurt any more than she's already been."

Kyle was protecting his sister the same way Ruby had always watched over him and kept him out of harm's way after their parents' deaths. It was ironic that Kyle thought his sister would be the one to get hurt in all of this. Because ever since Ruby had taken off her wedding rings and asked for a separation, Liam's own heart had been on life support.

* * *

Ruby had been sitting by Aidan's bed for about ten minutes now. At first he hadn't wanted her to come inside his bedroom, but once he'd allowed her entry, he had buried his face in his pillow and refused to talk to her.

Finally, Ruby reached out and gently turned him on his side.

"Hey, buddy. I know you're angry, but acting like this isn't the answer."

Aidan looked at her through red-rimmed, puffy eyes.

"Go away. You're just pretending to like me. I heard what you said to Uncle Kyle out there."

"And that upset you."

Aidan sat up and faced her. "Yes. Parents are supposed to love each other."

Ruby bit her lip. How in the world could she explain this so her son would understand it? He was only a little boy. One who seemed very invested in the idea that his parents would walk off into the Alaskan sunset together. She didn't want to break his little heart, but she also didn't want him to invest in a pipe dream.

"Aidan, right here, right now, I'm going to make a promise to you. I'm never going to lie to you. I've been away for two long years. You know all about how I lost my memory, so you have to remember that loving your father isn't something I remember. Love builds over time and I've only been back for two days."

"W-what about me? Do you love me?" His voice trembled. She could see the longing in his eyes, the heartfelt desire to be loved by his mother. It was the most natural thing in the world.

Ruby hesitated for a moment before answering. She

wanted to make sure she spoke from the heart. It was strange to acknowledge it, but she did love her son. Her feelings for him were the most natural, powerful emotions known to mankind. It was innate and instinctual. She knew without a doubt that she would sacrifice her own life to save his. Yes, indeed. It was love.

She reached out and tweaked his nose. "Yes, I love you, Aidan. As surely as the moon glows in the night sky, I do."

He scrunched his face up. "Then how come that's different than loving Daddy?"

"For some reason I don't need to have all my memories intact to tell me that what I feel for you is love." She put her arm around him. "Remember, I carried you around in my tummy for nine long months. We bonded before you even came into the world."

Aidan gifted her with a beatific smile.

"So maybe you can learn to love Daddy all over again. Right?" he asked with his head cocked. "Then we can be a real family."

"Um…well, it's possible, Aidan. But I don't want you to count on—" A knock on the door interrupted her.

The door opened and Liam peered in, his eyes full of questions. "How's it going in here?"

"What do you say? Did we get everything straightened out?" Ruby asked, leaning in to tickle him. Aidan burst into giggles and tried his best to fend her off.

"Better," Aidan said with a grin in his father's direction.

"Why don't you come out here and spend some time with your uncle before he takes off?" Liam asked. "He's meeting some friends in town."

"I still need to show him my fire truck," Aidan said, jumping up from his bed.

"And after your uncle leaves we're going to talk about throwing the fire truck," Liam said in a stern voice. "That was unacceptable."

"I'm sorry I did that," he said, his voice full of contrition. With a nod from his father, Aidan scooted out of the room.

As soon as they were alone, Ruby heaved a tremendous sigh. "I know you're probably wondering what happened. Long story short, Aidan overheard Kyle and I talking about us. He was pretty upset to hear I don't remember being in love with you."

Liam walked over and sat beside her on the bed. "He wants the fairy tale. With all the trimmings."

"And I burst his bubble. Great move on my part," Ruby said with a groan.

"I know this can't be easy for you."

"It's not. It's the worst feeling in the world to not be able to remember who I am and the things I felt, the people I cared about, the very things that made me Ruby Prescott," she admitted, sniffing back tears. All of a sudden she felt like a stranger in a foreign land. Nothing made sense at the moment. Her brain felt fuzzy and her soul was weary.

Liam reached out and grazed his knuckles against Ruby's cheek. Instead of shying away from his touch, she felt comforted by it. "Please don't cry. That could bring me to my knees."

"I feel like I'm letting everyone down." Her voice trembled. Seeing Kyle and disappointing Aidan had cemented it. She was fumbling through town without a clue as to anything more than her name and a few remembrances…snippets in time that didn't amount to a hill of beans in the scheme of things. She couldn't access the memories that mattered most. Loving and being loved.

What is the point of even staying here in Love? As soon as that thought escaped, her son's innocent face flashed before her eyes.

"What? Disappointing us? That's not true," Liam said. "I realize you agreed to stay on here in town because of our son. I don't think I've expressed in words how grateful I am. You could have left on the next seaplane back to Denver. But you didn't. You had a little faith in me. I'm asking you now to have some in yourself."

"I suppose I'm feeling a bit sorry for myself at the moment. Everyone remembers me and, on some level, they expect me to have memories of them. But, for the most part, I don't. At the Moose Café I saw the sadness in Paige's eyes when she realized it wouldn't be wise to hug me. She remembers me as her dear friend, but that doesn't really mean anything to me. And she could see it! Same thing with Kyle. I could see the love shining in his eyes and I felt a connection, but I keep beating myself up for not feeling more motherly." She pressed her hands against her heart. "What if these memories never come back? Where does that leave me?"

"Give yourself a break, Ruby. You've barely been back in town for forty-eight hours. The memories might come back to you, but if they don't, you can still build bridges with the people in your life who care about you. Look at you and Aidan! He still thinks you're a rock star."

"I wish that I felt that way about myself," she said. "At the café earlier, my hands were shaking like a leaf."

"We all get scared sometimes," Liam said. "You should see me when I have a patient whose illness is challenging to diagnose."

"I must have been brave to be in the search-and-rescue profession." Ruby hadn't asked many questions about her previous line of work. She was really curious about it and what had led her down that road. Liam had told her that both her parents had died in a car accident. Perhaps that had motivated her to rescue others so their families wouldn't have to deal with the loss and heartache.

She wasn't sure if it was her imagination, but Liam seemed to stiffen at the mention of her job. Maybe it was a touchy subject due to the Colorado mission.

"You weren't afraid of anything. Not ever."

"So I was tough?" she asked.

"As nails," Liam said. "Nothing ever scared you… not wolves or bears or delivering Aidan without a single pain reliever. You've always been a mighty warrior."

"What about you? Were you afraid when I went out on a mission?"

"I was always afraid of losing you…your job scared me. Not that I wasn't proud of you, because I was awed and humbled by your service. But in my heart I was always dreading the day when I would get a call saying you'd been injured or worse."

"And worse happened, didn't it?" She couldn't imagine Liam having to deal with the terrible news from Colorado. His wife had gone to rescue people, only to perish in the process.

"It did. And the bottom fell out of my world."

Something glimmered in his eyes that hinted of deep pain and loss. This man had been through the ringer. She wished she could do something to take away everything he'd endured at the loss of her. But it wasn't possible. At the moment all she could do was pray. She prayed for Aidan. And Kyle. She also prayed for her and Liam, that somehow all would be revealed to them in the weeks and months to come. And that whatever decisions they came to about their marriage and her future here in Love, they would both be at peace with them.

Chapter Seven

Liam sat in the office of his clinic, waiting for his ten o'clock patient to arrive. As it usually did, his mind wandered to Ruby. For the past week he had been trying to figure out ways to help Ruby settle into her old life. At the moment he remained stumped. How could he help his wife find her way back?

The situation was weighing heavily on him. He hated to see Ruby suffer. It reminded him way too much of how unhappy she'd been in those dark days before she'd left them for that last rescue operation. There had been a lot of tears and arguments leading to the unraveling of their marriage.

Just thinking about it made his chest tighten and sweat gather on his forehead. Losing Ruby seemed to be a recurring theme in his life. He didn't know how he could stand to do it another time if her unhappiness caused her to leave town. It was the main reason he was holding back and trying not to invest too much emotionally in their relationship even though she had decided to stay in town for an indefinite period to see how things played out. What if she ultimately decided it was too difficult to remain in Love and headed back to Colorado? The truth was that Aidan wouldn't be the only one with a broken heart. His own would be shattered…and not for the first time.

After hearing the jingle of the bell on the front door, he cast a quick glance at his desk clock. His patient, Myrtle Maplethorpe, was early today. Liam wouldn't be surprised if she had arrived early to get the scoop about Ruby's return. He got up from his chair and walked into the reception area. Cameron was standing there with Emma cradled against his chest. She had her thumb firmly rooted in her mouth and her eyes were closed. His niece looked as sweet as ever. Wanda, his receptionist, was gazing at Emma with adoration.

"I was just about to buzz you, Doctor Prescott," Wanda said, her expression sheepish. She walked behind the front desk and sat down.

"Hey, Cam. What brings you over here?" Liam greeted his brother.

Cameron's features looked pinched. A frown marred his brow. "I think Emma might be sick. She's been fussing quite a bit. She wouldn't go down for her nap today and she feels a little warm."

"Does she have a temperature?"

"I'm not sure. I figured I would just bring her over here so you could check her out. Paige is at that meeting over in Homer today, representing Lovely Boots. Declan flew her over. I'm on Dad duty."

Lovely Boots was a corporation based in Love that sold genuine Alaskan boots created by Hazel. A majority of the proceeds went toward the town of Love in the hopes of improving the local economy. "Let's go into one of the rooms so I can check her out," Liam said, ushering his brother down the hall.

Once they were inside, Liam reached out for Emma. At first she resisted, snuggling deeper into her father's chest. With all the gentleness in the world, Liam plucked her out of Cameron's arms and placed her on the examination table. Her eyes flew open and for a moment tears welled in her eyes. "It's okay, Emma. It's me. Uncle Liam." His voice was soft and tender.

Emma immediately turned and held her arms up toward Cameron. A small cry escaped her lips. "Shh, sweet baby girl. Uncle Liam needs to examine you so he can make you feel better."

He'd never quite seen such a tortured expression on Cameron's face. There was nothing like being a father to tie you up in knots.

"Why don't you hold her while I take her vitals?" Liam suggesting, realizing Cameron needed this for comfort as much as Emma did.

Relief washed over Cameron's face as he picked up Emma and rocked her in his arms.

For the next few minutes Liam examined his niece. "She has a temperature. It's 102."

"That's high," Cameron said, biting his lip. "Poor little thing. I knew something was off." He pressed a kiss against Emma's cheek.

The moment Liam checked in her ears he hit pay dirt. "She's got a double ear infection, Cam, which is no doubt making it difficult for her to lie down. It increases the pressure and pain in her ears. Has she had one before?"

Cameron shrugged. "Not that I know of. At least not in the last eight months or so."

Cameron's answer referenced the fact that he had

only known his daughter Emma since Paige had brought her to Love eight months ago. For the first fourteen months of her life, Cameron hadn't known of Emma's existence. Upon her return to town, Cameron and Paige had quickly fallen back in love and gotten married. They were now happily raising their daughter together.

"She's going to need a course of antibiotics and some drops for the ear pain. We don't want this infection to get any worse."

"I'm glad I didn't wait to come in. This way Emma will be on the mend right away."

"I'll call the prescription in to the pharmacy. I think I have some drops here somewhere." Liam turned around and rummaged in his cabinets. "Here we are." He handed Cameron a vial of drops that would take away some of Emma's discomfort. He winked at his brother. "This way you and Paige might not have to stay up all night with a screaming child."

"Bless you. It sure comes in handy having a doctor for a brother," Cameron said with a grin.

"Glad to hear it," Liam said. It made him feel good inside to know that he'd made his brother's road a bit easier. It was worth all the years of struggle and schooling to be able to make his beautiful niece feel better. Being a doctor in his Alaskan hometown was extremely gratifying. He truly believed it was his calling and that God had led him on this path.

"I've been meaning to catch up with you," Cameron said. "I know you've been really busy the last few days."

"It's been a whirlwind, that's for sure."

"So, how does it feel to be reunited with Ruby? It's pretty incredible, huh?"

"I feel blessed."

"And? What else? I know Ruby has amnesia, but has it been romantic between the two of you? Moonlight and roses?"

"No, it hasn't," Liam said in a curt voice. "Ruby doesn't remember me. She has no inkling of what we were to one another. The love we shared. The ups and downs."

Cameron frowned. "Downs? You two were perfect together. Blissful."

"That's not true," Liam snapped. Cameron's eyes widened. "Sorry," he apologized. "I didn't mean to snap at you. Before Ruby went on that Colorado mission, the two of us were having problems. We couldn't agree on her job. I thought she was tempting fate by putting herself at risk on these various missions, and she had no intention of giving it up. We went round and round about it with no resolution."

"Seriously?" Cameron asked, appearing stunned. "I had no idea you were going through that. From the outside looking in, the two of you seemed so content." He ran his hands over Emma's hair. She had fallen asleep on his chest.

"I didn't tell anyone. I thought Ruby and I would work it out ourselves. Until the day she took off her wedding rings and asked for a legal separation. It was the day before she left us. We had been fighting nonstop... I guess she had reached her breaking point. Truthfully, so had I. But I never imagined us not being together. Until she threw it out there."

"Liam. You would have worked through it if—" Cameron's words dangled in the air.

"If Ruby hadn't been presumed dead on that Colorado mountain?" Liam scratched his chin. "I don't know. It broke my heart when she took off her rings.

And even though I prayed we would find our way, we never got the opportunity."

"But you have it now, don't you?" Cameron asked. "She's back… God led her straight to Love and toward you and Aidan. That has to mean something."

Liam swallowed past the bile rising in his throat. "It's hard to put my heart on the line again, knowing that if she remembers the past she might toss me aside all over again. Maybe she really, truly, had fallen out of love with me. Perhaps that's why she hasn't had a single memory about me… and what we were to one another. And I'm starting to feel guilty about making her believe everything was peaches and cream between us, when that's far from the truth."

"Liam, you and Ruby were a love story. I can't believe you'd give up on that so easily. Most people don't get second chances at love."

"I'm not giving up. I just don't know how to protect my heart on this journey with Ruby. I want Aidan to have the thing he wants most in the world, but I also want my life back. The life I always imagined."

"Then go for it, bro. Don't let fear stop you." Cameron's voice was laced with encouragement.

Just then the clinic door jingled again, heralding the arrival of Myrtle Maplethorpe, aka the Duchess. Myrtle, the local historian, was also known as Love's resident town gossip. Liam could hear her high-pitched voice emanating from the other room as she greeted Wanda.

"I should get this little lady home and call Paige. It sounds like your next appointment is here."

They walked out into the waiting room together, both marveling at how soundly Emma was sleeping. The resiliency of children always amazed Liam, both personally and professionally.

Myrtle was standing there in front of the main desk, resplendent in aqua from head to toe. She peered at them through her Coke-bottle glasses.

"Well, hello, Dr. Liam. Cameron. Oh, and a darling little Prescott princess." Myrtle's tone trilled.

"She's a little under the weather with an ear infection," Cameron explained.

"Oh, those can be dreadful," Myrtle said. "I hope the wee one feels better."

"Thanks. Nice to see you, Myrtle." Cameron adjusted Emma on his chest. "See you later, Liam. And thanks for everything. If you need to talk, you know where to find me."

As Liam turned back to Myrtle, she narrowed her eyes at him. "Sounds like you've been leaning on your brother for advice. I've been called a good listener a time or two," she said. "If you need a listening ear."

Liam almost burst out laughing. Myrtle was notorious for spreading people's private business all around town. There was no way he was going to confide in her all his doubts and fears about Ruby. If he did, it would spread all over town like wildfire. Myrtle wasn't a bad person, but she certainly wasn't someone he could trust with his personal business.

"That's very kind of you to offer. Why don't we go check out your heartburn?"

As he led Myrtle into one of the examining rooms, he found himself wishing his issues with Ruby were as easy to solve as a simple case of heartburn.

Ruby felt a little bit nervous about showing up at Liam's clinic unannounced, but after consulting with Aidan, they had decided that surprising him with lunch was a brilliant idea. She needed to step out a little bit on faith and embrace the life she'd once made for herself. On some level she had to accept that the woman she'd once been had chosen this life for herself. She had picked Liam. Although she'd made strides with Aidan, she had deliberately been distant from Liam. Knowing they had been a storybook couple felt intimidating. Out of her reach.

How could she ever live up to the fairy tale of her and Liam? But was it right to not even try to forge something with her husband? She had once vowed to love this man for a lifetime. And with every day she spent here in Love, she was seeing the truth about this man with her own eyes. He was a loving father. Generous. And attentive. The fact that he could have been Mr. Alaska sure didn't hurt. He was the most eye-catching man she had ever known.

She had forced herself to take a good look in the mirror to examine her truths. Then she'd had a long talk with God. He had helped her see things more clearly. It was easier to have one foot in Love rather than invest everything in a life she couldn't quite grasp. That meant she had an escape hatch. If she wasn't fully invested, she could always head back to Denver. In the back of her mind, that's what she had been doing ever since she arrived in town. And even though she had agreed to stay on for a bit, there was no commitment to relocate to Love. Her hands weren't tied. But it also meant that she wasn't giving fully of herself. That had to change!

Now, armed with a fully loaded picnic basket, she was venturing out on a limb and seeing what came of it. And her pint-size companion seemed as excited about this outing as a kid on Christmas morning. He'd been the one to show her where to find the keys to the spare car sitting in the garage. Thankfully, due to Colorado's climate, Ruby was used to driving on snow-packed roads. She took her time and handled the unfamiliar roads like a pro.

Liam's clinic was situated in a small, white clapboard house at the end of Jarvis Street. A sweet sign welcomed them to Dr. Prescott's Office. A festive Christmas wreath hung on the door, adorned with bright red ribbons and candy canes. Adorable snowmen clung to the windows. Ruby couldn't imagine a more cheery-looking doctor's office.

As they walked through the front door, silver bells jangled from above them. Aidan giggled and pointed. He began swinging the door back and forth so the bells continued to chime. Ruby shook her head and laughed. The sound of footsteps alerted them to Liam's arrival before he came around the corner. The look of joyful surprise etched on his face was priceless. Warmth settled in Ruby's chest at the sight of him. All her nerves immediately settled.

"Hey! I didn't expect to see the two of you. I thought it might be Wanda coming back from her lunch break."

"We're taking you to lunch, Daddy." Aidan pointed at the picnic basket. "And you won't even have to leave your office."

Ruby held up the basket. "We hope you haven't eaten yet. A little birdie told me you usually eat around this time, so we decided to bring lunch to you."

Liam's face lit up like a Christmas tree. He grinned from ear to ear. "Thank you for thinking of me. It's always nice to break up the day like this." He motioned them down the hall. "Let's go set up in one of the empty offices. I have about forty-five minutes until my next patient."

Ruby trailed after Liam and Aidan. Once they were in the office she pulled a red tablecloth from inside her shoulder bag and began spreading it out on the small table.

"We brought chicken sandwiches and potato salad and cupcakes. Plus, a bag of my favorite chips." Aidan rattled off the menu. "And a bottle of sparkling cider."

"Cupcakes! Wow," Liam said. "You're going to spoil me."

"We did a little baking this morning," Ruby said. "For some reason I really enjoy making cupcakes." Ruby had discovered when she was living with Trudy and Ezra that baking was her forte. It had kept her busy in the weeks and months during her recovery. And the older couple had appreciated having someone help them around the house.

"You were always an excellent cook, Ruby," Liam said. "Your specialty was reindeer pizza."

Ruby turned toward him. "Reindeer pizza? Seriously?"

"It was your favorite." Liam rubbed his stomach. "Not only to eat, but you baked it to sheer perfection." Liam kissed his fingers and lifted them in the air. Ruby chuckled at the gesture.

Ruby began taking the plates and utensils out of the basket. She lifted the sandwiches out and placed one on each plate, along with a dollop of potato salad. Aidan and Liam sat at the table.

Ruby made a face. "No offense, but I can't imagine being partial to reindeer anything."

Liam shot her a knowing smile. "Don't knock it until you try it."

"Don't hold your breath," Ruby said in a singsong voice.

"Hey! Wanna see how long I can hold my breath?" Aidan asked. He puffed out his cheeks.

"After lunch you can impress us, A-man. Let's just focus on this wonderful meal for the moment."

"Let's pray over the food," Aidan said. He reached out his hands on either side of him. Both Liam and Ruby linked their hands with his.

"May I?" Ruby asked. Liam nodded.

"Go for it," Aidan said. His encouragement made Ruby grin. He was such a joyful child. It spoke well of the way Aidan had raised him in the aftermath of the tragedy. There wasn't a single thing about her son that she didn't love to pieces. Although the idea of caring so much about him scared her a little bit, she was enjoying her role as his mother.

She was acting on instinct and trying to listen to him and gauge his needs. *Fake it until you make it.* The expression popped into her mind. Ruby didn't have all the answers, but she was determined to try to be the best mother possible.

She bowed her head. "Thank You for this food, Lord, and for the blessings You continue to bestow on us. Thank You for this day and for all the ones to follow."

"Amen," Liam and Aidan said in unison.

They began to eat their lunch, enjoying a companionable silence as they devoured the chicken sandwiches.

This was nice, Ruby thought. For once her mind wasn't whirling with doubts.

"So, how is your day going, Dad?" Aidan asked, sounding older than his years.

Liam grinned. "Pretty interesting. A very familiar face popped by."

"Jasper!" Aidan guessed. "Was it his heart again?" he asked, referencing the heart problems that had side-lined Jasper almost two years ago.

"Nope. It was your cousin, Emma. She had an ear infection."

"Oh, that's yucky!" Aidan made a face. "I'm going to say a prayer for her tonight before I go to sleep."

"Praying for her is a wonderful idea," Liam said. He reached out and patted Aidan on the shoulder. Father and son. When they were sitting next to each other like this, Ruby could see the resemblance. They had the same dark brown hair and their facial expressions were identical. Aidan had her eyes, though—they were a warm shade of brown.

"Someone slipped this under the door this morning after you left." Ruby slid a brightly colored card across the table. Liam wiped his hands on his napkin then picked up the card and read it out loud. "'You are invited to a Get To Know Us tea party. Get dressed up and come spend some time with us. Tea will be served promptly at four o'clock at Hazel's Lodge.'" There were names scrawled across the bottom. Hazel. Grace. Paige. Sophie. Honor. And Annie.

Ruby had almost burst into tears the moment she'd read the gorgeous invitation. These ladies were being thoughtful and caring. They were trying to be sensitive of the fact that she had amnesia and didn't have memories to draw on. And they were pulling her into the fold by extending this thoughtful invitation to her.

Although she had acquaintances in Colorado, her closest friends had been Ezra and Trudy, who were senior citizens. Ruby loved them dearly, but there hadn't been any real common ground.

In Love, Alaska, she had blood relations and family ties. A best friend. A hunky husband who made her stomach do flip-flops. Whether she remembered it or not, she had history.

"So...are you going?" Liam asked. He was tapping his fingers on the table as if her answer was important to him.

"Of course. How could I say no?" Ruby asked. "It will give me an opportunity to renew some friendships and step out on that limb. Not to mention it will give me a reason to get a little gussied up. I'm getting tired of wearing nothing but jeans and leggings." She felt a little self-conscious as Liam's eyes honed in on her like laser beams.

"I think you look pretty awesome in jeans," Liam said, flashing her a cheeky grin.

She raised her hands to her heated cheeks. The compliment washed over her like warm rain. As if he needed to do anything else to make her heart go pitter-patter. During lunch she had struggled to tear her eyes away from his jaw-droppingly handsome face. Several times her gaze had lingered way too long. She'd been certain he had noticed her perusal, although he hadn't let on.

What had it been like, she wondered, to be this man's wife? To be adored and protected by such a strong, upstanding man must have been amazing. Liam was a hottie. It was undeniable. In his white lab coat and with his stethoscope hanging around his neck, he looked even more impressive.

But allowing her mind to veer toward romance wasn't smart. Not when she still didn't have any recollection of him or their life together. How could she allow herself to fall for Liam when she didn't know who she herself was?

"Well, we should get going and let you get back to work," Ruby said in a brisk voice. She stood and smoothed her hands against the fabric of her jeans. She began tidying the table and packing up the remnants from lunch.

"Aw. Is it time to leave already?" Aidan pouted.

Liam stood and lifted Aidan into his arms. "No worries, A-man. I'll be home before you know it. Maybe we can take a walk in the woods behind the house and leave some food for your reindeers."

"Yes!" Aidan cried as he raised his fist in the air.

Liam always knew what to say to make things better for their son. He did it so effortlessly, she couldn't help but feel a twinge of envy. Had she once had that particular talent? A memory tugged at her. She was pushing Aidan in a little swing to stop him from crying. Every time he went up in the air he pumped his little legs. For a moment she simply reveled in the recollection. It was real! She just knew it. And before long she would be remembering other things—perhaps about her friendship with Paige, her parents, Aidan's first moments… and her romantic journey with Liam.

Please, Lord, let me remember more about my life in Love. I don't want to walk around not feeling whole anymore. Let me learn more about myself so I can be a better woman. Not just for myself, but for Aidan and Liam, as well.

Chapter Eight

Ever since Ruby's return, coming home after work had been the highlight of Liam's day. As he drove down the private lane leading to the house, his chest always felt as if it might burst with expectation. It was a strange feeling since it reminded him of the early days when he'd first fallen in love with Ruby. Back then he had been full of a mixture of excitement and dread. He had been so afraid of losing her. It had always seemed to Liam that being with Ruby was like catching lightning in a bottle. It still stunned him to this day that all of his prayers had been answered when she'd fallen deeply in love with him.

God had blessed them both. And even though the current situation wasn't ideal, he had to remind himself to stay focused on the blessings.

Liam drove into the driveway and stared at the log cabin nestled in the woods. A soft, amber-colored light emanated from inside. This was his haven. He had always loved their abode, but now it felt like home again. During Ruby's absence he had tried to fill the house with as much love as he could, but he'd never been able to replicate all of the things Ruby had infused into their home. A woman's touch. A mother's nurturing instincts. A soft place to fall.

And despite her amnesia, she still brought her own ray of light along with her. It had subtly transformed their house into a home.

With each and every day that passed, he was finding it hard to imagine being without Ruby ever again. Although the question still remained. Would Ruby stay on in Love? Or would she return to the life she'd been living in Denver? The very thought of her leaving made his chest tighten with sorrow.

A flash of color caught his eye just as he was about to mount the stairs leading to the porch. A slight figure—bigger than Aidan—stood right on the edge of the area leading toward the forest.

The illumination from the porch shed a little light on the shadowy figure. It was Ruby. Placing his briefcase on the steps, he turned around and began walking in her direction.

The crunching sound of his footsteps on the snow-packed ground filled the silence with every step he took. Ruby swung her eyes toward him as he approached. With her red coat and white, tasseled hat and matching mittens, she looked utterly charming.

"Hi, Liam."

"Hey, Ruby. What's going on out here? It's pretty cold to be outside now that the temperatures have dropped."

She waved her mittened hand toward the woods. "I heard something out there. It sounded like an animal crying out. Aidan is watching television, so I figured I'd check things out." She shrugged. A sheepish expression crept over her face. "I thought maybe I could save whatever creature was out here raising a ruckus."

Liam cast his eyes toward the woods. "It was most likely a bird of some variety. A loon or owl. Or a beaver perhaps."

She bit her lip. "It was such a plaintive cry. Heartbreaking really. It stopped right before you drove up."

"You don't want to venture out in the woods at night, Ruby. I should have remembered to tell you that. It's fairly common to come up against wolves or even bears in these parts." He felt like kicking himself for failing to warn his wife about the potential dangers in Alaska. It was still hard to wrap his head around all of the things she no longer remembered.

Her eyes widened. "Yikes. So most likely a wolf was hunting its prey."

He smiled at her. "Most likely. They've been known to go after moose and caribou, as well."

Ruby nodded. "And they've gone after humans, too, which makes it foolish for me to have come out here to investigate." Her expression radiated frustration.

"Not foolish," he corrected. "Caring about animals is compassionate. Part of living in Alaska means being aware of the risks, however small they might be."

She huffed out a small breath. "It's strange to not remember such vital things." Ruby ducked her head. He could see her lip trembling.

He reached out and tipped her chin up, acting on impulse. "I know this whole experience must be scary for you. I can't imagine how difficult it must be to not remember so many things. For what it's worth, I think you're a brave woman, Ruby Prescott. You always have been."

They locked gazes. Her warm brown eyes flared with uncertainty. "That's the thing, though. I don't feel courageous. You told me earlier that I was a brave person, but maybe that was the old Ruby. Most days I feel like I'm stumbling around in the dark without a flashlight. I wish I could remember Aidan's favorite foods and the things that scare him."

"It's understandable that you feel that way. When I first opened my clinic here in Love, I had a lot of people questioning me." He let out a throaty laugh. "There were residents who still viewed me as a kid, even though I was a fully grown adult who was a medical doctor. It got to me. Pretty soon I was doubting my own qualifications and skills. I wondered if I'd bitten off more than I could chew."

Ruby's eyes blinked furiously as she looked at him. A fragile hope glistened in her eyes. Ruby wanted so badly to get her memories back. It shimmered from deep inside her like a beacon.

Liam ached for her. Had he been so worried about Aidan's feelings that he'd minimized how difficult this whole process must be for Ruby? Was he guilty of being selfish?

"And obviously you worked through it, right?" she asked, drawing him out of his thoughts.

"I did. Time worked wonders on my self-confidence. And with every day I became a little braver, just like you are."

"I'm trying to be patient, but sometimes I just wish all my memories would come flooding back to me. There are so many questions rattling around in my brain. I'm excited about the tea party invitation, but

I'm also fretting about it. What if I don't know what to say to them?"

"I know you're still getting back fragments of your memory, so you don't remember them just yet. But those ladies love you. Honor. Hazel. Paige. They'd walk through fire for you."

Tears welled in Ruby's eyes. "It humbles me to hear that."

"And don't worry about not knowing what to say. There's a saying that true friends know the song in your heart and can repeat it back to you if you've forgotten the words. That's the type of friends you have in your corner."

"That's a beautiful sentiment," Ruby said with a nod, the corners of her mouth lifting ever so slightly in a smile. She wiped her hand across her brow. "Phew. I guess that means I was a pretty decent human being," she quipped. "If I had been a total nightmare, I wouldn't have such amazing friends."

"You've always led with your heart," he said in a low voice. "And your kindness and loyalty to everyone in your circle never wavered."

Liam looked down at her, admiring the stunning beauty of his remarkable wife. He knew he was staring at her, but he couldn't help it. It might take him the rest of his life to get his fill of her after being under the belief that she was gone forever.

"Maybe we should go back inside," Ruby said, looking toward the house. "I'm sure Aidan is wondering where I am."

Liam chuckled. He could just imagine Aidan transfixed by his favorite science-fiction television show. "He's probably still glued to the screen."

Ruby giggled, showcasing the sweet sound of her laughter. "I have noticed that he can't be disturbed at this time of night. He really loves all the space travel and extraterrestrials."

He felt a surge of emotion rise inside him. This was pure Ruby. The infectious joy. Her utter radiance. The desire to protect a defenseless animal. It was all the best things about the woman he'd married. Bit by bit, she was coming back to him.

At this very moment he wanted to kiss her more than he'd ever wanted anything else in his life. And the way she was looking at him, with her face turned upward and her brown eyes brimming with emotion, made him think she wanted to be kissed.

Liam took a step closer. He reached out and placed his hands on either side of her face. "Ruby," he murmured, lowering his head toward her. He watched as she closed her eyes in expectation of the kiss. Her long, black lashes fluttered. He though he heard her let out a sigh.

"Hey! What's taking so long?" The high-pitched child's voice came out of nowhere.

"Aidan," Ruby said, her eyes blinking open. She turned toward the house where their son stood in the doorway, looking in their direction.

"Hey, Aidan. We were just checking on something," Liam called out. "We'll be right there."

"When's dinner?" Aidan shouted. "I'm as hungry as a bear."

Liam let out a groan. There was no way he was going to try to kiss Ruby with Aidan screaming in the background. Besides, their son had ruined the perfect moment for their kiss. He loved Aidan dearly, but his timing was horrendous.

"I have a casserole in the oven," Ruby said. "I need to take it out before it overcooks."

Liam simply nodded. He felt a stab of disappointment so sharp it made his ribs ache. Why did this feel like such a setback? He knew his feelings were tied up in wanting things to get back to normal and his fears that Ruby might not stick around Love long enough for them to work on their future. In this instance, a kiss would have allowed him to take a giant leap forward in their relationship. It would have given him hope. As it was, he felt as if he was continually walking on eggshells.

As they made their way, side by side, toward the house, Liam felt a tugging on his heartstrings as he enjoyed the steady presence by his side.

Thank You, Lord, for giving me another shot at getting things right in my marriage. I promise to be a little more patient and to learn from the mistakes I made in the past. I won't squander this opportunity.

There would be other moments for him and Ruby. He just needed to be patient and to appreciate the simple blessings.

Aidan was waiting for them at the door. Never in a million years had he believed his son would have the opportunity to spend time with his mother again and that the three of them would be able to live as a family.

God's grace was a mighty thing indeed.

"I'm so grateful for GPS," Ruby said as she navigated the winding back roads that led to Hazel's residence. She was driving Liam's truck rather than the spare car. Liam had told her that he felt better about her driving a truck with all-wheel drive and studded tires than a car that had been sitting in the garage for eons. If she hadn't been focusing so intently on the road, she might have been able to admire the stunning vista stretched out in front of her. Love, Alaska, was a picturesque fishing village straight out of a postcard.

Thankfully, between Liam and the Moose Crossing signs, she had been made acutely aware of the moose population in town. When three moose slowly made their way across the road, Ruby almost had to pick her jaw up off the floorboard. There was something majestic and beautiful about those humongous animals roaming freely about the land. But she also knew how dangerous they could be. As soon as they had crossed over, Ruby continued down the road. She sucked in a deep breath at the sight of large mountains looming in the distance. The raw beauty here in Alaska was unparalleled.

She let out a cry of triumph when she saw a wooden sign announcing the Black Bear Cabins. As she wound her way up the hill and drove past reddish-brown cabins, another sign with an arrow pointed the way toward the lodge.

As soon as Ruby rang the bell, the door swung open. Hazel was standing there, a welcoming smile on her face. She was wearing a bright pink sweater with a skirt that went all the way down to her ankles. Feeling a bit nervous, Ruby stuck out the bouquet of flowers she had brought as a hostess gift. "They're lovely," Hazel raved. "How did you know I loved forget-me-nots? Come on in."

"Thank you," she said as she entered Hazel's home. "Aidan helped me pick them out. And he told me that forget-me-nots are the official state flower, so that seemed perfect."

The moment Ruby entered Hazel's abode she felt as if she had been transported into a vintage era. There were so many elegant touches. Gleaming hardwood floors. Stained-glass windows. A grand spiral staircase. "Everyone is already in the parlor, so follow me," Hazel instructed with a wave of her hand.

Once they stepped inside, Ruby was greeted with a vibrant chorus of hellos. All the women had dressed up for the occasion. In addition to Hazel, she knew two of the women—Paige and Honor.

"I'm Sophie Miller." A stunning woman with fiery red hair and an infectious grin held out her hand to her. "Nice to meet you, Ruby."

"I'm Annie O'Rourke." Annie stepped forward and treated her to a warm smile. With her peaches-and-cream complexion and dark brown hair, she exuded sweetness. Her vintage emerald-colored cocktail dress was magnificent.

Hazel rubbed her hands together. "Well, we're just waiting for Grace to get here. Ruby, we wanted to host this tea party so you could see that you've got friends here in Love," Hazel explained. "And to extend you a hearty welcome back to the town that adores you."

"Everything is lovely," Ruby said as her glance swept across the table. It had been set with beautiful blue-and-white china. In front of every place setting sat a peacock feather.

"I'm getting pretty good at hosting these shindigs," Hazel boasted.

"You're a real pro," Sophie declared, gushing, her Southern accent on full display.

"One of these days we're going to host a party in your honor," Annie said, patting Hazel on her shoulder.

Hazel scrunched up her face. "Well, I'm overdue for a bridal shower," she grumbled. "Jasper has had me waiting so long for a proposal."

The parlor door opened. Grace was standing in the doorway with Boone right behind her, dwarfing his wife with his height. "Sorry I'm late, but I had a few technical difficulties."

Honor quickly reached her sister-in-law's side. "Is everything okay?"

Boone's eyes twinkled with merriment. His smile couldn't have been wider. For the first time Ruby noticed the resemblance between the three brothers. Liam was a bit more reserved, but he was the most devastatingly handsome of the trio. Her female appreciation of her husband made her cheeks warm.

"My wife's stomach made getting behind the wheel very tricky. I've never seen anything like it," Boone chuckled. "Her belly was actually touching the steering wheel."

Grace playfully jabbed him in the side. "You're enjoying this way too much, sheriff."

He leaned down and pressed a tender kiss on Grace's lips. "Give me a call when you're winding things up here and I'll swing back by and pick you up." He tipped his sheriff's hat in their direction. "Nice to see you, ladies. Enjoy your tea party."

As soon as Boone left, the room erupted into sighs of appreciation.

"Grace, if you weren't my best friend I'd be jealous of that dreamy husband of yours. And that goes for you too, Ruby and Annie. I don't know what's wrong with me." Sophie flung her hands in the air. "I came to this town as part of Operation Love, but I still haven't found anyone who inspires me for anything greater than friendship."

"Don't fret about that, Sophie," Honor said in a gentle voice. "You'll find him. They say you find someone when you're not looking."

"Well, that rules me out," she joked, "since I've been looking since the day I arrived in town."

All the ladies laughed at Sophie's animated expression.

"Why don't we sit down and start the festivities?" Hazel suggested. Everyone began moving toward the table. "Just sit anywhere. There's no assigned seating."

Ruby ended up next to Paige and Honor. There was quite a spread laid out for them. Gleaming silver dishes held cucumber sandwiches, lemon tarts, pastry puffs filled with lobster, scones with blueberry compote, mini pumpkin muffins and bagels with salmon spread. Ruby felt her tummy grumble in appreciation of the vast array of treats.

"Annie, could you serve the tea?" Hazel asked. "I'm Miss Butterfingers. I don't want to send anyone to Liam's clinic with hot tea burns. Jasper would never let me live that one down."

As Annie walked around the table and filled everyone's teacup, conversation began to flow as the ladies settled in and helped themselves to the food.

Grace spoke directly to Ruby from across the table. "I just want you to know, Ruby, that I haven't lived in Love very long myself. I came here as a journalist and ended up falling in love with Boone in rather quick fashion. When I first arrived here, I felt like I'd landed on a different planet. This must be very overwhelming to you. Although my circumstances were different, I can relate a little bit to how it must feel."

"I can also testify to how it feels to be a newcomer to Love," Sophie added, helping herself to another muffin. "Back in Saskell, Georgia, where I'm from, we hadn't seen snow since I was a little tyke no more than Aidan's age. So the climate here has been a little bit challenging. That was a shocker, along with getting used to the hours of sunlight depending on the time of year." She shook her head. "And I still can't wrap my head around all the single men roaming around this town."

"Add me to that list," Annie said as she placed the teapot back on the table and sat. "I came to Love to be town librarian and as part of Jasper's Operation Love campaign." She let out a sigh that sounded a lot like contentment. "I think my adjustment was easier because I was really looking to be part of a community. With no family to speak of, I found my haven here in Love."

"Sounds like you all did," Ruby said, moved by the fact that all three women had found their destinies in this quaint town. "It does feel like a whole new world sometimes. It's not the Alaskan lifestyle or the climate…at least not yet. What's bugging me is that I still can't access most of my memories." She let out a huff of frustration. "I have to accept the fact that I might never be able to recover the bulk of my past."

"Ask for God's grace in helping you face that possibility. If you lean on Him, He'll see you through this." Paige's words were heartfelt and wise.

Ruby had been leaning on God, but she needed to speak to Him about her fears and the things that were holding her back. And perhaps she needed to open up to Liam, as well.

"Why don't you and Paige go sit down and talk while we clean up?" Hazel suggested. "And, Grace, go sit on the settee. It makes me uncomfortable seeing you stand on your feet for long stretches of time. Your feet will get swollen."

"You don't have to tell me twice," Grace teased as she struggled to get up from her seat. Honor gave her a slight push until she was standing upright. She placed her hand on her belly and ambled off to the living room. All the other ladies headed to the kitchen, their arms filled with dishes to be washed.

"So, how are you settling in?" Paige reached out for Ruby's hand and squeezed it. The gesture felt like encouragement. Ruby hesitated for a moment. Paige was her sister-in-law, married to Liam's brother. She didn't want to say anything that could travel through the family grapevine.

"You don't need to worry about me passing any information along. We always had a pact that our conversations remained private." A gentle smile lit Paige's face. "That hasn't changed."

Ruby let out a sigh of relief. So far there really hadn't been anyone in Love that she could confide in. There was something calm and reassuring about Paige. She sent out very positive vibes. Ruby felt she could trust her.

"It's been a whirlwind, for lack of a better word. I'm sure it won't surprise you to hear that Liam has been patient and kind. I feel badly, though, because I keep seeing him look at me as if he's searching for his wife. But all he finds is me—a shell of my former self." She let out a little sob, shocked at the intensity of her own words.

"Oh, honey," Paige said in a comforting voice, "that must be so difficult...to feel as if you're disappointing him."

"That's exactly how I feel," she admitted, wiping away the tears from her face. "And I'm constantly wondering if I'm living up to the old Ruby as far as being a mother to Aidan. So far no one has given me a road map to follow."

"You have to remember, Ruby, that you aren't responsible for your amnesia. You were the victim of an accident. You lost two years of your life with your family. You're allowed to hurt and grieve and vent. And maybe you should express these feelings to Liam. I'm sure he's navigating through his own feelings of loss and confusion and pain."

Ruby allowed herself to cry. She'd been holding back for entirely too long. She felt Paige's comforting arm resting around her shoulder.

You never walk alone. She remembered Kyle saying that to her after the death of their parents. She would use her brother's advice now to guide her on her journey. Living in Colorado had been lonely at times. Her heart had yearned for connections. And now, sitting right beside her, was a dear friend who loved and supported her. She couldn't overlook that blessing.

"Thanks for saying that. I suppose I do feel guilty. My profession involved great risks to my personal safety. I can't help but feel that I caused my family a world of pain, and I'm still trying to connect to them in meaningful ways."

"Well, you need to know that in addition to being a first-class mother and a loving wife, you were amazing in your chosen field. You loved helping people and saving lives. You always said it made you feel ten feet tall to give them a shot at living another day."

Ruby found the topic of her profession fascinating. In the quiet hours between dark and dawn she had remained awake thinking about the fast-paced world of search and rescue. There were still so many questions she didn't know the answers to about her career. And she must have loved it immensely to risk life and limb on a regular basis.

"Do you know why I went into search and rescue?" She had a hunch it was tied up in the tragic loss of her parents, but she hadn't yet asked Liam.

"Yes. It was because of your parents. They died in a pretty horrific pile-up on a highway in Anchorage. Because of a delay in getting rescue workers to the scene, eight people died. There was a big outcry afterward in the media about it. Unfortunately, that was something we had in common. My mother also died in a car crash."

"So it bonded us?"

Paige grinned. "That, among other things. We were both in love with Prescott men, so that really jump-started our friendship."

"And we had to deal with Jasper," Ruby quipped.

Paige nodded enthusiastically. "Dealing with Jasper's antics and his constant comments about settling down with his grandsons bonded us for life. Now that I think of it, we should get medals of valor."

They shared a look that resulted in the two of them launching into fits of laughter.

Liam sat at the kitchen table filling out some paperwork. He'd closed the clinic early today so he could work from home this afternoon. Aidan was at a friend's house for a play date until suppertime. Ruby had gone to the tea party at Hazel's lodge, looking more gorgeous than ever. Without Ruby and Aidan puttering around, the house had a quiet, unnatural vibe to it.

How long did tea parties last, anyway? He missed his wife. And he had nearly passed out at the sight of her in her tea party finery. His breathing had definitely gotten shaky. Her long hair had hung loose in soft waves. Other than a slash of red lining her lips, her face had been devoid of makeup. Ruby had dressed to the nines in a red, knee-length, cocktail dress with black lace at the hemline. She'd found the dress at the back of the closet they had once shared. Try as he might, he hadn't been able to dispose of Ruby's things. His family had said he was holding on to his grief, but now he had to wonder if God had been telling him to hold on and not let go.

Ruby was a beautiful woman. It had taken every ounce of his self-control not to sweep her up in his arms and kiss her senseless. He frowned. What made him think she would want that type of intimacy with him? Even though she was starting to remember little nuggets about him, it still didn't mean they were going to ride off into the sunset together. There was still a chasm of unresolved issues standing between them, and those issues would come to light if Ruby's memories returned. They still had mountains to climb before they could ever hope to get back what they'd lost.

A loud knocking interrupted his thoughts. Someone was at the front door. Maybe Ruby had forgotten her house key. He pushed up from his chair and strode to the front door, pulling it open in one fluid motion. Instead of his wife standing there, he found himself staring into the bluest pair of eyes he'd ever known. A pair almost identical to his own.

"Pop!" He almost did a double take. His father, Gareth Prescott, was standing on his doorstep. Tall, leanly muscled and good-looking, his father cut an impressive figure. His tanned features hinted at a lifestyle inconsistent with Alaska.

"Hey, Liam. Aren't you going to invite me in?" He slapped him on the shoulder as he walked past him and into the house. "It's been a while."

Liam almost couldn't believe his eyes. Wasn't his father somewhere in South America helping with a search-and-rescue mission? Not that he had the up-to-date information regarding his whereabouts. His father had always been a rolling stone, living his life on his own terms without any apologies to his kids. After his parents had divorced and gone their separate ways, both had left Alaska for warmer climates. Gareth's profession as a search-and-rescue leader had placed him on several operations with Ruby over the years. Liam hadn't seen his father since Ruby's memorial service. Although he had called a few times, Gareth's contact with his family had been limited.

Liam closed the front door and trailed after his father, who was walking toward the kitchen. "So, kiddo. How's Ruby doing? Jasper called me about her return. I couldn't believe it when he told me she had resurfaced with amnesia."

Liam put a lid on his annoyance as his father opened up the fridge and began poking around inside. "What Jasper said is the truth. She has flashes of memory, but for the most part she's a clean slate. It's been improving, though, since she's been back in Love. So there's hope."

His father poured himself a tall glass of lemonade. He took a lengthy sip. "That's a tough break, Liam."

"So what brings you back to Love? It's been a while," Liam said. Every instinct was telling him his father wasn't just here to check in on his family. The past had shown him that Gareth Prescott was most comfortable at a distance.

"Well, to be honest, I've been asked by the higher-ups to find out if Ruby is interested in coming back to work. They flew me out here to talk to her, find out if she's interested, or if she's even capable of doing so, what with her memory loss and all."

Anger—hot and fiery—pulsed through his veins. Search and rescue had already taken enough from them. It wasn't getting Ruby back. Not if he had anything to say about it.

All this time he had been agonizing about the past coming back to bite him. How wrong he had been. He hadn't seen this coming. Not by a long shot.

Liam let out a harsh laugh. "I should have known. You would never come back simply to check in on your kids or Aidan or to meet your newest grandchild, Emma. It's all about the work, right, Pop?"

His father held up his hands. "Liam, don't take this so personally."

"Save it. I don't want to hear it. And I don't want you coming around buzzing in Ruby's ear about how wonderful search-and-rescue missions are."

"I'm not looking to make any trouble," Gareth insisted. "We worked together. I wanted to see how she's doing. After all, she did suffer her injuries in the line of duty."

Liam took a steadying breath. What was it about his

father that always pushed all of his buttons? He wasn't sure how to put into words how nervy it was for him to show up here. This was one big slap in the face after a lifetime of disappointments. Where had he been for the last two years when Liam had been mired in grief?

"Ruby is fine. I'll make sure of it." He spit the words out.

"She has to make her own decisions, Liam," Gareth said in a softer tone. "Despite everything that's happened, she's a big girl."

"How many ways can I say this? Ruby's career in search and rescue is over. She nearly lost her life due to that profession. There's no way I'm ever going to allow her to go back. Not on my watch!"

"Liam!" Ruby's voice crashed over him like a bucket of ice water. He turned toward the doorway.

Ruby was standing there, a look of horror etched on her face. Her eyes wide, she was looking back and forth between him and his father.

"I could hear the two of you shouting from outside on the porch. What in the world is going on here?"

Ruby felt as if she had just walked into a war zone. Liam—calm, cool Liam—looked wild-eyed and fierce. He practically had steam coming out of his ears. And the gentleman he was speaking to seemed just as agitated. His brow furrowed, he looked like a kettle about to boil.

"Liam?" she repeated in a tentative voice. "What's going on?" The tension hanging in the air was palpable.

He shoved his hand through his hair then jerked his chin in the man's direction. "This is my father. He was just leaving." Liam's voice was curt, bordering on rude.

Ruby frowned. Liam hadn't mentioned anything at all about his father to her, other than the fact that he'd been on her search-and-rescue mission two years ago. Clearly, there had been a reason for that omission. Their relationship seemed frosty at best.

Liam's father stepped toward her. "Since Liam doesn't seem inclined to introduce us, I'll do the honors myself. I'm Gareth Prescott. I can tell by the look on your face that you don't remember me, but we were friends."

"You were there that day on the mountain," she said. She practically had to push the words out of her mouth. It felt like there were cotton balls lodged in her throat. Every time she thought about the accident, dread rose inside her.

There was something about seeing Liam's father that made her want to ask him a hundred questions about that terrible day. What had he seen? Had she really saved lives on the mountain? Perhaps by finding out the answers to her questions, the fear bottled up inside her might dissipate.

He darted a glance in Liam's direction. Liam glared at him. Gareth turned back to her. "I was there that day." He shook his head. "I wish I could have done something more for you. One minute you were standing there and the next thing we knew the snow-slip swallowed you up."

"You saw it?" Ruby asked.

"Yes, with my own eyes." He shuddered. "I never want to see anything like it ever again, although in the search-and-rescue business that's unlikely."

Something had been bothering Ruby. It was a tidbit

of a detail. She wasn't sure it was from that mission, but she had to ask Gareth.

"Was there a search-and-rescue dog there that day? A German shepherd."

"Ruby, why do you want to dredge this all up?" Liam asked. He had a tense expression on his face.

"Because it's part of me. That day changed my life. I don't know why, but talking about it helps."

"It just drags you back into the past," Liam said with a shake of his head.

"And it might help me trigger some more memories." She turned to Gareth. "Was there a rescue dog?"

"Yes," Gareth answered. "There was a dog there that day. He didn't make it."

"Rufus," she whispered. Images of a sweet, brown-and-black German shepherd flickered in her mind like snapshots. Her mouth went dry. "Did I—?"

"You trained him, Ruby. He was yours," Liam said, his voice suddenly tender.

Ruby wrapped her arms around her middle. The memories flashing before her eyes were poignant and powerful. Rufus as a puppy trailing after her in the snowy yard. Aidan playing with him. Liam taking him for walks. Ruby training him as a certified search-and-rescue dog.

And he had died on that mountain in her arms.

She heard Liam's voice through a fog. He was telling his father it was time for him to leave. Out of nowhere it felt like she couldn't breathe. She began to breathe rapidly, her chest rising and falling with the effort.

Suddenly she felt Liam's strong arms around her. He was rubbing her back and trying to soothe her. Liam was holding her against his chest and it felt so good to be held in his arms. It was like refuge from the storms of life.

"Ruby. Are you all right? You're scaring me."

"I saw it. In my mind's eye. It felt like I was reliving it. Rufus located several climbers who were trapped. And then he slipped off the ledge. I rappelled down to see if I could help him, but it was too late. And then I remember hearing this horrific noise. It was coming at me so fast…and then there was nothing. Just nothing. I was gone."

"It's going to be okay. You're safe now," he crooned as he caressed the side of her face and pulled her against his chest.

"I remember you walking with Rufus…and Aidan," she cried.

"It's good to remember, Ruby, but I don't want you going through this emotional turmoil. It can't be good for you."

She pulled away from him. "You can't protect me from this, Liam. It happened. I lived it. And through God's grace I survived it."

Liam shook his head. "My father blew into town like a tornado and stirred everything up. I never wanted you to have to relive your darkest moments."

"I can't pick and choose what I remember," she said with a shrug. "I'm actually grateful to Gareth. It's painful, but what I just remembered is a huge event. And it gives me hope that I can remember other crucial moments in my life. And who knows? Maybe I can return to search and rescue if I'm healthy enough to do so."

Liam's entire body stiffened. His expression darkened. "How can you even consider doing that? I won't let you put yourself in harm's way. It's not going to happen!"

Liam had just thrown down the gauntlet. It simmered in the air between them.

"If I ever decide to go back to search and rescue, that's my decision, Liam. I never gave you permission to run my life," she snapped.

Hurt flared in Liam's eyes. She hated to see that wounded look, but he'd cornered her and forced her to stand up for herself. Over the last two years she'd had to make decisions for herself in her day-to-day life. Liam couldn't expect to just step in and make all her choices for her, especially when it came to something as huge as her former career.

"Point taken, Ruby," Liam said in a clipped tone. "I'll remember next time not to care if you decide to put yourself in harm's way and make Aidan a motherless child all over again."

Ruby sucked in a shocked breath. Liam's words served as a punch in the gut. They bordered on being cruel. Deliberately hurtful.

Ruby turned away from Liam without a single word more and made a fast retreat to the guest bedroom. In the past few days it had felt as if they were growing ever closer, despite her stalled memories. Now, it seemed as if rushing rivers stood between them. And she had no idea how they were going to bridge the distance.

Chapter Nine

Liam settled into his seat at the Moose Café. He looked around the place, admiring the festive Christmas decorations that were now on full display. Sprigs of holly hung by the window while a fully decorated pine tree sat in the corner. Gaily wrapped presents were scattered beneath it. Holiday tunes softly emanated from speakers. Liam tapped his foot to the beat underneath the table.

The café really had become a favorite of almost everyone in Love. He admired his younger brother for reaching for the stars and making his dream come true.

As he did at least a few times a week, he was treating himself to lunch at his brother's establishment. He looked up at the door just in time to see Boone striding through with his best friend, Declan O'Rourke, by his side. Declan, Boone's lifelong best friend, was the owner and one of the pilots for O'Rourke Charters, a private plane company he ran out of Love. Just married to the town librarian, Annie Murray, Declan was an unofficial member of the Prescott family.

"Hey, Liam," Declan greeted him. "Thanks for the lunch invite."

"Hey, bro," Boone said as he settled into his chair. "I'm starved."

"You're always as hungry as a bear. Poor Grace must be sick of cooking for you," Liam said, chuckling. "She probably can't keep up."

Boone peered at his brother from behind the menu. "I cook just as many meals as Gracie. I consider myself a Renaissance man."

Liam and Declan looked at each other and burst out laughing.

Boone rolled his eyes. "Laugh all you want. You two could take pointers from me. Annie and Ruby would thank me for it."

Declan looked over at Liam. "How are things going, by the way? Is Ruby getting acclimated to town?"

"Honor invited Ruby and Aidan to the Wildlife Center today, so that'll be a fun trip." Liam frowned. "Everything was going pretty smoothly until we were blindsided by a visit from Pops yesterday."

Cameron walked up just at that moment. He stopped in his tracks and gaped at Liam. "Pops is here in Love?" He sank into a chair.

Liam swung his gaze up at his brother. "At least, he was last night. Sorry. I thought you knew."

Boone slapped the menu down on the table. "What did he want?"

"Not to catch up on all times, that's for sure." Liam drummed his fingers on the table. "He came for Ruby."

"Ruby?" Declan asked. "Gareth isn't the sentimental type. It's hard to believe he heard about Ruby and was so moved he came back home. That's not his style."

"Something tells me Liam has more to tell us," Boone drawled. "Spill it!"

"He came to find out if Ruby was fit to return to duty. He was flown here by his employer to ask Ruby if she wanted to return to search and rescue." He clenched his fists on the table. "It took every impulse in my body not to toss him out on his ear. He basically wanted to be able to go back and tell his bosses that Ruby was ready to go back to work."

Cameron scoffed. "Maybe he got a bonus or something out of it. Wonder if Jasper knows."

"This is so typical!" Boone snapped. "Did he even see Aidan or ask about Emma? He's never even met Gracie. He didn't show up at Cam's wedding or mine. And I'm not even sure he's aware that Honor is back in Love."

"You'd think one of these days he'd get his act together," Declan grumbled. "You guys know my dad isn't any better. At least Gareth shows up once in a blue moon."

Liam grunted. "To stir up a hornet's nest. Ruby and I got into it about the whole idea of her returning to search and rescue. It didn't end on a good note, I'm afraid."

"Did I miss something?" Cameron asked, a quizzical expression stamped on his face. "How can she resume that career with amnesia?"

"They were sending out feelers about her coming back down the road. That's the sense I got from his probing. Little by little, Ruby is remembering bits and pieces, so it's very possible. She remembered me and Aidan. She even had flashbacks about Rufus and what happened to him during the rescue."

"So I take it you would have a problem with her returning to search and rescue?" Boone asked, gazing at him intensely.

"Of course I would." Liam frowned. "It cost my family everything. We lost Ruby for two torturous years. The truth is, we might never fully get her back. We're still in limbo, Boone. And there's no guarantee that we're ever going to get back what we lost. Why would Ruby ever want to go down that road again?"

Boone held up his hands. "I see where you're coming from, but as a member of law enforcement, I just have to tell you that it seeps under our skin…it becomes part of our identity. Ruby may feel compelled to go back to service."

His brother's words were not the ones he wanted to hear. But he couldn't afford to ignore them. Boone was one of the smartest, most perceptive people he had ever known. He was his go-to person for advice. As always, his words were golden.

"What can I get y'all to eat?" Sophie chirped as she walked up to the table with a pencil and small pad in hand. "The salmon frittata with red potatoes on the side is real popular today. And Hazel is making a mean frozen hot chocolate with three types of chocolate."

"Sophie, I'm going to have the bison burger with truffle fries," Cameron said. "And a tall glass of water."

"Just a cup of the caribou stew and some flatbread," Boone said, sitting back in his chair and folding his arms across his chest. "Oh, and one of those frozen hot chocolates."

Liam smiled. When Cameron had first opened the Moose Café Boone had been skeptical of the specialty drinks. Now Boone considered himself a connoisseur of all the various drinks on the menu.

"I'll have the same," Declan added. "That'll really hit the spot. I have to make a run to Seward later on. I might stay over if the weather kicks up. There's a storm brewing."

"I'm going to have the turkey wrap with avocado and bacon," Liam said, looking up at Sophie, who was patiently waiting with a perky smile on her face. Matter of fact, Liam realized, he couldn't remember ever having seen Sophie without a sweet disposition. She was a true Georgia peach.

"You always order that," Sophie said with a grin. "Next time I'm going to skip asking you," she teased.

"I'm a man who knows what he wants," Liam quipped, handing the menu back to Sophie.

Sophie leaned down so only Liam could hear her. "I met Ruby at the tea party. She's everything I imagined she would be. I'm rooting for the two of you. Your family is in my prayers."

Liam reached out and squeezed Sophie's hand. "I appreciate that, Soph."

As Sophie walked away, Liam jutted his chin in her direction.

"That gal right there is some kind of wonderful," Liam said. He shook his head, buoyed by Sophie's heartwarming words. It helped to know that his family wasn't an island. Thoughts, prayers and well wishes all helped him feel as if the whole fishing village was pulling for them. Somehow it served to ease the pain of his father's actions. It let him know he wasn't alone.

"She sure is," Cameron agreed. "Whoever ends up with Sophie better treat her right."

"Yep," Declan agreed. "And if he doesn't, he's going to have to deal with us."

They nodded in unison, knowing that no one better toy with Sophie's heart. She was under their protection just as much as Honor. With a heart of gold, a pretty face and a sunny disposition, it would only be a matter of time.

"You know that we're here for you, Liam. This can't be easy," Boone said, his eyes full of concern. "You grieved for Ruby for a very long time. I know your emotions must be all over the place. Joy. Confusion. Anger."

Liam blew out a deep breath. Boone had hit the nail right on the head. So far, no one had really touched upon his feelings in all of this. Outside of being grateful and happy about Ruby's return, there were a host of other emotions he was battling. And he really didn't have an outlet. Between providing a strong foundation for Aidan, helping Ruby get her bearings, and taking care of his patients at the clinic, he really hadn't had time to process everything.

"Thanks. Honestly, I think part of me is still in shock. And you're right, it's confusing. I don't think that I realized how angry I was until Pops started pushing my buttons."

"Who are you upset with?" Cameron asked.

Liam shrugged. "I don't know. The whole situation, I suppose."

Cameron, Boone and Declan shared a glance loaded with meaning.

"What?" he asked, looking around the table.

"It seems like you might be mad at Ruby," Declan said. He held up his hands, as if to ward off Liam. "I could be wrong. Don't shoot the messenger."

Angry with Ruby? Why would he blame her for everything that had transpired two years ago? She was a victim. She had suffered more than anyone.

"No!" he protested. "That's not it."

"Give yourself a break, Liam," Cameron snapped. "You're human. Ruby worked in a dangerous field. I know you weren't always comfortable with it."

Liam's shoulders sagged. "And the award for worst husband goes to Dr. Liam Prescott." He shoved his hand through his hair. "On some level I suppose I am angry that Ruby went on the search and rescue when it was something we had argued about."

"Don't say that you're a bad husband," Boone chided. "You've been the most loving, faithful partner in the world. Because of the way you two honored and respected each other, you made me believe that maybe someday I could have a love like that. And then I found Gracie." Boone's voice softened. "So don't ever say that…not when I'm around."

Liam was touched. Boone had never told him before that his relationship with Ruby had inspired him. Despite their fractured upbringing, the Prescott siblings had always shared a tight bond. And they had all idolized Boone, who had been their hero. To know that he had been a source of hope for his brother made Liam feel ten feet tall. He had given something back to Boone to repay him in some small way for everything he had done for him.

Boone's poignant words served to remind him of everything he should be fighting tooth and nail to preserve. So far he had been allowing fear to guide him. He hadn't been giving it his all with Ruby. He was so afraid of being rejected by her again that he had lost sight of everything they had been to one another. Rather than focus on the love, he had spent too much time dissecting the things that had gone wrong between them.

"I've got your drinks. Waters for everyone and two frozen hot chocolates!" Sophie said as she returned and placed the drinks on the table.

"Did I interrupt something?" Sophie asked as she looked around at them.

"No," Liam said, feeling humbled by Boone's words and the support offered by Cameron and Declan. "Boone was just reminding me of how blessed I am. Sometimes we lose sight of it for different reasons, but my big brother just gave me a reality check."

"That's what big brothers are for," Boone drawled. A wide grin broke out over his face.

Liam couldn't stop thinking about Ruby. His sweet, beautiful wife. He had been so out of sorts last night that he hadn't even allowed himself to rejoice at the fact that Ruby now had memories related to him. Real, tangible moments.

Despite their argument, Liam felt hopeful. There was nothing they couldn't fix if they worked toward that goal with hope and faith.

"Do you guys mind if I bail on lunch? I have the afternoon free," Liam asked as the germ of an idea began to percolate in his mind. "I think it might be nice to surprise my family at the Wildlife Center."

"Good call," Boone said with an approving grin.

"Better than sitting around with these two mugs," Cameron drawled, earning himself a jab in the side from Declan.

After saying his goodbyes, he jumped up from his seat and asked Sophie to wrap his sandwich as a to-go meal. As he left the Moose Café, Liam began to fervently pray.

Dear Lord. Please help me bridge the gap between Ruby and me. I don't want to walk in fear anymore. The past shouldn't be something to be afraid of. You have given us this wondrous gift. I want to celebrate Ruby's return without looking over my shoulder.

"I'm so excited! I can't wait to see Auntie Honor's animals."

Aidan's enthusiastic voice from the back seat served as a joyful reminder of what this outing was all about. Although she was curious about Honor's job and the animals, her true joy would be in seeing it all through her son's eyes. He was rapidly becoming the center of her world.

"This is a real treat for us," Ruby said, observing him in the rearview mirror. "Don't forget to thank Honor for inviting us."

"I won't," Aidan chirped, sounding like a contented baby bird.

She wished that her current mood was more in line with Aidan's cheerful outlook on life. Ruby didn't know how to explain the feelings coursing through her. Ever since the blowup with Liam yesterday, her mind felt like mush. She kept replaying it over and over again in her mind, wondering where she'd gone wrong. She had acted on instinct and stood up for herself. Liam had been tense and moody. Ruby still felt furious about his comment regarding Aidan. Her whole body tightened just thinking about it.

Why did she feel so out of sorts? People argued. But by all accounts, she and Liam had been sheer perfection together. She bit her lip, wondering if the conflict between them stemmed from her. After all, she wasn't the same Ruby. Not really.

Her chest tightened painfully at the thought of Liam. Although she was still angry at him, a part of her wished he was here with them. The word *heartsick* came to mind. It didn't make sense since she wasn't in love with Liam, but she couldn't ignore that her feelings for him were growing by leaps and bounds. Perhaps that was the reason for her feeling ill at ease. She was beginning to care for him, and the harsh words they had exchanged yesterday put them at odds.

She knew she should just live in the moment. Her therapist in Colorado had taught her how to focus on living in the here and now rather than dwelling on the past. That's what she needed to do right now instead of rehashing the terrible scene with her husband. She prayed that God would help them fix things.

Ruby let out a sigh of appreciation as the stunning Alaskan vista began to unfold around her. They were heading into a more remote area of Love where signs of habitation were scarce. Gigantic, snow-covered trees dominated the scenery. Mountains were so close she felt as if she could reach out and touch them. There were no houses or shops or cute little cafés that served up coffee drinks. Honor's wildlife center was in the boondocks.

As they pulled into the entrance, Ruby noticed the stallions in the paddock. They were beautiful, graceful animals, roaming wild and free in the snow. She slowed the car so Aidan could get a good look. He oohed and aahed from the back seat, making her chuckle with his over-the-top appreciation of the horses.

Ruby followed the signs along the way, turning left to continue on toward the main house.

Before they had even exited the car, Honor came running out of the ranch-style house. Dressed casually in blue jeans, a brightly colored T-shirt and a bomber-style jacket, she looked relaxed and enthused.

"Welcome!" she said, extending her arms wide. Aidan ran straight toward her and catapulted himself into her arms. "Hey, buddy. I'm so glad you guys came by today."

Honor, with her fresh-faced beauty, chestnut-colored hair and warm blue-gray eyes looked radiant.

"Thank you for inviting us, Auntie Honor," Aidan said, looking over at Ruby for confirmation he'd done a good job of following her instructions.

Ruby smiled at him, sending him an encouraging nod. "Aidan almost couldn't sleep last night. He was so excited. And to be honest, so am I."

"I hope you didn't have any trouble finding this place," Honor said, reaching out and touching her arm.

"Not at all," Ruby said. "I had my GPS and a set of directions I printed out. It gave me an opportunity to really enjoy the scenery."

"Well, you two made my day by coming to visit. I love it out here, but it does get a bit lonely."

"But you have the animals," Aidan chimed in. "Don't they keep you company?"

"You're right about that, Aidan. The only problem is that they don't talk to me when I ask them things," she said with a chuckle.

"What animals do you have here?" Aidan asked, looking around him as if he expected one to pop up right before his eyes.

Honor bent so she was eye-level with her nephew. She reached out and pulled his hat down over his ears. "So far we have eagles, wolves, moose, foxes and a lot more. Why don't I show you around and you can see for yourself?"

"Sounds like a plan." Ruby zipped up her coat. The December temperature had dipped even lower than it had been over the last few days. She glanced over at Aidan. His coat wasn't fastened all the way up. She reached over and adjusted it so that his neck wasn't exposed. Alaskan weather was no joke. Hypothermia could set in at any time of the year, mostly when the temps were between thirty and fifty degrees Fahrenheit.

Hmm. How do I know that? She smiled at the realization that more and more information was coming back to her.

All of a sudden they heard the low rumbling of an engine and the sound of tires crunching on the snow-packed road. Honor raised her hand to shade her eyes from the sun.

"That's Liam's car," she announced, turning toward Ruby and Aidan. A smile lit her face.

"Daddy!" Aidan called out.

Ruby felt her pulse skitter. She wasn't sure what emotion was roaring through her as she watched Liam step out of the car. Aidan ran toward him at breakneck speed then jumped into his father's arms. Ruby placed her hand on her stomach as butterflies did somersaults at the sight of the two of them.

As if in slow motion, Liam walked toward them, Aidan at his side. As he got closer, he locked eyes with her and she felt something shift inside her. It felt so right to have him standing there with them. She couldn't put her feelings into words, but despite everything brewing between them, she always felt better being in Liam's presence. Safer. More grounded.

"Hey! We weren't expecting you," Honor said. "I was just about to give the tour."

Liam still hadn't taken his eyes off Ruby. "Great! There's no place I'd rather be."

She looked away, feeling nervous at the intensity of his gaze. The heated exchange from yesterday still stood between them.

"Well, let's get started, then," Honor said, the corners of her mouth twitching in amusement.

Aidan planted himself right next to Honor, while Liam walked beside her. With his long legs, Ruby knew instinctively that he was slowing his gait so he didn't outpace her. Silence stretched between them for a few moments.

"I'm glad you decided to come," Ruby blurted. "You should have seen Aidan's face when you pulled up."

"Me, too," Liam said with a nod. "I've been here before, but Aidan's never gotten the full tour. There's nothing better than seeing something through a child's eyes."

"So, what determines which animals come to the center?" Ruby asked.

"The Wildlife Center takes in orphaned and injured animals. The goal is to rehabilitate them so they can go back into the wild," Liam explained.

"It's very important work," Ruby said, feeling very grateful to Honor for giving them the grand tour and giving them an up-close and personal look at something so special to her.

"It sure is," Liam acknowledged. "And she was born to do this."

Honor and Aidan stopped up ahead to wait for them as they reached the first structure.

"Come on, slowpokes," Aidan called out, waving them on with his arm.

As soon as they caught up, Honor ushered them toward the white, ranch-style building.

"Let's check out the aviary. I'll show you our newest friend," Honor said.

As soon as they stepped inside, Honor led them to an area where they could see the enclosure through a glass window. A gorgeous bald eagle sat on the ground, pecking at something in a round bowl.

"Cool!" Aidan shouted, pressing his nose against the glass.

"This is Dolly. She's a bald eagle with a severely injured wing. She can't fend for herself out in the wild due to her injuries, so we're taking care of her until she can do it for herself."

"What happened to her? Did a coyote get her?" Aidan asked.

"No, Aidan," Honor said in a solemn voice. "A bullet pierced Dolly's wing. We're hoping it gets better so she can learn to fly again."

"I can't believe someone would do that," Ruby said. "Aren't eagles on the endangered species list?"

"Not anymore," Liam said. "Although it's still illegal to try to harm them."

"We need to care for animals," Aidan said. "Like we did for Rufus."

"I can't believe you remember him," Ruby said. "You were just a little one then."

"I was almost three when he died, but I remember him giving me kisses and going for walks in the woods with him." Aidan looked up at her, affection shining in his eyes. "I remember loving him."

"So do I," she whispered as she nuzzled Aidan's cheek with her gloved hand. Being here at the center was bringing into focus her own love of animals, dogs in particular.

As they walked around the wildlife preserve, Ruby found herself in awe of Honor's knowledge. Honor explained to her that she had a master's degree in wildlife biology. To open the wildlife center, permission had to be granted by Alaska's Department of Fish and Game. Finding a visionary who could make it happen had been key.

"Opening this center was always my dream. Funding was the hard part. I'm fortunate to have partnered with people who really believe in conservation and animal activism. They put their money where their hearts lie. This place still needs the generosity of donors, though. We're hoping to have some fund-raisers across the state to ensure future programs."

For the next few hours Honor showed them around. They were able to get a glimpse of a wide variety of animals—bison, birds, wolves, baby elk, a sitka black-tailed deer, moose. Aidan was able to pet a baby wolf named Hercules who had been found abandoned in the woods.

"Do you have any dogs?" Aidan crossed his hands prayerfully in front of him as he asked the question.

"We do have a few. Let's go meet Rita." Honor led them toward an area where four dogs were in an enclosure. Three of them were running around and playing with each other while the fourth one was peacefully lying on a mat. Once they entered the enclosure all the dogs came running toward them. Ruby found herself being greeted enthusiastically by a black-and-white terrier who was missing a leg. His name tag read Diego in big letters. Ruby placed her arms around him and hugged him. The sound of Aidan's hearty chuckle rang out as Diego began licking her face.

Ruby felt the heat of Liam's gaze as he watched her bond with the dog.

How could she ever have forgotten how good it felt to be around dogs?

"Rita is about to have a litter of babies," Honor explained, moving toward the golden retriever reclining on the mat. "Any day now."

"Like Aunt Gracie?" Aidan asked, his brown eyes wide. He began patting Rita on the head.

Honor, Liam and Ruby burst out laughing. Out of the mouths of babes.

"Sort of, but not really. Rita is going to have several at one time and we're going to have to find homes for them," Honor explained. "Grace is expecting only one, unless they're holding out on us."

"Can we take one of the puppies, Dad? Pretty please with sugar on top." Aidan held his hands in front of him, crossing them in prayerful fashion.

Liam's expression was conflicted. "I don't know, Aidan. We have a lot going on at the moment and puppies are a lot of work."

"Please," he begged, shifting his eyes toward Ruby. "I'll feed him and walk him and teach him a bunch of tricks."

Liam turned toward her. He knit his brows together. "What do you think?"

Personally, she would love to own another dog, but Ruby wasn't sure she should even weigh in on it. So much about the future was uncertain. Would she be remaining in Love? If she and Liam couldn't even agree on her career, how would their marriage survive the challenge of her amnesia?

And there was still so much tension lingering between them from yesterday.

"I think it's something we should talk about at greater length," she said in a halting voice. She looked down at Aidan. Her heart sank as she recognized the signs of his vast disappointment. His lower lip trembled while his shoulders sagged. She bent over and tipped up his chin, so she could look him in the eye. Tears shimmered in his warm brown eyes.

"I know that's not what you want to hear," she said in a soft voice, "but bringing a pet into the home is serious business. Do you know that a lot of people make impulsive decisions to bring dogs home and then it doesn't work out? This isn't a no, it's simply a let's wait and see."

"I think that makes a lot of sense," Liam said with a nod.

"Why don't we head back to the main house for hot chocolate?" Honor suggested. Aidan's mood turned on a dime. Ruby sent her a grateful look for diverting her son's attention away from Rita and her soon-to-be brood.

Ruby was certain that Aidan's shouts of glee could be heard all the way back in town. As she walked hand in hand with Aidan as they journeyed back across the property, Ruby felt lighter and more joyful than she had in ages. The beauty of this day hadn't allowed her to dwell on the tension between her and Liam. It seemed that both of them had tried to put it aside so they could enjoy the Wildlife Center as a family.

Each day was bringing something new and wonderful her way. She just needed to look closely enough to see it. And to embrace the little boy who had swiftly stolen her heart.

Thank You, Lord. For gifting us with this wondrous day.

Chapter Ten

Later on that evening, Ruby stood at the sink washing dinner dishes. Her back was turned to Liam. He silently admired the graceful slope of her neck and the tiny little curls that had escaped her bun. She was radiant, even in all her simplicity. Her jeans and plaid-flannel T-shirt did nothing to diminish it. If anything, it only served to highlight it.

Liam still hadn't broached the subject of their disagreement from yesterday. Even though things had thawed between them this afternoon, the situation didn't rest easy on his heart. God had given him the tremendous gift of bringing Ruby back into his life and now he was squandering it.

He'd given it a lot of thought this afternoon. He could have handled the situation better, yet he'd lost control of his emotions and alienated Ruby in the process. Something had to give. They couldn't continue living under the same roof and walking on eggshells all the time.

Liam moved toward the kitchen counter. He stood close to her so that their arms were slightly touching. Her nearness caused a yearning he had stuffed down inside him for ages. The smell of lavender drifted toward him, causing him to take a good whiff of her light perfume. It was torture to be so close to his beautiful wife and not take her in his arms. So far he had reined himself in, but he didn't know how long he could continue to do so.

"Nice day out at the Wildlife Center," he remarked in a casual tone.

She nodded without looking at him. "Yes, it was."

"Don't you think we should talk?" Liam slightly raised his voice over the sound of the water from the sink.

"About what?" Ruby asked without turning around or shutting off the water. She continued to scrub the dishes.

"You're still angry with me. I get that. But we have to extend each other an olive branch. Sooner or later Aidan will pick up on the tension between us."

Ruby snapped her head in his direction. "That's a cheap shot, throwing Aidan into the situation."

"It happens to be the truth," he said in a curt voice. "Don't be so prickly about everything just because you're upset with me."

Ruby bristled. "I don't like being angry. It doesn't sit well with me."

"I don't like seeing you this way, either," he admitted. "It's not your way."

She turned off the water and wiped her hands on a dish towel. "I'm not backing down from my stance," she said. Her expression showed a fierceness he hadn't seen since she had returned. It was classic Ruby.

"Neither am I," he replied. "I've always done what's best for our family. You may have been the professional at saving lives, but I've always served and protected our family."

She folded her arms across her chest. "We can agree to disagree. Life's too short to harbor grudges or carry around negative energy."

"I agree. I know what it feels like to have the bottom fall out of my world in an instant. It feels silly to waste time being angry at each other."

"Ditto," she said.

She bowed her head. "But I'm still bent out of shape about the way you acted the other day. Not only toward me, but your father, as well."

His father? There wasn't time enough in the world for him to explain all the nuances of their fractured relationship. As a result, he looked like the bad guy in the situation.

"I've always regarded myself as your protector. Old habits die hard."

"Being protective is one thing, but bossing me around is another. Something tells me you didn't get away with that before the accident. Am I right?"

"You always gave as good as you got," he admitted. "You've never been the backing down type." They both laughed, which managed to ease the lingering tension a little bit.

"That's good to know," Ruby said.

"I'm sorry about what I said about you leaving Aidan motherless. It wasn't right." Just remembering his dig made his skin crawl. There had been some truth in his statement, but he'd known it would hurt Ruby to utter those words. That alone made him feel ashamed.

"Apology accepted," she said with a nod. "I would never willingly hurt Aidan. And I have to live with the fact that the repercussions of my career choices left him motherless for a time." She quirked her mouth. "Honestly, I didn't really need the reminder."

"Losing you in a rescue mission...that was always my worst fear. Then it happened. And just the thought of what might happen if you go back to search and rescue makes me crazy." He shuddered. "It plays on all those fears and the nightmare we've already lived through."

Ruby nodded. "I get where you're coming from, but it still isn't something you can lecture me against doing. That's not going to fly with me."

Although Liam liked the way Ruby was standing up for herself in true Ruby fashion, he hated that she was sticking to her guns about the possibility of returning to her career. As far as he was concerned, it was a nobrainer. Hadn't they decided Aidan's needs came first? Why tempt fate? They had already been put through the ringer because of her job.

Rather than stir up the hornet's nest any further, he needed to get a few things off his chest about his father. The topic of Gareth Prescott was one he usually avoided like the plague. But he needed Ruby to know where he was coming from so she didn't write him off as a jerk.

"With regard to my father, the friction between us goes back a long time. Whether you realize it or not, he came here with an agenda, Ruby. And that is galling to me, considering he was MIA for the past two years. Not once did he ever call to check in on us. Not an email or a text or a letter. Not even a smoke signal." He let out a harsh laugh. "And when Jasper had a heart attack, it barely registered with him."

"I'm sorry, Liam. That sounds awful. Has it always

been like this?" Ruby asked, her expression radiating compassion.

"Pretty much," Liam admitted. Even though he had convinced himself over the years it no longer hurt, the piercing sensation near his stomach proved otherwise. Even as an adult, Gareth Prescott still managed to tie him up in knots.

"When my parents divorced, neither one of them put their children first. Jasper became our surrogate parent and he did right by us. When Boone became an adult, he took all of us under his wing. He helped me foot the bill for medical school. He played the role of surrogate father. Neither of my parents were the warm and fuzzy type. And the truth is, they have both kept a far distance from us. It hasn't been easy for any of us, but Honor had it the worst since she's the youngest."

"I'm sorry," Ruby whispered. "It's unfathomable to me that parents would act like that."

"It is what it is," Liam said with a sigh. "All the Prescott siblings have had to come to terms with it the best we can. I think when they divorced they both decided they wanted to be footloose and fancy free. No real attachments or responsibilities."

"For the life of me I can't imagine that," Ruby murmured.

"When we got married I stressed the part about sticking it out because I came from the opposite of that. More than anything, I believe in honoring the commitments we make in this life…to each other and Aidan and our faith." In a strange way Liam felt as if he had just laid his heart down on the table for Ruby to dissect. He had told her in a nutshell his belief system and what mattered to him most of all. As a man who tended to go inward, it was a huge deal for him.

"Thank you for telling me about Gareth. I see why it was so tense the day he was here. I can't blame you for questioning his showing up here unannounced after he'd pretty much bailed out of your life."

"I appreciate your listening. As the saying goes, we can't pick our parents. On the flip side, it made me want to be everything I could be in Aidan's world because I never had it."

"And you are," Ruby said with a smile. "Watching the two of you together is such a joyful experience. You've done such a great job raising him."

"Being his father has been such a gift," Liam said, his voice breaking a little. When God had blessed him with the gift of fatherhood, it had been the greatest day of his life. He had never taken the responsibility lightly. And he never would.

Ruby bit her lip and ducked her head. She seemed to be having a moment of shyness. "I know things have been tense between us, but I wanted you to know that I had some flashes of you, in addition to the ones involving Rufus. Something opened up in me that day when Gareth visited. I remember the two of us being on a mountain and sledding down a hill. You were laughing and teasing me. You threw a snowball at me and it hit me right on the nose."

Raw emotion rose inside Liam. He remembered that day, as well. It had been one of the best days of his life. "We were out at Deer Lake. That afternoon you told me that you were expecting Aidan." He let out a ragged sigh. "Not many things in this life can ever compare to that moment."

"We were happy, weren't we?" she asked.

"Yes, we were, Ruby. I'd never call us perfect, but we sure had a great life. We laughed and we loved and we worked hard to build a life for ourselves."

And it had been truly wonderful. He wasn't exaggerating. They had been best friends. Co-parents. Two people who had been committed to living out their lives together with their son. Difficult times had come, but he'd never thought for a single moment those times had defined them.

A hint of a smile played around her lips. She twirled a strand of her hair around her finger. "That feels reassuring to me to hear you say that. It fills in the gaps."

"I'm going to call Honor and see if she can watch Aidan tomorrow night." Liam threw the comment out casually.

She frowned at him. "Why do you need a sitter?"

The idea had been percolating for a while now, but he knew this would be the perfect time to put his plan in motion. So far he hadn't been able to spend much quality time around Ruby without Aidan being present. And although he loved his son dearly, he wanted "alone time" with his wife. They needed it.

"Because I want to take you out on a date tomorrow night, Ruby. A good, old-fashioned date. How do you feel about that?"

A date with her husband? After all the tension between them, it was the last thing she had expected to hear Liam say. How did she feel about it? Excited. Nervous. It was thrilling. But she wanted to try to keep her cool and not act too giddy about it.

"That sounds nice," she had answered with a smile.

"Good. Tomorrow night at seven o'clock. Dinner."

Now, almost twenty-four hours later, she was doing her very best to make herself look date-worthy. With Liam's help, she had moved a lot of her personal items, including clothes, into the guest bedroom, so she was able to look through her wardrobe for an outfit to wear.

After narrowing her choice to three outfits, she settled on a burgundy wool dress that was flattering to her figure and stylish. She experimented with her hair, using the curling iron to create long, loose waves. Dangling earrings gave the ensemble a little pizazz. Having never mastered the art of makeup in the last two years, Ruby decided to stick with a mauve shade of lipstick and some mascara. She studied herself with a critical eye.

Yes, indeed. She sure cleaned up well. Hopefully, Liam would agree.

She smoothed her hand over her stomach. Butterflies were flip-flopping around inside, a direct result of her sudden case of jitters. This date was everything to her. It was an opportunity to test the waters with Liam, to see if these feelings brewing between them could serve as a foundation for the future. To know whether there was truly a place for her in this wonderful Alaskan community.

There was no need to be a bundle of nerves. This was Liam. She knew him. He wasn't just some stranger who had popped up in her life. She had strong, joyful memories of him. Each day more moments from the past were coming back to her.

And even if she hadn't recovered a few memories of her husband, he'd showed her in the here and now that he was a wonderful, kindhearted man. A giving man. Wasn't that the most important thing of all?

A few times she had answered the landline and spoken to patients seeking out Dr. Liam Prescott. Ruby didn't know of any doctors who regularly gave out their home phone number for emergencies. Each and every time, Liam had taken the call and spoken to the caller with compassion and warmth.

It was starting to feel like she had a crush on her own husband.

The sound of the doorbell ringing intruded upon her thoughts. A quick glance at her watch showed it was almost seven o'clock. When the pealing of the bell continued, she left the guest room and headed toward the front door. Who could it be? Honor was already inside, eating macaroni and cheese in the kitchen with Aidan. It was a little bit odd that Aidan hadn't run to the door to open it. More times than not, that's what he did.

Ruby swung the door open, letting out a squeak when Liam's tall frame filled the doorway.

"Good evening," he drawled, handing her a bouquet of white roses, baby's breath and red carnations. He was dressed in a dark jacket paired with a white shirt and a tan pair of slacks. He looked simply divine. She discreetly sniffed the air around them. He smelled pine-fresh like the great outdoors.

"Aren't you going to invite me in?" he asked, his lips twitching with merriment.

"Seriously?" she blurted. He was standing there looking handsome and swoon-worthy and capable of completely sweeping her off her feet.

He grinned, showcasing his perfect set of pearly whites. "Yes, seriously. This is a first-date move. Since you can't remember our real first date, I figured we should make this the first one. As I recall, I showed up at your apartment and rang your bell, presented you with flowers and took you out on the town."

If she hadn't already had a major-league crush on Liam, this would have pushed her straight over the edge. She ushered him in, firmly closing the door behind him. When she turned back to him, he was standing mere inches from her, staring her down with his magnetic blue eyes.

"You look amazing." Liam's eyes were full of appreciation as he looked her up and down, his gaze lingering a few beats too long. Something hummed and buzzed in the air—an awareness that felt palpable.

"Thank you," she murmured. "You don't look half bad yourself."

Suddenly, Honor and Aidan were standing there, grinning from ear to ear.

Ruby placed her hand on her hip. "I suppose the two of you were in on this, huh?" she asked.

"Yep," Aidan said. "Auntie Honor said it was romantic." Aidan made a face.

Ruby felt her cheeks blushing. It had been terribly romantic.

"Let me take your flowers and put them in a vase while you get your coat and purse," Honor suggested. She reached for the bouquet and pressed it to her nose. "If I can find a guy who'll give me flowers and moonlight, I might just marry him."

Although Honor's tone was teasing, Ruby sensed something lying behind her words. A true yearning to be connected with someone, she imagined.

After getting her purse and coat, Ruby joined Liam in the living room where they said their goodbyes to Aidan and Honor. As they set off into the freezing-cold night, Ruby couldn't resist asking Liam where they were headed.

"There's a restaurant over by the pier that only opens for dinner service. We used to be regulars there. It's called The Bay."

"So why only dinner service?" Ruby asked, feeling curious about the place.

"The owners are getting a little on in years. They came here from Italy more than thirty years ago. It was their dream to open a restaurant here and they did. But a few years ago this town had a recession. Everyone was hurting. Sal and Renata had to cut back their service to only one a day." He glanced over at her and smiled. "And the funny thing is they're doing better now than ever, since they streamlined the business."

"That's fantastic," Ruby said as she looked out the window at the scenery whizzing by. "I love hearing success stories like that."

"Me, too. It reminds me of Cameron. It took a tremendous amount of courage for him to open the Moose Café. He was coming off a huge town scandal involving Paige's father and embezzlement of town funds. There were a lot of naysayers."

"I'm sad he had to go through that, but I'm really happy he prevailed in the end. He and Paige and Emma seem so happy."

"They are. It hasn't been an easy road, though. They've endured a lot, but they've come out on the other side," Liam said. He turned off the road and entered a small parking lot near the pier. A red house glowing with brilliant lights stood about fifty feet away. A large tree decorated with twinkling ornaments stood in front of the farmhouse-style house.

Liam placed his hand on the small of her back and led her inside. The interior was packed with customers. It almost seemed as if every single table was occupied. Fantastic scents wafted in the air. The clanging of glasses and cutlery rang out.

"Liam! Nice to see you here." An older man with salt-and-pepper hair and a large frame greeted them. He locked gazes with her, then reached out and grabbed her by the arm. "Ruby! I'm Sal Terrazo. This is my place. And I'm very honored to have you here tonight. Let me show you to your table." He held out his elbow so Ruby could loop her arm through it. Once they arrived at the table, he pulled out her chair for her and then placed her napkin in her lap with a flourish.

"Your waiter will be over shortly. If the two of you need anything at all, don't hesitate to tell me." With a slight bow, he disappeared from the table.

Ruby almost gasped out loud when she realized they were seated right by the window overlooking Kachemak Bay. It was easily the best table in the whole place.

"Did you bribe someone for this spot?" she teased.

Liam flashed a knowing smile. "I didn't have to. Let's just say that the owners are the founding members of the Ruby Prescott Fan Club. They were more than happy to provide us with this incredible view."

She shook her head. "This is really nice. I wasn't expecting anything this incredible. Sal is amazing."

"He really is. There's a better view in the daytime, but there's something about the way the lights radiate off the water that really is spectacular." He peered out the window and pointed. "You can even see the mountains in the distance."

"I know this place," she blurted. "We had our first date here, didn't we?"

Liam nodded. "I can't believe you remember."

"It's hard sometimes because I'm not always sure if I'm remembering or if it's just a feeling. I do know this place, though. I remember eating pasta…lots and lots of pasta. And someone was teasing us about getting married one day. But that's all I remember."

Liam groaned. "That was Sal. Not exactly what a girl wants to hear on a first date. But you let me take you out on a second one and then a third."

"And we fell in love." Her words were a statement rather than a question. Those tender moments still eluded her. More than anything, she wanted to know how they'd fallen for one another.

"When we fell in love, I was the skeptic. It comes from having two parents who couldn't honor their commitment to one another. It made me very leery of relationships." He laughed—a rich, deep laugh that seemed to rumble through his chest. "But you came crashing into my life with your open heart and optimism. Even though I half expected you to break my heart into a million little pieces, I couldn't not be with you. I was a goner—right from the start."

Hearing about their early beginnings made her feel emotional. "Thanks for sharing that with me, Liam. I wish I could remember that night in vivid detail."

Liam locked eyes with her. "I have full confidence that one of these days you will."

He believed in her, supported her attempts at recovering her memories. He was her husband and the father of her child. In another life she had loved this man. And at this very moment she felt a gigantic shift in her heart. It was opening up—to Dr. Liam Prescott and all the possibilities a life with him would mean for her.

If only she could be brave enough to reach out and grab it with both hands.

As Liam drove away from the waterfront after a spectacular dinner with Ruby, he found himself not wanting the evening to end. He hadn't even admitted it to himself over the years, but he had missed female companionship. Not just any female. He'd missed Ruby. The love of his life. And despite the fact she wasn't a carbon copy of the woman she had once been, there was still a huge part of her that had stayed the same. His heart recognized her.

And being afraid of being hurt by her seemed shallow in the scheme of things. God had brought Ruby back to them and she had fought her fears and doubts to journey to Love. Couldn't he muster the courage to do the same?

She turned toward him as she sat in the passenger seat. "Thanks for showing me such a great time, Liam. It was a very special night."

He glanced at her, overwhelmed by her beauty set against the soft interior glow of the truck.

"You're very welcome," he said, feeling relieved that Ruby had enjoyed the evening as much as he had. "It's still pretty early. We could go to the Moose for a cappuccino. They're extending their hours of operation for the holidays. I think Cameron has a band from Kodiak playing there tonight."

"I'd love to. That sounds fun."

Liam made a left onto Jarvis Street and found parking a few spots down from the café. He walked around to the passenger side and helped Ruby down from the truck. On impulse he reached for her hand. He walked slowly with her, pausing to point out Christmas displays in various windows. He showed her the red toboggan, and she agreed that Aidan would love it.

On impulse, he pulled her into the alcove of a storefront. She looked at him with questions brimming in her eyes.

"I know you don't remember it, but we kissed on our first date."

Ruby smiled at him. "I kissed you on our first date?"

"Yes, you did," Liam said, trying to keep his voice solemn. "I seem to remember you saying something about me being irresistible."

"It would seem you have me at a distinct disadvantage, since I can't remember our first kiss," Ruby said in a light voice.

"I remember it vividly," he said.

She shook her head and laughed, her long tresses swaying with the movement.

"So, Ruby Prescott, in the event that you're really opposed to being kissed by me, I'm letting you know right here and now that I'm going to kiss you." He reached out and traced the outline of her full, soft lips with his thumb. He didn't think he could wait a second longer. It already felt like an eternity since their lips had met.

"Okay," she whispered. Her brown eyes were looking up at him with such a wealth of emotion. One step and he would tumble right over the edge into their depths.

He leaned down and placed his lips over hers. *Take it slow*, he had to remind himself. This kiss had been a long time coming. Liam reached out and gently pulled her closer to him. Her lips were warm and inviting despite the frosty December temperature. The heady scent of lavender surrounded her. She was kissing him back with such tenderness it made him ache inside. He felt powerful emotions roar through him. His heart was soaring well past the safe boundaries he'd set for himself. It was way too late to guard his heart against this.

Ruby. His sweet, unforgettable Ruby.

"Liam," she murmured against his lips as the kiss ended. He laid his forehead against hers, wanting to stretch out the moment until the stars were stamped from the sky.

Ruby couldn't seem to stop thinking about the kiss she'd shared with Liam. She replayed it in her mind during the rest of the walk to the Moose Café, going over every nuance and small detail. Liam had been so tender and romantic. Her heart had done somersaults. It was her first kiss, after all, since she couldn't remember another. And as first kisses went, it had been spectacular. Ruby had wanted it to go on and on, to savor the tender moment for as long as possible. She had known in the moments before he'd dipped his head that Liam was going to kiss her. Truthfully, she'd been praying he would do so.

Liam had kissed her! And she had joyfully kissed him back. His lips had tasted like cinnamon and sugar. His arms had been steady and sure. He smelled like fresh pine. And for the life of her, she couldn't stop thinking about kissing him again.

From what she'd observed so far, Liam Prescott was a good man. Honorable. Faithful. True. And with every passing day, he was nestling himself further and further into her heart. The kiss had just solidified everything.

Back in Denver she had dreamed about finding a man to share her life with. She had prayed to God to send her someone strong and loving and kind. Ruby looked up at the incandescent moon and felt a sweeping, soaring feeling rise inside her. At this moment she felt so happy she could almost soar as if on wings.

By the time Liam grasped her hand in his, Ruby wasn't certain she could contain her feelings. She felt as if she might burst with happiness.

"You're pretty quiet all of a sudden." Liam's deep voice intruded on her thoughts.

She looked over at him, admiring his strong jawline and the proud tilt of his head. Dr. Liam Prescott was an Alaskan hottie. And he was hers. All hers.

"I'm happy," she said, knowing she was beaming. "Thank you for this wonderful night."

Liam looked down at her, his handsome face lit with the same joy she felt. "The night's still young, Ruby." As he opened the door to the Moose Café and led her inside, Ruby found herself wishing that the happiness she felt at this very moment could last a lifetime.

Chapter Eleven

Considering it was a weeknight, the Moose was jumping. Although it was a tight crowd, Hazel managed to finagle a table for them so they could watch the show. Paige sat and joined them while Cameron was behind the scenes trying to ensure everything ran smoothly. The band from Kodiak had a big following, according to Paige. Cameron had said that some of their fans had even followed them to this gig in Love.

During the intermission, Cameron also came to join them at their table. He leaned over and pressed a kiss on his wife's forehead. It wasn't long before Hazel had pulled up a chair beside them.

"The band is the best we've had so far. And this place is filled to capacity." Cameron's face was lit like a kid in a candy store. Liam's chest swelled with pride. His brother had made lemonade out of lemons and earned his success through ingenuity and hard work. Now he was reaping the rewards.

"Proud of you," Liam said with a nod in his brother's direction.

All of a sudden Jasper came barreling through the

door like a man on a mission. His hair was sticking up and his expression bordered on wild. He reached their table in a few determined strides.

"All right, woman. I surrender." Jasper held his hands up in the air. His voice was as loud as a foghorn.

Hazel gaped at him. "What are you talking about? Did you rob a bank or something?"

He heaved a tremendous sigh as if he was carrying the weight of the world on his shoulders. "You've hounded, harassed, intimidated, finagled and bamboozled me all in your quest to coerce me into putting a ring on your finger." He dug in his pocket and pulled out a wooden box. After fumbling with it for a few seconds he managed to prop it open. A beautiful diamond ring sat inside.

Hazel's jaw dropped. She muttered something unintelligible.

Liam leaned in toward Ruby. "Oh, no. This is not going to end well," he whispered. Liam made a slashing motion against his neck in the hope that Jasper would see his gesture and figure out his message.

Ruby bit her lip and looked at him with big eyes. "This is not the sort of proposal a woman dreams about," she whispered back. "It's really a stinker."

All Liam could do was shake his head.

Everything hushed and stilled in the Moose Café. Everyone seemed to sense that a tornado was brewing. It was a good thing he and Ruby had decided to come by the café tonight. Jasper might very well need medical attention when Hazel got through with him.

Hazel stood and raised up to her full height. She was face-to-face with Jasper. "I've waited my whole life for this moment. I thought it would happen in my twenties, prayed it might happen in my thirties and despaired of it ever happening in my forties. Then in my late fifties I met you and I started to hope again. I fell in love with an ornery codger who can't seem to see the forest for the trees. And up until this very moment, I was willing to forgive your idiosyncrasies. Jasper Alistair Prescott, I wouldn't marry you if you were the last bachelor in Love, Alaska. I might not have all the answers, but I do know one thing for certain." She sneered at him. "I deserve way better than a bootleg proposal."

Jasper sputtered. "I—I gave you what you've been asking for, didn't I? A proposal of marriage."

"That wasn't a proposal. It was a hatchet job!" Hazel roared.

Jasper scratched his head. "Didn't you see the ring? I spent a small fortune on it," Jasper shouted.

"Don't take this the wrong way, but you can take that piece of tin and give it to your next girlfriend. Consider yourself dumped, Mayor Prescott!" Hazel turned on her heel and stomped off toward the kitchen.

"Hazel!" Jasper began, walking after her.

Paige reached out and grabbed him by the arm. "I think you've done enough. I'll go after her."

Ruby jumped up from her seat. She looked at Liam. "I'm going to go check on Hazel. She didn't look so good." She shook her head at Jasper. "You should be ashamed of yourself."

Jasper threw up his hands and looked at Liam and Cameron. "What's wrong with everyone?"

Liam shook his head at his grandfather. "At the risk of asking a dumb question, are you crazy?"

"What? What just happened?" Jasper asked.

"What just happened?" Cameron roared. "Surely you

can't be serious. You just hurt one of the most amazing, wonderful people in the world."

"Hazel shouldn't be hurt. She knows me. I'm not the sentimental sort. I'm not the type to get down on my knees and propose," Jasper muttered. The expression on his face showed that he was beginning to realize his huge misstep.

"Well, maybe just this once you should have done something to allow Hazel to live out her dream. It wouldn't have cost you anything, would it?" Liam pressed.

Jasper's face crumpled. "I…it's not my way. Hazel knows that."

"Really? Well, how's that working out for you right about now?" Cameron asked, his face a cold mask of fury.

Of all the Prescott siblings, Cameron shared the closest relationship with Hazel. She was his surrogate mother, employee and close friend. He was very protective of her.

As the band came back from their break and the intermission ended, Cameron left so he could resume his work duties. After a few minutes of sulking, Jasper got up and left the establishment. His shoulders were slumped, and he looked beaten. Liam couldn't help but feel a little badly for his grandfather. He suffered from a sort of blindness that wouldn't allow him to see his own faults and flaws. The way he had treated Hazel was shameless. And he didn't even seem to grasp what he had done wrong.

Liam felt a chill sweep over him as he realized something huge. He didn't want to be anything like Jasper. His grandfather was digging in his heels and refusing to acknowledge how wrong he had been. But what did his pride get him? He had lost Hazel and, from what Liam had seen, he would have an uphill battle getting her back.

Had he been walking in his own blindness? Refusing to even consider that Ruby's career was a calling rather than a threat to his family's stability? Protecting his heart rather than doing the brave thing—opening himself up to love. Putting oneself out there wasn't easy and it didn't feel totally comfortable, but Liam knew that Ruby was worth all the risks.

In the aftermath of her date night with Liam, Ruby found herself settling more and more into family life at the Prescott household. Things between her and Liam were good. More and more, she was imagining a permanent place for herself here in Love. With Liam and Aidan. With each passing day, Denver became nothing more than a blip on her radar. It was shocking how quickly she had shed her life in Colorado. And with each and every day, returning to Denver seemed less and less appealing.

Christmas was rapidly approaching. Ruby was getting really good at hiding presents all over the house. Some of her hiding places were so good she was beginning to fret that she might never find them. She had discussed with Liam the idea of buying Aidan a puppy for Christmas. Rita's litter hadn't been born yet, and they would need to stay with their mother for a few weeks after delivery. Aidan wanted a puppy so much, and since Liam was in agreement, Ruby wanted to make her son's dream come true.

Last night they had stayed in as a family and decorated the Christmas tree. Liam had brought her to tears by pulling out a box of antique ornaments that had been in her family for generations. Ruby had lovingly fingered them, admiring the stunning detail and the intricate craftsmanship. It made her sad that neither of her parents was alive to see Aidan or to help her navigate through life. No matter how old you were, there was always a yearning for a mother. She was no different. And she did have memories of the woman who had been her best friend and motivator. Most of her recollections were sketchy, but she had memories of a round-faced, cheerful woman who had loved to bake and shower her children with affection. Ruby could almost feel the tightness of her mother's hugs.

Her mother had passed on to her a love of the Christmas season. And now Ruby wanted to do something to pass on her family's legacy so that Aidan could know his heritage. That's where Kyle could be a big help. She was going to call him later today and invite him to Love for Christmas. Seeing how close Liam was to his siblings made her ache inside to strengthen her ties to her brother. And he could act as her living memory about their family traditions until those memories came back to her. Now, more than ever, she was optimistic about the bulk of her memories returning.

At the moment Ruby was sitting on the living room floor in front of the beautifully decorated tree, wrapping presents. Liam was right next to her, struggling with a tape dispenser and a roll of wrapping paper.

"Is there a secret to this?" Liam held up his hands. They were covered in tape.

Ruby chuckled and reached over to untangle him. "I take it that I used to do most of the wrapping?"

"Pretty much," Liam acknowledged. "Not that I didn't try, mind you, but you were way more talented at it than I was."

"It's okay. The true gift lies in the giving." She winked at Liam. "You've still got a shot at winning in that area."

Liam folded the wrapping paper and stuck the tape down. He held up the box. "It may not be the prettiest gift under the tree, but I stuck to it and I did it."

Ruby clapped. "Nicely done, Liam."

"I wanted to share something with you… My family has a Christmas tradition of going caroling a few days before Christmas. You used to love it. We go door to door, singing all types of Christmas songs."

"That's a great idea," Ruby said. "I imagine it's a real treat for the people whose houses you stop by. There's such joy in song."

"We're thinking of going tomorrow night. Are you okay with that? I don't want you to feel overwhelmed. The Prescotts can be a little wild and crazy during the holidays."

"Only during the holidays?" she teased. "Having just witnessed your grandfather's over-the-top proposal to Hazel, I'm going to hazard a guess that it's not just during the Christmas season."

Liam made a face. "Okay. I take that back. It's pretty much year-round with my family."

"The caroling sounds fun. Now that more of my memories have come back to me, I feel more comfortable being around groups of people. I don't feel like I'm stumbling around in the dark without a flashlight anymore."

"And you're developing friendships with Paige and

Grace and Hazel. And Honor thinks you hung the moon. You're not an island anymore."

"You're right," Ruby said. "It helps to have connections here in town. I really enjoyed the tea party. And having Honor invite us out to the Wildlife Center. Those ladies are all something else," she said. "Grace is so adorable. And Hazel—" She let out a laugh. "She's a character if I've ever met one. And Paige… I don't know how or why, but she already seems like a close friend."

"Trust me. Those women can be a real lifeline here in this town. Each of them in their own way is made of strong stuff."

It was nice to hear Liam speak so well of Hazel, Honor and both his sisters-in-law. She thought very highly of all of them. And she looked forward to making those connections with Annie and Sophie, as well. That was the beauty of community. She hadn't experienced it in Colorado, but right here in Love, it was as natural as breathing. It was enmeshed in the fabric of the town.

"So, I don't want to bring up a tricky subject, but we never talked about your dad. Is he still in town?"

"Not that I know of," Liam said. "I grilled Jasper about it, but he said Pops never swung by his house. Can't say that I'm surprised."

"How's Jasper doing? Hazel seems to be staying firm in her resolve to be done with the relationship."

"He's in a little bit of a tailspin at the moment. At first he was in denial, but now the anger is coming out. I'm hoping he just fast-forwards to the acceptance part."

Ruby made a tutting sound. "I feel kind of sorry for him."

"What? Why? He broke Hazel's heart," Liam said.

"Yeah, but I think his heart must be a little roughed

up, too. I think Jasper pretends not to care as much as he really does care deep down. Get it?" Ruby asked.

"I see what you're saying, but at this point in his life he needs to get his act together. Tomorrow isn't promised to anyone. We all need to own up to our truths." Liam looked over at her. He seemed slightly preoccupied about something, but he didn't seem inclined to share it with her.

She threw her tape down on to the carpet and turned to Liam. "I have an idea!"

Liam's mouth twisted. "Should I be worried?"

"No. It's brilliant. Why don't we play matchmaker for them? Hazel and Jasper! Think about it. Jasper is the one who created the Operation Love program. He's brought dozens of women to this town and helped Alaskan bachelors find love. Your brother met his wife through the program. So did Declan! Shouldn't we try and give something back to Jasper?"

Liam let out a sigh. "When you put it like that, I guess we do owe Jasper a little consideration. What exactly did you have in mind?"

It was a perfect Alaskan winter night for caroling. The temperature was a chilly fifteen degrees Fahrenheit. Snow was lightly falling as they headed out on foot from the center of town. With a full moon hanging high in the sky and the heavens lit up with sparkling stars, their path was made clear for them. There couldn't be a more perfect December night.

It was a full crew for caroling, but it truly did feel like the more the merrier. Liam had surprised her by inviting Kyle to come and join them. Jasper, Hazel, Boone, Grace, Cameron and Paige were also there. Jasper and Hazel were avoiding each other like the plague. Emma had stayed at home with her nanny, Fiona, since she had just recovered from her ear infection, and neither Paige nor Cameron wanted to run the risk of a relapse. Honor was there, as well as Sophie, Declan and Annie. And Pastor Jack Teagan, who made a point of telling Ruby he'd been the one to officiate her wedding.

Ruby was happy to see everyone. And she no longer felt like a stranger among the townsfolk or with Liam's family. She was part of them now. A citizen of this quirky Alaskan town. A Prescott.

They went door to door, singing beloved Christmas songs. More times than not they were invited inside for holiday treats and hot cocoa. Some townsfolk handed them candy canes or put their coats on and joined them in the revelry. Ruby couldn't think of a more festive way to spend an evening. And to make it even more special, she had a flash of being heavily pregnant with Aidan and going door to door, her hand firmly clasped in Liam's.

"I think that's it for the hot chocolate, Aidan," Ruby said. "You're going to end up with a bellyache."

"But, Mom, I don't feel sick at all," Aidan protested, his little mouth turned down in a frown.

Ruby stopped in her tracks, blown away by hearing Aidan call her "Mom." He continued to walk ahead with the group, totally unaware of what had just happened or how it had impacted her. Liam stopped and stood by her side. A smile threatened to take over his face. He looked almost as happy as she felt.

"Did you just hear that?" she whispered. "Or did I imagine it?"

"I heard it. I don't need to ask you how it feels to

hear him say that one very special word. It's written all over your face."

Tears pooled in her eyes. She began to sniff to keep them at bay. "I can't even put it into words. I feel like I could soar right now."

Liam reached out for her mittened hand and squeezed it. They began walking toward the group of carolers, hand in hand. For the first time in forever, Ruby felt like part of a couple. And it felt wonderful to know she wasn't alone in the world. She was tied to something so much bigger than herself. There wasn't any other place she'd rather be at this moment than right at Liam's side.

"Why don't we invite everyone over to the house for a small gathering? We were already planning to have people over. What's a few more?" Ruby suggested. The expression on her face was one of pure excitement. Her cheeks were pink from the cold, and he could tell from the way she was jamming her hands into her coat pockets that she was trying to stay warm.

"Everyone? Are you sure?" he asked, filled with surprise at Ruby's willingness to host a large gathering. It was a generous suggestion, particularly since she was still getting used to being around large groups of people.

"What about the plan for Jasper and Hazel? I'm not sure Jasper wants more of an audience for his big moment."

"Yes, I'm sure about including everyone. We have enough food to feed a small army, and Aidan will love having a house full of guests. Plus, it will make things more romantic when Jasper's plan comes to fruition. He owes Hazel big-time after the last one."

Liam hoped Ruby wasn't disappointed. His grandfa-

ther was a feisty, opinionated man who tended to dig his
heels in when he wanted to be ornery. There was never
a guarantee with Jasper that he would follow along with
anything, even a plan that might reunite him with Hazel
and put him back in her good graces.

As they stood on Jarvis Street, Liam put his hands
together and let out a whistle to gain everyone's attention. The group quieted and shifted their attention to
him. "Ruby, Aidan and I would like to invite everyone
back to our place for a light meal, fellowship and holiday cheer."

Judging by the reaction, everyone was excited about
attending a gathering at their home. There was clapping
and cheering from the group. Jasper let out a groan and
made a face at him. He didn't think he'd ever seen his
grandfather so nervous and agitated. He prayed this
didn't mean he was about to bail on the plan. Aidan was
doing a little dance in the snow and sticking his tongue
out so that he could taste the snowflakes. He dove into
the snow then picked up a handful, lifting in the air and
lobbying it in his father's direction.

Plop. It landed on Liam's shoulder. With a wild roar
he raced toward his son, who let out a shriek and began
running in the other direction. Before long, snowballs
were being lobbed in all directions by everyone. Liam
couldn't remember the last time he'd had this much fun.
Joy pulsed sure and strong in the air. The spirit of the
season could be felt right there on Jarvis Street among
this group of townsfolk.

Once they arrived at the house, Liam opened the
doors and let everyone in. He grabbed Ruby by the hand
and pulled her back outside.

"What's going on? Aren't we supposed to be inside?"

she asked with a laugh. "Jasper looks like he's about to jump out of his skin. You might need to settle him down so this can go off without a hitch."

"Jasper will be fine. I just wanted you to see something."

He pulled her into the yard so that they were facing their big bay window. "Look." He pointed up at the window.

Ruby let out a gasp of pure awe. "Liam. It's magnificent."

Liam and Ruby stood for a moment and simply admired the way their Christmas tree looked from outside. The lights shimmered and winked at them, dazzling in their beauty. The gold star glinted from on top of the tree. Their home looked warm and festive and inviting. In his heart of hearts, Liam had never imagined Christmas could ever feel this heartwarming ever again. It was true that a house wasn't a home. Ruby being back meant all the difference in their world.

She had brought so much along with her—hope, joy, heart. And he knew now that her return also served to provide him with a second chance to get things right. Part of doing that would be facing down his fears and telling Ruby the truth about their marriage problems. He simply couldn't exist in all this beauty while sitting on something so big. It was the only way he could save their relationship from future bumps and bruises. If they were going to have an open and honest relationship, he was going to have to be transparent.

"It's simply beautiful, Liam." Ruby let out a sigh. "This whole evening has been so joyful. Being with family and friends. Seeing Aidan so happy. The caroling door to door."

Liam grinned with pleasure. "It was a night to re-member, that's for sure."

"I felt like a kid again singing like that. I was in the choir, you know," she boasted. Yet another thing she felt blessed to have remembered.

"It's a good thing you're easy on the eyes because your singing voice needs some work," Liam teased. Her singing voice had always been something he'd been able to tease her about.

Ruby swatted him with her mitten. "Hey! That's not very nice."

Liam was laughing so hard he clutched his stomach. "Maybe not, but it's true."

"I'm very insulted," she said in a prim voice.

"I'm sorry. It's just that you're amazing at everything under the sun. That's the only thing I could ever tease you about," Liam admitted.

"It's not the sound of the voice that's important. It's the way you put your heart and soul into it," Ruby said, trying not to chuckle.

All of a sudden Liam stopped laughing. Her words represented way more to him than she realized. It sig-nified the way he wanted to walk in the world. Heart. Soul. Truth. He couldn't imagine being wrong when being led by those values.

"You're right about that, Ruby. And no one sang to-night with more heart than you did. You radiate from inside."

"I'm happy. I think that explains it," she said in a soft voice.

Happiness. It wasn't a concept he'd allowed himself to think about for some time. Not since his entire world had fallen apart in the wake of Ruby's "death." His feelings for Ruby were more powerful than he could put into words. He had always loved her, but now he was falling in love with her all over again. Step by step, moment by moment, she was making indelible impressions on his heart. And the sheer power of it scared him to death.

"You're a beautiful woman, Ruby Prescott. Inside and out." Liam reached out and ran his palm across her cheek.

He lowered his head and captured her lips in a stunning kiss that took her breath away. Her legs almost gave way beneath her. It felt as if she was being swept away. Despite the frosty cold, Liam's lips were warm and inviting as they moved against hers. Ruby reached up and grabbed the fabric of his coat, pulling him closer. She wrapped her arms around his neck, anchoring herself to him. Ruby wanted to show him that she was in this—with every fiber of her being she wanted to be Mrs. Liam Prescott. She wanted him! And Aidan. And a life filled with all the blessings that had been on full display tonight.

As the kiss ended, she found herself standing on wobbly legs. With a grin, Liam steadied her by holding her arms. Who would have thought a simple kiss would feel so earth-shattering? The attraction between them was electric. It even managed to cut through the chill in the frosty night air.

"Let's head inside. We need to give those two lovebirds a push in the right direction," Ruby whispered.

"Just don't be too disappointed if it doesn't work out the way you plan," Liam warned. "As a Prescott, I've learned to expect the unexpected."

"Have a little faith," she said as they walked inside.

After taking off her winter parka, Ruby made her way into the kitchen, pleased that everyone was helping themselves to food and drinks. Prior to leaving for the caroling outing Ruby had laid out most of the food on the dining room table. Although they had only planned on a small number of guests, Ruby felt grateful they had enough food to accommodate a larger number of people. She busied herself filling up the punch bowl with egg-nog and taking the shrimp and deli platters out of the fridge and placing them on the table. Honor had set up all the desserts on the side table. At the moment Aidan and a few of his little friends were helping themselves to cookies and brownies.

All of a sudden Jasper appeared at her side. He tugged at her arm. "Ruby, I need to talk to you in private."

"Now?" she asked with a frown. "Is this about you-know-what?"

"If you-know-what involves the diamond ring sitting in my pocket…then, yes," he responded with a loud whisper. "I'm about to burst."

Ruby quickly led him to the office at the back of the house that Liam used when he worked from home. Once they were alone and she had closed the door behind them, Jasper began to vent.

"I'm not sure about this plan anymore. Seems to me that I would be groveling. Jasper Prescott doesn't beg."

"Jasper, this isn't about your pride. It's about repairing the damage you did the other night. That went down in a public arena, so it's only fitting that you reverse things in the same way."

His lips trembled. "But what if she says no, Ruby?

I'm not sure this old heart of mine could take the rejection again."

Sympathy flared inside her. At his heart Jasper wasn't quite the curmudgeon he appeared to be. He was a man who hid a lot of his feelings behind a façade of irreverence. It was a mechanism he had most likely developed after the death of his first wife and the heartache he had suffered as a result of that huge loss. After all, it took a man with a mighty big heart to conceive of the Operation Love program.

"I'm not going to lie to you and say that it's not possible, Jasper. But how will you ever know if you don't try?" She reached out and squeezed his hand. He was trembling. "I know what it feels like to be afraid. I've been dealing with fear for the last two years. One of the bravest things I've ever done is get on that seaplane—destination Love, Alaska. And the second will be laying my heart wide open for Liam to claim it. Am I afraid that he won't? Of course. But I can't let that stop me. God led me home for a purpose. And I can't run from that, even if it terrifies me at times."

Jasper reached up and cupped her face between his palms. "You belong to us, Ruby. You're a Prescott through and through, but you're also a big part of this town. Love needs your big heart and your courage. I feel blessed to call you my granddaughter."

Jasper pulled her into his arms. Ruby blinked away tears as she sank into the hug. Deep down, Jasper was a cuddly teddy bear. She loved this man, warts and all. And she wanted him to have his happy ending with Hazel.

"I think I'm going to need to borrow some of your courage," Jasper said in a raspy voice.

"You've got this, Jasper. Just speak from your heart and try to focus on what Hazel brings into your life."

"Hmm. Good things, right?" he asked with a frown.

"Jasper!" Ruby cried out, gently swatting him.

He threw his head back and laughed. "Just a little joke. I had to get it out of my system before I make my pitch."

Ruby studied him. "Are you ready?"

"As I'll ever be," he muttered as he wrenched the door open and strode back into the party.

Ruby trailed behind him, not wanting to miss his moment.

Jasper walked into the living room, where the majority of guests were gathered. He looked around the room and finally spotted Hazel sitting next to Grace on the couch. When she spotted him approaching, she gave him the stink-eye. She did it so well Ruby thought she could give lessons on it.

"Hazel! We need to talk," Jasper announced. Ruby made a face at Jasper. He was starting off on the wrong foot. He needed to be tender, not gruff.

"I don't need to do anything! We're no longer an item in case that addled brain of yours forgot!" Hazel said. She made a slashing motion in the air with her hand. "We're history! Kaput!"

Yikes! This was not going to be easy, Ruby feared. She met Liam's eyes from where he was standing across the room. His expression was doubtful.

"I love you, Hazel Tookes!" Jasper shouted.

The room got extraordinarily quiet. All eyes were glued to the unfolding drama. Guests began to trickle in from the other rooms to watch.

Hazel's eyes widened. Ruby imagined she'd never

heard Jasper declare his feelings in such a public forum. He moved closer and took Hazel's hand in his. "The other night I made a plum fool of myself. And in the process, I dragged you down with me. I'll regret that for the rest of my life.

"Hazel, you know that I already had the love of a lifetime."

Hazel nodded. "Yes. Your wife, Harmony."

Jasper nodded. "She was a fine woman. I lost her due to a mixture of my pig-headedness and her pride. I never imagined God would bless me twice in my life. But he did, Hazel. He brought me you. He sent me a supportive, beautiful woman who is my best friend. Someone I can laugh with and confide in, a woman who knows me inside and out, yet still thinks I'm worth loving. Half the time I know that I don't deserve you, Hazel. What you've brought me and the entire Prescott clan is beyond anything I can articulate with mere words."

By this time tears were streaming down Hazel's face and she was choking back sobs. Ruby felt moisture on her own cheeks. A quick look around the room showed that most were becoming emotional. The raw emotion emanating from Jasper was undeniable.

"Would you make this old fool the happiest man in Alaska and consent to marry me?" He dug in his pocket for the ring box and popped it open. The diamond glinted and winked at Hazel from its throne. "I'd get down on one knee, but I'm not sure I would be able to get up."

The room broke into laughter. Ruby looked over at Liam. He seemed as if he might burst with pride. Hazel stood and wrapped her arms around Jasper's neck. She stared deeply into his eyes. "Jasper, you've made me the happiest woman in the world. All I ever wanted was to know that you loved me. And if you really want me as your bride, my answer is yes. A thousand times yes." She leaned in and placed a smooch on Jasper's lips that sealed the deal.

The room erupted into chaos. Shouts. Cheers. Whistles. The next thing Ruby knew Liam and Aidan were both at her side, sharing the heartwarming moment with her. Liam reached for her hand and squeezed it. It felt so right having their hands linked, as if they belonged together.

Ruby blinked back tears.

Jasper taking this leap of faith and putting his pride aside was a mighty thing indeed.

This had been a perfect evening, capped off by the knowledge that Jasper and Hazel had been blissfully reunited. Finally she could allow herself to believe in the possibility of a happily-ever-after with Liam. If someone as set in his ways as Jasper could make this huge shift, anything was possible. And she needed to believe, since she'd fallen in love all over again with her husband.

Hope shimmered in the room like the gold star on the Christmas tree.

Chapter Twelve

Ruby sat in the kitchen, studying one of her favorite cookbooks. She had volunteered to make the turkey for Christmas dinner at Jasper's house, and she had no intention of delivering a dry, pathetic excuse for a turkey. Nope. It wasn't happening. This turkey was going to go down in Love, Alaska, history as the juiciest, most succulent bird of all time. Liam would be so proud of her. And she would be extremely proud of herself, as well.

Something had been bothering her all morning. She had a slight headache and there was a strange feeling of dread hovering over her. It didn't make any sense, considering all that was right in her world. Aidan was now calling her Mom. Her memories were slowly but surely coming back to her. And her relationship with Liam had turned romantic. Last night's kiss had definitely moved them out of the friend zone. There was no doubt in her mind that she was falling in love with her husband.

Just the thought of it gave her goose bumps.

Meeting Liam for lunch at the Moose Café would serve as a nice treat in the middle of the day. And it felt much better to spend time with him than to sit around daydreaming about the tall, dark and handsome doctor who had captured her heart.

Aidan sat at a little table with Emma, who was hanging out with Cameron at work today. From what Ruby observed, the two kids did more playing than eating. It was nice to watch the two of them together. Although there was a three-year age difference, they got along like two peas in a pod.

Liam swung his gaze from Aidan to her. "Something tells me Aidan wants a little sister or brother someday. We always wanted a big family."

Ruby took a sip of her coffee. "We did?" she asked, her heart thundering inside her chest.

"At least ten," Liam drawled.

Ruby's jaw dropped. "Ten? Seriously?"

Liam's grin threatened to take over his entire face. "No, I'm teasing, but we did want more."

She looked over at Aidan and smiled. "He'd be a great big brother."

"It's obvious to me that you're feeling more settled now in Love," Liam said as he gulped down his coffee.

"I am," Ruby said. "There were a few bumps on the road. It was hard for me to know what the future held for me without my memories. But that's changed quite a bit. A lot of my memories have trickled back. I feel more grounded now."

"I admire you," Liam said. "When you first arrived in Love, your head must have been spinning. You really held on to your faith."

"I have no doubt that God sent me here. Imagine if I hadn't come seeking answers." She shuddered. "You and Aidan might never have known that I survived the accident." The thought of it was terrifying. Her whole life would have been different. It was painful to even think about not reuniting with Liam and Aidan.

Liam reached for her hand and raised it to his lips. "I will always be grateful for God pointing you in the direction of home."

"Me, too," Ruby murmured, overwhelmed by the magnitude of how much her life had changed in the past few weeks. Before coming to Love she had been pretty much a loner, one who wasn't tied to anything or anyone. Now, she had a family, one she loved with all her heart. And her future was ripe with promise.

After lunch ended, Ruby took Aidan to the library to pick up a few books. He was at the age when he needed to get started on the road to reading. Next fall he would be headed to kindergarten.

Annie greeted them as soon as they walked inside. With her sweet nature and extensive knowledge of the library's catalog, Annie made their visit engaging and wonderful. They ended up with both of their arms full of books by the time they departed.

When they finally arrived home, it was Aidan's nap time.

Ruby stuffed her library books into a shopping bag she had tucked away in the trunk. She placed the strap of the bag over her shoulder and prepared to help Aidan lug their finds inside.

"Hi, Ruby. Aidan." Gareth was on the porch, sitting in one of the Adirondack chairs. He stood as they came closer.

Aidan reached for her hand and warily studied his grandfather.

"Do you remember me?" Gareth asked, bending over until he was at Aidan's eye level.

Aidan shrugged and looked up at Ruby. He turned to Gareth and said, "Not really, but I've seen pictures of you from when my daddy was little."

Gareth winced. "I'm sorry I haven't been around more often, A-man. It's great to see you, buddy."

Ruby frowned at her father-in-law. "What are you doing here, Gareth? Liam thought you left Love."

His smile twisted. "I was visiting some friends in Homer. But I didn't get very far before I realized that I needed to come back and talk to my children."

"Liam is at the clinic." She frowned at him. "But I'm sure you know that already."

He had a sheepish expression on his face. "I'd like to have a few minutes to talk to you, Ruby. To apologize. To explain myself."

"Come on in, Gareth." Once they crossed the threshold, she turned to him and whispered, "I'm only extending this courtesy to you since you're Liam's father. A bit ironic, I'd say, considering you haven't given any of your kids much of that."

Turning toward her son, Ruby said, "Aidan, you need to go take your nap. You're about to crash."

"But I don't want to go to sleep," he complained. The way his lids had been slowly creeping closed had showed he was fighting sleep.

"Listen to your mother, kiddo. I promise we'll do something fun together really soon." He stuck out his hand. Aidan grinned and shook it, then retreated to his room.

"Come on into the kitchen," Ruby said, leading the

way. She took down two glasses and filled them with lemonade. Gareth sat across from her at the table.

For a moment he looked down, avoiding her gaze. "I was your mentor, so I feel a little bit of responsibility to keep tabs on you. I know that might sound strange to you, considering how I've dropped the ball with my own kids."

Anger on Liam's behalf rose inside her. "You did more than drop the ball. Your vanishing acts have really hurt your children. That's unacceptable."

Gareth looked up at her. His eyes were full of shame. "I know. I'm determined to change all that moving forward. I really want to try." He reached for his glass and took a sip of lemonade.

Ruby nodded. "I respect that."

"If you have even the slightest inclination to return to search and rescue, I'm here to answer any questions. And I know that might place me in the crosshairs of my son, but this isn't personal. It's professional. I was the one who called you in for that Colorado mission." His face blanched. "I feel responsible for everything that happened."

Ruby shrugged. "You shouldn't feel that way. Life happens. And with regard to my career, I'm just going to have to wait and see. It's too soon to know anything."

"I can appreciate that. You've been through a lot, Ruby. I'm really happy that you and Liam got past all of your marital problems."

Her heart constricted. She frowned at him. "Problems? What are you talking about?"

Gareth's face fell. His mouth opened then quickly closed.

"What problems?" she persisted. The pounding inside her chest was getting louder by the second.

He held up his hands as if to ward her off. "Ruby, please. I didn't come here to make trouble."

"Tell me, Gareth." She wasn't taking no for an answer.

He let out a sigh and shook his head. "You were struggling with a few marriage issues. It would have blown over. I know it."

Marriage issues? Hadn't everyone said that she had enjoyed a perfect marriage? If something had been wrong in their marriage, Liam would have told her. He was a straight shooter, not the type to harbor secrets.

"I've said enough!" Gareth said in a fierce voice. "It's all in the past. Liam will never forgive me for opening this can of worms." With a tortured groan, Gareth rose jerkily from the table and pushed his chair in. "I really did come here today to make inroads." He strode from the room, quickly making his way to the front door.

"Gareth!" she called after him. Without turning back to her, he wrenched open the front door and disappeared from view.

Once she opened the front door Gareth was already in his car, taking off down the road. She closed the door and sagged against it, filled with confusion about Gareth's revelation. She didn't necessarily take Gareth at face value, but she was of the mind that his comment had been truthful. The immediate look of regret on his face once he had realized his mistake had been authentic.

She began to tremble. Gareth had been telling her the truth. She knew it instinctively. This was the thing she had been so afraid to discover. This was the monster hiding under the bed. And she had been so afraid to remember it because on some level she knew it might change everything between her and Liam.

Ruby began to knead her head with her fingers. Her head ached. She sat on the couch and wrapped her arms around her middle. She began rocking slightly back and forth.

Suddenly she had a flash of the fight with Liam. His face had been a cold mask of anger. She had been crying and speaking in a raised voice. As if she was watching a movie, she heard herself ask for a separation. She saw the hurt look etched on Liam's face followed by his blistering anger.

It had been about her job! The words "dangerous" and "Aidan" and "mission" had been flowing in the conversation. She had wrenched her rings off and placed them in a red-velvet box in his dresser drawer. There had been tears and raised voices between her and Liam. Then resignation as she calmly began packing her duffel bag.

It made sense. For so long she had wondered about where her wedding rings were and what had happened to them. She had never asked Liam about it, nor had he given her the rings back. That in itself was a red flag. Wouldn't Liam have mentioned her wedding rings? Unless, of course, he hadn't wanted to bring them up, knowing she had made the decision not to wear the rings shortly before the accident.

Dear Lord. Please let this be a false memory. Please don't let this be real. I want so badly to believe in Liam...to believe in us and our marriage. I don't know how I can do that if Liam hasn't been honest with me.

* * *

Filled with determination, Ruby took a deep breath and headed down the hall to the master bedroom. She slowly turned the knob and stepped inside. Goose bumps popped up on her arms. This was the scene she remembered from her flash. She looked toward the twin dressers standing side by side. It wasn't right to go through Liam's private belongings, but she had to know if what she remembered had really happened.

She pulled open the top dresser drawer. There were a few items inside…mainly socks. In the corner sat a crimson box. Taking it out, she lifted it open with shaking fingers. Inside were two rings—a solitaire diamond and a wedding band with a row of smaller diamond stones.

Ruby let out a small cry. She felt as if someone had just placed a twenty-pound weight on her chest. It was difficult to breathe. All she wanted to do at the moment was to curl up on the floor and sob.

Footsteps sounded behind her on the hardwood floor. Startled, she whirled around. Liam was standing there, a look of unease stamped on his face.

"I couldn't bear to tell you. I tried several times, but I never could do it." His voice sounded ragged.

"You didn't try hard enough," she cried. "All of this time you could have said something to me. You had plenty of moments."

He took a step toward her. She held up her hands to ward him off. She needed to keep him at a distance.

"You were trying to get your life back and bond with our son. Flashes of memory were returning to you. Maybe it was selfish, but I didn't want to run the risk of everything falling apart if you found out."

"I took off my wedding rings. We were breaking up. That's huge." She felt numb. How she had prayed this one memory wasn't true. But it was true, and now she had to figure out what it meant for her marriage to Liam.

He nodded. "It's true that we weren't in a good place, Ruby."

His admission frightened her. Suddenly every ounce of security she had established in Love felt as if it were slipping out of her grasp. She raised her hand to her mouth as a sob bubbled up inside her. Why had he allowed her to believe they were a storybook couple?

"I can't believe this! Everything I believed about us is a lie."

"No! It wasn't a lie. Relationships ebb and flow, Ruby. Sure, we were grappling with certain issues, but we loved each other. That's the biggest truth of all."

"But we were separating. Breaking up," she cried out.

"We would have found our way back to one another. I know it!"

She sank onto the bed as if her legs were too weak to hold her up. "It feels like I don't know much of anything. Everything between us since I've been back in Love has been based on what I thought we had. Everyone here in town told me we were this amazing couple, but the truth is, they didn't know our struggles or that we might not have stayed together."

"I know this is confusing to you, but it doesn't change what we were…the love we shared. We were devoted to each other, Ruby. Head-over-heels, besotted, crazy-in-love fools. Did we have rough times? Yes. Did we fall short of what we wanted to be? Yes. But the good times far outweighed the bad." A sheen of tears shone in his eyes. "I know we would have stuck it out because I vowed it to you on the day we got married."

She shook her head. "If all that is true, why weren't you honest with me?"

"Because after losing you, I couldn't stand the thought of going through it all over again. I wasn't confident that I could tell you without losing you. I allowed fear to cloud my better judgment. I was afraid for Aidan, as well, and what it would mean for him if you took off back to Colorado."

"Stop hiding behind Aidan! Ever since I came back you've been avoiding the elephant in the room. You made me believe that we had this beautiful, perfect marriage. And so did everyone else in this town—" Suddenly she wasn't just furious with Liam. She was angry at the townsfolk for giving credence to the fairy tale. And she was furious with God, for allowing her to believe she had found her way back to the place she belonged.

"It wasn't perfect, but it was everything we ever wanted it to be."

"That's not true," she said in a steely voice. "I remember the fighting and the bitterness. We were planning a separation. That's not what most couples dream about."

Liam grimaced. "You brought up the idea of a separation after things got heated between us. I hated the fact that you were going out on these dangerous missions and putting your life at risk. One of your search-and-rescue colleagues had been killed in a previous mission. I wanted you here in Love, with us, where it was safe."

Ruby raised her hand to her head. It still ached. "And I told you that my profession was a big part of me and that I wouldn't be whole without it."

Liam nodded, his expression grim. "Neither of us was willing to budge."

"So we broke?" Ruby's lips quivered. She had bought into the fairy tale of her blissful marriage to Liam. The perfect couple with the high-powered careers and the adorable son. Not a single person had described them as anything other than euphoric. Suddenly nothing made sense. Liam wasn't the man or the partner she had believed him to be. And it hurt terribly. The pain threatened to strangle her.

"We weren't broken. A little chipped and frayed around the edges, perhaps. But none of that is what's most important. We're two people who were given an opportunity to repair the pain in our marriage. Try to remember us, Ruby. Who we truly were. What we can be again."

She shook her head. "Nothing beautiful or lasting can be built on deception. I remember enough to know that, Liam. It wasn't pretty."

"I think you're falling in love with me all over again. You already have my heart, Ruby. There's nothing standing in our way. Let's not put up obstacles."

She gathered her strength and stood. "So, tell me one thing, Liam. Would you still hold me back from doing search-and-rescue work?"

"Don't ask me that question." Liam gritted his teeth.

She locked gazes with him, letting him know in no uncertain terms that she expected an answer.

He let out a groan. "My head says no, but my heart says yes. I lost you once due to unacceptable risks. How could I ever be on board with you returning to that line of work?" His brow was furrowed. His features radiated intensity.

Ruby shuddered. Up until today it had felt as if they were moving toward their own happily-ever-after. But now, after what she had discovered, it felt as if everything was falling apart.

"I need to go, Liam. I can't keep going around and around this with you. Aidan is taking his nap." She began walking toward the door. Liam reached out and grabbed her arm. She shrugged him off.

"Please don't go. Stay and talk this through with me. There's not a thing we can't figure out together." There was a pleading quality to Liam's voice that made her want to stick around and hash things out. But she was so confused about everything. At the moment she didn't know up from down. And she needed time to sort things through.

"I can't. Truthfully, it's really hard for me to look at you right now."

She raced to the living room, picked up her purse and keys and headed out into the Alaskan afternoon. Ruby had no idea where she was headed, but the one thing she knew for certain was that she no longer felt safe and secure in her world.

Liam watched through the bay window as Ruby roared off down the road. Pain ricocheted through him like bullets. He closed his eyes and prayed to God for a reprieve. This was what he had been so afraid of—losing Ruby all over again. It was the reason he had steeled his heart from her until she had worn down his defenses. Once again, he felt like he was being ripped up inside. And there was nothing he could do to stop the tidal wave of pain. He just had to endure it.

He had failed Aidan. And Ruby. And, ultimately, himself.

"Daddy?" Liam turned at the sound of Aidan's sleep-infused voice.

"Hey, A-man," he said. He was trying his best to keep his voice normal. The last thing he wanted was to upset Aidan. "How was your nap?"

"I had a bad dream. There was a snow monster and it came to take Mommy." His lips trembled and he raised his arms to be lifted up.

Liam scooped Aidan into his arms and patted his back to soothe him. "Aw, I'm sorry. Nightmares can be really scary. They seem so real, don't they?"

Aidan nodded as he wiped away tears with the back of his hand. "Where's Mommy?"

"She had to go out for a little bit."

Aidan frowned. "But what if something happened to her? What if the snow monster got her again?"

Liam walked over to the couch and set Aidan down. He sat next to him. "She didn't get eaten by the snow monster. That's not going to happen again."

"Promise?"

"Yes. I can't promise that nothing bad is ever going to happen, but I can tell you for sure that the snow monster isn't going to hurt your mother. Not ever again."

Aidan nestled his head against Liam's chest. He felt his heart tighten painfully. The love he felt for his son knew no bounds. It literally threatened to bring him to his knees. And it terrified him to think his actions had jeopardized their family's future. Because of him and the pressures he'd placed on her, Ruby might choose not to stick around.

Please, Lord. Don't let Ruby walk away from us. She's the love of my life. The mother of my child. Give me an opportunity to make things right and to show her that there's nothing we can't get past.

Ruby drove around Love with her thoughts jumbled and chaotic. She had no idea of where to go. Every tie she had in this town led straight back to Liam. Liam. The man she loved. It was too late to rein herself in. She had already fallen deeply, completely, in love with him. And now, knowing their marriage had been in trouble, she had no clue what it meant for their future.

Did they even have one now? Liam hadn't been honest with her. How could their future be built on a lie? She didn't know if she could trust him moving forward. She felt almost as confused as she had when she'd first arrived in town.

After riding around for a while, Ruby parked her car in front of the Love Free Library. It was such a beautiful place. Maybe she could go in and sit somewhere soothing so she could think. Annie seemed to be the sort of person who wouldn't pry and, if she needed to, she would be someone to confide in about Liam.

Ruby walked toward the library and looked up at the gold-and-cream library sign. She stopped to read the words etched on the front of the library. *Love is patient. Love is kind.* The verse from Corinthians. She knew it on a deep level. It spoke to her.

Liam had recited it to her at their wedding. It had been part of their vows. And she had recited it to him, as well. She could see it all in her mind's eye. Her romantic, elegant wedding gown. Liam looking handsome in his dark tux with his brothers at his side. In her hand she'd held a bouquet of forget-me-nots as she walked down the aisle on Kyle's arm. There had been such a look of love stamped on Liam's face as Pastor Jack pronounced them husband and wife.

More than anything, she recalled the way she had felt that day. Hopeful. Certain. Committed. She had known on that day that she had wanted to be married to Liam Prescott more than anything else in the world.

Ruby quickly reversed herself and headed straight back to the car. At this moment all she felt was overwhelming love and gratitude for the man she had vowed to love for a lifetime.

Liam heard the front door open with a bang. Ruby! He walked toward the hallway. Ruby was standing in the foyer. He stopped, uncertain as to what he was walking toward.

"Liam!" With a wild cry, Ruby dropped her purse and beat a fast path toward him. He met her halfway, reaching down and gathering her up by her waist so that she was in his arms.

He was cradling her against him, not wanting to ever let her go. Although he'd known it wasn't likely, he'd feared that she might never come back to him. The very thought of it had been unbearable.

He set her down, gazing into her tear-filled brown eyes. "I'm so happy you're back. I love you so much."

"Oh, Liam, I never should have walked out. I should have stuck around to listen and try to understand."

He smoothed her hair back and kissed her on her forehead. "Shh. I don't care. What's important is that you're here. And I plan to show you how much I love you, Ruby. You'll never have to doubt us ever again."

Tears streamed down Ruby's face. "No, I won't ever question it again. I love you, Liam. After I left here, God pointed me in the right direction. He shined a bright light on our love. I remembered our wedding day and the vows we exchanged. Love is patient. Love is kind."

Liam blinked past his own tears. "Love never fails."

"Love never fails," Ruby repeated, reaching up on her tiptoes to place a tender kiss on her husband's lips.

"I'm going to support you, Ruby, no matter what decisions you make in the future about your career. There's no way anything is going to tear us apart. After everything we've been through, the rest should be a cakewalk."

"What matters is that we're in this for the long haul. That's what we promised each other on our wedding day. That we would stick it out come what may." Tears pooled in Ruby's eyes. She was getting choked up. "I promise never to forget the road that led us to where we are today."

"Marry me, Ruby." He cupped her face between his palms.

"Did you forget? We're already married," Ruby said with a chuckle.

"In some ways that was a lifetime ago. Let's renew our vows. At Christmas. Let's remind all our friends and family that our love has endured…and is thriving. Let's serve as an example that love is worth fighting for."

"I'll marry you again, Dr. Prescott. Today. Tomorrow. Any day of the week."

Liam dipped his head and placed a triumphant kiss

on his wife's lips. He hoped it conveyed everything he felt for her and all the hopes he held for their future.

"I'm going to hold you to that, my beautiful Ruby."

The lights from the Christmas tree sparkled brightly as Liam and Ruby kissed to celebrate their happy news. Years ago at Christmas they had committed themselves to walking through life together. Now, all these years later, they were going to do it all over again. Ruby and Liam knew the most important thing of all was to love one another.

Epilogue

"So what's my job again?" Aidan asked as he looked up at his father.

Liam and Aidan had just finished changing into their tuxedoes in one of the waiting rooms inside the church. Liam bent down to fix Aidan's crimson bow tie so it would sit straight instead of crooked.

"Your job is to stand up for me as my best man," Liam said. He reached out and tousled his son's curly hair. "You have to hand me the rings when it's time to put them on Mommy's finger."

Aidan grinned, showcasing a missing front tooth. He had lost his very first tooth two nights ago and had been showing it off ever since. "She's going to be happy about the new stone you added. It's awesome."

Liam took the ring out of his pocket and admired it for a moment. The ruby stone sparkled next to the diamonds. It signified a new beginning. The past had been their foundation, but they were looking forward to a future ripe with promise. Over the last few weeks they had both learned what mattered most. Above all else, their family reigned supreme. And despite any obstacles that might come their way, they were in this for life. *Till death do us part.*

"I'll hold on to these until we get to the altar," Liam suggested, tucking the rings into his jacket pocket.

"Phew," Aidan said, wiping his hand across his forehead. "That's a lot of responsibility for a kid."

A slight tapping noise drew their attention to the door.

"Come in," Liam called out, wondering if Pastor Jack or one of his brothers had stopped by to check in. The door slowly opened to reveal Ruby standing at the threshold in her ivory wedding gown.

For a moment all Liam could do was gape at her. Her long hair had been swept up in an elegant twist, with tendrils of hair framing her beautiful face. The dress— the same one she'd worn at their original wedding—was romantic and ethereal. A crown of holly and red berries sat on top of her head, serving as a glorious reminder of their Christmas wedding.

Liam couldn't form a sentence for a few seconds. The sight of his bride in her full wedding regalia was mind-blowing. "Ruby, you look…magnificent."

"Mom, you look so pretty." Aidan chimed in.

"Thank you," Ruby said. She winked at Aidan. "Both of you look incredibly handsome. You sure clean up well."

Aidan frowned at her. He looked back and forth between his parents. "Hey! I thought the two of you weren't supposed to see each other before the ceremony."

"Technically, that is the tradition…" Ruby hedged. "But since we're already married, I don't think we're breaking any rules."

Aidan shrugged. "Sounds good to me."

"Hey, buddy, why don't you go see if Jasper is here?

I think your mom might want to tell me something in private," Liam said.

"Sure thing," Aidan said. "I'll be right back. I'm going to go check on the uncles and make sure they know what they're doing."

"Don't mess up your tux," Ruby called after him.

As soon as the door slammed behind him, Ruby and Liam exchanged a tender smile.

"I wanted to tell you something before we renew our vows."

He studied her face. "I can tell there's something lying on your heart."

She reached out and entwined his hands with hers. "I've decided not to get recertified in search and rescue." She let out a deep breath. "That's all over for me now."

Liam's mouth opened. He fumbled for words. "What? But it's always been so important to you."

"It has been. And it was a wonderful career. But it was part of the past. My life is leading me in another direction."

"Are you sure about this? I want to make certain that you're fulfilled, not just in our home life but professionally, as well. That's important to me."

"I'll always value the work I did, but I don't want to take risks like that anymore. I want to close that chapter of my life. All I'll ever need to be fulfilled is you... and Aidan and our faith. And whatever other little ones we may be blessed with down the road."

"Oh, Ruby, as long as it's something you're willingly letting go of... I'll never stand in your way. Not ever again."

"I know," she said with a fierce nod of her head. "You showed me that you would support all of my dreams and aspirations. It actually made my decision all the more meaningful, knowing that it was my decision to make."

She took a deep breath. "So that brings me to my next venture."

He raised an eyebrow. "Which is?"

"Training search-and-rescue dogs," she said in a triumphant voice. "Like Rufus."

Liam shook his head. He wasn't even surprised at his wife's ingenuity. Once a road closed she was planning to travel down another avenue. "That's a wonderful idea, Ruby. It's a nice way of staying tied to the search-and-rescue community. And with your love of dogs, it's perfect for you."

"I'm really excited about this, wherever it leads me. I've done a bit of dog handling before, but I'm really intrigued by all the possibilities." She crossed her hands in front of her. "I'm going to start small at first but, hopefully, I'll be able to really expand it into something much bigger. Hazel has been a real inspiration for me with her Lovely Boots."

Liam closed the gap between them and placed his hands on either side of Ruby's face. "Have I ever told you how much I love your tenacity? And your vision? There's nothing you can't do, Mrs. Ruby Prescott."

The door opened with a bang. "Smooching again?" Aidan asked with a loud groan. "Everyone is out there sitting in the pews. They're waiting for the wedding to start." He scrunched up his face. "Jasper is walking back and forth and mumbling to himself. He told me to tell you to get a move on."

Liam rolled his eyes. Ruby giggled and raised her hand to her mouth.

Liam locked eyes with Aidan. "Are you ready to do this?"

"I was born ready," Aidan said with a cocky tilt of his head.

Ruby chuckled. "Uh-oh. You've been hanging around Declan way too much."

"In the famous words of the mayor of this town, 'let's go get hitched,'" Liam said, placing his hand on Aidan's shoulder.

"Amen," Ruby said. "I can't wait to be your bride all over again."

A few minutes later Ruby walked down the aisle of the church to the strains of the "Wedding March." Kyle was at her side, ready to give her away to the man she adored.

As she walked past pews filled with friends and family members, she couldn't help but feel incredibly blessed. Her fears had all been put to rest. In the end, love had been her healing balm. The love she felt for Liam and Aidan stamped out all the darkness. And the tremendous way they adored her in return made her feel as if she could do anything…be anything. God had placed her exactly where she needed to be. She would never take it for granted again. Love, Alaska, was home.

Never again would she focus on the memories she had lost. From this moment forward she and Liam would be stepping toward their brilliant future, secure in the knowledge that nothing could ever shake this union or derail them from their path. From this point forward they would be walking in faith as husband and wife.

* * * * *

**WE HOPE YOU ENJOYED
THIS BOOK FROM**

LOVE INSPIRED
INSPIRATIONAL ROMANCE

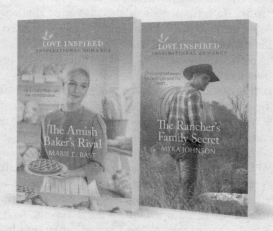

Uplifting stories of faith, forgiveness and hope.

Fall in love with stories where faith helps
guide you through life's challenges, and discover
the promise of a new beginning.

6 NEW BOOKS AVAILABLE EVERY MONTH!

LOVE INSPIRED

Stories to uplift and inspire

Fall in love with Love Inspired—
inspirational and uplifting stories of faith
and hope. Find strength and comfort in
the bonds of friendship and community.
Revel in the warmth of possibility and the
promise of new beginnings.

Sign up for the Love Inspired newsletter
at **LoveInspired.com** to be the first
to find out about upcoming titles,
special promotions and exclusive content.

CONNECT WITH US AT:

Facebook.com/LoveInspiredBooks

Twitter.com/LoveInspiredBks